A Royal Runaway Road-Trip

Story of a Princess and her Bodyguard

A. Goswami

Free Lesbian Romance Novel by A Goswami

Hello Dear Readers,

Please don't forget to download your free 300-page Lesbian Romance Novel by me that I would like to give to you as a thank you for reading and enjoying this book.

Download it right now by clicking here

Chapter One

Penelope

Pink Poison's about to blaze up the stage and my heart's hammering like a kid in a candy store. Alexa's about to be mere feet away. Close enough for me to count the specks of glitter on her cheeks. Can't get better than that.

Perched in the VIP section, because, hello, princess here, I take in the energy of Wembley Arena, sizzling like a live wire, ready to combust any second. The crowd's buzzing, an infectious rhythm that has me bouncing on my seat, anticipation skittering under my skin.

Beside me, Kriti, my PA, is trying to play it cool, but the star-struck twinkle in her eyes gives her away. Pretty as a picture and sharp as a tack, she's a firecracker, that one. Not that I can talk with my security squad looming over us. You'd think they were guarding the crown jewels, not a 21-year-old at a rock concert.

And then, there it is - the hush. The world sucks in a breath as the lights dim. I lean forward, heart thundering. It's showtime. The first chord rips through the silence like a thunderbolt, and I'm no longer Her Royal Highness Penelope Victoria Windsor. I'm Penny, a girl with a mega crush on a rockstar, drowning in the pulsating waves of Pink Poison's music.

As the stage lights burst into a kaleidoscope of colors, a silhouette emerges. Alexa. She's pure dynamite, a ticking time bomb of energy ready to explode, dressed in leather and lace, looking every bit the rockstar. Hailee Steinfeld could be her twin sister, but the raw, unapologetic power Alexa exudes puts her in a league of her own.

As Alexa struts down the walkway, microphone in hand, the floodlights catching on her cascading brown hair, it hits me. I am so incredibly gay. Watching her is like a crash course in what it means to desire, to yearn.

I pivot toward Kriti, perched primly at my side, and I toss her my wishful question. "Kriti, what do I need to do to get some one-on-one time with Alexa?"

A confident smile dances on Kriti's lips. "You're the Princess of England, Your Royal Highness. All you need to do is... make a wish."

A flush of pleasure lights up my face, a grin broad enough to let her know my wish. "Consider it made, Kriti."

Her dark eyes glimmer with amusement. "And when would this wish be granted?"

My eyes wander back to Alexa, standing out like a sun amidst the mediocre stars. "Sooner than yesterday," I reply, my heart thrumming along with the bass vibrating through the venue. Alexa was all I cared about now, the rest of the band fading into the background like...well, straight porn.

My mind whirls into a world of scandalous fantasies. "Do you reckon she's sleeping with the other members of her group? Do you think they engage in secret trysts after rehearsals, bodies still slick with sweat?" The question is more for my racing mind than Kriti, but she humors me.

Kriti chuckles, an amused huff escaping her lips as she tucks a loose strand of hair behind her ear. "Your Royal

Highness, you're making it sound like a second-rate porno," she teases, her gaze locked onto the stage where Alexa and the band are executing flawless choreography. "I should've never let you near the unprotected internet."

"I was seconds away from being exposed by the royal internet. I was in a state of desperation - if another day had gone by, the queen would have been informed that her daughter had some rather, ahem, royal peculiarities," I said sarcastically.

"They are called kinks, Your Royal Highness," Kriti informed me.

"I know. I am not a child. And I also happen to know that you have one as well."

"What? Rubbish!" Kriti says with an air of surprised amusement, "I am as vanilla as they come."

"Well, my sources tell me...vanilla does not make you cum!" I giggle and watch Alexa slowly hump the mic stand provocatively, her sultry doe eyes taking up all the space on the giant screen.

"I choose to remain quiet. However, if you wish to indulge in your royal peculiarities, I would advise you to meet with Alexa at Highgrove House instead of Buckingham."

"And why would you assume I have any intention of...indulging in such activities with Alexa?" I ask, a smirk playing on my lips. Alexa's hypnotic moves still hold my attention hostage.

Kriti raises an eyebrow, looking at me with bemusement. "What else could you possibly want a private meeting for? To discuss her hair routine?" she jokes, but I can tell she's dead serious.

"I'm shocked by your audacity, Kriti. Is this how you address your princess?" I snap back, feigning hurt. "One word from me and you could be tossed off this balcony."

Our staring contest is broken by Kriti's whisper, "I apologise, Your Highness. I'll keep the jabs to a minimum. I know you're easily...butthurt."

The glare I shoot at her is matched by her innocent look, and then we both erupt into laughter. "Piss off, Kriti. If my mother ever caught wind of our antics, she'd have your head."

"She's tried. But you always come to my rescue."

"One of these days, I might just let her win."

Kriti grins, her Indian features glowing with amusement. "And that would be the day your life becomes unbearably dull, Your Royal Highness."

Standing in front of the ornate mirror in my chamber at Highgrove House, I glance at my reflection. A beautiful, hand-stitched gown covers me from neck to toe, as royal protocol demands. "Might as well be a nun," I mutter to my reflection, a frustrated sigh escaping my lips.

This wasn't exactly the 'come hither' look I had in mind for my rendezvous with Alexa. In my ideal world, I'd be in something sultrier, leaving little to the imagination.

My dark eyes gleam back at me from the mirror, a playful spark dancing within them. The perfectly coiffed waves of my chestnut hair, cascading down my shoulders, frame my youthful face with an air of regality. And there's my secret weapon: my lips - full, plush, and perfectly shaped, a tantalizing lure I know I can always count on. A smudge of deep crimson adorns them tonight, an added allure.

"Well, Alexa," I murmur to my reflection, pulling my lower

lip in a sultry bite. "Even in this royal monstrosity, you won't stand a chance."

My gaze travels upward, to a small mole that perches right above the right corner of my upper lip. An unexpected beauty spot that gives my sophisticated visage a touch of eccentricity, a hint of rebel amidst the royal.

I laugh, a sound that echoes around the room, filling it with youthful energy and determination.

I take a deep breath, my hands smoothing over the rich fabric of the gown before they impulsively make a detour to tug the neckline down a tad. There. That's a little more cleavage for our dear Alexa. *Who says royalty has to be boring, eh?*

A small sigh escapes me as I wonder why I'm fluffing feathers for a chick who might not even bat for my team. But then, Alexa's numerous cozy moments with her bandmate, Lily, play like a highlight reel in my head.

The borderline flirty touches, the giggles that echoed a tad too intimate in countless interviews, they keep the flame of hope alive.

Then there's that grainy video — a beach, a sunset, and a lip-lock that certainly wasn't sisterly. Alexa in the arms of another girl. And just like that, my doubt takes a backseat, hope maneuvering the wheel again.

If love's a game, hope's my ace in the hole. Plus, it makes one hell of a story, doesn't it? Princess charms the rockstar, and they lived gaily ever after. Fingers crossed!

"Try the wine." I point at the bottle of the expensive red

resting on the table, a mischievous glint in my eyes. "It's a personal favorite."

Alexa's gaze flickers from me to the wine and then back to me, a small smile tugging at the corners of her lips. "I'm not sure I'm much of a wine person, Your Royal Highness."

Ignoring the flutter in my chest, I lean forward, my gaze locked with hers. "Enough with the formalities, Alexa. We're beyond that now. Call me by my name."

A sharp intake of breath on her part is my only clue that I've affected her. "Alright, Penelope," she utters, my name rolling off her tongue with an intimate rasp that I feel deep in my belly.

I lean back, a victorious grin spreading across my face. "So, what tickles your fancy? A cold beer? Shots of tequila?"

Alexa chuckles, the sound like music to my ears. "I'm more of a whiskey girl," she says, her eyes sparkling with mirth.

"Actually, I already knew that. I don't know why I asked," I declare, crossing my legs and wishing my gown had a slit that ran up to my thighs.

"And how did you come to know that?" she questions.

"I may have indulged in a bit of stalking, Alexa. I am a huge fan of your work...and your beauty," I admit without any qualms.

Raising an eyebrow, Alexa mirrors my pose, crossing her own legs. Her dress, unlike mine, boasts a daring slit. My eyes linger on the path it reveals, tracing the smooth expanse of her skin up to where her thigh meets her waist. I lick my lips, an unspoken wish that the slit didn't have to end.

"It's an honor to be stalked by the future Queen of England," she teases.

"But that's not all who I am," I counter, a wave of

seriousness washing over me.

"I'm aware. I've done my research too. You don't exactly revel in your royal duties, do you? You seem to enjoy ruffling the queen's feathers."

"It's not about the rebellion, Alexa. It's about control. Control over my own life. The one thing I can't seem to have, as the future Queen of England."

I sit back, running my fingers through my hair. "You're quite well-informed, aren't you?"

Alexa shrugs, her dark eyes sparkling with mischief. "I believe in knowing my audience."

"And am I your audience, Alexa?" I query, the question hanging between us, as palpable as the electric charge in the air.

"You could be," she replies cryptically, her gaze piercing mine.

"But that would mean you're my performer," I counter, unable to wipe the smirk off my face.

"And would that be so terrible?" she challenges, leaning forward, the teasing glint never leaving her eyes.

"Well, no. But only if you're up to the task," I volley back, sipping from my glass of wine.

Alexa chuckles, a sound that reverberates through the room, echoing my racing heartbeat. "And what task would that be, Princess?"

"That depends," I answer, setting down my glass and meeting her gaze with newfound determination. "Are you looking to entertain, or make history?"

"Both," she declares, her smile widening. "I like a good challenge. Keeps things exciting."

I lean back in my chair, a thoughtful expression painted on my face. "Interesting. Because, you see, I am not just looking for excitement. I am looking for...a revolution."

Alexa quirks an eyebrow, a slow, mischievous smile tugging at her lips. "Is that so? And what sort of revolution are you envisioning, Penelope?"

"Of fucking anyone I want to, whenever I want, without having to think how the country will be affected by my orgasms," I reply, my tone dead serious.

"I can get behind that revolution," Alexa says, running a languid hand through her hair, her gaze taking on a sizzling quality that makes my blood rush south.

Her outfit, a pencil skirt with an inviting slit, and her eyes, a smoky mystery, is making me hotter than a midsummer day in London.

God, I need her more than Britain needed monarchy.

"Are you willing to lay your life for the cause, baby?" I bat my eyelashes at the singer, who visibly swallows and seems momentarily at a loss for words.

The poor girl can't believe this is really happening. I can't blame her. It's a lot of pressure knowing you have to please the Princess of England in bed.

Alexa drains the wine from her glass, takes a deep breath, and fixes me with an unwavering gaze. "I'm more than willing, Your Highness. Just tell me what to do, where to do it... how long to do it... how... hard... to do it, and your loyal soldier will be at your service."

Our lips collide, the moment lighting a spark that quickly

becomes a wildfire. Alexa's pressing into me, and I forget the regality that's part of my everyday, losing myself in the heat of the kiss. Her hands are everywhere, tracing patterns on my body, pushing all my buttons, driving me crazy.

Then she pulls back, leaving my lips cold and wanting more. My gown's off in seconds, my body bare and trembling under her heated gaze. The approving smile on Alexa's face makes my pulse race, her gaze intoxicating me more than any wine ever could.

Alexa's hands roam my body freely, leaving me feeling more alive than I ever felt at a royal gathering.

I reach for her, sliding my hand along the tempting slit in her dress, up her thigh, my touch making her gasp.

"I have never had clothes taken off my body by a princess before," Alexa purrs in my ear, as I unzip her skirt and push my cold, trembling hands inside.

"I have never been fucked like a naughty girl before," I say, grabbing a handful of Alexa's meaty ass and kneading it in a very unroyal way.

"I guess it's going to be a night of firsts for both of us, Your Highness."

I am thrown onto the massive bed made of dark wood.

The canopy over my head and the drapes on the wall are a deep red, almost brown. The bedding is detailed with gold trimmings, and it looks like it costs more than the average peasant makes in a decade.

The crash of Alexa's body onto mine feels forbidden, rousing an intoxicating thrill. Within the castle walls, I, the Princess, am being dominated by a commoner. The scandalous thought floods my senses, and I instinctively lock my legs around Alexa's waist, pulling her closer with a force born of desperation.

Her lips trace a path from my neck, journeying downwards to my breasts. As her tongue playfully circles my nipple, teasing it to a peak, I arch my back into her, welcoming her intimate exploration. Slowly, she descends further, her every move marked by tantalizing kisses. Suddenly, a gasp claws its way from my throat as her fingers sneak their way between my thighs, pushing in...

She bites down on the insides of my thigh, leaving a mark of her teeth. Then she licks over it, as if to soothe the pain.

Little does she know, the future queen of England is a submissive who can tolerate more pain than the average British citizen calculating his taxes.

I lift my lower back off the bed, grab Alexa's wavy, soft hair in my fist, and feel the first lashes of her tongue attacking my clit.

"Fuck me while you taste me," I command, and she obliges. Her fingers dive inside me and I buck my hips in response.

"Another!" I gasp out, and she adds another finger, my moans ringing out, echoing around the grand room. The pain and pleasure intermingle, and I savor every throb, every gasp. I'm crying out her name, each syllable a testament to her skill, and it spurs her on.

Her gaze is ferocious, her mouth slick as she devours me. I'm writhing, arching and bucking like an animal, losing myself in the waves of pleasure cresting within me. As the pressure builds, I sense the imminent explosion of ecstasy.

Then it hits, crashing over me like a tidal wave, rippling through me, seismic waves of pleasure radiating from my core. As I open my eyes, I see Alexa panting, a proud grin spread across her face.

"Long live the revolution," I whisper, pulling her into an

embrace.

Jessica

Strolling down the hallway, surrounded by chattering college kids who seem to live in a world of their own, I can't help but feel out of place. 'Not Afghanistan,' I remind myself, pushing down the old habits that want to treat every unfamiliar sound as a potential threat. Then again, a lecture on Freud can feel like a war zone in its own right.

Ahead, I spot the professor at the classroom door, quizzing a tardy student. A girl, tall and blonde, pretty in the way that models like Josephine Skriver are - almost unreal. Can't help but roll my eyes a bit. 'What would she know about the real world?' I think, watching as she fumbles to answer the professor's question.

I know the answer.

It's one of the many things that war teaches you, the things that lurk in the darkest corners of the human mind. I whisper it, low enough to be drowned by the noise but loud enough for the girl to hear. She blinks, turns to look at me, then repeats the answer to the professor. She's allowed in by the professor, who calls her Sophie, and I trail behind, invisible as always.

Throughout the class, I feel her gaze on me. Makes me feel almost... seen.

It's a strange feeling, not entirely unwelcome.

I've been alone for a long time, celibate even longer. A brief, stolen thought of what it would be like to be with her flickers through my mind. It's brief but leaves a lasting impact. 'Not here, not her,' I chide myself. But the thought lingers, and I can't help but wonder

The chalk on the board squeaks, droning on like the professor. A discussion on Freud and his Oedipus theory. Heavy stuff for an early morning.

My gaze slides sideways. Sophie's notes in neat handwriting fill up her page. My page? Almost empty. But my mind is filled with experiences no textbook can teach.

Her clothing choice fascinates me. Tight leggings hugging her sculpted legs, a crop top leaving little to the imagination. I'd chided many soldiers for less revealing gear in the desert, but this is a different battlefield. My gaze slips up to her ponytail, the blonde strands bouncing with her every move, not a single scar marring her skin. A stark contrast to my own. She's the untarnished picture of youth; I'm a relic with wounds that run deep.

Our eyes meet.

A bolt of electricity.

Her smile is wide, full of life. I don't return it, the muscles in my face unaccustomed to that exercise. It's a game I stopped playing years ago. She holds my gaze, undeterred, her smile dimming but never quite leaving her face.

The professor's voice fades out; the clatter of chairs signals the end of class. I pack my books, the urge to leave stronger with every passing second. But Sophie stands in my path, a living, breathing roadblock.

"Hi, I'm Sophie," she chirps, extending a hand. Her nails are painted a soft pink, matching the blush in her cheeks.

"Jessica," I reply curtly, taking her hand. Her grip is surprisingly firm, a fact that registers in my brain before I quickly withdraw.

'Thanks for earlier, Jessica,' she says, the gratefulness in her voice pulling at something deep inside me. I shrug it off, reminding myself of who I am. A soldier. A protector. Not a student looking to make friends or catch feelings.

I muster a gruff, "Don't mention it," before walking away, the echo of her voice trailing behind me.

"Jessica," she calls out, the echo of her voice sending a shiver down my spine. I stop in my tracks, already regretting it. "I heard you were a Marine." Her voice holds a hint of awe, admiration painted on her face.

"Yeah. So?" My response is clipped, an icy barrier I erect with practiced ease.

She seems undeterred. "Just... fascinating," she gushes, stepping closer. "Why psychology, though?"

I sigh.

It's my life she's poking at.

But something in her gaze tells me she genuinely wants to know. "To help others," I say simply. "PTSD is a silent killer. And if I can learn to help, why not?"

Her eyes light up, her fascination with me growing. "That's amazing, Jessica. You're amazing."

I roll my eyes, not used to the compliments. "Just doing my part."

But she continues, the words spilling out of her like a dam breaking. "And you're gorgeous too. Like if Romee Strijd decided to drop her angel wings and become a commando."

I bark out a laugh, surprised at the comparison. Romee Strijd? A Victoria's Secret model? Me? "You need to get your eyes checked, Sophie."

She shakes her head, a stubborn set to her chin. "No, really. You've got this... rugged charm. Your toned body, that tall height...and that skin, it's like bronze. Like you've been kissed by the sun."

I feel a blush creeping up my neck, unfamiliar heat spreading across my face. "Alright, that's enough," I cut her off, uncomfortable with the attention, the compliments.

"But—" she starts, but I'm already walking away. "See you tomorrow, Jessica!" she calls out after me.

I just raise a hand in acknowledgement, not trusting myself to look back. 'Guard up, feelings down,' I chant to myself. But for the first time, it feels more like a desperate plea than a steady reminder. And that's a slippery slope I can't afford to tumble down.

∞∞∞

Stepping into the university gym, my gaze immediately lands on a familiar figure in the corner. Sophie's in a deep squat, her firm thighs straining against the tight fabric of her leggings. A frisson of desire ripples through me, a quick, surprising jolt that I hastily push down.

Pushing aside the unnerving image of her, I focus on my routine. I load the plates onto the barbell, my hands steady despite the turmoil inside.

'Guard up, feelings down,' I remind myself again, even though the mantra is starting to lose its calming effect.

My eyes, as if on their own, flicker towards Sophie again. She's moved on to lunges, her movements fluid and rhythmic, a dance of strength and beauty. I clench my jaw and lie down on the bench, ready to push the heavy barbell.

As I start my reps, an old memory floats up to the surface. Maria Sanchez, another Marine, a lover. A memory of our bodies tangled together, her dark eyes flashing with intensity, heat, and fear. The room, an abandoned building, somewhere in the outskirts of Baghdad. The sound of distant gunfire roaring in the background, while our bodies moved in a silent rhythm of longing and urgency.

The metal clinks, the noise echoing in the gym as I complete my set. I sit up, my heart pounding more from the memory than the exercise. I wipe the sweat off my brow, a bitter chuckle escaping me.

'Maria, if only you could see me now,' I think, my gaze inadvertently falling on Sophie. She's looking at me, a question in her eyes.

I look away, my past threatening to crash into my present. An uneasy feeling settles in my gut. I shake off the disquiet, my mind reaching for the familiarity of my mantra. 'Guard up, feelings down.' I wonder how long I can keep it up.

As I'm busy stacking the weights, I sense a presence.

Before I can turn around, a voice rings out, "Hey, Jessica." It's Sophie, her light blue tank top clinging to her, sweat trickling down her collarbone and disappearing into her cleavage.

I feel a stab of desire, quickly followed by frustration. 'Guard up, feelings down,' I remind myself, clenching my jaw.

"Need something?" I manage to sound unaffected, turning my gaze towards the floor. She's beaming, and it's too damn infectious to ignore.

"Just admiring your routine," she says, a faint blush coloring her cheeks, "It's impressive."

I shrug. "Comes with the territory. Military discipline."

Her eyes light up. "That's what I need! Discipline." She clears her throat, tugging her lower lip between her teeth. She's nervous. Good. Makes two of us.

"Sophie, if you're trying to get me to be your personal

trainer, it's not happening."

"No, no," she rushes to explain, "I'm a sprinter, 100-meter. Just... thought maybe you could... spot me?"

A sprinter. Figures. Explains the tight body, the long legs. I respect a good athlete. Still, the request catches me off guard.

I narrow my eyes at her. "You need a spotter for squats?"

"Well," she flushes, glancing at the floor, "yeah."

I stifle a laugh. "I don't usually spot sprinters doing squats, but I guess there's a first time for everything."

My mind is a whirlwind of contradictions. I don't want to be near her, yet I find myself walking over to her squat rack. It's all so damn confusing, and I hate confusion. I prefer black and white, right and wrong, ally or enemy.

Sophie, with her blue eyes and easy smile, is in the gray area. It's a territory I'm not comfortable in.

Yet here I am, spotting a sprinter in the gym, trying to keep my 'guard up, feelings down.' I'm starting to believe my mantra needs an update.

Sophie sets herself up for her first set of squats, her form impeccable, her breathing steady. I watch her closely, my eyes tracing the curve of her spine, the way her muscles ripple under her skin. The desire is still there, a simmering heat that refuses to be ignored. I curse myself silently. This is exactly why I avoid fraternizing with civilians, especially women. It only leads to complications.

But as she lowers into the squat, her thighs trembling with effort, I can't help but feel a certain admiration for her. She's strong, resilient, and unafraid of pushing herself to her limits. It's a quality I can appreciate, as a Marine and as a person.

Sophie steadies herself, focusing on the barbell in her

grasp. "What's life like for you, outside the university?" she asks, a note of genuine curiosity in her voice.

I'm taken aback, a little. People don't usually show interest in my life. "Quiet," I offer, focusing on the rhythm of her squats.

Sophie looks at me. "No hobbies, past times? No drinking at bars, picking up cute college girls?" Her tone is teasing, a glint in her eye that sets off alarms in my head, plus I wonder how she knows I like girls, or women, for that matter, as I had not been with a girl in ages.

I give her a sideways glance. "I box. And read, sometimes."

She looks surprised at the reading part. Then her eyebrows furrow. "Boxing, huh? That's... different."

"Yeah," I smirk, "A soldier who likes to punch things, unheard of, I know."

But I notice her form is faltering, the previous fluidity replaced with a stiffness that looks uncomfortable. I step closer, my hands hovering over her hips. "You're off balance," I tell her, trying to keep my voice steady. "Let me…"

I guide her hips, correcting her posture. Sophie looks at me, a strange, charged silence between us. Then she dips into a squat, her back brushing against my front, her hips moving in a way that sends a jolt of heat through me.

I want to step back, break contact. But I can't.

My senses are hyper-focused on her – the smell of her sweat, the curve of her body, the softness of her skin beneath my hands. It's all-consuming, throwing me off balance, much like the girl in front of me.

As Sophie straightens, the movement dislodges my grip on her hips. I stumble back, a wave of dizziness washing over me. Sophie turns, a look of concern in her eyes.

"I… I need to leave," I say, my voice sounding distant to my ears.

Sophie's hand fastens around my waist, halting my escape. "Wait," she breathes out, those pretty blue eyes of hers wide and pleading.

There's a stirring deep inside me, a spark of something dangerous that had been flickering for a while now but suddenly flares up.

My heartbeat picks up pace, and for once, it's not in response to the imminent threat of a gunman jumping out from behind a door. This... this is something entirely different, something I'm not equipped to deal with.

"I... I wanted to ask you out," Sophie stammers, her grip on my wrist tightening.

"Dates aren't really my thing," I reply, blunt as ever.

"Well, what is your thing, then?" she counters, a teasing lilt to her voice.

"What's your endgame here, Sophie?" I ask, frustration creeping into my tone.

"I just... I want to know you, Jessica."

I can't help the scoff that escapes me. "Hate to break it to you, Sophie, but I don't do the 'getting to know you' dance. I only ask questions when I'm interrogating a target. Chit-chat isn't part of my repertoire."

Unfazed, Sophie steps closer. The smell of her sweat mixes with the metallic scent of the gym equipment and it's unexpectedly intoxicating. I can feel the pull of her, a relentless gravity that's threatening to suck me in.

"Damn it," I murmur under my breath, taking a step back. This isn't a battlefield I'm prepared for. I'm in uncharted territory and, quite frankly, I'm scared shitless.

"So don't ask questions. Don't take me out. Just...fuck me

till I can't feel my knees, baby. You are the hottest thing on campus, and everyone wants you. But they're all too scared of you. Not me though, Jessica. I think I can handle you. In fact, I want to run straight into the eye of the storm."

My heart is pounding a rhythm in my chest that's not unfamiliar, but its cause certainly is. Not adrenaline. Not fear.

Desire.

Lust.

They're not unfamiliar to me, but it's been so long since I've felt them, it might as well be a lifetime ago.

"Do you even know what you're asking for?" I bite out, my voice rougher than I intended it to be.

But she doesn't back down. "More than you think, Jessica." Her voice is softer now, but her eyes still hold a challenging glint.

The internal struggle rages on inside me, but I can't ignore the burning need any longer. Loneliness, I've found, is a ruthless beast. It gnaws at you, bit by bit, until you're nothing but a hollow shell of your former self. And the only way to quiet that beast, if only for a little while, is through a moment of fleeting connection.

"I hope you know what you've signed up for, Sophie," I whisper into her ear, before grabbing her hand and leading her towards the showers.

I had significantly underestimated my desperate yearning for sexual release, and Sophie, it seemed, had miscalculated the brutal intensity of the tempest she'd so eagerly chosen to confront.

Years of loading and unloading firearms, operating heavy machinery, and wrestling with fellow marines had instilled an aggression in my hands that was more than I'd intended.

Despite every precaution I took to temper the strength of my touches, I found myself fiercely ripping off Sophie's clothes.

"Is this what you wanted?" I growl, my hands pawing at Sophie's sports bra, yanking it from her breasts with unrefined movements.

"Yes," she answers, appearing pleased at being so roughly handled by me.

"Even this?" I question further, nipping at her shoulder blades.

"Ohh... fuck yes!" Sophie responds, her hand twisting to turn on the shower.

The warm water envelops us, showering droplets cascading down my back, flowing in rivulets along my spine. Her skin is beautifully pale, a stark contrast to my bronze, creating a striking juxtaposition.

I grab hold of the elastic bands of her leggings, sinking down onto my knees. I tug at the damp material, the water from above making it stick to her skin. Patiently, I peel her leggings down, revealing her long legs and freshly-shaved intimacy.

Stepping out of her leggings, Sophie looks at me with the same intensity as a police dog hunting for its target. I feel my heart racing and my chest pounding.

Still on my knees, I grab her around the waist and turn her to face me. She squeals and starts laughing, reminding me of days past when I was in high school and just discovering my passion for young women's bodies. As she bends over, presenting her toned behind to me, it brings back all the excitement of that time.

I shower her ass with kisses before sinking my teeth into the fleshy part and letting out a loud groan.

Sophie squeals again, but it is not followed by giggles this time.

I bite her again, and Sophie throws her head back, whimpering and groaning from the intoxicating cocktail of pain, pleasure and submissiveness.

Taking a handful of her hair, I roughly pull her head back and demand: "Is this what you want?"

"Yes! God yes," she pants back, her brow creased in a delightful display of abject pain and utter pleasure.

The only response I allow myself is to nip at her bottom lip one more time. The sensation of giving pain and receiving pleasure is not new to me, but it has never been quite so... fulfilling.

She is a beautiful sight, a true treat to the eye: her arms extended above her head, her hips thrusting forward, her ass jutting out towards me, waiting for my touch.

I feel like a beast has been let loose within me. I feel free and ready to take on more.

I rise to my feet, hug Sophie from behind, and whisper in her ear, "Thank you for this," and then I drop my hands to Sophie's legs, and slide them between her thighs.

Chapter Two

Penelope

"Penelope, are you listening to me?" my mother's voice filters through my distracted haze, pulling me back to the present moment.

I tear my gaze from the intricate designs etched on the teacup, the heat of the drink having long since faded. "Yes, Mother," I reply, feigning a smile and masking the longing in my eyes with the ease of a seasoned royal.

"We had a successful trip," she continues, a satisfied smile playing on her lips. "The trade agreements we've established will greatly benefit our economy, especially in these trying times. It's a lot of diplomatic mumbo jumbo, but it's crucial for our relations."

"Diplomatic mumbo jumbo, right," I echo, my fingers tapping lightly against the china, as my thoughts meander off to Alexa. The way she laughed, how she looked in the morning light... even her impudence was something I found myself yearning for.

"Well, Mother," I murmur, forcing myself to focus. "It sounds like you've had quite the time out there in the wild, wild world of trade pacts and diplomatic schmoozing. Tell me again, how many hands did you have to shake?" A chuckle slips out before I can contain it. God, I'm such a terrible listener.

My mother's voice, polished and practiced, pours over me like warm tea, filling the room with soothing mundanity. I can't help but admire her as she sits opposite me, the very picture of regal grace. Imagine Anne Hathaway in 'The Devil Wears Prada', but with a couple of decades added, minus the devilish part, plus a whole lot of Queen.

Her eyes, sharp and shrewd, are studying me now, probably wondering why her only offspring can't keep up with a simple conversation. "Penelope, you seem to be elsewhere today. Is something the matter?"

I shoot her an apologetic smile. "Oh, just a bit tired. All those charity balls and galas, you know. Dancing and looking pretty is such tough work."

With a knowing nod, she goes back to her cup, her elegant fingers clasping it with such finesse, it's like watching a ballet. It's in these quiet moments I'm reminded that I'm not just dealing with my mother, but the Queen.

"Remember, Penelope," she says, her voice carrying a soft sternness, "we are born for duty, not for desire. Our lives are not entirely our own."

Yes, I know, a bit of a buzzkill. But then again, she isn't entirely wrong.

Before I can conjure up a suitable reply, my phone lights up, the screen displaying a text from none other than Alexa. "Hey, Penny, did you ask your mom about that trip to the US yet?"

I blink at the screen, biting back a laugh. Oh, Alexa. Your timing is, as always, impeccable.

"Mum, do you think it'd be...erm... acceptable if I took a short trip to the States?" I ask, trying to sound as nonchalant as possible.

"The States? Whatever for?" She raises an eyebrow, her teacup halfway to her lips.

"Oh, you know... just sightseeing. Might swing by to say hello to our lovely cousins, the Obamas."

Mum places her tea cup back onto the saucer, a small frown creasing her brow. "Penelope, you wouldn't be planning on meeting that rock singer, would you? The one who stayed at Highgrove?"

I choke on my tea. Damn, she's good.

"No, of course not," I cough out, dabbing at my mouth with my napkin. "Just sightseeing, really."

Her gaze narrows slightly, the silence between us suddenly heavy. "Penelope, I won't beat around the bush. People are talking. About you, about your... proclivities."

My blood boils at her insinuation. "What I do and who I do it with is none of their damn business!" I snap, slamming my teacup down, the liquid sloshing over the edge.

"Penny, dear," she sighs, clearly unphased by my outburst. "It's not about what's right or fair. It's about perception. The monarchy depends on the nation's goodwill. If they don't accept their future queen..."

"Well, they damn well should!" I interject. "It's the 21st century, for God's sake! If they can't accept a queen who likes women, then maybe the monarchy deserves to crumble!"

Mum's face hardens at my words. "Careful, Penelope," she says, her voice ice cold. "Some words, once spoken, can't be taken back."

"Alright," I say, taking a deep breath to cool my temper. "What if I was going to visit Aunt Martha in Washington? She did say she's been missing us terribly."

Mum's gaze flicks back to me, a knowing gleam in her eyes.

She doesn't comment on the obvious lie, instead choosing to play along. "That's... more palatable," she replies slowly. "But I still need some time to think it over."

And then, as if she wasn't already muddling enough with my plans, she decides to bring up the ultimate guilt trip. "You know, your father wouldn't have been too keen on this."

Dad.

The mention of his name cuts through me. "Yeah, well, Dad wanted a boy, didn't he?" I retort, bitterness seeping into my voice. "And we all know how that turned out."

"You know he loved you, Penelope," she replies softly.

"Did he?" I scoff. "Or did he love the idea of having a son that he could pass his legacy onto? A legacy that I'm apparently tarnishing with my 'proclivities'."

"Penny," she starts, her eyes softening, "your father..."

I rise, cutting her off. "You know what, Mum? I'm not really hungry anymore. I'll be in my room." With that, I leave the room, leaving behind a queen who looks more like a saddened mother and a conversation that has left a sour taste in my mouth.

Queen Beatrice Victoria Windsor

The minutes tick by as I wait patiently in the grand meeting room of the palace. Each tick is a thud, resonating through the cold silence of the room. But patience, I've learned, is a virtue of the monarchy.

The door finally swings open, and in walks Prime Minister Anthony Mathews, a tall man with silver hair, his presence filling up the room. He's a man of action, of decision - qualities that made him fit for the position, qualities that currently have me on edge.

"Your Majesty," he greets, dipping his head. "How do you fare this fine day?"

"I am well, thank you, Prime Minister," I respond, my tone measured. "You?"

"Fit as a fiddle," he chuckles. "Although, I've always wondered, why a fiddle?"

"I suppose it's because when in tune, a fiddle produces a fine sound," I answer, offering a smile.

"Ah, well," he says, "Onto business. We've received intelligence that the Russians are responsible for shooting down our cargo plane in Ukrainian airspace."

My heart skips a beat. "What?"

"It's been confirmed, Your Majesty," he replies grimly. "And so, the cabinet has decided we must send troops to aid Ukraine."

A cold dread seeps into me. "This could very well lead to war, Prime Minister."

"I'm aware, ma'am. But our allies, the United States and Germany, are of the same mind. We can't sit idle while Russia flexes its muscles in Europe," he argues.

I nod slowly, understanding the gravity of the situation. "What about the Commonwealth? Have they been informed?"

"Yes, Your Majesty. We've already received support from Canada and Australia, and we're in talks with the other member states," he informs me.

"I see," I say, taking a deep breath. "We must act in the best interest of our nation and our allies. But we must also think of the consequences of war."

"Of course, Your Majesty," he agrees. "We'll ensure that

our diplomatic efforts are maximized before we resort to any military action."

"Very well," I say, feeling the weight of the crown upon my head. "We'll support Ukraine in any way we can."

"Thank you, Your Majesty," he says.

Staring back into Anthony's piercing blue eyes, I hesitantly open the topic that's been playing at the back of my mind. "My daughter wishes to visit the States," I confess, my voice quieter than I'd like. "You know about the rumors circulating her and that...American singer, Alexa. My concern is, this trip might add more fuel to the fire."

Anthony, always the composed statesman, doesn't betray any surprise. Instead, he leans back in his chair, fingers drumming on the mahogany table. "Yes, Your Majesty," he murmurs. "I've heard the whispers, seen the headlines."

"Then you understand my concern?" I press, hope flaring briefly in my chest.

Anthony nods, his gaze never leaving mine. "I do, ma'am. But may I offer a different perspective?"

I nod, curious despite myself. Anthony rarely suggests without reason.

"Right now," he starts, "we're on the brink of a conflict that might very well draw America into war alongside us. Having Princess Penelope in the States during this time could show unity between our nations. It's a calculated risk, indeed. But it might just work to our advantage."

I consider his words, feeling the weight of his suggestion. It's a bold move, but it might just work. "I see your point," I say finally. "But the public might not be as forgiving."

"It's a risk we must take," he says firmly. "If we want to show that the monarchy is adaptable to the times, we must make a statement."

"And what statement would we be making by sending the Princess to her rumored lover, who happens to be a girl?" I ask, my frustrations rising to the fore.

"That the monarchy is not an outdated organization, based on long forgotten principles that reflect archaic thinking."

The Prime Minister narrows his eyes, and I like how he is unafraid to voice his opinion in front of me.

"I happen to be the Supreme Governor of the Church of England, and Defender of the Faith, which still adheres to some archaic concepts you just mentioned. How can I, the Defender of the Faith, allow my daughter, who will be the future queen of England—to publicly engage in a same-sex relationship?"

"We can work out the details, Your Majesty. We can keep things under wraps, until we know the way ahead."

"Until that time comes, Prime Minister, I don't want my daughter meeting that singer. The monarchy will adapt when the time comes, but now is not the time for that."

"As you say, Your Majesty."

I nod slowly, feeling the weight of my responsibility heavy upon my shoulders. "Very well," I say, making my decision. "Princess Penelope will go to the States. But I want the press to be kept at bay. We don't want any unnecessary attention drawn to her."

"Understood, Your Majesty," he agrees, rising from his seat. "I'll make the necessary arrangements."

"Thank you, Anthony," I finally say. His reassurances have done little to quell the storm brewing inside me, but at least, it has given me a new perspective. I find myself looking out of the window, the setting sun casting a brilliant glow over the carefully manicured gardens of the palace. A storm is brewing, of that I have no doubt. But perhaps, just perhaps, we might weather it yet.

Chapter Three

Penelope

10 Days Later

I find myself snuggled up in a corner of my suite, an old, worn-out tome titled 'British Diplomacy: A Legacy Unravelled' lying open in my lap. As I skim through the pages, my mind wanders back to the earlier times, particularly the War on Terrorism and the fateful decision that linked Britain and the USA in an unyielding alliance.

What if I could go back in time? What if I had been the one in the PM's office when the call from the States came, a request for assistance cloaked in diplomatic niceties and political code? Would I have sent our troops to Iraq, knowing the consequences?

I shake my head at my reflection in the glass of the old-fashioned lantern sitting on my side table. Me, a politician? The idea seems ludicrous, yet I can't help but wonder. The weight of the decisions that have shaped our country's present is heavier than any royal crown.

The room falls quiet as I immerse myself deeper into the book, but my mind keeps wandering. Would I have given the same answer, assuring our allies of our full support, even if it meant sending our soldiers off to a foreign land, knowing not all would return?

The book slips from my hands, falling onto my lap with a soft thud. The reality of leadership, of decision-making at a national level, is so different from what we're led to believe. I lean back against the plush cushions, feeling a twinge of sympathy for the long line of leaders who've shouldered this burden.

It's easy to criticize from the sidelines, to say I would've done things differently. But in the hot seat, under the weight of responsibility and the glare of public scrutiny, would I have done any better?

Buried deep in the labyrinth of thought and books, I'm startled out of my reverie by a knock on the door.

"Who is it?" I call out, already knowing the answer.

"It's me, Kriti," comes the inevitable response, along with the familiar sound of the door creaking open.

I don't look up as I hear her footsteps approach. Instead, I run my fingers over the spine of the book, finding comfort in its solid presence.

"Princess," she says, her voice formal. She only calls me that when she's about to deliver news from my mother.

"Yes?" I reply, finally looking up from the book. "What's the verdict?"

"I've been told that Her Majesty would like to see you in the Blue Drawing Room," Kriti relays, her tone neutral.

The Blue Drawing Room? That's where mum holds her private audiences. I raise an eyebrow, intrigued.

"The Blue Drawing Room?" I echo her words, "Is this a court summon?"

"Apparently, yes. She didn't elaborate further." Kriti

shrugs, a smirk playing on her lips. "All I know is, she's made her decision about your American jaunt."

I roll my eyes. "Well, isn't that a cliffhanger?"

"Only one way to find out, princess," Kriti responds, emphasizing the title with a playful wink. She knows how much I despise the formality.

"You're enjoying this, aren't you?" I retort, tossing a cushion at her. But I'm smiling despite myself. It's impossible to stay too serious with Kriti around.

"Just doing my duty, princess," she grins, expertly catching the cushion. "Now, don't keep the queen waiting."

∞∞∞

As I walk into the Blue Drawing Room, I am immediately taken by the grandeur of the setting. The room is dominated by hues of cobalt and cream, with the sun's rays making the room glow through the heavy velvet drapes.

There, at the far end of the room, sits my mother, looking every bit the queen she is.

"Ah, Penelope," she says, beckoning me over with a wave of her hand, a glint of amusement in her eyes. "I see you haven't lost your knack for promptness."

"Can't keep the Queen waiting, can I?" I reply, giving her a mock salute as I take a seat across from her.

"Tell me, did you finish the book I sent your way?" she inquires, changing the subject.

"The one on diplomacy suggested by the PM? It was an interesting read," I nod, trying to steer clear of the underlying question. "Gave me a whole new perspective."

"Good. Good. Anything you'd have done differently, if you were in the hot seat?" She chuckles, raising a delicate teacup to her lips.

Before I can answer, I seize the opportunity to turn the tables. "Speaking of hot seats, have you been taking all your medications, Mother? You remember Dr. Harrison was quite insistent on it."

"Ah, yes." She grins. "My daily cocktail of pills. From blood pressure, heart disease, arthritis, diabetes, to even depression! Penelope, why do you insist on making me feel old?"

"Well, I just want you to stick around for a while longer. You're not exactly easy to replace, you know," I quip, with a playful smile. "Plus, who else would I tease about their pill intake?"

The room fills with our laughter, a sound that's become rare these days. It's moments like these that remind me how much I treasure these times with my mother, the Queen. She's not just a monarch; she's a mother, a friend, and most of all, a woman I deeply admire.

"And on a more serious note," my mother starts, her tone shifting to one of authority, "I have come to a decision about your trip."

"Go on," I say, my heart pounding in anticipation.

"You may go to the United States," she says. My heart leaps with joy. But then she raises her hand. "Under certain conditions."

"Conditions?" I retort, my joy quickly sinking into a pit of disappointment.

"Yes," she replies, cool as a cucumber. "Firstly, you will be staying with Aunt Martha in Washington."

I squint at her. "So, no freedom of movement. Just stuck in

D.C.?"

"Exactly," she confirms. "You are also expected to attend at least one diplomatic event. It's vital to maintain appearances, after all."

My fingers dig into my thigh under the table. "Right, maintain appearances. Got it."

She doesn't seem to pick up on my irritation. "There will also be a bodyguard with you, 24/7. This individual has already been selected."

"A bodyguard? Seriously, Mother?" I snort, incredulous. "I'm not five!"

"Furthermore," she barrels on, ignoring my outburst, "you are not to engage with the press, nor post about your trip on social media. This is a confidential journey, Penelope."

"Well, isn't this just peachy," I grumble, crossing my arms. "Anything else?"

"And lastly," she says, pausing for effect, "if you wish to meet your...friend, it will be on my terms. I will arrange for her to come to the ambassador's house, where you may meet her."

I stare at her, my jaw practically on the floor. "You're joking, right? Are you trying to cage me in, Mother?"

"These are the rules, Penelope. If you want to go, you must abide by them," she insists, her eyes never leaving mine.

"And what if I don't?" I ask, already knowing the answer to my question.

"Then you won't be allowed to go."

I smirk and feel the anger rushing through my veins.

"Why are you even sending me then? Is there a ruse that I am not able to see through?"

"There is no ploy. You should be thanking me for

arranging for you to continue your scandalous affair with that singer." The queen's words fly through the air like daggers.

"If Alexa would have been Alex, and a well-settled British diplomat or a military man, then there would have been nothing scandalous about my affair, right?"

Mother sighs, and places both hands on the armrests of the throne-like chair. "Yes."

"I don't like your conditions."

"I know. I don't like wearing this crown sometimes, but I still do."

"You love it, Mother. Don't lie to me. You like controlling people."

"I control them when I see that they are going down the wrong path."

"Yes, because you are the only authority on judging which path is right or wrong. You don't get to choose paths for others. They should be allowed to make their own paths, and learn from them."

"As a royal and Queen-in-waiting, you don't have the luxury of making mistakes."

I scoff. "I don't have the luxury of freedom, the luxury of loving who I want to...the luxury of having a normal life...a normal mother. You left a lot of things off the list."

I have to bite my tongue to keep from adding more to my rant.

The audacity of this woman...and yet, she is my mother, and a queen. My opposition won't change a thing, but it felt good to let it out.

My mother's face is blank, but her eyes tell a different story. There's pain behind them, pain that I have caused. But it's too late to take back my words. I sit there, feeling the weight of my anger, the weight of my words. I know I have hurt her, but I can't bring myself to apologize. Not yet.

"Is that all, Mother?" I ask, trying to keep my voice neutral.

"Yes," she says softly. "That's all."

I stand up, my anger still simmering just below the surface. "Then I shall take my leave. Thank you for seeing me, Your Majesty."

I turn on my heel and walk out of the room, my head held high even though my heart is heavy.

The weight of my anger and disappointment follows me out of the room.

Jessica

I'm sitting in a cold, dimly lit room with more brass than a trumpet factory. The big guys, the powers that be. There's General O'Grady, with his eagle-eye gaze that doesn't miss a single fidget.

O'Grady, the man who dragged me out of a dusty, hostile Iraq hut and threw me onto a chopper just as it was lifting off.

"This isn't a request, Thompson, it's an assignment," says Admiral Ryan. She's all gray hair and serious eyes, looking at me like she's already seeing me fail.

"Fantastic," I mutter. "So, I'm a glorified babysitter now?"

"Yes, to the future queen of England. That's an important position."

"Respectfully, ma'am," I grit out, "I'm in the middle of my semester. My psych classes won't complete themselves."

"Your country needs you, Thompson," Admiral Ryan retorts with an unwavering gaze.

"My country needs me to babysit a princess?" I can't help the sarcasm dripping from my words. "Can't the Brits handle their own?"

O'Grady cuts in, his stern face softening a smidgen, "Jessica, you remember when my team pulled you out of Fallujah?"

It's a low blow, dragging Iraq into this.

He knows I owe him. I barely nod, still hating that my name and Fallujah are in a sentence together.

"You owe me one, Thompson. This is me calling it in," O'Grady says, his gaze locked with mine. There's no escaping it. I'm cornered.

"Fine, but you owe me," I retort, bitterness edging my voice. I can already see my attendance plummeting and my grades in freefall. Great.

They hand me a thick folder. It's the princess in all her royal glory. Itineraries, likes, dislikes, daily schedules.

It's like she's a pet and I'm getting the owner's manual. As I skim through it, I realize this isn't just any assignment. This is a 24/7, 'forget your personal life' gig.

"They're paranoid about her safety," says Ryan, her tone unyielding. "There've been threats. You're to stay with her at all times, ensure she's secure."

"Just peachy," I grumble, my annoyance apparent. I'm picturing royal tea parties and paparazzi-chased car rides. I'm just a grad student doubling as a PTSD-riddled vet, for God's sake. But I know the game - once you're in, you're in for life. A part of me hates that I'm a pawn in their international chessboard.

Another part just shrugs it off.

After all, what's another war to a veteran?

I take a deep breath and nod my head. "Okay," I say, my voice resigned. "I'll do it."

The two of them exchange a look, and I can tell they're relieved that I'm not putting up much of a fight. They probably expected me to protest more, to argue and make a scene. But I'm too tired for that. Too tired to fight the big guys, too tired to argue with my own destiny.

I stand up, folder in hand. "When does she land?"

"The day after tomorrow," O' Grady says, reminding me of a disaster movie by the same name, and I wonder if it is an ill omen about the assignment I am about to undertake.

As I exit, I feel a small sense of dread start to bubble in my gut. I've never dealt with royalty before. I'm not sure I'm cut out for this kind of work. But I push the feeling aside, reminding myself that I can handle anything.

After all, I survived Fallujah.

On the drive back to my little studio apartment, I glance through the princess' Instagram profile.

She looks incredibly young, younger than she should be for someone of her royal status.

She's also beautiful, that much is sure. Her face is perfectly symmetrical, her big eyes a mesmerizing shade of brown. She has chestnut hair which cascades down to her shoulders in smooth waves. Her features almost resemble those of a popular French actress - Lea-Elui - and she even has a small mole above her lip.

She may be pretty, but I can already tell she's got a bit of snobbishness about her too.

Who knows what kind of drama this assignment will bring? On the one hand, she could be fun to baby-sit... or maybe it's just more reason for her to act like a bitch?

I can't tell yet. All I know is this will surely prove to be an interesting assignment.

Penelope

I'm hunched over my laptop, the cool glow of the screen casting a ghostly pallor on my face as I share my recent woes with Alexa, the rockstar who's been igniting some interesting feelings within me lately. The screen is filled with her charming grin, framed by that dark hair which refuses to behave - not that I'm complaining.

"So, I'm supposed to be the diplomatic golden child in Washington while you party it up in La La Land?" I grumble, running my fingers through my own stubborn locks in frustration.

A sigh filters through my speakers from Alexa's end. "Pen, if I could, I would drop everything and jet over. But, the album launch...the interviews...it's one big, unmovable circus."

I lean back, raking my hands over my face. I get it. She's got commitments. Doesn't make it any easier to swallow though. "I don't suppose my royal woes are enough to tempt you?" I ask, pouting for effect.

Her laughter rings out, easing the sting. "Well, if you're offering to parade around in a bikini for me, I might reconsider..." she teases, tossing me a wink.

I can't help the laugh that escapes me. "You wish," I retort, shaking my head at her antics. "I've been assigned a babysitter. A bodyguard who'll be with me 24/7."

"Ooh, a bodyguard? Why not seduce him into doing your bidding?" She wiggles her eyebrows suggestively, her grin widening.

"You're incorrigible," I mutter, though I'm grinning back at her. "And it's not going to be that simple. Rumor has it, the bodyguard is an ex-American marine, and also a woman."

Undeterred, Alexa starts shedding her jacket, revealing the tank top underneath. "Marine, huh? I'm sure you'll find a way... and when you do, I'll make sure it'll be well worth your time to sneak away to L.A."

Casting a playful smirk her way through the screen, I shoot back, "Would you get all green-eyed if I tried?"

Her chuckle echoes through the room, mirth dancing in her eyes as she deliberates. "I don't think I would," she finally drawls, an impish grin playing on her lips. "I've got faith that you'll be cunning enough to get your way - even if it means wrapping your bodyguard around your little finger. As long as you come back to me in the end, I've got no reason to be jealous."

Raising an eyebrow at her, I lean closer to the screen, my voice dropping to a sultry whisper. "And what if I can't rein myself in? What if I get carried away with the bodyguard's chiseled abs and biceps?"

That earns me a full-blown laugh, her eyes twinkling with mirth. "Don't think female six-packs are quite your scene, Princess."

Feigning indignation, I retort, imitating Alicia Silverstone from 'Clueless', "As if! Honestly, a woman - a proper woman - with icy eyes and a strong, silent vibe might be just what this caged, tired, pent-up princess needs!"

Alexa leans forward then, a devilish glint in her eyes, and my gaze involuntarily drops to her cleavage. A fading mark of our last rendezvous on her skin captures my attention, causing a pulse of desire to flare within me.

"In that case," she purrs, her tone teasing, "we might

have to consider sharing this bodyguard of yours on our honeymoon, hmm?"

I can't help but laugh, even as my heart pounds in my chest. Scandalous fantasies, intoxicatingly rebellious rockstars...and potentially, bodyguards with washboard abs? I was learning about weaknesses I never thought I could have".

I watch as Alexa's image pixelates before vanishing completely, her words still hanging heavy in the air. "Blasted," I grumble, flipping the laptop shut. I'd been hoping for some empathy, but instead got a tempting offer of shared bodyguard shenanigans. Who does she think I am, some kind of Regency rake? I shake my head; even for me, that's a ludicrous idea.

On cue, the heavy door to my suite swings open, and my lady-in-waiting swans in. "Presenting Ms. Kriti Gill," she announces, her voice bouncing off the marble columns and richly embroidered drapes. I quirk an eyebrow at Kriti. We've been chums since our diaper days, and the formal introduction is beyond ludicrous.

With an easy smile, Kriti takes a seat across me, plonking a daunting stack of papers on the coffee table. "Your life for the next seven days," she announces, pushing it towards me with a grimace. My life in print, neatly bounded and planned to the minute.

Joy.

Kriti interrupts my sour musings. "Don't look so tragic, Penny. I've managed to squirrel in some you-time," she says, trying to brighten the mood.

I can't help but smirk.

"What's that, a whole five minutes between the meeting with the President and Aunt Martha's infamous tea parties?"

"I thought you might enjoy a run in the maze... alone."

"Oh, the sheer delight," I reply, with a roll of my eyes. But my gratitude for Kriti's efforts shines through my sarcasm. "Really, thanks, Kriti."

She nods, then leans back, her gaze turning serious. "About your bodyguard…" she starts, making me straighten in my chair.

"Meet Jessica 'Jess' Thompson, a native New Yorker," Kriti announces, handing over a stack of papers. My eyes land on the photo at the top of the stack, the determined face of a woman staring back at me.

"A New Yorker babysitting me? Now, this will be fun," I quip, but my words lack their usual bite.

"Her parents died in the 9/11 attacks when she was only nine." Kriti's voice is quiet, somber. I feel a sudden pang of sadness for the little girl she was, losing everything in an instant.

"God," I utter, my fingers absently tracing the edge of the photo. The tragedy is unfathomable.

Kriti nods and continues, "She moved to Texas afterward. As soon as she turned eighteen, she joined the Marines."

Turning the page, I study her in uniform, in the heart of a desert far away. I flip to another photo: Jess, in regular clothes, looking like a rock-hard version of Romi Strijd. The same beautiful face, but with ice-blue eyes that hint at her hardened past.

"She served in Iraq and Afghanistan, was part of a deadly encounter in Fallujah, got a medal and an honorable discharge," Kriti recounts, the rhythm of her voice grounding me.

"A bona fide hero, then," I respond, a new level of respect seeping into my tone.

"Well, the story doesn't end there. She dealt with PTSD post-service, is currently enrolled in her psychology degree, and wants to help others in similar situations," Kriti adds. A survivor and a helper, a rare combination.

"And now she's assigned to babysit me. Excellent," I mutter, a strange feeling coiling in my stomach.

"Indeed. Jess Thompson is anything but your average bodyguard." Kriti smirks.

"Clearly." I rest back in my chair, dropping the papers on my desk. There's an undeniable pull about Jess that intrigues me. She's more than a survivor; she's a warrior.

"But she's not what I expected," I confess, musing over her photos again. "I thought she'd be more...muscular, tomboyish. But she's sexy, tall, and with those blue eyes, she's downright stunning."

Kriti chuckles. "Surprised, are we?"

"Mmm, it's just...I have to figure out how to handle a bodyguard who looks like a supermodel and fights like a soldier," I muse aloud, wondering if this war-hardened guardian might just become the biggest hurdle to my LA escape plan. God save the Queen, I think, because this princess is about to embark on a seriously wild ride.

Jessica

The neon luminescence of the city bleeds through the grimy windows of Joe's, casting long, distorted shadows over our worn leather booth. A covert spot frequented by the soldiers and scarred, this dimly lit bar has been my solace for years. Maria Sanchez, a firecracker I once sort of dated and who still remains my closest friend, already sits there, nursing her whiskey, looking like Sommer Ray's Latina doppelgänger.

"Hey, Thompson," she purrs, her brown eyes flashing with mischief, "gonna keep a girl waiting?"

"I like to keep you on your toes, Sanchez," I respond, sliding into the seat opposite her, feeling the familiar, cool touch of whiskey filled glass she pushes towards me.

"Hah, you wish," she scoffs, tossing back a mouthful of her drink. Her eyes sparkle with an unholy glint as she nudges my foot under the table, "So, are you gonna talk about your rendezvous with that college girl? Sophie, was it?"

"Should've known you'd ask," I sigh, downing a swig. "What happened to not sticking our noses into each other's business, Maria?"

"Come on, Jess. Since when do we keep secrets?" she retorts, her lips curling into an impish smile. "We're exes, not strangers. Plus, you've got that 'I've-got-laid' glow about you."

"Oh, do I now?" I chuckle, raising an eyebrow at her. "And here I thought I was blending in perfectly with the crowd."

Maria lets out a hearty laugh. "Yeah, like a bull in a china shop," she retorts, her laugh subsiding into a grin. "Now, stop evading and spill the beans."

"Alright, alright," I admit defeat, rolling my eyes. "It was fun, a good distraction. But she wanted a relationship, and I..." I shrug, "I just needed a release."

"Ahh, there's the Thompson I know!" Maria raises her glass, a gleam of understanding in her eyes. "Bailing out of emotional entanglements since... forever?"

"Four years and counting," I respond, clinking my glass with hers.

"And I thought I was the queen of commitment-phobia," Maria chuckles. She clinks her glass against mine, her smile warm, familiar. "Here's to your four more years of monkhood, Thompson."

And with that, we down our whiskey, the taste of bittersweet memories lingering on my tongue.

As the laughter subsides, Maria swipes at her eyes, the remnants of her mirth lingering in the sparkle of her gaze. "You know, Jess, you really should've been a comedian," she snorts.

I shrug, a sardonic smile pulling at the corner of my lips. "Yeah, right, as if the world needs more of my cynical humor," I retort.

"Perhaps," Maria concedes with a smirk, "But what the world definitely doesn't need is more of your mysterious 'too cool for school' aura. So, spill it. What's bugging you, Thompson?"

The playful banter of a moment ago dims, replaced by a thick cloud of trepidation. With a sigh, I toss back the rest of my whiskey and set the glass down with more force than necessary. "I've been assigned a new mission," I start, rubbing my temples.

Maria's smirk vanishes, her demeanor turning serious as she leans in, "What is it this time? Syria? North Korea? And aren't you retired?"

I chuckle dryly. "I wish. No, Maria. It's a bodyguard detail. To babysit a bratty, spoilt princess who's on a tour of the states," I reveal, grimacing at the thought.

Maria blinks, surprise morphing into incredulous laughter. "You're kidding! The Marines are turning a badass war vet into a nanny? No way!"

I nod, echoing her disbelief with a sarcastic smile. "You're telling me. Imagine Jessica 'Hardass' Thompson, trailing after a royal highness, Princess Penelope of England, no less. I've heard she's a pain in the ass. A stuck-up, rude snob who likes to raise hell wherever she goes."

Maria's eyes crinkle in amusement. "Oh, Jess, the thought

of you two prancing around in matching tiaras... it's stuff for the books!"

"Far from it," I counter, rolling my eyes, "Have you ever seen her?"

Her face scrunches in distaste. "Can't say I have. Frankly, I don't fancy keeping tabs on the daily lives of imperial bigots."

I can't help but empathize with Maria's disdain. The scars left by the monarchy in her homeland run deep.

"Can't blame you. But she's pretty," I admit, waving over the bartender for another round. "In that overly pampered, doll-faced way. Reminds me of those brats at the Officers' Club, strutting around like peacocks just because their daddies outrank ours. Utter nepotism, I tell you. A pretty face and a tiara, none of which she earned."

Maria's eyebrows shoot up. "Now you've got me curious, Thompson." She pulls out her phone, typing away, "Let's have a look at this royal Barbie."

A few swipes later, she thrusts her phone in my face, a photo of Penelope gracing the screen. The princess is caught in a candid moment on some Spanish beach, dressed in nothing but a bikini.

"Damn, they let royalty get snapped in bikinis these days?" Maria asks, an edge of admiration creeping into her voice.

I shrug. "Not generally. But this one doesn't play by the rules."

Maria grins, holding the phone out for a second glance. "Well, I have to say, I admire her defiance. And her ass. You should definitely check out the view, Thompson. You've always been an ass woman. That's why you went for me, right?"

I roll my eyes, smirking at Maria's teasing. "Sure, that's the only reason," I retort, snatching her phone to get a better look at the princess. And there she is, Penelope of England, with her long chestnut-brown hair and almond-shaped eyes - and a body that could make even the most disciplined of soldiers weak in the knees. I have to admit, Maria is right about one thing: the view is definitely worth checking out.

But I can't let myself get distracted by a pretty face and a killer body. Not when there's a job to be done.

I hand Maria back her phone and drain the rest of my whiskey. "I'll try to keep my eyes on the job, not her ass," I mutter, grimacing at the thought of playing babysitter to a royal brat.

Maria chuckles. "Good luck with that, Thompson. I've seen you in action. You're not exactly subtle."

I roll my eyes, feeling a pang of frustration. It's true - I've never been good with authority figures, especially not ones who think they're above the law. And from what I've heard about Princess Penelope, she's the poster child for privilege gone wrong.

But orders are orders, and I'll suck it up and do my job. Even if it means pretending to be interested in a spoiled princess's daily routine. It's not like it's the first time I've had to put up with entitled jerks. I've been in the military long enough to know how to put on a fake smile and make small talk with the best of them.

"Thanks for the vote of confidence," I quip, signaling for the check. "But I better get going. I've got a flight to catch early tomorrow morning. The royal Barbie lands in Washington at noon, and it's a long flight from San Francisco to DC."

Maria nods in understanding as I stand up from the bar stool. "Stay safe, Thompson," she says, giving me a quick hug. "And don't let that princess get under your skin."

I return the hug, grateful for Maria's support. "I'll do my best. See you soon."

Chapter Four

Penelope

Touching down in Washington at the break of dawn on the tenth of June, I am met by a solemn airport deserted for my clandestine landing.

A convoy of black GMCs driven by men in suits resembling Men in Black whisk me away to my destination.

Seated next to me, in this high-speed roller-coaster of anticipation, is Kriti Gill, my partner-in-crime, the Jeeves to my Wooster, her wit as sharp as her style.

"C'mon Penny, that frown doesn't suit your face," she quips, her eyes twinkling with teasing warmth.

"Hmph, it's easy for you to say," I retort, my attention fixated on the majestic blur of cityscape outside. The Washington Monument pierces the sky, a reminder of America's fierce patriotism. The Lincoln Memorial stands tall, stoic, almost intimidating, like a headmaster at a school assembly.

The palpable air of power in this city sends shivers down my spine.

"Busted!" Kriti breaks my reverie, the corners of her lips curled in a knowing smirk. "You're more transparent than the

Queen's tea, love."

"Stop spying on my thoughts, Gill," I grumble, turning to face her.

"Well, I wouldn't need to if you'd just talk," she shoots back, her gaze steady and comforting.

"Fine! I'm a nervous wreck, alright?" I blurt out, throwing my hands up in exasperation. "I don't get how I'm supposed to rub shoulders with the world's powerhouses without tripping over my words or, even worse, my heels."

Kriti's laughter fills the car, her amusement a balm to my rising anxiety. "Penny, you worry too much. You have the world wrapped around your little finger. You've become an icon for the younger generation, someone who's not afraid to challenge conventions. Trust me, those big shots will be more starstruck than you."

I ponder her words, letting them seep in.

It's true, I've always followed my heart, let my rebellious nature guide my actions. Still, the prospect of making small talk with world leaders feels as daunting as walking a tightrope in my six-inch stilettos.

"But Kriti, you know how I tend to let my foot meet my mouth in moments of pressure. I'm afraid I might upset someone and spark World War III!"

Her laughter echoes once again in the spacious interior, her hand coming to rest on mine. "Oh, Penny! Your honesty is your strength. You speak from your heart, and that's what people appreciate. Just be yourself, and remember they're only humans, not a pack of hungry lions."

A deep breath inflates my lungs, my heart pounding against my ribs. As our car pulls into the grand driveway of my aunt's stately Washington residence, I feel a mixture of exhilaration and fear. Welcome to the American adventure,

Penelope!

∞∞∞

In the palatial dining room of the ambassador's residence, I find myself seated next to the most delightful pair. My Aunt Martha, her face a radiant sun in the sea of fading evening light, her lips never tiring from spouting tales of yore.

Then there's her consort, my uncle, the dignified British Ambassador to the United States, a man who upholds the very epitome of British grace and sophistication.

Aunt Martha chatters on, her vivacity filling the air like sparks from a firework. "So Penny, darling! How was your flight? I hope it was smoother than my wrinkles," she giggles, sipping her wine while patting at her laugh lines theatrically.

Giggling, I reply, "Smooth as a baby's bottom, Aunt Martha. Your charm must've spread its wings and taken us under."

"Ha! Such a sweet talker, just like your mother," she twinkles, her blue eyes echoing her high spirits. "Oh, speaking of spreading wings, your London Fashion Week appearance. God, girl! You had jaws dropping, tongues wagging, and hearts thumping. You looked as pretty as a picture, better than the models themselves!"

"Thank you, Aunt Martha. Although I was a bit unsure about that slit..." I admit, a blush creeping up my face.

The gleam in her eyes turns mischievous. "Oh, pish posh! It was scandalously perfect. I remember this slit gown I wore on my honeymoon..."

Before her story starts to gather more... explicit momentum, Uncle saves the day. "Ahem, Martha, my love, don't you think that story is a tad too colorful for dinner?"

Martha shrugs nonchalantly. "Oh fine, keep your trousers on, love!" She then winks at me, and we both dissolve into laughter, leaving the men in the room clueless.

"I can assure you, Penny," Uncle begins, successfully regaining our attention, "Your stay here will be quite enlightening. We're hosting a party in your honour, inviting Washington's finest. It's a golden opportunity for you to mingle and understand the crème de la crème of American society."

My heart skips a beat. "Sounds... interesting. Who all are on the guest list, Uncle?"

"From politicians, diplomats, to influencers and A-listers, my dear. It will be a glorious mix of power and charm," Uncle informs, the soft glow of anticipation in his eyes. "Don't worry, I'll be right by your side, to steer you clear of any potential faux pas. We'll make a splendid team."

I offer him a grateful smile.

If there's one person I'd trust to navigate this tumultuous sea of political sharks and social butterflies, it's my charming uncle. "Thank you, Uncle. I really appreciate it."

"Penelope," Uncle Robert intones, a tone of seriousness replacing his usually jovial demeanor. "There is someone you should meet."

"Go ahead, Uncle," I reply, brows arched in intrigue.

In response, he gestures towards a shadowy corner of the grand room.

Out of the darkness steps a figure that steals my breath away. Long, lithe legs glide forward with an assurance that only comes with years of self-confidence, carrying a tall, powerfully built frame towards us.

The woman who emerges is stunning in the most unconventional sense.

Dressed in a tailored pantsuit of slate grey that clings to her athletic build, her every stride radiates a raw power.

Golden hair cascades down her back, loose and wild, framing a face that looks like it has been sculpted by war itself.

But it's her eyes that truly rivet me, those icy-blue orbs, fierce and indomitable. They remind me of a stormy sea, beautiful yet formidable, and equally capable of destruction if provoked.

"May I introduce Jessica Thompson," Uncle Robert announces, oblivious to the electric charge sparking through the room. "She will be your bodyguard during your stay."

As he rambles on about her commendable past and decorated service, I struggle to keep my reaction concealed.

Here stands a woman who is not just my bodyguard, but a stark embodiment of resilience and bravery, a silent testament to a world much harsher than my own.

"She won't be a bother to you, Penelope," Uncle Robert reassures, somehow reading the hesitation on my face. "Jessica is quite adept at blending into the background while ensuring her charge's safety."

Feigning indifference, I turn to Uncle Robert, the words escaping my mouth a pitch higher than usual. "I appreciate your foresight, Uncle."

Back to her, I manage a nonchalant nod in her direction, a feeble attempt to assert my unaffected stance. Yet, there's something in her respectful bow and the way she says, "Your Highness, I'm honored to serve. I look forward to ensuring your safety," that stokes a fire of intrigue within me.

Beneath my haughty exterior, my heart thunders against

my ribcage, my cheeks flush, and my palms sweat.

Suddenly, I find myself staring into the abyss of the most compelling and intimidating woman I've ever encountered.

"May I speak candidly, Jessica?" My eyes find it hard to lock with Jessica's for too long, and I cast them away to play with the spoon on my plate.

"Of course, Your Highness."

"When my mother, the omnipotent, all-knowing queen of England, told me I was to be assigned a bodyguard, who would shadow me around like Penn Badgley from 'You', I was far from thrilled."

"Understandably so, Your Highness," Jessica offers in a muted tone.

"I wasn't done talking, Jessica." The words tumble out before I can reel them in, surprising even me.

What's gotten into you, Penelope?

Am I resorting to rudeness as a defensive mechanism again?

"I apologize, Your Highness."

"However, I took a look through your file, and I must say, I was rather impressed. It's a bit of a disservice to a decorated war hero like you, relegating you to babysitting duty. Therefore, I would prefer if you could be a friend, and nothing more. Is that something we can agree on?"

There's a pause as Jessica absorbs my proposal. Her expression gives away nothing of her thoughts.

"I take my job very seriously, Your Highness. While I usually prefer maintaining the roles of bodyguard and client, I'm open to attempting a friendship."

"That would be ideal, Jessica. Would you care to join us for dinner?"

"No, I have to liaise with your head of security to familiarize myself with their security protocol. Please, enjoy your dinner, Your Highness." With a bow, Jessica turns to leave.

As I watch her confident, long strides and the wavy blonde hair bouncing with each step, I'm filled with awe.

That woman is fucking hot!

I confess to myself, swiftly chiding my own weakness for women who can intimidate me.

Is it mommy issues...or daddy issues?

I can never quite put a finger on it.

"That was a tad rude, don't you think, Penny?" Uncle Robert's words hold a note of reprimand.

"Umm...no, I think I was just being forthright. That's just how I am, Uncle," I reply, with an unwavering smile.

"Well, just be careful not to step on any toes, my dear. Jessica is a force to be reckoned with," Uncle Robert advises, his expression softening. "But I'm glad to see you're taking an interest in her. She's quite the enigma."

I raise an eyebrow. "Oh? Do tell, Uncle."

"Well, for starters, her military records are classified. Even I don't have clearance to access them," Uncle Robert reveals, leaning in conspiratorially. "But from what I've gathered, she's been on the frontlines since she was eighteen. Fought in some of the most dangerous warzones in the world. Survived a few explosions, lost a few comrades, but always emerged as a true leader of her squad. Hence, the commendations and awards."

"I'll keep that in mind, Uncle. I may be dealing with someone who has talked to aliens!" I laugh, and so does Aunt Martha, but Kriti and Uncle Robert are silent.

Uncle Robert scrutinizes me for a moment, as if trying to decipher the real meaning behind my words. But eventually, he seems to let it go and turns to address the rest of the table.

"Well, let's resume our dinner, shall we? We don't want the delicious food to go to waste."

Jessica

The nerve of that spoiled brat! I fume as I stalk down the hallway, heels clicking ominously against the polished marble, the echo amplifying my annoyance.

"And I wasn't done talking, Jessica," I mimic Penelope's high-handed tone under my breath, fury crackling in my veins. Just because she had a silver spoon lodged permanently in her mouth, she thought it was acceptable to talk down to everyone.

Well, not on my watch.

I push through the double doors leading to my assigned room, letting out a frustrated huff.

Why is it that those born into privilege always end up being the most difficult to handle? What was the need for her to interrupt me mid-sentence and snap at me like I was a disobedient schoolkid?

Ridiculous!

My room is a functional, impersonal space with a solid oak desk and an oversized bed, complete with an en-suite bathroom. It's probably the closest thing to luxury I'll get in my time as a royal babysitter. However, instead of appreciating the upscale decor and plush comforts, I'm nursing my simmering outrage.

I toss my jacket onto the back of a chair and start pacing, mulling over my recent encounter with the princess. All the while, the silence in the room amplifies the pounding in my head. Was her arrogance a result of being coddled all her life? Or was it the entitlement of being born in the lap of luxury, far removed from the realities of a world where people actually worked for a living?

With a sigh, I glance at the clock.

It's late.

The briefing with Penelope's security detail was exhaustive. They run a tight ship, leaving me with a pile of documents and protocols to go through before dawn.

I decide to grab a quick shower before diving into the paperwork, hoping the hot water would ease my frazzled nerves.

Stripping off my clothes, I step into the shower, letting the water wash over me. It's a momentary escape from the madness of my new job. I close my eyes, reveling in the warmth. The sound of the water beats against my skin, soothing my senses. It's a luxury I can hardly afford in my day-to-day life, let alone in a foreign palace. But here I am, naked and wet, in a shower fit for a queen.

I shake my head, determined to focus on the task at hand. The paperwork won't go away, no matter how much I wish it would. And neither will Penelope. I have to find a way to work with her, despite her condescending attitude. The sooner I can establish a rapport, the better for both of us.

The hot water from the shower pours over me, but it does nothing to wash away my annoyance. I'm staring at the bathroom tiles, an intricate mosaic of blacks and whites, but all I see are flashes of that interaction with Princess Penelope.

Each drop splashing against my skin reminds me of her stubborn, privileged character.

Her demanding demeanor.

The way she didn't even bat an eyelid while talking to me. Hell, she was even sitting there in a mini skirt and stockings, radiating her regal, feminine power.

A snort escapes me, breaking the monotonous sound of water hitting tile.

A princess.

And not just any princess, but the royal pain-in-the-ass of England herself had managed to ruffle my feathers, something not even the toughest drill sergeants could do.

I turn my face up to the shower head, letting the water drench my hair and run down my face. For a moment, I close my eyes, hoping the water might blur the image of Penelope's arrogant face in my mind.

But it only makes it clearer.

Her damned mole on her lip. Her polished exterior. And let's not forget her nerve - her fearless, unflinching nerve. She didn't show a hint of intimidation, a rarity I've come to appreciate.

I find my hands involuntarily balling into fists at my sides, the water from the shower making my grip slip.

I wish she wasn't such a hard-ass. I wish she wasn't... No, I'm not going there. I am not letting the image of a pampered, spoilt princess to get under my skin.

With a frustrated growl, I punch the glass of the shower. The noise echoes around the room, bouncing off the cold tiles. The impact sends a dull throb through my hand, but it's not enough to distract me.

This assignment... I swear it's going to be the end of me.

Penelope

I tuck my legs in and wrap my hands around them, wishing I hadn't been such a bitch.

There was absolutely no need for me to talk to her like that, but my damn defense mechanism—with its proclivity to land me without friends—has always been my downfall.

I let out a frustrated sigh, roll over on my belly and press a button on my nightstand.

"Please send in Jessica Thompson," I say, jumping out of bed.

For the next few minutes, I'm a blur of activity: combing my hair, putting on a fresh layer of lipstick, changing from my comfy but washed-out shorts and tank top to my satin nightdress that barely covers my ass and shows a bit too much of my royal titties.

I examine my own reflection and notice an unexpected burst of colour staining my cheeks.

Now, where the devil did that come from?

An ominous echo of footsteps reverberates behind me and my head whips around so fast, I'm left slightly dizzy.

"Ms. Jessica Thompson, Your Highness," announces the lady-in-waiting, before taking her leave with an obligatory curtsey.

Caught off guard, Jessica manages to muster, "I apologize for my state of undress. I had just taken a shower...Your Highness," with a shred of wavering confidence.

My eyes involuntarily scan the length of her, catching sight of her muscular, battle-scarred legs peeking from behind the fabric of her bathrobe.

"Late night shower enthusiast, I see?" I throw in a comment, desperately attempting to divert my gaze from her tantalising thighs, directing it instead to the icy chill of

Jessica's stare.

As if that helps any!

"Indeed. Helps clear the fog," she says, casually running a hand through her towel-dampened hair.

"Very true," I add, "and it also serves as an excellent opportunity to indulge in a bit of the ol' rumpy-pumpy!" My grin stretches across my face as the words spill out.

Her stoic, expressionless face screams 'not impressed'.

"The what, Your Highness?" she inquires, the question hanging in the air.

"Oh, never mind... Regardless, I asked for you...err...I requested your presence because I think we may have stumbled out of the gate, Jess. Can I call you that?"

"Certainly, Your Highness."

"Brilliant! So...I thought we might start afresh. Hi! I'm Penelope Victoria Windsor, the future Queen of England and purported destroyer of the monarchy, if you believe a word Mother spouts," I declare, extending my hand for a handshake after a swift three-stride approach.

Her hand engulfs mine, offering a grip strong enough to rival any seasoned military official, practically crushing my dainty fingers.

"Staff Sergeant Jessica Thompson, retired marine, at your service, Your Highness," she declares.

"So, Jess, have you been thoroughly briefed about my illustrious engagement schedule? I hope my head of security didn't give you too much trouble," I begin, propping myself up against the doorjamb.

Jess responds with a smirk that flickers and disappears as quick as a shooting star. "Believe me, Your Highness, I've faced worse," she says, in a tone more akin to a threat than a complaint.

I lean in a little closer, an intrigued grin creeping onto my face. "Really now? So, do you generally consider yourself the toughest woman in the room?"

"No," she replies succinctly, but a playful glint in her eye makes me think there's more to it.

"No? That's surprising. Do tell more."

"I consider myself the toughest person, not just woman, in the room."

My interest piqued further, I let out a chuckle, appreciating her cheeky confidence. "I love the sound of that. More power to you, Staff Sergeant."

I decide to share a bit of my current mental tumult, letting my guard down a smidgen.

"Honestly, I'm not thrilled about spending seven days cooped up in Washington. Mother insists, of course. But I'd much rather be in New York, enjoying the city's vibrant energy."

I pause for a moment, fishing for a response, hoping for some sort of rebellious solidarity from her.

Maybe even an offer to smuggle me out to the city that never sleeps?

"Perhaps it would be best to do as your mother says, Your Highness," Jess advises, not even a hint of rebelliousness in her voice. "Disobeying orders from authority, in my experience, tends to end poorly."

My hopes for an impromptu New York adventure deflate faster than a popped balloon.

"Oh, come off it, Jess! Since when did 'authority' become the end-all-be-all? It's people like us who should be challenging the status quo, isn't it?"

Jess crosses her arms, her eyebrows furrowed. "We all have roles, Your Highness. Yours is to be a representative of your country, and mine is to protect you. That requires order, discipline, and yes, authority."

We lock eyes, the room suddenly seeming far too small for the debate brewing between us.

"Or perhaps," I retort, stoking the coals, "it requires a dash of defiance, a pinch of unpredictability, and a healthy dollop of living on your own terms. I'm not just a princess, Jess. I'm a person, too. And people need to live a little, don't you agree?"

Her frosty gaze doesn't waver. "And live you shall, Your Highness. But my duty is to ensure you live...safely."

"Even if it comes at the cost of living fully?" I push back, setting the stage for an argument that promises to be as titillating as it would be challenging. But what's life without a bit of a verbal joust now and then, especially with someone as fiercely intriguing as Jessica Thompson?

Jess stands there, unmoving, her face a mask of composure. "There are ways to live fully without risking your safety, Your Highness," she finally replies, her tone even.

I narrow my eyes, sensing that my efforts to incite her have fallen flat. "You're impossible," I grumble, throwing my hands up in the air.

Jess's lips quirk up in one corner, a hint of amusement evident in her eyes. "I've been told that before."

I roll my eyes, feeling a smile tug at the corners of my mouth despite myself. "Well, I suppose I'll just have to find a way to crack that tough exterior of yours," I say, stepping closer to her.

Her expression remains neutral, but I can see a spark of something in her eyes. Is it...interest? I can't be sure.

But I'm determined to find out.

"Jess," I say, climbing up onto my bed and knee-walking to the headboard, and then turning around to face my ex-marine babysitter, "I once stole a horse from the palace stables and rode it all the way from Balmoral Castle, the one in Scotland, to Aberdeen, by the sea. I rode for four hours straight and hid in one of the lighthouses, a crumbling old mess, infested with rats, just so I could live one night of my life how I want to." I lean against the headboard, lift my leg up, and point my toes at Jess. "Could you help me with my socks?"

"Absolutely," Jess retorts, her form shifting slightly beside the grandiose bed.

A fleeting instance catches my attention; her eyes linger on the expanse of my exposed legs before she gently captures my foot within her secure grasp.

"Once, Your Highness, I was part of a team tasked to track down a terrorist. Hidden deep within the labyrinthine caves of the Iraqi desert, he was like a ghost. I lost two of my comrades and was ordered to return to base. Five days later, I returned alone, the severed head of the terrorist in my backpack." Jess's voice reverberates in the room, her words causing a ripple of tension to slice through the silence.

A soft gasp escapes my lips when her fingertips make contact with my bare skin.

Yet, she remains stoic, her eyes locked onto mine, unwavering.

My heart starts pounding a mad, erratic rhythm against my ribcage. It's a feeling I hadn't felt before, a nervous excitement mingled with an undercurrent of something far more intense. This isn't diminished as she proceeds to address the other foot, her movements precise and controlled.

"I think we are cut from different cloths," I utter,

struggling to maintain a semblance of composure.

"Your cloth is still fresh, Princess. You're only twenty-one. I, on the other hand, am thirty-one. My cloth has been repeatedly stitched and patched. It's become complex and rigid. I don't think it's going to change anytime soon," Jessica admits, her voice carrying a hint of finality.

Jessica

Nestled in the quiet embrace of shadows, I watch the royal show play out in front of me. Princess Penelope, flanked by the ever-grinning Uncle Robert and the over-enthusiastic Kriti, is engaged in the most taxing task of her royal highness's day: going through the guest list for tonight's diplomatic ball.

What a chore, right?

From the ornate Victorian couch, she wrestles with a flurry of names and titles.

I can practically hear the cogs grinding in her head. "Sir Edmund Fitzgerald, Governor-General of Canada and his wife Lady Francesca... Minister Zhang Wei of China's Ministry of Foreign Affairs... the flamboyant Ambassador Kato Tetsuro of Japan... and who on earth is this Dr. Moyo from South Africa?"

She struggles and stumbles through the seemingly endless list. The daunting web of international diplomacy, laced with the nuances of their individual personalities and political climate, is proving too much for the young princess.

I almost find it amusing.

There are young women out there, raising kids all on their own, hustling between two, sometimes even three jobs just to keep the lights on. And here we have a princess, the future queen of England, whining about a few names she can't remember and an event she has to attend in designer threads.

"I need to get out of here," Penelope declares, her voice echoing the frustration that had crept into her body language.

She looks tired.

"I need a Starbucks."

Uncle Robert, ever the diplomat, nods sympathetically. "That sounds like a wonderful idea, Penelope."

Kriti, already standing, declares, "I'll accompany you, Your Highness."

"No," Penelope's hand is raised in protest, "I want to go alone."

Uncle Robert's voice comes in then, the veneer of his jovial demeanor replaced by the sterner tone of an experienced diplomat, "That isn't possible, Penny. You'll need to take Jessica with you."

I watch as she rolls her eyes, a small frown marring her features. "Do I have to bring her everywhere I go?" she grumbles under her breath.

Uncle Robert's voice is firm. "Yes, you do, Penny. It's protocol."

Penelope lets out a dramatic sigh before turning to face me. "Fine. Let's go, Jess," she says, rising from the couch.

There I am, parked across Penelope, tucked into a dim corner of a Starbucks. Her face is obscured by a low-hung baseball cap and colossal Dior sunglasses, drinking her latte as if it's a rebellious act of defiance.

Frankly, it's amusing to see this royal figure cloaked in Nike, her toned stomach peeking out from beneath the fabric of her cropped top. Hell, the girl even has the start of a six-pack.

The loose joggers she's sporting does wonders for her hip curves but falls baggy down the rest of her legs. Suddenly, I feel underdressed in my worn-out white tank top, skinny jeans, scuffed sneakers, and budget Walmart shades.

"Are you going to keep staring at me?" The annoyance in her voice is palpable. She's got nerve, I'll give her that. "Or are you going to use that Marine training of yours to help me calm down?"

"Well, Your Highness," I respond, not missing a beat. "Last I checked, my training was more about evading bullets, not remembering the names of politicians and their pets."

Penelope glares from behind her sunglasses. It's clear she's not in the mood for my humor.

Right, she's royalty and I'm just a bodyguard.

"Alright, alright. Step one, recognize your stressor. What's causing this anxiety?" I ask her, taking a sip from my drink.

"It's the event. It's the people. I just...I just don't want to mess up, you know?" she replies, fidgeting with the lid of her cup.

"Okay, you've got that figured out. Now step two, control your breathing," I explain, leaning back in my chair. "Try 'box breathing'. Inhale for four, hold for four, exhale for four, then wait for four. Repeat until you feel calmer."

She gives it a shot, following the counts on her fingers. I watch as the tension seems to slowly ebb away from her shoulders.

"Lastly," I continue, "positive self-talk. It sounds cheesy, but remind yourself that you can handle it. You're prepared. You're capable. It might help."

For a few moments, she remains silent, processing my advice. I down the last of my coffee, hoping she finds my Marine anxiety-reducing techniques a little helpful.

If only remembering names was as easy as diffusing a bomb.

The little calm I see Penelope acquire quickly dissolves and her face scrunches up in frustration. "It's not working," she says, staring back at me behind her sunglasses.

"Then you're not being honest about your stressors," I state matter-of-factly. It's not a reprimand. Sometimes the worst lies we tell are to ourselves.

Penelope's gaze drops to her coffee cup as she chews on her bottom lip, lost in thought. After a beat, she finally says, "There's... there's someone."

"Oh?" I keep my tone neutral, not betraying my surprise.

"Alexa," she divulges, rolling the name around like a prayer. "She's a singer. Having an album listening party in LA in a week."

"And you want to go." It's not a question.

I can see the longing in her eyes.

"I need to be there. But Mother has practically put me under house arrest. I really like this girl, Jessica," she confides, leaning in. The way she says my name is intimate, the way you'd talk to a friend.

"And because she's a girl..." I venture, letting the implication hang in the air.

"I can't see her because I'm the future queen of England and apparently, a same-sex relationship isn't...conventional," she finishes for me, a bitter edge to her words. "All I want is one last, crazy time with her. And then I can come back and play my part. I promise."

She almost sounds like she's begging, and it's a punch in the gut. Not just because she's the princess, but because she's just a 21-year-old girl infatuated with someone, wanting to break free.

I'm taken aback, I admit. But I push the surprise back. It's not the time to let my personal feelings cloud my judgement. "Penelope..." I start, but then stop, unsure of how to navigate this conversation.

In front of me, Penelope waits, hopeful yet nervous, a girl ready to break the shackles of her birthright. And suddenly, I find myself on the precipice of a decision that could change everything.

This job isn't as straightforward as I thought it would be.

I look at Penelope, trying to quell the churn of emotions within me. Duty, the age-old weight on my shoulders, tells me to say the words I do. "Penelope, maybe it's better to listen to your mother," I begin, keeping my tone even. "Mothers know best. As for Alexa, why don't we try to arrange a private audience for her here? A secure location, a hotel maybe? I can manage that."

But my words don't land well. Penelope's face hardens, her eyes sparkling with anger. "You're a coward," she spits. The accusation stings, but I hold my ground.

"Penelope, I'm just--"

"Doing your job? Is that it, Jessica? You want to look good in front of your superiors. It's all about covering your own ass, isn't it?"

"Princess, I assure you--"

"I thought I could trust you, Jessica," she continues, her voice a bitter note in the calm of the café. "I thought you could be a friend. But you're just like them. You've lost all emotions in the war, and become nothing but a robot. You've forgotten what it feels like to be a human, to feel, to want something so desperately it hurts."

Her words cut, and I find myself taking a step back. Suddenly, I'm not in the café but back in the dusty streets of Iraq, amidst gunfire and chaos. I blink, forcing myself back to the present.

"I'm sorry, Penelope. I--"

"Don't," she cuts me off, her voice trembling with unshed tears. "You were my mistake, Jess. I thought you could be different, but you're not."

Her words hang heavy in the air, a sentence passed and served. She gets up, tossing a few bills on the table, and without another word, she storms out of the café, leaving me to chase after her.

After all, I am still her bodyguard, if not her friend.

I'm mute as we trail out the café door, Penelope's words echoing in my skull, ricocheting off the insides, producing an annoyingly persistent pang. Her anguish, her frustration, it's all palpable, yet I'm gagged by my role as a protector, a bloody statue with emotions locked away somewhere, gathering dust.

What is safety without a dollop of joy, eh? Is it worth burying yourself alive for?

I stalk behind her to the car, maintaining a sombre distance. She nimbly settles into the passenger seat, tossing me an expectant look. So, I grudgingly squeeze into the driver's seat and navigate the route back to Uncle Robert's fortress.

Our journey is cloaked in a veil of silence. Neither of us speaks, nor do we exchange glances. Yet, her simmering wrath fills the car, hanging in the air like an ominous cloud.

"You're right," I break the silence, my words echoing in the tense quiet. "I've become numb to people's pain. Seeing humans ripped apart by bombs, watching homes crumble into dust, witnessing families torn to shreds, day in and day out, you'd go mad if you didn't numb yourself to it. So, maybe I've become a cold, obedient robot, a ruthless war hound, programmed to kill without feeling. But that's what we've got to be, Princess, if we want to shield people, the nation."

"Each person has their own kind of pain, Jess," Penelope says, her voice cold but calm. "It would be unfair for me if you belittle my suffering just because I'm not caught in a warzone or because I wasn't born in poverty."

I can't help but scoff at her comparison. "You're right," I say, pulling the car to a halt in front of the ambassador's house. "We can't be friends. Our worldviews are just too different."

And with that, I kill the engine, marking the end of a heated car-ride. The silence that follows is a brutal end to a budding friendship that could've been, should've been, but just wasn't.

Chapter Five

Penelope

As the evening rolls on, I manage to slide into my diplomat role as smoothly as a swan slides into water.

As if the earlier outburst in the car was simply a figment of my imagination.

I engage in charming conversations, expertly discussing politics, trading anecdotes, and laughs, never missing a beat.

"Minister Watson, I must say, your work in providing medical facilities to underprivileged areas in London is commendable," I praise, a warm smile gracing my features.

"Thank you, Your Highness," Minister Watson replies, a broad grin spreading across his features, "Your mother was a great supporter of this initiative. I'm pleased to see you share her values."

Clinking glasses with the Swedish ambassador, exchanging pleasantries with the Indian delegate, sharing laughs with the French representative – it's all part of the game. A game I've been trained to play, a game I have to win.

After my diplomatic duties are somewhat satisfied, I sneak away to a quiet corner, seeking refuge in the company of Kriti, my most trusted aide.

We hold flutes of champagne in our hands, the twinkling bubbles reflecting our shared amusement.

"Kriti," I say, swirling my drink absentmindedly. "I have a task for you."

She cocks an eyebrow, interest piqued. "A task? For me? This ought to be good."

"I need you to find out if Jess..." I pause, gathering my thoughts. "If she's straight or not."

Kriti chokes on her champagne, her eyes wide behind her glasses. "Excuse me, what?!"

"Don't make me say it again!"

"Penny, my dear princess, I am not a toy or a hot undercover spy that you can parade in front of someone to extract their secrets!"

"But you can be for me! I am your future queen!" I say with mock seriousness.

"Don't play the 'I am your future queen' card again. Just tell me you'll get me that Gucci bag I have been eyeing."

I almost spit out my drink. "Gucci?"

"Yes."

"I am sending you to seduce a woman who any girl would be happy to flirt with! Have you seen her? She drips with sexuality!"

"Yes, for a girl who is bi or gay. I am straight, Your Highness!"

"A CCTV footage of you tonguing that French waitress in the royal kitchen says otherwise," I say with a chuckle.

"That never happened. Okay, I'll do it, but from the sound of your voice, I get the feeling you want to know Jess's sexuality for more than one reason."

I roll my eyes. "Jess is ten years older than me."

Kriti raises an eyebrow and says curiously, "Out of all the things you could say, it's curious that you said that. Anyway, let me get this over with."

Jessica

In the silent shadows, my frame is nothing more than a background accessory to the grand tapestry of the ongoing diplomatic soirée. Nestled in my corner perch, I take in the royal extravaganza with a trained, strategic eye. Yet, as my gaze cuts across the glimmering hall, it's inexplicably drawn to one person - Princess Penelope.

She's an ethereal vision in a blush-rose gown that dips sinfully low at the back, revealing acres of milky skin that's dotted with the softest sprinkling of freckles. The fabric hugs her curves, snaking its way down her body in a symphony of silks and sequins. Her hair, a molten waterfall of curls, tumbles down her back like a soft, silken river.

The girl who'd been struggling with diplomatic niceties a few hours ago now converses with world leaders like she was born to do it. Damn, it's impressive, and yes, a part of me begrudgingly acknowledges she's stunning.

Before I can delve too deep into that thought, I spot a familiar figure slicing through the crowd of tuxedos and sequin-clad socialites.

Kriti Gill, the princess's ever-present shadow. The tall British-Indian woman exudes a palpable aura of sultry sophistication. Her raven-black locks, streaked with rebellious blonde, cascade down her shoulders, framing a face that could rival any Bollywood starlet. Her gown, a sapphire blue number, plunges dangerously low at the front and cuts high on the leg. I take in her approaching figure, the glamour of her outfit accentuating her statuesque silhouette, making her an undeniable vision.

As she strides confidently towards me, I straighten my posture, mentally preparing for whatever this encounter may bring. One last glance across the room catches the princess, bathed in chandelier light, sparkling like a crown jewel.

I sigh quietly, shifting my gaze back towards the approaching Kriti.

"Hi," she ventures, a nervous edge cutting through her usually confident demeanor.

It's uncharacteristic; it's intriguing.

Returning her greeting, I watch her with a narrowed gaze, an all too familiar dance of observation and evaluation. "Hi."

Kriti attempts a coy smile, her fingers fiddling absently with the strap of her shoulder bag. "It's nice to see you dressed up tonight."

I can't help but let out a dry chuckle. "Yeah, it took me a while to figure out how to wear this gown. They are complicated things. I am better equipped at dismantling assault rifles."

She simply nods, her eyes flickering with a hint of amusement. "So, are you having fun?"

The loaded question hangs in the air for a moment before I retort, "Having fun babysitting your future queen?" There's a challenge in my tone, a subtle invitation for her to join this verbal duel.

She takes the bait, her eyes hardening a notch. "Don't speak about her like that!"

I shrug nonchalantly, prodding further. "I didn't know you British were so defensive about your royals. I always took you guys to have a good sense of humor and bad food."

Her reply is quick and sharp. "We have both. You should try our men...or women, if you are into that." A telltale hesitation hangs on the end of her sentence. Is this...flirting?

Choosing to not give her a clear answer, I deflect, "I'll stick with your humor, thank you." My eyes stray towards Penelope, her figure catching the chandelier's glow as she dances through the sea of guests.

"Why? Don't you like our men...or women?" The question is sharp, like a carefully aimed arrow.

"I don't care for men of any country, darling."

My gaze keeps drifting back towards Penelope, observing the sway of her hips as she gracefully moves around the room.

Kriti pushes on, "So...women?"

"Yeah, if I'm in the mood. Why...are you offering?" I lock my gaze onto hers, issuing a silent challenge.

"Erm...maybe," she stutters, her champagne sloshing over the rim of her glass and onto her dress.

"You need to get out of that dress," I state, watching her eyes widen in surprise. "Because of the spill," I clarify, indicating the stain on her gown.

Her response, a sultry, "How about...you get me out of it?" sends a jolt of surprise through me.

Kriti steps in closer, her perfume a heady mix of jasmine and lavender, the scent curling around my senses. "I know a place."

"As the head of security here, I am sure I know more," I quip, stepping into her personal space and leaving it to her to decide her next move.

A heavy pause ensues, her deliberation evident in her wide, calculating eyes. I, too, am evaluating the situation.

After Sophie, the desire for a no-strings-attached encounter is strong, and Kriti Gill doesn't strike me as the clingy type. Perhaps she's seeking the same release...

"Okay, take me to one of these secret places," says Kriti, locking her exotic, smoky eyes onto mine.

I lead Kriti to a hidden alcove, concealed behind an intricate tapestry. The space is small, intimate, and faultlessly appointed with plush pillows and soft blankets. The room is dimly lit by flickering candles, casting shadows that deepen the mystery of the space.

Kriti brushes past me to gaze at the space in awe, her fingers tracing over the sumptuous fabrics.

"Wow," she whispers breathily, turning to face me. "You weren't kidding. This is definitely off-limits."

In the quiet of the alcove, she pushes me against the wall, her lips attacking mine with a renewed hunger.

I can feel the warmth emanating from her body, the scent of her perfume consuming me. My hands roam her body, tracing the curves of her hips, the swell of her breasts, before slipping under her dress. She moans, the sound vibrating through my lips, and I deepen the kiss, tasting the sweetness of her mouth.

In the dimly lit space, Kriti's dainty hands find my ass and give it a hard squeeze. Not to be dominated, and now filled with hunger, I wrap my hands around Kriti's slim waist and turn her around, pinning her like a dart to a dartboard.

"Aren't you overstepping your boundaries?" I ask Kriti as I take a lick of her lips.

"What boundaries? I can fuck whoever I want."

"Yes, but that's not why you approached me, is it? The Royal Barbie put you up to it, right? Getting you to seduce me so that I comply with her rebellious plans."

Kriti lets out a gasp as I nibble on her shoulder. "Not that I am complaining," I say.

Suddenly, I am being pushed away and a distraught, scared Kriti stands in front of me.

"How the hell..."

"I am a trained marine. I have seen through people who have successfully lied to the CIA. So what if I know your secret...you came to only seduce me, but now you realize you want the whole package. Come and get it!"

"No, I can't. I have to go," says Kriti, adjusting her dress before darting out of the alcove through the tapestry.

Penelope

Ensconced within the luxurious palace washroom, I stand before the ornate mirror, meticulously correcting the smudged red lipstick staining my otherwise perfect porcelain complexion. The feathery touch of the Gucci Rouge à Lèvres Voile against my lips brings me back to my reality.

As I finish dabbing a touch of the Dior highlighter on the high points of my cheeks, a small hint of worry tugs at my heart. Why did Kriti and Jessica rush out of the hall?

Suddenly, the gilded bathroom door swings open, and Kriti stumbles in, pale as a ghost, panting like she's run a marathon in her Versace heels. She clutches at the golden vanity table for support, her normally perfect lipstick smeared wildly across her face.

"Kriti! What happened?!" I exclaim, rushing to her side.

"Your...your Jessica...she's..." she pants, not making much sense.

"She's what, Kriti?" I ask, feeling a twinge of apprehension.

"She's...a fucking sex goddess," Kriti gasps, finally getting her breath back. "She knew about the plan... and she..." Kriti's face turns an adorable shade of crimson, "She made me want her."

A bark of laughter escapes my lips. "So, you fell for her charms, did you?"

"No, Penny, I didn't. This is not funny, I'm serious!" Kriti groans, covering her face with her hands.

"Wait, let me get this straight," I say, struggling to contain my laughter. "You, who claimed to be as straight as a ruler, got seduced by Jessica, and now you're standing here, telling me that you're attracted to her?"

Kriti only groans louder, which makes me laugh even harder. But underneath the laughter, a twinge of jealousy pulses within me. The thought of Jessica with Kriti... it pinches more than I anticipated.

"I am not attracted to her! But yeah, for a moment, I wanted her, and I swear, I thought I was straight."

"But...how? Did she put some spell on you? Mix some sort of a love potion in your drink?" I question, reaching over to fix the haphazard smear of lipstick across Kriti's face.

"No, it's a couple of things I think, her blue eyes, and the smugness...the confidence."

"That's three things," I tease, struggling to keep the tremor out of my voice.

"There could be more."

A pang of something I don't want to recognize shoots through me. "How far did things go?" The question falls from my lips before I can stop it.

"No, it didn't go that far. We kissed. That's all. And she wanted to take it further, but I didn't."

"Of course you didn't," I respond, barely concealing the biting sarcasm in my voice. I push away the unwelcome images that try to invade my mind.

"No, I swear! I stopped us in time."

"Why? You didn't have to."

The words tumble out, bolder than I feel.

Kriti looks taken aback by my bluntness.

"She caught onto us, Penny. She knows you sent me to seduce her although she has no idea that you were planning to use info on her to try and seduce her on your own. She didn't think that far ahead, or found it incomprehensible that you would try to seduce her."

Chewing on my lower lip, I manage to keep my budding jealousy at bay, for now at least. "So, you're saying, our hardened ex-marine is...what's the word...seduceable? Is that a thing?"

"I don't think so, but yes, she can be seduced," Kriti corrects me.

I mock a deep bow. "Gratitude, Ms. Oxford," I quip, rolling my eyes. "Don't forget though, you've just violated royal protocol by linking up with my personnel!"

Kriti's eyes widen. "Oh, my God, you set me up..."

"Relax, darling, I'm merely teasing, just as Jessica did with you. You naughty girl." I wink, moving on quickly. "But tell me, what was your approach? How can I get to her?"

I lean against the cool marble countertop, smiling with a shrewd glint in my eyes.

"You look like the Queen having successfully lied about

the country's economic stability to the masses," Kriti retorts.

"Bored now, Kriti. Spare me your wit. What did you do?" I press her, impatient.

"All I did was ask her if she was into British men...or women. That was enough, it seems. Let me tell you, Princess, she's the most intelligent, sexiest, scariest, yet..."

"Yes, yes, she's everything you're not, I get it," I cut her off, grinning. "I think I've got it, though. If she doesn't believe I could seduce her, that's exactly what I'll do. Once she falls into my trap, I'll blackmail her into escorting me to LA."

Kriti gives me a look of disbelief. "So, the ex-marine, an actual trained killer, is going to fall for your kindergarten-level scheme?"

"No." I turn, pressing my lips together, evening out the layer of lipstick. "She's going to fall for this ravishing body and the allure of my royal title."

When the chandeliers were dimmed, and the last vestiges of aristocracy had retired, I decide it is time to reel in the bait. It wasn't just about Los Angeles anymore; it was about winning this game, this electric, forbidden tango with the ex-marine.

My eyes seek out Jessica, and I make my way toward her. As I approach, she stands up, a soldier bracing for battle. My lips quirk as I drew closer. Before she can say anything, I speak in a low voice.

"Can you escort me back to my room?"

Her brow furrows at my request. "Isn't that Kriti's job, or any of the ladies-in-waiting?"

"I'm afraid she's a bit under the weather," I lie smoothly,

meeting her gaze with innocent wide eyes.

With a sigh that suggests she knew she was being ensnared but couldn't resist the intrigue, Jessica nods. "Lead the way, Your Highness."

We move through the winding corridors, their imposing stone facades whispering tales of ancient liaisons and illicit rendezvous. I can feel Jessica's steely gaze on me, her trained eyes taking in every movement, every sway of my hips as I guide her to my boudoir.

"God, it's so warm in here," I complain once we enter the room. The guest rooms are designed to retain heat, making it an ideal stage for the next part of my plan.

Jessica immediately turns to leave, presumably to fetch some water. I reach out to stop her, my fingers brushing lightly against her arm. "There's no need. Just... could you help me with this dress?"

Her expression is an amalgamation of surprise, doubt, and a hint of intrigued curiosity. She takes in the sight of me, dressed in layers of heavy, ornate fabric, a damsel in distress pleading for her assistance.

With a hesitant nod, she approaches, her fingers lightly brushing against the intricate lacing at my back.

The closeness is electric. Her scent, a blend of leather, metal, and something uniquely Jessica, fills my senses. I turn my head slightly, catching her eyes in the vanity mirror. They are focused, steely blue under the soft glow of the room's chandeliers, but I also spot something else in them, an unspoken curiosity.

"So," I start, trying to keep my voice steady under her intense gaze. "This isn't exactly what you signed up for, is it?"

Her hands pause on my laces. "I'm adaptable," she replies, a faint smirk playing on her lips.

"Good," I say, my eyes never leaving hers in the mirror. "Because I have a feeling that this won't be the last time I require your...services."

Our eyes lock in the mirror, her hands still at the small of my back. "And what makes you say that?" she asks, a challenging lilt in her voice.

"I always need someone else to undress me," I say, and then continue in a very innocent voice, "Your fingers seem to have stopped moving."

Jessica continues undoing the laces and stops at the last one. "If I undo this one, the dress will fall to the floor."

"So?" I arch an eyebrow.

"I think you can take care of this one, Your Highness," Jessica says, turning around to face the other side.

"I can't. I command you to untie the knot...right down to the last one."

I watch her turn around in the mirror, her cool, blue eyes filled with apprehension and confusion.

She is a vision, a red, hot burning vision, in her short, black, off shoulder dress and bright golden hair, parted all to one side.

Her shoulders look delectable, worthy of having a tongue running up and down their length, outlining the crescent scar on her shoulder blade.

My breath hitches as she slowly reaches for the last lace, her fingers trailing over my skin. The dress falls to the floor, pooling around my feet. I step out of it, standing before her in nothing but my lingerie.

Jessica's eyes roam over my body, a hint of desire flickering in her gaze. I can feel the heat rising between us, intensifying with each passing moment. I take a step towards her, my hand reaching out to touch her cheek.

"You're beautiful," I whisper, my voice barely above a breath.

Jessica

"You're beautiful," the Royal Barbie says, throwing a confetti of beauty and lead-melting sexiness my way.

My throat is dry, my hands sweaty, and my heart a thumping, throbbing ball of excitement, and desire.

Any other day, any other profession, and I would have been sprawled on this royal brat, straddling her pretty face with my legs, and riding her until she felt incapable of uttering another snarky remark.

But I am on an assignment, and I am a loyal soldier.

Fuck, if only I was a disloyal traitor!

I force myself to meet her gaze, my voice low and steady. "I'm not here for your amusement, Your Highness."

Her lips quirk into a smile. "Oh, but I think you are here for exactly that. You're intrigued by me, aren't you, Jessica?" Her hand trails down my arm, sending shivers down my spine. "You want me, just as much as I want you."

I try to resist, to push her away, but her touch is electric. I feel myself giving in, my body responding to her like a magnet. "I can't..." I breathe, my voice barely above a whisper.

"But you want to," she insists, her lips grazing my earlobe. "You want to feel my lips on yours, my hands on your body."

She is standing on her toes now, breathing hot air onto my neck, and intertwining her fingers with mine.

Her eyes are bright with hunger, her breasts moving with every heaving breath. Her hair is like silk, flowing in the wind, reflecting the moonlight.

What sorcery is this?

What kind of a witch is she?

Her hot, sweet breath is intoxicating, and I feel myself getting drunk on each puff of air she blows into my ear.

"In a life as decorated as yours," she husks in my ears, and grips both of my wrists, "it would be a pity if..." she places both my hands on her waist, "you don't top it off with a royal...fucking," she says the word like she means it, enunciating each vowel.

"It would definitely be a pity," I reply, as I slide my hands down from her waist and feel both her butt-cheeks with my palms.

I am close to defeat.

I can see the next few minutes of my life flash before my eyes, a royal fucking, followed by a royal firing.

I see all my medals being thrown down the drain.

But I am so close to not giving a fuck and tearing her panties off her ass.

"It would definitely be a pity, to lose all that I have ever worked for, only to satisfy the cravings of a rebellious princess," I finish and take my hands off Penelope's hips.

"I'll see you tomorrow, Your Royal Highness, and before you plan anything else to get me to take you to LA, keep in mind that I am very close to snitching on you," I say, catching my breath and rushing out the room like it was on fire.

Well, in a way, it was.

Chapter Six

Penelope

I wake up with my head pounding like a construction site. My tongue feels like a cactus, dry and prickly. Last night's memories are a blurred mix of royal charm and unexpected humiliation.

How had Jessica, a mere marine, defied me? Me, Penelope of the High Court, who's been turning heads since forever. I've had lords and ladies, barons and baronesses, fall at my feet, drawn in by my charm.

Yet, somehow, Jessica has managed to evade my web, the first to do so. It stings my ego, I'm not going to lie.

Then, there's Alexa's constant calls. Ugh! I've been avoiding them since yesterday. The incessant ringing of my phone feels like a mocking reminder of my failure. But right now, I couldn't care less about Alexa. My mind, my wounded pride, are fixated on Jessica.

And vengeance.

"I need Kriti," I mutter to myself, pressing the buzzer by my bed that calls my faithful confidante. The door swings open in a moment, Kriti, ever so prompt, walks in with a question in her eyes. She's no doubt added two plus two.

"So...how did it go?" she asks, in a voice barely louder than a whisper.

I grimace. I don't need her pity. But I do need her assistance. I manage to mumble out, "Plan B."

"Plan B?" She blinks at me, her face a mask of confusion.

"Yes, Kriti. Plan B. We are going to Los Angeles, by hook or by crook. And for that, I'm going to need your help."

"What's Plan B?" Kriti asks again. Her eyes are wide with apprehension.

"Well, darling," I grin, savoring the dramatic pause, "I am going to be sick. As a dog. I am going to be throwing up all over the place."

Kriti looks horrified. "Oh no, Penny! Are you feeling alright? Do you need a doctor? Maybe you shouldn't..."

"Calm down, Kriti." I chuckle, halting her mid-sentence. "I am not really going to be sick. I am just going to act it."

"But... why?" Kriti looks more confused than ever.

"Just you wait and see, darling," I say with a smirk. Plan B has never failed me. But this time, my trickery will be directed at others, people less cunning and intelligent than Jessica, and with more emotions than that war robot.

In a swift operation worthy of a Royal Commando Unit, Kriti and I spin the manor into a pandemonium of worry and concern.

She is perfect in her role, all worried eyes and hushed whispers. And I, with the right mix of ghostly foundation and red eye shadow under my eyes, play the ill-fated damsel to the hilt.

When Aunt Martha and Uncle Robert rush into the room, their faces are a study in surprise and alarm. Uncle Robert, the stoic ex-Army Colonel, is uncharacteristically disconcerted. And Aunt Martha? Oh, she's the perfect audience for my grand act, a mother hen, always fretting about her chicks.

"Penny, dear, what's wrong?" Aunt Martha asks, her hand trembling on my forehead.

I keep my act up, my voice weak, my body slack. "Nothing Aunt M," I reply, my voice barely a whisper.

"But something is clearly wrong, my dear," she insists.

And in a masterstroke, I say, "I...I can't tell you."

Just the right dose of melodrama, coupled with an air of mystery.

Aunt Martha, alarmed, orders Uncle Robert and Kriti out of the room. Once they are gone, she sits down by my side, holding my hand. "You can tell me, Penny. I am here for you."

I launch into my story, a cleverly woven tale of teenage distress. My best friend's album listening party in Los Angeles, the house arrest by the Queen, the insurmountable FOMO. I make sure to convey the urgency of my situation, of feeling like my life is slipping away, of having to grow up sooner than most of my age.

"Oh Aunt M," I whimper, "it's all just too much. I feel like I am drowning."

Aunt Martha looks at me, her eyes filling with sympathy. I have her where I want her. I can see her mind churning, her empathy bubbling over.

"No girl should ever have to let go of her youth. Not like this, not like..." she trails off, a sorrowful look in her eyes.

"Penny, I was much like you once. Carefree, rebellious, full of life. But life...life had other plans," she says, her voice filled with melancholy. "I had to give up on a lot of things, and grow up fast."

I listen to her tale, a sad story of lost youth and assumed responsibilities. And I realize that the key to my freedom is right here, sitting next to me, telling me her story.

"Promise me, Penny," she implores, "promise me you won't let go of your youth. Don't make the same mistakes I did."

I promise her. Not because I mean it, but because it's part of the grand play. The stage is set, the actors are in place.

It's showtime.

Aunt Martha takes a deep breath, her eyes shimmering with determination. "I will talk to Robert, Penny," she assures me, her grip tightening around my hands. "And I will make sure you get to go to Los Angeles. You deserve to enjoy your youth, not be trapped inside these manor walls like some damsel from the medieval ages."

I look at her, feigning gratitude. "Oh, Aunt M, you're my knight in shining armor," I whisper, my voice trembling for added effect. She smiles, the glint of a fighter back in her eyes.

"I know what it's like to be trapped, to feel like a bird with clipped wings," she murmurs, her eyes distant. "And I'll be damned if I let you go through the same thing."

She rises from her seat, her every move radiating strength. I watch her stride across the room, a woman on a mission. I can't help but admire her spirit.

As Aunt Martha leaves the room, my lips curl into a sly grin. I've pulled it off. The stage is set.

LA, here I come.

∞∞∞∞

The grand hall is awash with tension, everyone's faces bearing a different shade of apprehension, except for mine. I'm practically glowing with triumph. Uncle Robert, the stoic ambassador, looks like he's swallowed a lemon. Aunt Martha is a picture of quiet victory, her reassuring smile practically lighting up the room. Kriti is her usual serene self, giving away nothing of her thoughts.

And then there's Jessica. The brooding ex-marine looks as if she's preparing for a war, her eyes storming with an indescribable mix of anger and determination. Seeing her like this gives me an odd thrill. She thought she had me cornered, thought she could play me, but here we are.

With a grim face, Uncle Robert finally speaks. "Alright, Penny. You can go to Los Angeles," he grudgingly allows, causing my heart to do a joyous flip. "But there are a few guidelines that you will need to follow."

I'm about to protest when he holds up a hand. "We cannot risk anyone spotting you, not even the Royal staff. I'll tell the Queen that you're unwell and need rest. All your engagements can be postponed."

The room is silent, and then Uncle Robert drops the second bombshell. "Jessica will drive you to LA. You will always be in disguise and if you dare defy her orders, I will personally fly you back."

My smile freezes at that. This is not how I had imagined it. Jessica, my escort? But I know better than to argue. With a nonchalant shrug, I counter, "I think I can handle Sergeant Stoneface."

The room tenses as Uncle Robert turns to Jessica, who

offers a curt nod. "I can arrange for a private plane, Sir. It's more covert. I have contacts in the Army."

I scoff, unable to resist the urge to retort. "And what's the fun in that? The whole point of this trip is to see America up close. What's the use if I'm in LA in a few hours?"

I can feel Jessica's glare burning into me, but I don't care.

"I have a plane as well, Sergeant. But the Princess insists she wants to experience the heartland of America. She will fly back from L.A," the ambassador announces, "and you will be back within a week, is that understood?"

I nod, but my eyes find Kriti's, who barely manages to contain a victorious smile.

"But, sir, the distance from Washington to L.A. is huge. The chances of the princess being spotted are great. Do you really think this is a good idea?"

"Jessica, know your place!" I snap, and Uncle Robert raises his hand once more.

"Your job is to follow orders, Sergeant, just like me," says Uncle Robert and gives his wife an irritated look.

"I understand, sir," Jessica concedes.

"You will leave today, without wasting any time. Pack your bags, and don't pack anything designer, or something that costs an entire ranch in Texas. You need to blend in."

"Tell her," I point at Jessica, "she sticks out like a sore thumb. Please wear clothes that an average woman would wear, and not a man going through a mid-life crisis!"

Jessica does not reply, but I know every fiber in her body wants to retort.

Ooh! This is even better than sex!

Jessica

Some missions, I find myself crouched in the dank, musty corner of a warehouse, waiting for arms dealers to show their ugly mugs. Others, I'm wading through the treacherous jungle, grappling with the unknown threats lurking in the shadows.

Today, it's babysitting duty. Correction, royal babysitting duty. I'm herding a princess who thinks she's Marilyn Monroe and an assistant who, despite her docile appearance, is as cunning as they come.

All cramped in a Range Rover driving across America.

"You know, I always imagined my first road trip with a hot American girl," Penelope muses, her gaze lost in the open road before us. The wind tousles her chestnut hair as she leans out of the window, the evening sun casting an ethereal glow on her face. For a fleeting second, I'm captivated. Not by her beauty, no. I've seen my fair share of pretty faces. But the genuine smile gracing her lips, the one that's hard to find under her layers of bravado, it's... refreshing.

Before the moment becomes a memory, she turns to me, her chocolate-colored eyes twinkling with mischief. "I guess, you will have to do, Sergeant."

"Well, forgive my appearance, Your Royal Highness. Perhaps a few drinks would make me more appealing, as they did last night?" The words rolled off my tongue, laced with sarcasm.

A swift glance towards our esteemed princess, her majesty, the Royal Barbie herself, indicates she didn't expect that jibe.

"Don't flatter yourself. Last night was all part of the plan. You didn't even register on my interest scale," Penelope fires back, eyes firmly glued to the road ahead.

"Yeah, nor on mine," chimes in Kriti from the back seat. The chorus of denial was music to my ears.

"Sure, if that's what helps you ladies sleep at night." A smile tugs at my lips, victorious. The reflection of Kriti glaring at me in the rear-view mirror is almost as gratifying as the smirk on Penelope's face. Annoyingly sexy yet smug, it somehow suited her.

Free from royal constraints, her highness had chosen a more provocative attire. Denim booty shorts coupled with a black bustier. The result was less royal heiress, more sexy beauty influencer. The bustier, a blatant provocation, accentuated her curves while revealing just enough skin to be tantalizing. A fleeting glance her way has me questioning if it's a tactic to provoke me.

"Eyes on the road, Sergeant," Penelope advises, catching my glance.

"Checking the side mirror," I retort, trying to sound convincing.

"We've seen no other cars for miles, Jessica."

Good lord, this woman could argue with a wall and win.

As the urban jungle of Washington recedes, we traverse unpredictable winding roads. The austere grid of the city is replaced by quaint suburban houses, before being swallowed entirely by boundless green fields.

We've now entered the outskirts, where America morphs from the land of dreams to an endless watercolor painting. The air is a refreshing cocktail of freedom and possibility, flavors foreign to our confined Princess.

Would this trip offer a glimpse into a world beyond her golden cage? But who am I kidding? I'm not a life coach. I'm an overqualified soldier chauffeuring a stubborn princess to a party.

Looking at her, lounging with a content smile, bathed in the rural tranquility, she appears almost...soft. For a fleeting moment, I can forget the haughty princess, the constant need to be alert. But then, her eyes flicker open, that familiar fire of defiance burning bright, pulling me back to reality.

"I'm getting bored. Let's stir up some controversy," declares the princess languidly.

I suppress a sigh.

"I've got a question for you, Sergeant," she begins, her voice as silky as her smile is sharp. "It's been nagging at me for a while now."

"Oh?" I reply, trying to sound nonchalant while my brain scrambles to prepare for whatever verbal minefield she's about to drag me into.

"Between Kriti and me," she continues, the playfulness back in her voice, "who did a better job of seducing you?"

It takes me a second to process her question. It's like a punch in the gut. I knew she was testing my patience, but I didn't expect her to go this far.

Behind us, Kriti laughs nervously, clearly as blindsided by Penelope's question as I am.

"I am not answering that," I retort, my voice colder than I'd intended. There are limits to what I'll tolerate, and the princess just bulldozed past one.

"Why? Afraid you might offend one of us?" she shoots back, her eyes gleaming with wicked delight.

"No, because it's none of your business," I say, matching her stare. I may be her driver, but I'm not her plaything. "And frankly, it's a grossly inappropriate question."

Her smile falters for a second, but it quickly morphs into a smirk. "Touchy, aren't we?"

"Respectful," I correct her. "Something you should learn a thing or two about."

"Respectful, huh? You're implying it was something different when your hands conveniently slid down to grab my ass last night. Could've kept your distance, Sergeant, but you couldn't resist a feel, could you?" Her words are a punch to the gut, but I keep my face blank.

"That's not how it went down," I spit out, clenching the wheel.

"I think that's exactly how it happened," she shoots back, leaning forward, daring me to contradict her.

"No, I wanted you to think your little games worked, before I shut you down. Let me make this clear... shut you down, Your Highness. In fact, to answer your question, I was looking forward to taking things to the next level with Kriti, not you."

"I don't want any part of this!" Kriti tries to intervene, but gets hushed by the princess.

"Really? So, the heavy breathing, the shaky voice, beads of sweat on your forehead...all of that was just acting?"

"Yup," I reply, hoping my nonchalance masks the truth.

"What a liar!"

"I never lie."

"I could see in your eyes that you wanted me!" Penelope insists, leaning back into the seat like she's just delivered the final blow.

"Could say the same about you. I wonder, how's your singer friend gonna feel when she realizes you threw yourself at your bodyguard?"

"She won't care, 'cause she's cool."

"Or 'cause she doesn't like you enough?"

"She's nothing like you!" Penelope retorts, fire in her eyes, "She's an artist! Artists are emotional!"

"Yeah, R. Kelly was an artist too. Not very emotional, was he? Degenerate, yeah, but hardly emotional."

Kriti can't suppress a laugh, and Penelope, too, smiles and then quickly goes back to glaring at me.

"Nice to know you have a funny bone in you, and it's not all muscles and scars." Penelope's voice softens, a trace of a smile in her tone. It's a subtle change, but one that doesn't escape my notice.

Deciding to take advantage of her seemingly good mood, I choose this moment to broach a subject that I'd been avoiding for a while.

"Umm...is it okay if my friend, Maria, joins us in Nashville?" I glance at Penelope, gauging her reaction. "She needs to get to LA as well, and honestly, I would also like someone in this car who doesn't want to verbally challenge me at every opportunity."

A moment of silence follows my request. Penelope's eyes narrow slightly, a speculative look crossing her face. "Is she an ex-marine too?" she inquires, her gaze locked on me.

"Yeah, but she's nothing like me. She's free-spirited," I clarify, trying to pitch Maria as someone she'd like.

Penelope lets out a chuckle, an unexpected sound that somehow lightens the tension in the car. "Yeah, you are definitely not that!" she responds, amusement clear in her voice.

With a playful smirk, she turns to high-five Kriti, who reluctantly raises her hand to return the gesture.

"Alright then, more the merrier. I'm sure she'll be a great addition," Penelope finally declares, her lips curling into a smile as she throws me a wink.

"Thanks," I say with a genuine smile.

"So, you have friends? That's a surprise!" Penelope continues the banter after a temporary break.

"Yeah, we were stationed together in Iraq," I start, my gaze fixated on the hypnotic pattern of yellow and white lines on the highway. The memories of those years, intense and raw, wash over me. "We got on the same unit, same squad. It was... a challenging time, to put it mildly."

A look of genuine interest crosses Penelope's face, drawing me out of my recollections. There's a vulnerability in her eyes, a longing to understand a world that's so far removed from her own. The sight disarms me a bit, prompting me to share more than I initially intended to.

"We saw a lot together, went through a lot together," I add, my voice dropping to a barely audible whisper. "And well, during that time... we kind of got together."

Her eyebrows shoot up at that, her mouth forming a small 'O'. I can't help but chuckle at her reaction. It's oddly endearing. "You mean you and Maria...?"

"Yeah," I nod, feeling an unexpected tightness in my chest. "We weren't officially together or anything, just... finding comfort in each other, I guess."

I can see her mind processing the information, her expression softening with understanding. But then her brows furrow, a frown appearing on her face. "What happened?"

I sigh, gripping the steering wheel tighter. "She was called back home. Her father was sick, and she had to take care of things. And I took another posting, in Afghanistan."

"Why? Do you enjoy being stationed in hostile, far-flung places?" Penelope queries, her eyes studying me intently.

"It gives me a sense of purpose," I respond, feeling a strange kinship with this city princess who knows nothing of my world. "What are we without purpose in life?"

Her mouth closes, her gaze drifting towards the vast expanse of the fields around us.

Maybe my words struck a chord.

Maybe she's merely bored. It's hard to tell with her.

After a pause, she breaks the silence. "Where do you spend Christmas?" she inquires, her voice softer now. I can see Kriti shifting uncomfortably in the rearview mirror.

"In a shooting range," I reply. "It's become somewhat of a tradition."

She chews on her lower lip, a sight that has haunted me since our paths crossed. "You're a good woman, just a bit too stubborn," Penelope comments.

"You're a good girl, just a bit too royal," I whisper in response, stealing another glance at her, at those lips.

Eager to shift the mood, Penelope swivels in her seat towards Kriti. "On a lighter note," she says, a playful spark in her eyes, "Kriti, if I were to permit it, would you care to continue your little tryst with Jessica, which you had to abandon because of me? I feel like doing something nice for my bodyguard, now that I've learned about her rather bleak existence."

"You don't need to answer that, Kriti," I interject quickly, my protective instincts flaring up. "You're not a prize to be won."

"But I'd say yes," Kriti fires back, igniting the atmosphere in the car, "if the sexual tension between the two of you wasn't so thick."

"Oh, shut up!" Penelope retorts, spinning back to face the road once again.

"So, Jessica," Penelope begins, pulling her legs up on the seat and wrapping her arms around them. "What are your likes and dislikes?"

This sudden shift in conversation surprises me. Why would she care? I grip the steering wheel tighter. "I like my coffee black, my days sunny, and my nights quiet," I reply, stealing a glance at her. She is smiling at me, her eyes glittering with an innocent curiosity that I have never seen before.

It's disarmingly charming.

"And dislikes?" she prompts further.

"Liars, unnecessary attention, and overly-sweet tea," I reply, adding the last one with a smirk. She giggles at that, a sound that catches me off-guard.

"And what about a car ride with your ex-lover and two women who, according to you, couldn't keep their hands off you just a day ago?" she teases, her eyes sparkling with mischief.

"Couldn't care less," I shoot back, devoid of any emotion.

Sure, the prospect of being stuck in this motorized capsule with three alluring women was unnerving. But it wasn't because of their beauty; it was the unsettling idea that one of them, Penelope, was slowly worming her way into my heart...and maybe some other places. And the last thing I wanted was Maria picking up on this during our ride.

"Oh, you are such a buzzkill," Penelope laments. "I hope Maria isn't as stony-faced as you. I plan to get some juicy gossip from her."

"Like what?" I ask, curiosity piqued. I wanted to know her

limits, maybe give Maria a heads up to not spill unnecessary beans.

"Like, what physical signs do you show when you're turned on."

"Why would you want to know that?" I ask, taken aback.

"Because I'm pretty sure your 'acting' last night wasn't just acting, Jessica. Your hand on my ass wasn't incidental. It was a surrender flag."

"Why are you so hung up on making people surrender to you? I'm the soldier here, shouldn't that be my job?" I question, a tinge of sarcasm lacing my voice.

Penelope's response is a giggle, her laughter echoing in the confines of the car. She turns in her seat, her chest forming an enticing vista. "How would it feel if an enemy you thought you'd beaten refused to admit defeat? Wouldn't you want solid proof of your victory?" she says, her extended leg and toe carelessly playing with the AC vent.

"I'd be okay knowing I won. I wouldn't need to prove it," I counter.

"Well, I do. I am a brat, as you would have already figured out, and I like to show off my wins. And by the end of this trip, I'll have you admitting that you were dying for me last night."

"Keep dreaming, Your Highness," I retort, stomping on the accelerator to drown out Penelope's triumphant laughter with the engine's roar.

Penelope

Nashville is out to celebrate pride month, and wow! In all the pride and chaos that is Nashville, my eyes can't help but return to the rearview mirror where Jess is locked in a steely gaze with the road. Pity, she's missing all the fun. The city is a riot of color, a true carnival for the senses, a beautiful tribute to freedom and love in all its forms.

"I love this city!" I shout, pressing my hand against the window like some starstruck tourist. Except, I kinda am.

Back home, my life was all stuffy royal parties, pompous nobles, and pretending to care about diplomatic ties. Out here, it's a celebration of life and individuality.

Nashville is vibrant, exploding with life, and rainbows. That's right, rainbows, as far as the eye can see. It's like someone took a massive paintbrush and splashed colors all over the city.

Rainbow flags billow in the wind, storefronts are adorned with shimmering banners and garlands, and the people, oh the people, are a living, breathing embodiment of the Pride spirit.

In Washington, I could hardly notice that it was Pride month, but Nashville was screaming it in my face.

I find myself entranced by women walking arm in arm, their faces painted in bold stripes of red, orange, yellow, green, blue, and purple. Women, kissing and laughing, their bodies intertwined with each other, celebrating their love for each other, openly, and without any fear. They're free to love whoever they want, however they want. How I wish to be a part of this world! A place where I can hold my girlfriend's hand and not have to worry about the paparazzi snapping photos or the public judging me.

I've known about my sexuality since I was a teenager, and the reality of being a closeted queer in the British Monarchy? Well, it's a royal pain. The stiff upper lip doesn't really vibe with the rainbow spirit. But, here in Nashville, I am starting to understand what it means to live with pride, to be open about who I am and who I love.

"We'll have to stay in Nashville for the night. I don't want

A ROYAL RUNAWAY ROAD-TRIP

to risk being on the road with you after dark," Jessica asserts, while a group of frolicking young men, dressed in rainbow colors, walk past us. "And please wear your cap and shades. People here will recognize you in an instant."

"What makes you say that?" I ask, snapping on my NY baseball cap and sliding on Dior shades that are comically oversized for my face.

"You are a queer icon, don't you know that?" Jessica says, shooting me a look of surprise.

"Really? Why? Nobody knows I'm gay."

"All it takes is a quick YouTube search with your name and 'exposed as a lesbian' to find a treasure trove of theories and evidence," Jessica states as if she's talking about the weather and not my personal life.

I can't help but let out a giddy laugh at that.

It's a strange sense of liberation, to know that I'm not as trapped in the proverbial closet as I thought.

"I see," I muse, "That explains the influx of rainbow flag emojis on my latest Instagram post."

Turning my attention back to the lively streets of Nashville, I can't help but feel a strange sense of pride. Me, a queer icon? The thought sends a shiver of excitement down my spine.

"But," I drawl, turning my head to meet Jessica's ever-watchful gaze, "I'm not hiding. It's just that no one has ever asked me the right questions." A teasing smile stretches across my face, inviting her to read between the lines.

"Right," Jessica snorts, her eyes hardening behind her aviator glasses. "And I'm sure the paparazzi hounds just haven't had the time to ask."

"Exactly," I chirp, undeterred by her skepticism.

I click open the visor and regard my disguised reflection, adding in an offhanded manner, "I'm a real master of deception, aren't I?"

"Ah, the female 'James Bond' herself," Kriti purrs, sarcasm heavy in her voice.

"That just earned you the smallest room in the suite," I retort, but she only cackles in response.

"We aren't scoring a suite," Jessica chimes in, "They'd want IDs. And you're not exactly traveling incognito with your royal passport, are you?"

"I thought you were my passport?" I volley back with a smirk.

"I'm just your bodyguard..."

"Who has a habit of copping a feel off her charge!" I can't hold back my laughter at the indignant look on Jessica's face.

"I love how that's become my defining trait...anyway, we're staying somewhere they won't ask for IDs. And we're sharing one room."

"You mean, all three of us?" Kriti's face distorts with disbelief.

"Yes, unless the princess here wants to sleep in the car," Jessica shoots back, her focus still primarily on navigating the Nashville traffic.

"I suppose it'll be like a sleepover," I muse aloud, choosing to see the silver lining. "We can do each other's hair, tell scary stories, and gossip about boys...or girls, in our case."

I don't see it, but I am sure Jessica rolled her eyes behind her Aviators.

I don't remember the name of the hotel where we are staying, or I simply did not care. The room itself is nothing to write home about.

It is barely furnished, with a large bed in the center, and a couch tucked in one corner, where I assume Jessica would spend the night.

Everything in the room has a layer of dust on it, except for the bed, thankfully. The once-white walls are now marked by water damage and grime, creating abstract art of decay. A small wooden table stands at the foot of the bed, holding a decades-old telephone and an outdated TV guide. A dresser stands against one wall, its varnish chipped and dull.

All in all, it was just the sort of place one would expect a group of fugitives to hide out in.

I huff as I throw my bag onto the bed, sending up a cloud of dust. "Where's the full-length mirror?" I ask, looking around in despair.

Jessica lets out a small laugh. "I'm afraid the five-star amenities are a bit lacking here, Princess."

"I noticed. The bed's too small," I complain, poking the sagging mattress with a grimace. "And there's a cockroach in the corner."

"Think of it as part of the experience." Jessica smirks, throwing her bag onto the lone chair. "When I was stationed in Afghanistan, I once had to stay in a hut in the middle of the desert. No AC, no running water, and the only other inhabitants were scorpions."

Her attempt to make light of the situation does little to lift my spirits. "Well, that's comforting."

Meanwhile, Kriti has been quiet until now, but her face is thunderous. "This is ridiculous. We could have rented an Airbnb. Only one of us would have needed to provide ID."

"Too risky," Jessica cuts in before I can even respond. "We can't leave a paper trail. And the same goes for calling in any favors. The less people who know we're here, the better."

The Oxford graduate looks like she might burst a blood vessel. "So we're stuck in this... this roach motel?" She glares at the offending insect in the corner, which scuttles away as if sensing her wrath.

"Yes, stuck in a roach motel with a giraffe," I say, giving Jessica half a smirk.

"Well, lucky for you. I am stuck in this room with a bitch!"

I completely ignore Jessica's jibe but appreciate the quality of the comeback internally.

I pick at the loose threads of the old quilt on the bed, wrinkling my nose at the pungent odor. "I can't spend another second in here," I declare, rising from the bed, "Let's get fresh, change, and step out for dinner. Or hit a bar, I don't care which."

Kriti's eyes light up at the prospect of escape. "Sounds like a plan to me," she agreed.

But Jessica is shaking her head before I even finish speaking. "Too risky," she insists.

A sudden rush of rebellion floods through me. "I'm not asking to parade through the streets in my tiara, Jessica," I counter, my voice rising. "I will do everything you say, disguise myself...but please, don't make this harder for me than it already is!"

I am met with silence.

I can see the war raging in Jessica's eyes, the part of her that wants to keep me cooped up in this room for my own safety, and the part that wants to grant me this small reprieve. In the end, it's the latter that wins out.

"Fine," she sighs, conceding. "But if anything happens, we're getting out of there, quick."

I try to keep my victory grin from becoming too pronounced. "Deal."

In an hour, we are dressed in unrecognizable attire, thanks to the clothes we had managed to pack. It felt almost surreal, staring at my reflection, sans the designer wear and royal glamour.

Just an ordinary girl out on the town.

Despite the simplicity of our accommodations, our change in attire holds an oddly exciting element. Stepping out of my comfort zone – and closet – is refreshing.

In place of designer gowns and sparkling tiaras, I chose a simple pair of blue jeans – bought on the way from Walmart, because all my jeans were designer – and a black loose-fitting shirt. It's a look that was chic and casual, quite a departure from my usual royal glamour. As a final touch, I wear a beanie over my hair, tucking most of it inside, leaving only a few loose strands out.

Kriti, usually seen in office wear, is transformed into a punk rocker. She wears a red plaid skirt paired with a white graphic tee that screamed 'I Love Nashville', which was handed to us by a group of teenagers while we were wafting through Nashville's traffic for a dollar each. Her hair is tied in a messy bun, and black-rimmed glasses complete her look.

As for Jessica, her attire mirrors her personality – practical and minimal. She wears khaki cargo pants and a white tank top, her lean, muscular arms on full display. Her brunette locks are pulled back into a no-nonsense bun. A black cap and a pair of aviator shades make her look every bit the incognito marine.

We are a trio that could not be more mismatched –

a princess in disguise, a personal assistant turned punk, and a muscular marine looking like she stepped out of an action movie. But, oddly enough, in the vibrant and buzzing atmosphere of Nashville during Pride month, we somehow fit right in.

∞∞∞

Venturing into the sultry night air of Nashville, our little party land on the steps of a pulsating lesbian bar found after a quick Google search. The electric buzz of anticipation that wraps around the place is like a living entity, both intimidating and exhilarating. "Remember, no flirting, no making out," Jessica warns me, a firm note in her voice as we step into the tantalizingly forbidden territory.

"Why, Sergeant," I tease, "it sounds like you're worried about having to watch me kiss someone else."

Her retort dies on her lips as she concedes, "Maria will be meeting us here."

The bar is an explosion of color and light, festooned with the brilliant hues of the rainbow, alive with the energy and enthusiasm of Pride month.

The crowd is dense, the air electric with chatter, laughter, and the rhythmic thumping of bass that thrums through the floorboards. A sea of women – all shapes, sizes, and flavors, their bodies swaying to the beat, their faces lit up with abandon and joy. The vivacious atmosphere tugs at my heart, pulling me into its joyous embrace, and I can't help but feel a sense of longing. A realization tugs at me, a pang that this kind of freedom was something I could never truly have back home in Britain.

We claim a booth in a corner, Jessica slipping away

momentarily to return with an array of drinks. Cocktails for Kriti and me, the glasses adorned with tiny colorful umbrellas that bob with the movement of the liquid, and whiskey for herself.

I sigh, looking at the dancing crowd, an itching in my feet making me bounce in my seat. "I wish I could just take off this cap and dance," I confess, the whirling, frenetic energy of the dance floor drawing me in. Jessica, ever the pragmatist, reassures, "You can dance, Penelope. Just keep the shades and cap on."

"The entire point of this stupid disguise is to not draw attention to myself, and if I go and start dancing alone, with huge, black shades and a baseball cap, I would look like a meth addict."

"Then, you can just dance here, in the booth," Kriti offers.

"That's even more depressing! What a load of crap! I want to dance!"

Jessica takes a sip of her whiskey, then decides she's gonna need to drink a lot more if she is going to survive the night with me and empties the glass in one go.

"No dancing, no kissing, no flirting, no 'being a brat'," Jessica commands, pouring herself another drink from the pitcher.

I roll my eyes but comply with her rules – for now. Instead, I sip on my fruity cocktail and take in the scene around me, watching as the crowd grows increasingly wild. The music is getting louder, the bass vibrating through my bones, and I can feel the energy pulsing through the air. I want to be part of it, to feel the rush of freedom and adrenaline that comes with letting go. But I know that it's too risky, that one wrong move could blow our cover and jeopardize everything. So I stay put, content to watch from the safety of our booth.

As the night wears on, the crowd thickens, and Maria finally arrives.

Her resemblance to Sommer Ray is undeniable - a beauty molded in the same mold as the curvaceous goddess herself. Richly textured curls of blonde hair tumbled down her shoulders, framing a face of undeniable beauty. Her eyes, strikingly reminiscent of Sommer's, are the color of storm clouds – a mix of gray and blue with hints of green. They are magnetic, drawing you in, full of stories of their own.

Her body, perfectly proportioned with curves that threatened to spill out of her form-fitting black dress, is a testament to her Latina roots.

There is a natural, raw sexuality about Maria that makes you do a double take - a testament to her appeal that transcended her marine uniform.

She is a living, breathing, walking sex symbol.

As she approaches our table, I feel a prickle of intimidation, but I soon put these thoughts aside and greet the newcomer.

Maria is a whirlwind from the moment she joins us, giving a playful curtsy as she beams. "I'm a huge fan. This is so surreal for me to be standing here with you." The sincerity in her voice is touching, to say the least.

Once settled, Maria has a good laugh about our stern, always-so-serious Jessica in such a vibrant, energetic bar. "I never thought I'd see the day!" she exclaims. "Sergeant Thompson, in a lesbian bar, with all this music and fun. The world really is full of surprises!" Her words pull laughter from both Kriti and me as we join in teasing Jessica. Our stern, stoic bodyguard can only roll her eyes in response, her grumbling only stoking our laughter further.

"And who's this then?" Maria's eyes alight on Kriti, a

playful twinkle brightening their depths. "You British too, love?"

"Indeed, but my parents hail from India," Kriti replies, her smile unveiling a set of pearly whites.

She likes Maria. I didn't see that coming!

"India? I've got to put that on my to-do list, Jess. The place that makes stunners like her." Maria clinks her glass with Jessica, who smiles with some reservation.

"Oh, you're too kind," Kriti gushes, her cheeks flushing prettily.

I can't believe I was blind to Kriti's leanings for all these years. I say, "Kriti's been a hot commodity of late," and catch Jessica's eye. She's giving me the 'don't-go-there' look. Is she trying to keep her escapades from her ex?

"How so?" Maria enquires.

"Umm...let's just put it this way, my personal assistant here, has her fair share of admirers who are keen on some private...appointments," I quip.

Kriti's blush deepens and I see Jessica ease back into her seat.

"Can't blame them! She's a catch," Maria shoots back. "And speaking of catching, my favorite song's playing. Fancy a twirl on the dance floor, Miss India?"

Jessica's shaking her head, not quite believing what she's witnessing. But Kriti? Kriti's all nods and smiles.

I watch, mouth agape, as Maria sweeps Kriti onto the dance floor mere minutes after making her acquaintance.

"Has she always been this...forward?" I ask Jessica, who nods her affirmation, her attention half on me and half on her rapidly depleting fourth drink.

"Maria's quite something, isn't she?" I watch the curvaceous bombshell twirling Kriti on the dance floor, her agile, hourglass body effortlessly in tune with the music.

Jessica snorts into her whiskey, nodding. "She's always been... vivacious."

"Jealous much?" I lean in closer, our arms touching, the scent of her perfume mingling with the smoke and alcohol that pervades the bar.

She laughs, a deep, throaty sound that sends shivers down my spine. "Jealousy isn't my style, Princess."

"But you and her...?" I ask, the question hanging in the air like an uninvited guest.

Jessica shrugs, her gaze fixed on her rapidly depleting glass. "We had our thing, but it wasn't love."

"What was it then?" I prompt, curious, and confused at the same time.

"Sex," she says, simply. The word rolls off her tongue, casual and unapologetic. A hint of a smile tugs at her lips, and I find myself blushing like a schoolgirl caught reading a risqué novel.

"So, if it was only about sex... was she good in bed?" I ask, half-teasing, half-serious.

Jessica splutters on her drink, coughing and laughing at the same time. "Princess Penelope! That's some question."

"But seriously, Jess," I persist, grinning like a Cheshire cat. "You guys are soldiers. I've heard rumors... soldiers are rough in bed, so are you like that?"

Jessica gives me a side glance, her blue eyes sparkling with amusement and maybe, just a hint of... arousal? "Are you asking for a friend?"

"No, I am asking for myself," I say, my voice a bit husky, my heart pounding. "Come on, Jess, spill the tea."

Jessica rolls her eyes but the smirk on her face tells me she's more amused than annoyed. "Fine," she finally relents, the whiskey probably loosening her lips. "The last time... it got a little rough."

I blink, a swarm of butterflies taking flight in my belly. "How rough?"

"The lady left my apartment with a couple of love bites, some scratches, and... a rather satisfied grin." Jessica leans in closer, whispering the last part.

The visual of Jessica in bed, her soldier's strength coming to play, marking a woman with primal intensity, sends my imagination into an erotic tailspin. The dim lights, the pulsating music, and the taste of the cocktail all merge into a sensual haze. The desire I felt when seducing Jessica, the feeling of her hands on my ass, it all rushes back, making my heart pound louder, drowning out the music.

I gulp down the rest of my cocktail, the cool liquid barely managing to douse the fire Jessica's words have ignited. And all the while, Jessica sits next to me, smirking into her whiskey, oblivious to the storm she's stirred up in me. Or maybe not. With Jess, you can never be too sure.

Suddenly, I'm not so interested in watching Maria and Kriti dance anymore.

"And what about you, Princess? This whole running-away-from-royalty gig, it's for Alexa, right?" Jessica throws the question in the air casually, but her eyes don't leave mine.

I sigh, wondering how to frame the whirlwind that is my feelings for Alexa. "It was her music at first," I confess, "I saw her in music videos, and her voice...it was like she was singing just for me."

Jessica chuckles, shaking her head. "The ol' celebrity crush, eh?"

"But it was more than that," I insist, the memory of Alexa's dark eyes and captivating smile filling my mind. "When she performed at Wembley, it felt as if there was no one else in the room. Just us. Her voice...it touched something inside me. I wanted her."

"So you seduced her," Jessica states, not as an accusation, just a fact.

"Yes," I admit, my heart pounding, "And she was good, Jess. So good. I felt something...something more than just desire."

"Love?" Jessica ventures the L-word cautiously.

I shake my head. "I don't know, Jess. But I need to find out. That's why I'm going to her. To see if there's more than just sex."

"But even if there is," I add after a moment's pause, "I can't date her. I can't marry her. Not out in the open at least. Not in my world."

My heart aches as I say those words, the reality of my life, my title, hitting me hard.

"So, in the end, it's just about sex?" Jessica's voice is soft, almost sympathetic.

"In the end," I nod, looking straight into her eyes, "I guess it will be."

The unspoken words hang heavy between us, a realization that what we're seeking – connection, passion, love – may be just beyond our grasp, curtailed by the walls of our own lives.

"Why don't you just marry a bloke and carry on an affair like so many other royals?" Jessica's voice breaks the silence, her question catching me off guard.

I blink, taken aback. "That's what you think I should do?" The idea is repugnant.

"Well, it's not unheard of," she shrugs, "And it keeps you in line for the throne. You get to have your cake and eat it too."

"But I don't want just the cake, Jess," I retort, "I want the whole damn bakery."

She chuckles at that, but I continue, "I am a girl who believes in love. I want to proudly display my love, not hide it. I don't want to live out the rest of my life without ever truly living out a fairy tale."

"And what is a princess without a fairy tale?" I finish softly, hoping she understands what I mean.

She's quiet for a moment, her eyes distant. Then she says, "What if you say you don't want to be queen? Would that make it easier?"

"But that's the thing, Jess," I reply, shaking my head, "I *do* want to be queen. Not the kind my mother is, or the queen my ancestors were. I want to make changes to the monarchy."

I continue after taking a sip of my cocktail. "I want the crown, the responsibility. I want to rule. But more than anything," I pause, my eyes meeting hers, "I want to do it all with the love of my life by my side."

Jessica doesn't say anything for a moment, her eyes unreadable. Then she breaks into a grin. "Damn, Princess. You sure know how to dream big."

"I am a royal, after all. We don't do things by halves," I reply with a smirk.

"You know what? I like that about you. You're not willing to compromise your happiness, not even for the crown. That's brave," Jessica says, raising her glass to me.

"And downright foolish," I add, clinking my glass against

hers.

"We're all a little foolish when it comes to love, aren't we?" Jessica grins, and I can't help but agree.

We're both silent for a while, watching as Maria and Kriti move rhythmically to the beat of the music, their bodies a picture of harmony. Their arms are wrapped around each other in a dance that seems more intimate than public.

"Seems like things are escalating quite quickly between your ex and my assistant," I remark, my gaze never leaving the dancing pair.

Jessica chuckles. "Maria was never one for wasting time. She knows what she wants, and she isn't shy about going after it."

I can't help but smile. "Sounds like a woman after my own heart."

"Let's just hope Kriti knows what she's in for," Jessica replies, taking another sip of her whiskey.

"I think Kriti can handle herself," I say, although I can't help but feel a pang of concern. Kriti might be a personal assistant to a princess, but she's also my friend, and I don't want her to get hurt.

"And Kriti is not one to only get into a relationship for sex." I look at Jessica with a look of concern.

"Then I'll make sure Maria clears this to her. Because Maria is all about sex."

"And...I am also not all about sex," I say, as an afterthought.

"I didn't say you were, Your Highness." Jessica meets my gaze, and for a while we look into each other's eyes.

A snake uncoils itself, and writhers up my windpipe, and makes me breathe like I may need oxygen support any minute.

Jessica is like a tortoise in a hurricane.

"But..." I continue, "I also can't help myself, when it comes to women who are...different."

"Define different," Jessica says and unpins her bun, letting her blonde hair loose.

I gulp and lick my lips.

Jessica's eyes follow my tongue and then look back up into my eyes.

"Women who don't give a fuck..."

"About what?" Jessica tilts her head.

"About rules, regulations...orders, consequences."

"So...someone completely opposite to me?" Jessica grins.

"Or...someone who hides her true nature, under the pretext of...discipline." I cross my legs, and my thigh rubs against Jessica's.

In the distance, Kriti and Maria are doing some form of 18-plus version of the salsa.

"I follow orders, and that's my true nature." Jessica shuffles in her seat, so that our legs rub together.

I shuffle closer to the ex-marine and place a hand on her shoulder.

I lean into her ear, like I had on the night of the diplomatic party, while seducing Jessica. "Who says I was talking about you?" I whisper, in the most seductive voice I can muster.

I can feel her skin, soft and smooth, a slight perspiration forming on her shoulders and arms. Her hair brushes against my face, strands of it touching my nose and ears.

I can hear you swallowing,

I can hear the breath that you try to hold,

I can hear your heart beat,

and your breath through your nose,

I can hear you screaming for me, Jessica...

"Princess," Jessica intones, her hand gently cradling my chin, forcing my gaze to meet hers, "I must confess. That night, my hands on your hips... It wasn't an act. It was me, in every raw and uncensored way. I wanted to feel you. Yet, I withdrew. It wasn't out of duty or hesitation, but fear of defeat. If I had surrendered to my desires that night, I would've been the one losing. So, if you genuinely crave to feel the touch of an ex-Marine, if you wish to discover how rough I can truly be, you mustn't tease me with mind games. For me to disregard orders, you need to communicate your desires plainly. You need to tell me how much you really want it, how far you're willing to... beg for it."

I can't help but let out a laugh, pulling away from Jessica's intimate hold. "Begging is hardly fitting for the future queen of England. Beheading, though... what about that?"

Jessica grins, her eyes sparkling with a devilish light. "Behead me or beg me, it's all the same. I've always lived on the edge, courting death. Why else would I willingly accept assignments teetering on suicide?"

"You're mad!" I exclaim, shaking my head in disbelief.

"Precisely. And that, Your Highness, is why you will end up begging," Jessica retorts with an air of certainty that somehow stirs a whirlwind of anticipation within me.

Before I get the chance to counter, the booth is stormed by Maria and Kriti, who are closely tailed by another couple, two women who carry a certain grace and seasoned joy about them.

"Jess, Penny, look who we found!" Maria trills, her hand firmly entwined with Kriti's as they saunter over, bringing with them two women who seem to be in their early fifties, their eyes sparkling with unadulterated delight.

"Who?" Jessica inquires, raising an eyebrow at the newcomers and eyeing them with suspicion.

It's a good thing I still have my cap and shades on.

"This is Rita and Sharon," Maria gestures towards the pair, "They were tearing up the dance floor right beside us."

"Guilty as charged," Rita proclaims, sending a playful wink in our direction, "We couldn't help but notice these two beauties and just had to get to know their story."

"And quite a story they have," Sharon chortles, nudging Rita affectionately.

"I hope it's not a crime story," I joke, earning a ripple of laughter from our booth's occupants.

"Oh, nothing of the sort, dear," Rita dismisses, "These two are just a couple of adventurous souls on a thrilling journey, much like you two, right?"

"Umm...I guess?" I glance at Kriti from behind my shades, who looks guilty as charged.

"Two ex-marines, falling in love with two actors! When I found out, I just had to meet the two of you," Sharon, the more boisterous of the two, exclaims with a face that's becoming redder with each passing second.

"Wow!" I marvel, "Quite a picture you've painted there, Maria and Kriti, for our new friends." My lips curve into a smile, but my eyes are already screaming 'you are so fired' at Kriti.

"We're actually on our 'Pride Bus' trip," Sharon elucidates, her eyes gleaming, "A whole bus of us, traveling, stopping at pride parades across the country, all the way to Dallas."

"And we've just managed to convince these two to join us,"

Rita points at Maria and Kriti who are beaming, "Wouldn't it be wonderful if you two also hopped on board?"

I can see a glint of mischief in Maria's eyes. Kriti's lip curls up slightly, clearly pleased by the offer.

Clearly, alcohol has been working overtime in my assistant's system.

I glance at Jessica, the thought unspoken yet clearly reflected in her eyes – we were being mistaken for a couple. The seriousness of the situation somehow morphs into something comical.

"Thank you for the offer, but we would have to decline," Jessica finally chimes in to rain on our parade, as she usually does.

"But...I think it would be so much fun...baby!" I wind my arm around Jessica, who regards me like I'm a target she's been assigned to terminate.

"No...*baby*, remember we have to get to LA? As soon as possible?" she retorts.

"I think LA can wait," I challenge.

"Can Alexa wait?" Jessica drops the fake smile from her face.

"Who is Alexa?" I peer into Jessica's eyes, trying to communicate how desperately I want to be on that pride bus, now more than ever because I know it would piss off my bodyguard.

"No, it would derail our plans," Jessica states, emptying her glass and looking away from me.

"Can I talk to you in private for a second?" I ask, my tone mirroring the seriousness of Jessica's.

I tug Jessica into a corner and let out my frustration. "Look, woman, I am not a toy, or a donkey, or a ship that you can steer around, boss around, and...play with however you want! I am a damn princess, and you are a soldier! You are supposed to be following my orders, not the other way around!"

I am breathing hard, and anger is coursing through my veins.

Jessica's nonchalance is only stoking the fire in my temper.

"There's a hundred ways we could be recognized on that bus, Penny," Jessica reminds me, her voice flat and authoritative, a tone that's designed to quell any argument. "And it takes only one leak for our cover to be blown."

"But what if... what if we make them promise?" I suggest, my anger quickly giving way to my desperation. "They're queer, just like us. They would understand the need for privacy, for secrecy, wouldn't they? I am a queer icon, right? Won't they understand?"

Jessica says nothing, her eyes distant. She's thinking, I know. She's weighing the pros and cons, the risks and rewards. Her job is to protect me, keep me safe.

But I am asking her to take a risk, to go against her instincts, all for a bus ride.

"Jess..." I start, reaching out to touch her arm, but something in her eyes stops me. There's a fear in them that wasn't there before, an unmistakable terror.

Suddenly, her knees buckle and she crumples to the ground.

"Jessica!" I cry, falling to my knees beside her. Her eyes are glazed, her breathing uneven.

"Jessica!" My voice breaks the pulsating rhythm of the club as I drop to my knees beside her. Her eyes are vacant, losing the lucidity I've come to know. They're like distant galaxies, swirling with unknown dangers and uncharted territories, completely lost in the vortex of their own cosmos. Her lips are parted as uneven breaths escape in hushed, ragged gasps.

"Jess?" I reach out tentatively, a strange trepidation gripping me as I feel her cold skin under my fingertips.

It's like she's here but somewhere else entirely, trapped in an invisible prison I can't perceive. I can't understand, can't fathom what's happening.

My voice becomes a distant echo as I call out for Maria, for Kriti, for anyone who might know what to do.

In a haze of uncertainty and escalating anxiety, I find myself rooted on my knees, Jessica's hand still clutched in mine. The echo of her name hangs heavy in the air as Maria and Kriti sprint towards us.

In an instinctive motion, I discard my shades, tossing my cap aside. It falls to the floor, forgotten, in the face of the unfolding crisis.

My vision clears, the world now bare and too real.

I can see Jessica, her face a terrible tableau of raw terror that strikes me to the core. It's as though I'm looking at a ghost of her usual unwavering self, the warrior spirit dimmed by an unseen enemy.

What the hell is wrong with her?

Jessica

I wake up in a cold sweat, heart pounding like a jackhammer in my chest, the air in the dingy room stifling, as the lingering remnants of the nightmare cling on, refusing to let go.

Stale, moth-eaten drapes hang loosely from the rusted rails, the pallid yellow walls reek of abandonment, and the chipped-off ceiling paint hints at the tale of dilapidation the place has borne witness to. It's as if I've woken up in the remnants of a past life, my old world where the air was always thick with smoke and the earth permanently soaked in blood.

The deafening echo of gunfire is still fresh in my head. The rapid staccato of machine guns, punctuated by the thunderous eruptions of mortars.

A cacophony of war that once was my constant companion.

Then there were the bodies. A memory that doesn't fade, no matter how much I want it to. I still see them, just as they were. Disjointed. Shattered. Broken. Lifeless eyes staring into nothingness, their stories ended abruptly, snuffed out in the unfeeling crucible of war.

But this isn't the battlefield, I remind myself, shaking off the phantoms of the past. I'm thousands of miles away, in a run-down hotel room, my current sanctuary from the chaos outside. And there's no war here, no life-or-death battle.

Well, except maybe for the battle in my mind.

There's a soft rustling sound and I turn my head towards it, feeling a dull ache spread across my neck muscles. Maria and Kriti, I realize, are perched on the edge of the bed. They look tense, weary, their expressions reflecting the silent strain of the situation. Maria's hands are clasped tightly in her lap, knuckles white, while Kriti is biting down on her lower lip, an act of anxiety that seems far too normal in this moment. Her touch is a comforting presence amidst the whirlwind of my thoughts, her concern palpable.

In the dim light of the room, my eyes struggle to focus on Penelope. The woman who I'm supposed to guard, the woman who, right now, seems to be guarding me. Her royal highness, the princess, in this dreary room with her supposed bodyguard. If there's a more bitter irony, I can't think of it at the moment. Her eyes are fixed on me, filled with worry that's unusual for her usual teasing, playful demeanor.

She isn't a princess in this moment. She's a friend.

In the quiet, broken only by the sporadic noise from the old ceiling fan, I let the realization sink in. I'd hoped to guard her, to protect her. But it seems, in some twisted turn of fate, I might need her just as much as she needs me.

The room seems to heave a collective sigh of relief as I pull myself into a sitting position, my back against the worn-out headboard. A dry laugh escapes me. "Well, it's official. I've had better wake-up calls."

Penelope withdraws her hand from my forehead so quickly it's as if she touched a hot stove. She covers her awkwardness with a sheepish grin, a child caught red-handed.

Maria, her eyes reflecting a lifetime of worry, shoots me a piercing look. "So, which place was it this time?" she asks. "Iraq? Afghanistan? Pakistan?"

"Little bit of everything," I reply, massaging the sides of my temples, attempting to erase the echoes of distant warfare. "Kind of like a global tour of hell. How did I end up here?" I ask.

"We rolled you into the back of a cab, and Maria, with the help of the receptionist, dragged you to the room," Kriti answers my question, and I groan.

I must have looked pathetic…a weakling.

Penelope's voice interrupts my cynical reverie. "Maria told me about it… your PTSD, your hunger to understand it… how you are pursuing a degree in psychology to help others."

I arch an eyebrow, glancing at Penelope. A faint smile tugs at the corner of her lips. "You know, seeing you like this, vulnerable, it doesn't make you any less badass. Just more… human."

I don't know whether to laugh or to snap at her for the sheer absurdity.

In the end, I do neither. Instead, I change the subject. "So, are you still mad at me for the Pride bus?"

Penelope shakes her head, though her eyes are sombre. "No, not anymore. Rita and Sharon recognized me after I took off my cap and shades. But you don't have to worry, they promised not to reveal my secret, and, crazy as it sounds, I trust them."

I chuckle to myself, and find Penelope's naivety cute. "Well, if you trust them, then I trust them. Pack your bags, princess, we're going on a Pride bus!"

But before I can even move, Penelope places a hand on my arm, her touch gentle. "Not yet, Jess. You need to rest first."

I am stunned into silence. It's been years since anyone has shown concern for me. In my self-imposed isolation, I'd been taking care of myself, protecting myself from the world, but here she is, Penelope, caring for me. And as much as I try to hide it, to push it down, her words hit me like a wave, washing over the stony shore of my well-guarded emotions.

Also, it feels nice to hear her call me 'Jess'.

I shake my head, forcing a weak chuckle. "I guess that makes you my princess-in-shining-armour, huh?"

But as I laugh, I can't help but wonder, why does Penelope's concern feel like a storm, raging within the calm sea of my stoic resolve?

"I don't need rest, Penny," I grumble, waving off her concern, and also using her nickname. "It's not like I've been physically injured. Just a little mental hiccup, that's all."

"Ha! A little mental hiccup? Jess, you and sanity were never in the same zip code," Penelope quips, her grin infectious.

The laughter subsides as Kriti steps in, drawing our attention. "So, I heard from Rita and Sharon. There's a pride parade tomorrow here in Nashville. The Pride Bus is part of it... an open-top bus. They've invited us to be part of it. The bus leaves tomorrow evening after the parade. Are we going?"

I glance at Penelope, catching the hopeful twinkle in her eyes. I blow out a sigh, shaking my head in disbelief. "What the hell, why not? What's the worst that can happen? Adding a royal princess and a Pride parade to my global PTSD tour might even be a pleasant change from Afghanistan."

Before I know it, Penelope has wrapped her arms around me in a hug.

I stiffen at the unexpected contact. She whispers into my ear, "I might have to beg if you keep this up."

I search for a witty reply, but Penelope's words have thrown me off-guard and sent my head into a tizzy.

I watch her sitting across from me on the couch, legs crossed, a picture of elegance and royalty, even in a beanie and a simple, black shirt.

Guess you can't keep the royalty out of a princess, even if you dress her up as a poor college student.

She is eyeing me, and there is something off in the way she is looking at me. I notice an absence of the mischievous glint, or the spark of a ready comeback in her gorgeous, almond-shaped eyes.

Instead, I notice concern, filled out with a deeper understanding of something.

But what?

Kriti and Maria chat amongst themselves about what we should order for dinner, while I sit back, and keep observing the princess out of the corner of my eye, who is now busy with her phone.

I can't help but feel drawn to her, a magnetism that I try to ignore, but it pulls me in nonetheless.

As she types away on her phone, her lips curve into a soft smile, and I can't help but wonder who she's talking to. Is it a friend? Family? Or could it be...someone else? The thought sends a wave of jealousy coursing through me, and I clench my fists to keep from showing it.

"Jess, are you alright?" Penelope's voice pulls me from my thoughts. I glance up to find her studying me, her eyes intent on mine.

"Yeah, I'm fine," I reply, attempting to dismiss the lingering sense of unease gnawing at my chest.

"Are you sure?" she presses, setting her phone aside.

"Who were you talking to?" The question slips out before I can check it, and I immediately curse myself. Why am I behaving like a jealous girlfriend before we're even... and why am I even considering scenarios where I might be her girlfriend?

"Alexa," she responds, and it feels as though a truck has just been dropped onto my chest.

"Oh... is she eagerly awaiting your arrival?" My words drip with sarcasm, a poor shield for the jealousy seething beneath.

"She says so, but she hardly replies to my texts. I mean, considering the risks I'm taking for her, shouldn't she be practically sending me nudes every day?" Her words ignite a fury in me I didn't know I possessed.

"Maybe... she's busy with her album launch," I offer, struggling to keep my voice even.

"Yeah, maybe," Penelope agrees, her voice trailing off into silence.

Meanwhile, Maria and Kriti seem to have completely forgotten about dinner in favor of discussing their favorite rock bands.

"Hey, lovebirds, I'm starving, and so is the princess. Cut the swooning and order some food," I announce, rising from my seat to peer out the window, checking if the lesbian couple has kept their word or if we're now surrounded by paparazzi.

"We can't decide on something to order," Kriti admits.

"Turkish," I grumble, turning back to face the mismatched pair.

"Why Turkish?" Penelope asks, now simply sitting and playing with her hair.

"Once I was holed up in a safehouse in Istanbul, and all they fed me was Doner Kebab for twenty-five days straight. My mission officer nearly fell off his chair when I landed back in the States and the first thing I ordered was... yep, you guessed it, a Doner Kebab. Could've eaten it for thirty more days, honestly."

Penelope's dazed expression tells me she has no idea what a Doner Kebab is.

I laugh at her expression, finding it endearing. "You've never had one, have you?"

She shakes her head, biting her lip. "I don't even know what it is."

"It's a Turkish dish, basically meat cooked on a vertical rotisserie. It's usually served in pita bread with salad and sauce. Trust me, you'll love it," I assure her, my mouth already watering at the thought of the savory meat.

"Don't they have Doner Kebabs in England?" Maria asks, leaning against the wall.

"They do," I answer on Penelope's behalf. "But not in Buckingham Palace, I suppose." I glance at Penelope, who's suddenly become very somber.

"I wonder how many things in the world I'll never taste, experience, or enjoy just because I'm too highborn to be exposed to them. It sucks, honestly. Sometimes, I'd rather have been born a commoner."

"No, you wouldn't," I reply firmly. "Trust me, stay in your palace. The world of the commoners is... unbearably painful."

"But pain forges superhumans like you and Maria. A life of luxury and stability can make people soft," Penelope counters.

"Why do you need to be a superhuman, Penelope?"

"Because you never know when everything can be taken away from you. It's better being a warrior in a garden than a gardener on a battlefield."

Penelope's wisdom takes me by surprise, and I furrow my brows at her. "Well said, Princess. England could really use a queen with such wisdom."

"Are you suggesting my mother lacks wisdom?"

"No," I say, my expression distant. "But she could certainly use some guidance on how to treat people who love based on the beauty of the heart, not the gender they were born with."

Penelope eyes me curiously.

"What would you do if you were queen and also the head of the church in England, which frowns on same-sex marriage?"

"Me?" I smile, tucking a loose strand of hair behind my ear.

"I'd leave the country and go to Iraq or Afghanistan. Because really, there wouldn't be much difference. I'd find the same ideology there."

Penelope appears taken aback, her brows furrowing as she digests my words. "You make it sound so dire," she says, her voice small.

"Because it is, Penelope," I reply, my gaze turning towards the window. The Nashville skyline is lit up, its vibrancy belying the depth of our conversation.

A silence ensues, the four of us lost in our own thoughts. Maria breaks it eventually, her voice light, "Well, if Jess is queen, can I be her royal adviser? I mean, who wouldn't want a front-row seat to that shit-show."

Kriti laughs and the moment eases, the heaviness of our discussion lightening. "Only if I can be the royal jester," she adds, "I've always wanted to pursue a career in comedy!"

"Now, that's a good joke," Penelope says, managing a small smile. Their jests might seem trivial, but in moments like these, they're lifelines.

"As much as I love this alternate universe you're building, we've been waiting on Turkish food for ages now. Who's placing the order?" Penelope continues, directing the attention back to the here and now.

"All right, all right. I'm ordering," Maria says, pulling out her phone.

As the room fills with the light chatter of food choices and Kriti's laughter, I turn my gaze back to the window.

Tomorrow, we'll take part in the parade, riding atop a Pride bus, celebrating love, and freedom. There's a long road ahead, both literally and figuratively.

I cast a sidelong glance at Penelope, the 'royal gardener'. I hope she's ready for the battlefield.

Tyra

Member, Pink Poison

The rich aroma of garlic butter dances in the air, it's hypnotic scent enough to draw any bystander's attention. But I'm too wrapped up in my nervous fumbling with the straw in my strawberry daiquiri to really appreciate it.

Darren, the object of my relentless infatuation, sits across the table, his eyes a blazing blue inferno of curiosity. It's unnerving how charming he is today, his smile alone enough to disarm me.

"Alexa's really counting on this stunt, isn't she?" Darren posits, a gentle smile lurking on his handsome features.

Exhaling a sigh, I shoot him a disbelieving glance. "Darren, she's totally sold on this idea that the princess showing up will miraculously save us. It's... unsettling. Plus, how will it help the band, when she is showing up at the listening party of her solo EP, and not the band's album? She is such a conniving little... "

His lips curl up further. "Well, the public does love a royal scandal. It could work, but yeah, only for her. I don't see the PR helping the band in general."

Something in his casual dismissal irks me. "It's just..." I begin, struggling to find words, "It feels wrong. To exploit someone like that."

His grin expands into a full-fledged smile, the kind that radiates mischief. "Ah, a sudden moral compass, Tyra?"

I laugh, flinging a piece of lettuce at him. "Shut up, you!"

His laughter rings through the restaurant, infectious

and comforting. "So, this royal rescue mission... when is it happening?"

"Next week, I think," I say, twirling my Caesar salad in absent-minded circles. "The album listening party is on Saturday."

"Cool, cool," Darren nods, his attention seeming to drift towards the football game playing on the restaurant's flat screen. He always had a knack for making everything seem utterly casual. "And who's she hitting the road with? Anyone interesting?"

"Just some old bodyguard, and her personal assistant, I guess," I shrug, dabbing my lips with a napkin. "Why, planning on crashing their road trip?"

"Ha! As if," Darren snorts, giving me a playful wink. "Just curious."

His curiosity had always been endearing, his interest in the minutiae of my life charming in a way I never expected. "Oh, and Alexa and Penelope... how're they, you know...?" Darren asks, an eyebrow raised suggestively.

I can't help but laugh. "Oh wow, you're really getting into the gossip, huh?"

He shrugs, his face the picture of innocence. "What? I can't be interested in the drama?"

"No, it's adorable," I giggle, reaching across to give his hand a reassuring squeeze. "As far as I know, they're just close friends. But with Alexa, who knows?"

"And, Alexa told you all of this...herself?" Darren's eyes have practically lit up, and they are more expressive than I have ever seen them to be.

"Yeah, she is a loudmouth. Can't keep things to herself, anyway, I don't want to keep talking about her on our special lunch. You tell me, how are the rehearsals shaping up?"

Darren

In the cold, impersonal sanctuary of my car, the charm fades away, the endearing smile morphs into a hard, grim line. My eyes, reflecting the harsh city lights, flicker with a calculating coldness. My hands, previously gentle, now grip the steering wheel with a firm precision that belies my earlier demeanor.

I flip open my phone, dialing a number that's etched deep into my memory, my heart pounding with a mix of adrenaline and a rising sense of urgency.

The line rings. Once. Twice.

"Speak," a voice at the other end commands in thickly accented English.

"Subject is en route. Repeat, subject is en route. Next week. She'll be at Alexa's album listening party," I say, my voice low and steady. The agent on the other end grunts, acknowledging the information.

I glance at my rearview mirror, at Tyra's shrinking figure disappearing into the crowded city streets, her innocence and trust completely blind to the dark underbelly she's unknowingly entangled in.

A twinge of regret gnaws at me, but I push it aside. I can't afford to feel. Not when the stakes are this high.

"'Foxhound' is traveling with Jessica, a former marine, and friends Maria and Kriti," I add, holding my breath as the agent makes note of the intel.

"And the target?"

"Alexa. She's the key," I tell him. "She's Russian, might even be sympathetic to our cause. Turning her could be our ticket to 'Foxhound'."

For a moment, the line goes silent. Then, a gruff acknowledgment echoes through the call. "Understood. We'll proceed accordingly."

I hang up, my pulse roaring in my ears. The game is changing, the stakes mounting, and the board is set. The pawns are in place, oblivious to their roles in this high-stakes play of power and politics.

As I drive away, the cruel reality sinks in. We're not just dealing with a rebellious royal and her band of misfits anymore. This... is the beginning of a silent war. And the battlefield is about to become a lot more dangerous.

The chill of the night seeps through the glass, a haunting echo of the icy undercurrent running beneath my words. I take one last glance in the rearview mirror, Tyra's figure now completely consumed by the bustling city, before steeling myself for what's to come.

God help us all.

Chapter Seven

Jessica

With the sun beating down on us, Nashville feels like the inside of an oven. Not the best day to be squeezed into a street full of people, but here we are.

Amidst a sea of colors and sounds, there's Penelope, moving through the crowd like she's walking a runway. And why not? With her short white denim shorts and a black bikini top that's practically invisible, she's dressed to kill.

On her insistence, I too, am stuck in a similar getup.

A bikini top, denim shorts, and an increasingly nagging feeling of discomfort. I mean, I've been in some dicey situations in my life, but never have I been this...exposed.

Maria and Kriti have gone the summer dress and leggings route, looking far more comfortable in their own skins than I am. And as if being a fish out of water isn't enough, there's a whole new problem waiting at the Pride Bus.

Rita and Sharon, the good folks from the lesbian bar, are there with smiles as wide as the Grand Canyon. And they are still under the misconception that Penelope and I, just like Maria and Kriti, are a couple. It's a bit jarring, but hey, no harm done, right?

Except there is.

I drag Penelope to the side, needing to talk about this whole 'fake couple' situation. Being a pretend girlfriend? That's a whole new level of strange for me. But Penelope's all chill about it. She even cracks a joke, asking if she's not my type.

"Got no type, Princess," I shoot back, crossing my arms. "And if I did, I doubt it'd include royals who are ten years younger than me."

She belts out a laugh that eclipses the surrounding chaos of the parade. And hell, it's infectious. It rattles my nerves and eases something inside me that I hadn't realized was wound so tight.

"Jess, darling, you sure you're not lying about your age? Because honey, you're rocking the second-best look I've seen all morning," she teases, grinning like a Cheshire cat.

"Second best?" I ask, squinting into the sun, and trying to discern who's caught her discerning eye.

"Obviously, darling. The best-looking woman in any room - or parade, for that matter - is always going to be yours truly!"

Penelope strikes a pose as she says this, hands on her hips, hips popping out and all, and I feel a stirring within me.

Damn, those shorts are criminally short.

"Look, pretending to be a couple isn't rocket science. Just call me 'baby' every now and then, peck me when Rita and Sharon are watching - tongue strictly off limits - and just be my little puppet for the day. Easy peasy!"

"Why do I feel like you're going to exploit this... arrangement to your advantage?" I retort, giving her a skeptical look.

Her only response is an impish grin that makes my stomach flutter in a way I'm not entirely comfortable with.

"Who knows?" she shrugs, "Maybe I'll ask you to give me a piggyback ride when my royal feet start to ache."

"In that case, I might just stumble over a conveniently placed rock and 'accidentally' dump you," I retort, adjusting my shorts to regain some semblance of control.

As if sensing my discomfort, Penelope approaches me, looking every bit like a cat eyeing a canary. "Here, let me help you with that," she purrs. The way she's looking at me makes me feel like I'm on display.

Before I can protest, she's already reaching for the front of my shorts, deftly unbuttoning them. "What the..." I sputter, half expecting her to laugh at my startled expression.

"Relax, darling. Unbuttoned shorts are all the rage right now," she reassures me, stepping on her tiptoes to land a swift peck on my lips. "For Rita and Sharon, remember?" she whispers, pulling away just far enough for me to see her smirk.

My eyes drop to her lips, which she licks, then my eyes drop to her cleavage, which I...*desperately*...want to lick.

This is worse than being tortured by a few ISIS militants.

Back at the pride bus, Kriti and Maria are in their own little world, lost in each other's eyes, two bodies intertwined in the world's sweetest dance.

It's cute, really.

The lawns around us are a splash of rainbow colours, filled with happy, dancing people, their faces bright and painted in vibrant hues. Amidst this chaos of colour and laughter, Penelope spots a Harley Davidson, all polished chrome and black leather, parked conspicuously near the front of the bus.

"Wow, Jess, look at that beast!" Penelope exclaims, her eyes lighting up like fireworks at the sight of the gleaming Harley. "Imagine riding that in the parade."

Just then, I realize she isn't wearing her disguise.

"Wear your shades, and cap, Penelope!"

"Oops," Penelope says, cutely, and dons her disguise.

I then follow her gaze to the machine, the Harley.

It's impressive, alright. The thought of riding it sends a thrill through me. But the parade? That's another matter. It's just at that moment, a burly guy with rainbow-coloured hair, muscles bulging in all directions, steps up on a makeshift podium.

"Attention, ladies and gentlemen!" he bellows, his deep voice easily rising above the din. "The push-up contest is about to begin! Winner takes a ride on the Harley, with their partner, at the head of the parade! All they gotta do, is beat my count. Which has been a record in these parts of the town for many years! Two hundred push-ups!"

Penelope turns to me, her eyes sparkling mischievously. "Jess, you have to win this! I want that ride."

"I haven't belted out two hundred push-ups in ages, Princess," I say, staring at a man who fails at fifty.

"You are lean, and lighter than most of these men. You can do it. Come on, Sergeant, I really want to ride that Harley! I have seen people do it in movies, and it's so cool!"

I groan internally but manage to keep a straight face. "Alright, I'll give it a shot," I say, even though I'm dreading the embarrassment that is sure to follow.

There goes Hollywood raising women's expectations, yet again.

As I step forward to take on the challenge, laughter ripples through the crowd. "Oh, this is going to be good!" someone says, trying to suppress their laughter.

"Go, girl!" another voice chimes in, a little too sarcastically for my liking.

I see a muscle-bound Goliath warming up to go after me, a smirk on his face. They all see a David stepping up to him, a denim and bikini-clad woman with lean muscles.

The mismatch is comical.

"Don't judge a book by its cover," I say, stretching my arms and winking at the crowd. That gets them laughing even harder. Even Kriti and Maria pause their love fest to watch me.

"Don't worry, Jess, we believe in you!" Kriti says, Maria by her side, giggling.

What follows is a blur of activity. The crowd starts to count as I get down to the ground and begin the push-ups.

One... Two... Three... I keep going, fueled by the adrenaline rush, and the desire to wipe that smug smile off the beefy man's face. Ten... Fifteen... Twenty... The crowd's laughter slowly turns into a stunned silence. Then the cheers start, slowly at first, then growing louder.

I push past a hundred, and then finally, with my muscles burning wildfire, I hit two hundred. I've got this. For Penelope. For the parade. For the damned Harley. For respect. The crowd erupts into cheers and applause. Maria's and Kriti's voices stand out, their proud shouts acting as the icing on the cake.

As I stand up and turn towards Penelope, her face is a sight to behold. I am sure her eyes are wide behind her blingy Dior shades, her mouth hanging open. She looks absolutely thrilled, and I can't help but feel a wave of satisfaction wash over me. I've not just won a silly push-up contest. I've won Penelope's admiration. And quite possibly, the respect of everyone at the parade.

"And that, ladies and gentlemen," I announce, slightly out of breath, "is how it's done!" The crowd roars in response, their cheers echoing around the parade ground.

∞∞∞∞

Straddling the Harley, I feel the rumble of the engine between my legs, like a mechanical heartbeat. As I glance around, I see a sea of painted faces, rainbow flags billowing in the wind, and sparkling eyes full of pride and joy. There's a buzz in the air, the electric charge of unity, freedom, and acceptance.

Penelope wraps her legs around my waist and sits facing me, in the little space between my crotch and the fuel tank.

"I was expecting you to sit behind me," I say, trying hard to keep myself from grinning with anticipation.

"What's the fun in that?" her Royal Highness responds and tugs at my waist with her thighs.

She's one hell of a sight, my own personal Aphrodite in denim and bikini.

Every curve, every laugh line, every sun-kissed strand of hair escaping her cap, god, it's messing with my head. And I thought disarming a bomb in the blistering heat of the desert was hard.

"Can you believe it, Jess?" she turns her head, her eyes twinkling with excitement, "This might just be the best day of my life!"

Her words hit me with the force of a hurricane, ripping apart my carefully constructed walls. The last time I felt this rush was at Marine school graduation. But this, this is different. This isn't a rush of adrenaline, of accomplishment. No, this is... something else.

"Sergeant Jess," she purrs, making my pulse stutter.

"You've given me the best day of my life. Thank you!"

Her gratitude, raw and honest, is a physical blow, leaving me reeling. The churning in my stomach isn't anxiety, it's a whirlpool of feelings I've been trying to dodge. Feelings that have a face now. A beautiful face with a banging body and laughter that echoes in the hollows of my heart.

Damn it.

I'm falling, aren't I?

Plummeting headfirst into something more terrifying than a warzone. Yet, something so exhilarating, so goddamn right that it's sending my heart into overdrive.

The fearless Marine Sergeant is being blindsided by a woman's smile and a parade.

Ridiculous? Maybe.

Unexpected? Definitely.

Terrifying? You bet.

"Can't we go faster?" the Princess requests, and I shake my head.

"We are at a parade, Your Highness, not a race."

Penelope pouts, her bottom lip jutting out in a way that makes me want to bite it. "I know, but I want to feel the wind in my hair."

I chuckle, "You're wearing a cap, Your Highness."

She rolls her eyes. "You know what I mean, Sergeant Jess."

I know exactly what she means.

I want to feel the wind in my hair too, to feel the rush of the world around us as we speed down the parade route. But it's not just the wind I want to feel.

It's her, it's the heat of her body next to mine.

As we continue down the parade route, I steal glances at her, taking in the way her hair whips around her face, the curve of her hips, the way her eyes light up with every passing float.

She keeps rating the floats out of ten, as they overtake us, and then tells me exactly why she gave the float that rating. And then, from time to time, she leans back, over the speedometer, and stretches like a cat, her long limbs reaching out to their full length, her breasts straining against the fabric of her bikini top.

I try not to stare, to keep my eyes on the road, but it's impossible. My gaze keeps flickering back to her, drinking her in like a woman dying of thirst.

We pull over for a breather, the Harley purring beneath us, our hearts in sync with its rhythm.

There's a chant rising above the din of the parade. A demand. A battle cry, if you will. I ignore it at first, tuning out the voices, tuning into Penelope. Her gaze meets mine, a question in her eyes, a challenge. "Should we oblige them?" she asks.

I strain my ears to the chant, understanding seeping in. "Kiss! Kiss! Kiss!" The crowd, thirsty for a spectacle, has its eyes on us. They want the tall, lean woman, the winner of a push-up contest, and the petite, charismatic young woman to put on a show.

They want us to kiss.

Our companions trail behind us, clinging to the Pride Bus, their eyes wide with shock and awe. I see Maria and Kriti among them, their expressions echoing the crowd's chant.

My world narrows down to the sea of expectant faces and Penelope's mischievous smile. And then, it's just us.

Just Penelope and me.

The crowd fades into the background, their chant a mere whisper against the roar of my racing heart.

There's an expectant hush as I lean into Penelope, a tremor of excitement zipping through the crowd. The world telescopes into the space between us, electric and charged, the rhythmic beat of the parade a distant drum in my ears. "Well, I never back down from a challenge," I tell her, my voice rough with a strange mix of anxiety and excitement.

Her eyes widen as I close the distance, her surprise giving way to understanding just a second before our lips meet. The crowd erupts around us but it's all background noise now. The only thing I feel, the only thing I hear, the only thing I see, is Penelope.

The kiss starts slow, tentative. A peck, a tease.

And then it's more, so much more.

Her lips are warm and soft against mine, moving in rhythm with a dance that's as old as time yet as new as the Nashville dawn. Her hands find my face, fingers threading through my hair, pulling me closer, deepening the kiss. And I respond in kind, my own hands roaming to her waist, pulling her into me, the feel of her lithe body against mine sending a jolt of electricity up my spine.

There's a sudden intensity that catches us both off-guard. The kiss deepens, lasts longer than we'd planned. There's an unspoken understanding in the way her tongue brushes against mine, a silent agreement in the way my hand splayed against her back. It's not just a spectacle anymore, not just a show for the crowd.

It's raw, it's real, it's us.

A soft moan escapes the princess' mouth, and suddenly, she breaks the kiss, as if the voice from her throat gave too much away for her liking.

Pulling back, I take a moment to look at her. Her lips, a bit swollen from our kiss, curve into a smile, her eyes sparkling with mischief and something else, something I dare not name.

We turn to the crowd, their cheers and whistles filling the air, their approval, their support resonating in our ears.

With Penelope still in my arms, we raise our hands in a triumphant wave. The crowd responds with a deafening cheer. But amidst the cheers and the music and the colors, amidst the celebration and the love, all I see, all I feel, all I know, is Penelope.

Penelope

The nightlife in Nashville is vibrant and alive, and we've found ourselves in the throbbing heart of an R&B club, a local hotspot famous for showcasing rising talents. The four of us, still high on the energy of the parade, immerse ourselves in the electric atmosphere.

The stage is bathed in a soft, moody glow, as a sultry voice caresses the notes of Rihanna's "Umbrella". The singer is a revelation, her voice lending a depth to the song that is at once heartbreaking and inspiring. As she croons the familiar words, "When the sun shines, we'll shine together...", I can't help but get lost in the rhythm, the sentiment.

Jessica and I haven't exchanged many words since our kiss.

There's tension between us, crackling like electricity in the charged air of the club.

Every once in a while, our eyes meet, a silent conversation carried in a shared look. I glance at her, her profile illuminated by the stage lights, her eyes closed, lost in the music. Her stoicism seems out of place here, amidst the laughter and the music, and I wonder what she's thinking.

As the singer's voice rises, hitting the chorus with an impressive intensity, my mind wanders back to our kiss. The memory hits me with a force that is staggering, the taste of her, the feel of her, a sensory overload that leaves me breathless. It's as if the passion we shared in that one moment has eclipsed the love I've experienced in all my past relationships.

"Because when the sun shines, we'll shine together..." The singer's voice echoes through the room, mirroring my thoughts. I had never thought a kiss could do that to me. More than a physical connection, it felt like an awakening, a realization of something deeper, something visceral. A shiver runs through me, not entirely from the air conditioning.

My gaze flits over to Jessica again, her tall frame leaning against the bar, her eyes still closed, and I wonder about her. About her life. The way she throws herself into danger to feel something... it resonates with my rebellion, with my need for freedom.

The singer's voice swells, hitting a high note that vibrates through the room. "Know that you're not alone..." The words resonate with me, bringing unshed tears to my eyes. Jessica isn't alone, she doesn't have to be, and suddenly, I find myself wishing she could let herself rely on someone.

I watch as Jessica finally opens her eyes, her gaze meeting mine. Her face is still unreadable, but there's an intensity in her eyes that takes my breath away. It's then I realize that our lives, our rebellions are not so different. We are two sides of the same coin, seeking freedom and connection in our own ways.

I find myself thinking of Jessica's childhood, of what made her the woman she is today. I want to know her, truly know her, beyond the surface-level banter and shared danger.

As the song comes to an end, the club erupts in applause.

Yet, amidst the noise and cheer, all I can hear is the echo of a single thought - I want to know Jessica's story. I want to be part of her story. I want to be her 'umbrella', even if in the limited capacity of a friend, because I know Jessica Thompson is a person I would like to have in my life, because she is that unique...that amazing, and maybe because I think, even with all our differences, we are the only two people who can understand each other.

Back at the hotel, night seeping into every corner, the room buzzes with energy from the day's activities. We're not alone.

Rita and Sharon, that charismatic lesbian couple we met earlier, have joined our merry gang. Even now, amidst our lively chatter, their eyes hold a special spark, a quiet joy, reflecting a day well spent.

But I'm not myself.

There's a fever prickling under my skin, the result of the day's excitement and exertions. I try to shake it off, keep the smile intact, but it's a losing battle. Something's up, and the others know it.

Jessica. Reliable, trustworthy Jessica. Always alert, always ready to jump into action. She's quick to spot my discomfort, her eyes scanning me over with a worry that tugs at my heart. But she doesn't hover. Instead, she slips away silently, leaving me to the tender mercies of Kriti and Maria. Their concern is touching, if slightly overwhelming.

As I sit curled on the plush couch, my senses heightened from the fever, I strain to hear Jessica's conversation in the hallway. There's an intensity in her voice that stirs a warmth within me, fever notwithstanding. She's talking to Rita and Sharon, asking if the pride bus can delay its departure till tomorrow. She mentions how much I want to be a part of it, and how much it means to me.

A night's rest, she says.

She thinks I just need a good night's sleep and then I'll be up and running, ready to conquer the world again.

Such faith she has in me.

The muffled voices from the hallway filter back into the room, the sound of gratitude mingling with the gentle hum of the hotel's air conditioning.

I hear Jessica thank Rita and Sharon profusely, while they tell her how lucky I am to have a partner like Jessica.

My fevered mind almost produces a chuckle, the irony of their statement tickling my fancy. Were I not besieged by my body's refusal to keep its temperature in check, I might have succumbed to a full-fledged bout of laughter.

As it stands, I simply watch as Jessica strides back into the colourful chaos that is our room, her aura of calm a stark contrast to the whirlwind around us.

She sinks into the seat opposite mine, her gaze sweeping over me with an intensity that's hard to miss. "How are you feeling now?" There's an unmistakable note of concern in her voice, tucked neatly behind a veneer of casual indifference.

I know you care for me, you old, sexy Marine.

Kriti breaks into our little moment with her typically matter-of-fact question. "How many cocktails did you have again?" Her tall frame acts as a welcome barrier between me and the glaring, dreary fluorescent lights overhead.

I offer her a half-hearted smile, my mind preoccupied. "Enough to drown out my sorrows for the night," I admit, my gaze straying back to Jessica.

I see Jessica fiddling with her smartwatch.

Yeah, she wears a smartwatch to track her daily steps,

calories, the million push-ups she does each day, and how hard her abs are. Things like that.

Things that I have started to find adorable.

"Do you have Viking blood in you?" I inquire, my words punctuated by a small cough.

She pauses, her attention fully on me. There's a glacial intensity in her icy blue eyes, cutting through me with startling ease. "My parents were Dutch, I'm sure there are some Viking genes in there."

I can't suppress the shiver of delight that travels down my spine. "I think that's hot," I confess, another cough escaping my lips.

She arches an eyebrow, a smile playing at the corners of her mouth. "You are hot... with fever. And you should rest."

She's right, of course, but the question pressing on my mind refuses to be ignored. "Are we still going on the Pride Bus?" I ask, my eyes wide with anticipation, like a cute puppy.

Why do I like being smothered by this tall piece of Dutch sexiness?

Jessica's eyes soften, the intensity melting away. "We are," she confirms, her voice gentle. "But you need to take care of yourself first. We can't have you collapsing on the bus." It's almost a joke, but the concern in her voice is palpable.

I nod, a small smile tugging at the corners of my lips.

"Okay, boss," I concede, playfully saluting her. She chuckles, the sound like music to my ears.

In the midst of my delirium, I observe a rare moment - a manifestation of Jessica's playful side. She's turned her attention to Kriti and Maria now, her sharp wit and dry humor transforming the room's ambiance. She leans back into the couch, her arms folded across her chest as she raises an eyebrow at the two women who, in turn, are trying to suppress their amusement.

"So, you two," Jessica begins, her voice low and mirthful. "Your little performance at the R&B club was quite the spectacle. I've seen Marines with less commitment during drills. What's up with that?"

Maria shoots a sheepish smile at Kriti. Kriti shrugs, feigning innocence. But their conspiratorial grins betray their façade.

Jessica smirks. "And don't even get me started on your antics with Rita and Sharon. You two had a more fleshed-out backstory than most characters in a Michael Bay movie."

"Look, Jessica, we both know you're an ace when it comes to interrogation," Maria starts, her eyes steady on Jessica. "You've made terrorist kingpins crumble with your techniques, but this is no covert operation, alright? Kriti and I...we're just two people bored out of our minds."

"And Kriti, she's fed up with playing Penelope's glorified butler." Maria tosses in for good measure, only to backtrack when she catches sight of my incredulous expression. "Oh, I didn't mean it like that..."

"What? This is news to me!" I glare at Kriti.

"No! That's not what I meant! Maria!" Now it's Kriti's turn to glare at Maria, and amidst all this, Jessica has an evil smile plastered on her face.

"Well, I see a little crumbling going on here. Kriti, is it true that you truly despise being Penelope's personal errand woman? A glorified butler, if I may dare to venture?"

Jessica is relentless, and I am loving this side of her.

"No! I love Penelope. She is my best friend, and she got me this job. But, I am also an Oxford graduate...so, I just feel that, sometimes, my skills are not being utilized."

"But Kriti...when I ascend the throne, you'll be my royal advisor. It's a position of honor," I argue, feeling my throat scratch with each word.

Kriti appears dumbstruck, looking like she's caught between a rock and a hard place. "Penny, I'm never leaving this job. I love this job...and you."

"And Maria, it seems," Jessica interjects. I can't help but laugh at her audacity.

Kriti is gaping at Jessica. "Sister, what's gotten into you?" she demands, her expression a mixture of annoyance and amusement.

Jessica shrugs, a playful wink directed at me. "Maybe I'm just as bored as you guys."

Jessica senses the shift in the room's vibe and, with the agility of a seasoned diplomat, deftly changes the topic.

A part of me is relieved, the rest of me is downright intrigued. "So, Kriti, what's your type? Is it muscular marines with an insatiable hunger for blood and the ability to squat as much as an ape?" she says, a mischievous grin stretching her lips, as she raises her eyebrows suggestively at Maria.

Caught off-guard, Kriti blushes, something I'd hardly seen in all my years of knowing her. "Well...I, uh..." she stammers, before finally collecting her thoughts. "It's not about that, Jessica. Sure, Maria's strength is...attractive, but it's more than just physical."

She takes a deep breath, seeming to gather courage from the air around her. "I mean, yes, those squats have definitely helped shape a...particular part of Maria's body to perfection, but it's more than that."

We all chuckle at this, and Maria blushes, a rare occurrence for her as well.

"But, Jessica, let me turn the tables on you. Why did you hook up with Maria back in Iraq?" Kriti's counter-question lands with a thud, ricocheting around the room.

Jessica, unfazed, brushes it off with her signature nonchalance. "Well, when you're stationed in Iraq, the dating pool is rather limited. Maria wasn't so much an option as she was a necessity." She grins at Maria, who throws a cushion at her.

I can't help but feel a pang of envy at the ease with which they banter with each other, their laughter filling the room. It's a camaraderie I've always wanted to be a part of, but I never quite fit in. I've always been the odd one out, the outsider looking in. Even with Kriti, my closest friend, there's always been a distance between us, a wall I can't seem to break down.

Suddenly, Maria decides to dive into her own pile of ammunition. "Hey Jess," she begins, leaning back on the plush couch, a smirk playing on her lips, "remember how you didn't want this job? How you claimed that babysitting a royal was beneath your dignity? Funny how things have changed, isn't it?"

Jessica raises an eyebrow, attempting a stoic exterior, but her eyes are glinting with good-natured humor. "Well, can't a person change her mind?"

"Change her mind or change her heart?" Maria teases.

Jessica rolls her eyes, a grin creeping onto her face.

Then, Maria swivels towards me, her grin widening into a full-blown smirk. "You know what's really funny, Penelope? When I first showed Jess your picture, she couldn't stop talking about how great your ass looked."

A giggle escapes my lips before I can stop it. I return Maria's smirk, my feverish mind delighting in the shared joke. "Well, she certainly wasn't complaining when she copped a feel a few days back."

Maria's smirk disappears, replaced by a look of surprise. Jessica, on the other hand, chokes on her drink, her face turning a shade of red that can only be described as 'Royal Guard Uniform.'

"Wait, what?" Maria gapes at me, then whips her head towards Jessica. "You...she...what?"

"Oh, didn't I mention?" I say, feigning innocence. "I tried to seduce her into taking me to LA. Things got a little...physical."

Maria sniggers, giving Jessica the 'you naughty dog' look. Even Kriti is snickering into her hand. Jessica, still beet red, gives me an incredulous look, which only makes me laugh harder.

"I swear, you royals...you're all completely mad," Jessica grumbles, but there's a smile tugging at her lips. She's outnumbered, and she knows it.

Chapter Eight

Jessica

The morning sun is barely scratching the horizon, and I'm standing next to Penelope in front of a Pride Bus which is about as subtle as a brick in the face.

It's painted in all the colors of the rainbow, adorned with ribbons and sequins. It looks like the love child of an acid trip and a gay rights parade.

Rita and Sharon are waving us in, their smiles infectious. The two women look like they've been cast in a glamorous rock music video. Decked in glitter and rainbow-colored accessories, they're the quintessential images of Pride.

Kriti and Maria, on the other hand, are managing their act as the fake couple brilliantly. The two of them enter the bus holding hands, perfectly in sync, while I just stand there, trying to wrap my head around the theatricality of the whole scenario.

Penelope and I are trying to portray a similar facade, but to be honest, the whole acting thing isn't really my cup of tea. She, on the other hand, is brimming with excitement, as if she's been waiting for this all her life. She's draped in a tastefully minimalistic, all-white ensemble with a dash of color on her hat and shoes.

I look at her, the unmissable exuberance in her eyes, the radiant smile on her face, and feel an overwhelming surge of protectiveness. And then, we step onto the bus.

As soon as we do, a hush falls over the bus. It's as if someone's pressed the mute button on a TV. One by one, the passengers turn to look at us, and then, as if on cue, they begin to bow. Curtsy, actually. I watch in amazement as each person, one after another, pays their respect to Penelope.

And then, it hits me. These people know who Penelope is. I remember how Sharon and Rita had stumbled onto our secret in the lesbian bar, and now, others on the bus know who Penelope is. They recognize her. Not as the 'spoilt, rebellious royal' that the tabloids paint her to be, but as a symbol of hope, a beacon for the queer community. Here, in this bus full of queer individuals, Penelope is royalty in the truest sense.

The love and respect that fills the bus is almost tangible, and it's aimed at this young woman standing next to me, who's trying so hard to hide her blushes and failing adorably.

I glance at her again, my mind a whirlpool of emotions.

As I'm processing the admiration radiating towards Penelope, I feel a sudden shift. Eyes turn towards me as well. Not with suspicion or wariness, but with respect. Similar curtsies are now directed towards me, paired with expressions of reverence. This doesn't make sense. I'm just a bodyguard. I'm... then it clicks. They think I'm going to be the queen's wife, Penelope's partner in ruling, and her partner in life.

Their assumptions, however ludicrous they seem to me, warm my heart. It's not about the perceived status, or the respect that comes with it. It's about being acknowledged and accepted as a part of this community.

One by one, people start approaching us.

There's a burly man with a mustache that looks like

it belongs in the 80s, dressed head-to-toe in pink. He tells Penelope how her rebellion against her family resonates with him, how it gives him hope. A couple dressed in matching rainbow flag capes say they know about her struggle and promise to stand by her side.

A transgender woman, with blue hair cascading down her shoulders, hugs Penelope and whispers in her ear that she's a beacon of light for them all. A drag queen, towering over everyone with stilettos that are death traps, promises Penelope that they won't let her secret out. They're the family she chose, and they will protect her.

Overwhelmed, Penelope takes a moment to compose herself. A single tear escapes her eye, but her voice is clear when she speaks, "I am humbled by your support, but I must ask you to keep my identity a secret. I want to be the one to share it when the time is right."

They nod, understanding her predicament. Their expressions remain full of love, but now with a sense of duty. They'll protect their royal sister, and they'll do their best to give her and me, who they believe to be her chosen one, the best time.

Surreal as it is, standing here amidst all these vibrant souls, being accepted, being respected, I feel a pang of gratitude. These people don't know me, but they're willing to accept me, accept us, simply because they believe in love, in freedom, and in the courage to be oneself.

I trail behind the princess as we're led to our seats, a position of importance at the back of the bus, where we can overlook the rest of the passengers. Kriti and Maria are seated in front of us, while the others, numbering around 20, occupy the rest of the bus.

The bus is a double-decker, and the seats on the top have an aerial view of the surroundings, which Penelope is excited to try out once the bus hits the freeways.

As we settle into our seats, I can't help but notice the way Penelope's eyes flicker to me every so often. It's almost as if she's trying to gauge my reaction to everything that's happening around us. I give her a small smile, letting her know that everything is okay.

Rita and Sharon, dressed in glittering tops that sparkle like a disco ball and rainbow pants that scream Pride, take center stage. Sharon clears her throat, and her deep voice cuts through the excited chatter in the bus.

"Alright, folks! Here's the plan. Our fabulous bus will be journeying through the heart of America, making its way to Dallas by tomorrow morning. We'll be camping overnight just outside Arkansas. So, brace yourselves for some wild fun!"

"Wild fun?" I ask, trying not to sound too skeptical. I'm having trouble imagining Penelope, the royal highness, camping in the wild.

"Oh yes," Sharon winks at me, "We have games lined up, music to shake the bus, and plenty of alcohol. It's going to be Pride like never before!"

Penelope perks up at the mention of games, her deep-brown eyes sparkling with curiosity. "What kind of games are we talking about?"

Sharon lets out a hearty laugh. "Your Highness, let's just say you'll have to shed your royal elegance to fully enjoy these games."

The bus erupts into laughter, and even I find myself chuckling. Penelope pouts playfully. "Well, bring it on then. I'm ready to have fun!"

Seeing Penelope's delighted reaction to the camping announcement, I feel a knot of concern in my stomach.

We're going to be out in the open, vulnerable to elements

and prying eyes. I need to voice my worries. As discreetly as I can, I tug at Penelope's sleeve.

"Hey," I say, trying to keep my voice steady and casual. "Are you sure about this camping thing? It's not exactly a five-star hotel..."

Penelope blinks at me, then a slow smile spreads across her face. "Oh, so the rundown motel was fine, but camping under the stars is where you draw the line?"

"Well..." I scratch at the back of my head, feeling oddly embarrassed. I'm not used to this feeling. As a marine, I'm always in control, always ready for whatever is thrown at me. But with Penelope, things are different.

She laughs then, a soft sound that sends a warm sensation coursing through me. "Are you melting for me, marine?" she asks, her voice low and teasing.

"No..." I say, too quickly. She tilts her head, studying me with those almond eyes that see too much, know too much.

"I've been on camping trips before, Jess, back in England. Mother and I go for an annual camping trip into the wild English forests."

"How wild can the English forests be?" I joke.

"Wild enough." Penelope grins at me, and I can't help but be drawn to her infectious energy. "Besides, I'm not afraid of getting a little dirt on my dress."

Yes, the dress. Did I tell you about the white summer dress?

The white summer dress, or the 'other revenge dress' as I have since then named it, is a white, knee-length, figure-hugging, flared piece of garment, that Penelope has decided to wear, the day after our kiss left me questioning everything about me...and her.

The dress is white, with straps thinner than a finger, connecting behind her neck, leaving her shoulder blades and back bare. The fabric is so light that it seems to float around her, and I can't help but feel a pang of desire as I imagine what it would be like to have her in my arms, the dress fluttering around us like a cloud.

The dress hugs her breasts and waist, while the skirt flows and flares around her waist. Her skin is alabaster white, glowing in contrast to the dark brown of her hair as it cascades down her sides. The dress's hem is inches above her knees, making it easy to see her long, toned legs.

Shedding the 'hot girl summer' look, and donning the sexy, understated elegance of an English girl, Penelope has decided to go all out to rupture my heart and to make me long for her.

As I sit back, and watch her stroll up and down the aisle, obliging people with small talk, warm smiles, and a random hug, I see Penelope in a different light.

I watch a queen in waiting work her magic; I see the glimmer, the hint of brilliance that will surely come to define her reign. She is confident, charming, and oh so beautiful, that it makes me ache in all the wrong...or the right places.

For the first hour of our journey, I can't tear my eyes away from her dress, her legs, or the enticing swell of her breasts. It's only when Maria joins me that I snap out of my fantasies involving her highness.

"Look at us, lusting after two British flowers, surrounded by people you wouldn't say 'hi' to on a street," Maria comments, her eyes following mine and landing on Penelope.

"Who says I won't say 'hi' to these people? I find them...endearing," I shoot back.

Maria grins knowingly. "She's changing you, isn't she?

Turning you into someone I always hoped you'd be." Her words yank me from the enchantment of Penelope's charm.

I snap my attention back to Maria. "You were just interested in screwing me. When did you suddenly want me to...change?" Maria sighs, her gaze locked on Penelope, engaged in conversation with a woman decades her senior.

"I mentioned it once...I could see us as something more, if sex wasn't your only interest."

"I don't remember," I lie smoothly, the memory of her words a sharp note in my mind. I had never intended to change, not for Maria.

But admitting that seemed crueler.

"I get it, Thompson. I was just a distraction, until the real thing came along. Never thought you'd fall for a delicate little flower, though."

"She's not delicate. She's a force, ready to take on an entire monarchy," I defend, surprising myself.

The last person I'd ever thought I'd be defending was Penelope, but here I was.

"So, what is it then? Lust or love?" Maria asks, pulling me back to reality. I find myself stalling, unsure.

"What about you and Kriti?" I deflect.

"I don't know yet," she confesses.

"Same here."

"But I'm definitely finding out how Kriti tastes by the end of this road trip!"

I can't help but laugh at Maria's audacity. "Easy, Sanchez. She doesn't strike me as the kind of woman who's used to... earth-shattering sex," I advise, though I can't resist adding, "Although, she did have quite the fire when she kissed me."

"No worries, Thompson. Your kiss with Kriti doesn't bother me." Maria shrugs, and my curiosity piques.

"Why? I kissed Kriti first. Shouldn't that... annoy you?" I question.

Maria grins mischievously. "No, because that means I can kiss Penelope... if she's willing."

"Back off, Sanchez," I snap, irrationally territorial.

"I can see it's more than lust, Thompson. Even Kriti can. The question is, when will you acknowledge it? Or will the princess beat you to it? Maybe she can help you with your emotions, eh?"

"No one can help me, until I want them to," I continue in my irritated voice, "and you...keep your paws off her."

"I never intended to paw at her. I was just testing you, trying to get a reaction out of you, and guess what, for the first time ever, I beat you at your own game. Now, if you will, there is a tall, Indian goddess waiting for me to regale her with my heroics in Iraq. You continue...gawking at your flower," Maria says, leaving me with a wink and a smile that irks and humors me at the same time.

Penelope

Locked in chit-chat with this sweet old lady, my ears catch the lilt of her seasoned tales. But her words, they kinda fade into white noise, cause I've got a much louder distraction going on.

In the glossed-up window ahead of me, a certain reflection has my heart doing somersaults and my head spinning faster than a merry-go-round. My pulse is tap-dancing, racing with every beat as I catch sight of those blue eyes I've grown so fond of.

Jessica. Just a few seats behind, but her gaze – it's like a homing beacon locked on me. Even as I moved about the bus, sharing laughs and swapping stories, I felt the heat of her stare. Like invisible threads pulling me back to her. It's one hell of a sensation, knowing you're the focal point of someone's attention.

My mind darts off on a wild tangent. If just her eyes on me set my heart pounding like a drum, what about her touch? Or, heaven help me, her lips? My thoughts take a sharp, thrilling turn, and it's kinda hard not to get swept up in the whirlwind.

The old lady's voice trickles back in, like an anchor, pulling me back to the here and now. But even as I focus on her words, Jessica's reflection in the window is a constant, delicious distraction.

I can see the soft curls of her blonde hair, swept to one side, reflecting the sunlight like a beacon on a snow-capped mountain.

I can see the toned cheekbones, the fleshy, pink lips begging to be mauled and devoured.

The abs, peeking from below her sports bra, inviting me for a taste.

I want to touch her, to feel her skin against mine, to taste her.

But I know that's not possible. Not when... she's just a reflection in the window.

As I listen to the elderly woman sitting next to me, I find her life story to be as colorful as the pride flag she proudly wears, painted on her aging but vibrant skin.

Her name is Stella, a name that suits her sparkling personality.

"I've been on quite the journey, love," she continues, her

eyes a delightful blend of nostalgia and mischief. "You see, me and my partner, Grace, we were best friends since we were kiddies, always at each other's side."

The bus rumbles along the road, and I lean in closer, entranced by Stella's tale. She has a way of talking that's as comforting as a cup of hot cocoa on a chilly day - warm, sweet, and slightly spicy.

"We married the men we thought were the loves of our lives. We were happy," she continues, her voice steady but filled with memories. I can almost see the younger version of Stella, a woman experiencing love in all its joyful messiness. But then her tone shifts, her voice dipping lower.

"But you know, life is quite the drama queen. It threw us a curveball when both our husbands died on the same fishing trip. They were inseparable, even in death," Stella sighs, her voice carrying a current of lingering sorrow.

I reach out to hold her hand, a silent gesture of support. To my surprise, she gives me a warm smile, not the least bit deterred by the dark turn in her tale. She pats my hand, the twinkle in her eyes returning.

"But as they say, after a storm comes a rainbow," Stella quips. "In our shared grief, Grace and I found solace and...eventually, love. We were 60 then, starting over when most are winding down."

Her story is so powerful that it leaves me momentarily speechless. Stella and Grace, finding love in the most unexpected of places, at a time when society was far less accepting.

"We run a quaint bookstore in Arkansas now," she shares, her voice filled with pride. "But with people preferring screens over pages, we've been thinking of switching to a café. Grace can cook Italian food like a dream." She laughs, her eyes twinkling.

"Tell me about your bookstore," I inquire, eager to hear more about Stella and Grace's lives.

Stella's eyes brighten at the question, and a soft smile dances on her lips.

"Oh, dear, it's a haven for book lovers. Old wooden shelves, brimming with stories of every kind, from mystery thrillers to soppy romances. A little nook in the corner with comfy armchairs for those who just want to lose themselves in a good book," she describes, her eyes shining with pride and affection.

"But..." she hesitates, and I see a trace of sadness creep into her features. "But times are changing, dear. Paperbacks are becoming relics, and we can't afford to be relics too."

The bus lurches a bit as it goes over a pothole, but neither of us pays it any mind. We are both lost in thoughts of a small bookstore in Arkansas, clinging on to its past.

"What about the café?" I ask, nudging her gently out of her reverie.

"The café...oh, we've been dreaming of it for years now. Grace's spaghetti alle vongole could make an Italian nonna weep! But dreams cost money, love," Stella sighs, her bright eyes clouding over, "I wish she could meet you, but she is waiting for me in Dallas. Rita and Sharon were kind enough to let me onto this 'couples only' bus without her, although being here and watching all you folks being in love is making me miss her even more."

Stella shares her struggles with me, about finding capital for the café, about their friends who cut ties with them because of their lifestyle. Stella pulls out her phone and shows me their GoFundMe page.

The page is charmingly done, full of cute doodles and a heartwarming photo of Stella and Grace, both donned in Italian dresses, beaming beside a massive, perfectly cooked pizza. There's something so genuine, so raw about their dream that it strikes a chord within me.

My mind wanders, and for a moment, I envision a future where I stand alongside someone I love in Buckingham Palace, echoing Stella and Grace's beaming smiles.

But the thought seems like a distant dream, wrapped in layers of royal protocols and expectations.

"I have a feeling your café will soon become a reality, Stella," I say, my voice radiating a warm certainty. I can't help but lean in to give her a hug, the strength, and resilience of this woman stirring an unexpected fondness in me. I hold onto her a few seconds longer than necessary, her frail form comforting in its own unique way.

"Stella," I confess in a hushed voice, "I haven't hugged my mother in years, ever since I became an adult." I can feel her stiffen in my arms at my confession. "The Queen, she says that hugging your child after they turn eighteen...that it's allowing them to be weak."

For a moment, there's silence, only the hum of the bus and the murmur of conversations filtering through. Then, Stella gives a soft laugh, and her arms tighten around me, pulling me closer.

"Well then, Penelope," she says, her voice full of gentle defiance. "If the Queen won't hug you, then surely, you can. The next time you see her, give her a long, bear hug. And don't let go. Show her that strength isn't always about standing alone, but sometimes, it's about holding onto each other."

Her words, simple yet powerful, resonate within me, stirring up a well of emotions. Maybe, just maybe, I can take Stella's advice to heart. For now, though, I hug Stella again, tighter than before, grateful for her wisdom and kindness.

With a final squeeze to Stella's shoulder and a promise to

catch up later, I totter back to my designated spot in the royal carriage... I mean, the back of the bus.

Plopping down next to Jessica, I find her engrossed in a thrilling session of Candy Crush on her iPhone, which should probably be in a museum by now.

"Do you know even the sweet nonna upfront has given that game the boot, Jess?" I quip, wrinkling my nose at the screen.

Jessica barely glances at me, her fingers swiping deftly across the screen. "What others do doesn't put the crown on my head, Princess," she retorts, eyes still on the game.

"Do you have a box of these punchy one-liners tucked away in your pocket?" I shoot back.

"Nah, they're all battle scars. You'll earn your own when you cross the thirty-one-year-old finish line," she counters.

"Huh, can't wait," I mutter, my thoughts drifting back to Stella and Grace and their six-decade supply of one-liners. On a whim, I turn back to Jessica. "Ever thought about yourself at sixty, Jess? How do you think your story will end?"

Jessica's fingers freeze over her phone, and she lifts her gaze to meet mine, those sharp blue eyes slicing through me like sushi-grade tuna. She pauses, seeming to weigh her words as the world outside the bus melts into a watercolor smear of greens and browns. Then she inhales, her shoulders dropping a fraction of an inch.

"At peace," she murmurs, and graces me with a smile that's more of a sunbeam than her usual smirk.

I don't need to hear anymore.

I smile back, taking in her chiseled features, that tiny warrior scar above her upper lip, and whisper, "And here's to you not having to wait until sixty to find it."

∞∞∞∞

The madness is about to begin, and to my utter surprise, it's the liveliest our bus has been since the departure. From poker-playing pensioners to hard-rock rebels, everyone's gathering around our unofficial game organizers, the incomparable Rita and Sharon.

These two, they're a spectacle in their own right. Rita, a firecracker with her mane of curls , has enough energy to power a small city. On the other hand, Sharon, with her sleek ebony bob , is the perfect cool, composed yin to Rita's spirited yang. Their combined humor and repartee manage to hook even the most reluctant of us into their charade.

"Listen up, lovebirds!" Rita booms, her hand waving a pile of question papers as though she's about to issue royal decrees. "We're about to dig deep and see just how much you really know about your other half!"

"Now, here's the twist," Sharon chimes in, a devious smirk on her lips. "One half of each couple will get a sheet of questions. Answer 'em secretly, and no peeking, mind you!" A ripple of chuckles runs through our audience. "Then we'll ask your partners the same questions. If your answers match, bingo! You're one step closer to being crowned 'Bus Couple Supreme'."

There's a shared groan of hilarity, some scoffing, and I spot Jessica's gaze meeting mine - the reluctant amusement in her eyes mirroring my own. We're in for a wild ride, alright. As I see it, we're on a one-way trip to couples' humiliation, and there's no emergency exit.

Not far from us, Maria and Kriti are caught in a similar turmoil, their faces a mix of startled amusement and what

I can only describe as mortal fear. I lean over to Kriti, whispering a sly, "Well, darling, say goodbye to your 'perfect couple' reputation."

I get a gentle thwack on my arm as my reward, but it's worth it. As we brace ourselves for the storm of intimate inquiries, I can't help but feel a thrill.

"And there's more!" Sharon chimes in with the biggest grin on her face, one that screams mischief.

"For every correct answer, you lovely couples are going to share a kiss, right here, right now." Giggles break out, the couple in the front row already snogging as if they've won. Sharon raises a brow at them, waiting for them to disentangle before she proceeds. "And mind you, each subsequent correct answer requires a steamier, naughtier, even... should we dare to say... pornographic kiss!" At this point, the bus is in an uproar. The couple in the front row are turning a deeper shade of red, and Jessica and I are sharing a glance that is one part amusement, two parts mortified.

"But hold on," Sharon's finger shoots up in the air, silencing the rowdy bus, "with each wrong answer, there's a forfeit. One of you will have to spank the other." A split second of stunned silence follows this revelation before the bus erupts into laughter and hoots. "Usually, it's the one who answers incorrectly who gets the, er, bottom end of this deal."

The rules are laid bare, and Sharon, with a queenly sweep of her arm, directs us to sit in pairs. Amidst the frantic shuffling and raucous laughter, Jessica and I glance at each other.

Our expressions mirror each other's disbelief and hilarity as we prepare for a game that promises to be as scandalously entertaining as it is cringe-inducing.

"I'm answering the questions on that sheet," Jessica murmurs, her voice low in my ear, hot and immediate.

"Good, because I've been dying to get spanked." I lean in, my lips practically grazing her earlobe as I deliver the cheeky retort. The urge to nip at her earlobe sparks like an electric current, then fizzles out, leaving a warm glow in its wake.

Something about Jessica's presence has become an addictive pull, an itch that's begging to be scratched. I'm shocked by this growing desire to touch her, to feel her since our kiss at the parade. The memory of her lips against mine sends a pulse of heat through me.

What's going on?

Is it the intoxicating remnant of that stolen kiss?

Or is it the way she's looking today, more tempting than I've ever seen her? But wait... she's just dressed in tight leggings and a sporty Nike bra, her hair pulled up into a careless ponytail.

What's so damn sexy about that?

I groan internally. The answer is painfully simple: Everything. Everything about Jessica is unbearably sexy, and I'm caught in her pull, helpless and wanting.

I watch Jessica, totally engrossed in her sheet, her forehead furrowed in concentration. Across from us, Maria mirrors her, studiously penning her responses. A glance shared with Kriti communicates our shared love for spankings by sexy marines.

I scan the rest of the bus, taking in the couples. Some share whispered jokes, others steal kisses, filling the downtime as the game trudges on. Unable to resist, I attempt a stealthy peek at Jessica's sheet, only to be caught red-handed by Sharon.

"No royal privileges in the game, Your Highness!" Sharon calls me out. The bus erupts in laughter, making me feel like a mischievous child who's just been busted for stealing cookies.

"I was merely... trying to steal a look down my Jessica's top," I improvise. My lame excuse hangs in the air and I'm mentally awarding myself the 'Lamest Excuse Ever' trophy.

Jessica flicks a glance at me, her eyes clearly asking, 'Have you lost your bloody mind?' I lean back, raising my hands in surrender as the sound of scribbling and rustling paper fills the air.

Another battle lost in the war of the Bus Games. Oh well, bring on the next round!

∞∞∞

The game is on and the bus is buzzing with palpable anticipation. Our self-appointed hosts, Rita and Sharon, are doing a splendid job, dishing out questions with saucy smiles and a sprinkle of drama.

Up first is the dynamic duo: Sam, a sturdy woman with tattoos crawling up her arms, and her transgender partner, Alex, an ethereal vision with hair as blue as a midsummer's sky. Alex is posed with the question: "What is Sam's guilty pleasure?"

Her reply comes without a hint of hesitation: "Watching 'RuPaul's Drag Race' while feasting on Nutella straight from the jar." A wave of laughter sweeps through the bus. Sam's face flushes a glorious pink, confirming the truth in Alex's answer. She pulls Alex into a smoldering, celebratory kiss that sparks a chorus of hoots and cheers. Even the blushing faces scattered throughout the bus add to the hilarity of the moment.

The next duo in the hot seat is the charming gay couple: the brawny, gentle giant Hank, and his skinny, quick-witted partner, Gary. The question directed at Gary is: "Who is Hank's celebrity hall pass?"

Gary's smirk turns impish as he answers, "The Rock, Dwayne Johnson." The bus erupts into giggles and hoots, but Hank just shakes his head, blushing up to his ears.

"Wrong, babe," he corrects, a playful scowl on his face. "It's Chris Hemsworth, thank you very much." The bus morphs into a collective groan as we digest Hank's Thor fantasy.

As per the rules, Gary leans across Hank's lap to accept his playful punishment. Hank's light smack is more a love pat than a spanking, prompting another round of laughter.

The show keeps rolling and next up are Maria and Kriti.

Sharon winks at them, a mischievous glint in her eyes. "Kriti, darling," she drawls, her voice laced with a teasing, playful edge. "Can you tell us what Maria's most used phrase during lovemaking is?"

You could hear a pin drop in the bus. Kriti's cheeks flare into a hot, tomato-like red, her eyes darting to me in panic. I shrug helplessly, a bemused grin on my face. Next to me, Jessica raises an eyebrow at the question. I lean in, my lips brushing against her ear as I whisper, "Well, you must know the answer to this one."

Jessica snorts, then her eyes widen a bit before she smirks at me. "Honestly, Penny," she whispers back, her voice dropping into a husky, suggestive timbre that sends heat rushing to places I won't mention. "Usually, when I'm with a girl, all they manage to do is make choking noises." She punctuates the sentence with a cocky, self-assured smirk.

The image this plants in my mind does things to me, very naughty things.

My heartbeat quickens, and I can feel a blush creeping up my neck. But before I can even get my bearings, Kriti's nervous voice fills the bus.

"Uhm... 'Oh God?' she mumbles, squirming under the

expectant gazes of everyone.

A round of laughter echoes in the bus as Maria chimes in, shaking her head with an indulgent smile. "Wrong, babe," she says, pulling Kriti towards her and planting a soft kiss on her cheek. "I usually go for the Spanish version. 'Ay Dios mio.'"

"I guess Kriti's mind is usually elsewhere when making love," says Alex with a chuckle.

"Yeah, busy imagining Natalie Portman in Maria's place, probably," Sam fires off a quip, that has the bus laughing, but Maria and Kriti looking like lost sheep.

"Time for the spanking! And this time, we want to hear a sound, like a loud thwack!" I say, and Kriti looks at me with eyes raging with thunder.

"Yeah, Sanchez, you don't want us marines looking weak!" Jessica joins me and gives me a low-five.

Kriti takes a deep breath, and then leans over Maria's lap, her pert backside up in the air. The bus falls silent, all eyes on the couple. Maria raises her hand and then brings it down with a loud, satisfying thwack that echoes through the bus.

Kriti lets out a yelp, but her face says she enjoyed it more than she should have.

As Kriti leans back into her seat, she looks over at me with a glint in her eye. "Your turn next, Pen," she says with a smirk. "Let's see how you handle it."

"We can opt out of this if you want. We can tell them we are not a couple. I am sure they won't kick you out of the bus. They love you!" Jessica mutters under her breath, while rubbing her hands, an act that is supposed to scare me.

"No way! It is more fun pretending to be a couple. Now, don't hold back, okay? I want you to spank me like you spank your Spanish women."

"I don't think I have seen this version of Titanic," Jessica jokes.

The wheels turn again, and now, it's Jessica and me under the spotlight.

Rita fixes me with a penetrating gaze. "Penelope," she says, her voice deceptively soft in the hush of the bus. "What is Jessica's biggest fear in life?"

An anticipatory silence hangs heavy in the bus.

I close my eyes, a sudden wave of nerves washing over me. This isn't some trivia question or a fact check; it's an intimate look into Jessica's soul, her very being.

What could a Marine be scared of?

I start analyzing the shards of Jessica's life I've seen so far. Her toughness, her loss, her solitude, her daring, even her reluctance to let people in... and then it hits me. Like a stray piece of a jigsaw puzzle, it falls into place.

Slowly, I open my eyes and meet Jessica's guarded gaze. "Her biggest fear is losing people she loves," I say, my voice ringing clear in the quiet bus.

A beat passes.

Two.

Then Jessica's eyes widen slightly, a wave of vulnerability, surprise, and something else—something softer—flashing in their deep blue depths. And then, before I can even blink, she's reaching for me, pulling me into a breathtaking kiss as applause erupts around us.

It starts as a mere pressing of lips, tentative yet yearning, and then Jessica is the one deepening it, an arm snaking around my waist to bring me closer. Our surroundings blur, the cheering crowd fades into the background, and it's just her and me, lost in our own world, kissing each other like there's no tomorrow.

As our lips move in perfect sync, my hands wander down to her hips, feeling the curves of her body through her clothes. I pull her closer, wanting to feel every inch of her against me. Her hands knot in my hair, pulling me closer still, and I let out a low groan of desire.

The bus erupts into catcalls and hollers, but I barely hear them. I'm too lost in the moment, in the feeling of Jessica's lips on mine, her tongue exploring my mouth, her hand tugging lightly at my hair.

Oh, how I wish she would tug harder!

I can feel her heart pounding against my chest, matching mine beat for beat.

When we finally pull apart, gasping for air, the world comes rushing back to me. I'm greeted by catcalls, shouts, and whistles, and the latest round of applause.

I turn to look at Jessica, and I don't know what I see in her eyes; it could be affection, it could be desire, it could be something else. Something I have never seen in anyone's eyes.

Something I don't know how to name.

"You know, you are a pretty good actress, Penelope."

"Thanks," I reply, my gaze still locked on Jessica, "but I think you are better."

Jessica

As the bus roars on, so does the game, the banter and the laughter filling the air. Alex and Sam are still going strong, their answers hitting the mark more often than not. Hank, however, looks like he's about to burst into tears with each wrong answer from his partner. At least he's having a good workout for his bottom, though, which is more than can be said for Kriti.

Kriti.

That demure Oxford graduate has lost again and is now grinning like a maniac as Maria lines up for another spank. Only this time, there's something different about her request. "Harder," she practically purrs, her eyes twinkling with a mix of defiance and anticipation. Maria obliges, two more swift slaps landing on Kriti's behind, the smacks echoing throughout the bus. Each spank elicits an appreciative sigh from Kriti, and a collective cheer from the rest of us. *I should get her a "I ♥ Spanks" t-shirt after this.*

The wheel of fortune spins again, and it lands on Penelope.

I gulp, my heart pounding like a jackhammer in my chest. Damn, I can't believe I'm nervous about this. I want to kiss her. No, I *need* to kiss her. God, it's like I'm a teenager again. What's next? Writing Mrs. Jessica Windsor in my diary?

Rita, the sprite of a woman with cat-eye glasses perched precariously on her nose, turns her gleaming eyes towards Penelope. "Alright, Princess," she purrs, a mischievous grin lighting up her face. "What's Jessica's favorite move you pull off in bed?"

The bus lapses into a silence so thick you could cut it with a knife. You could almost hear the collective holding of breath, the undercurrent of prurient interest crackling through the air like static. Hell, even I am curious, despite being the subject of the question.

How the bloody hell is Penelope going to answer this?

"It's a tough one," I find myself saying, a mad impulse seizing me. I meet Penelope's eyes, her intelligent gaze locked onto mine, as if I'm a puzzle she's determined to solve. "Almost like riding a mechanical bull in a pub, wasted and high."

Penelope, bless her quicksilver wit, does not miss a beat. She pauses for the right amount of time, her eyes never leaving mine. "Well, Jessica is quite fond of... when I straddle her and... move about."

The gasps echo through the bus like a chorus of surprised pigeons, while Maria shoots me a look that says 'I know what you did there'. I, on the other hand, find myself utterly, stupidly impressed by the astuteness of the princess.

It appears she might indeed be capable of running a kingdom someday.

Sharon throws us a wink, lighting the fuse. "I guess it's time for the royal couple to make out again. But remember, we're making this PG-18."

Stella, the sweet old lady from Arkansas with the bookstore that's fighting its last stand against digital giants, giggles and adds, "Wasn't it 18 plus the last time?"

But then, the peanut gallery joins in, and things quickly spiral out of control. Kriti, the usually demure Oxford graduate, decides to be the ringleader. "We need the princess to demonstrate her move. It's only fair!"

Even a grizzled old cowboy, who makes up one half of a gay couple with matching hats, hollers, "Yeah, that would be fitting. Come on, Your Highness, it's time to straddle your marine!"

As much as I'd love to see Penelope straddling me in public, I find myself praying for the bus to have a sudden brake failure or something.

Just anything to distract this crowd.

But it seems like divine intervention is not on my side today. Penelope, the little minx, just looks at me with a twinkle in her eyes and then, as if it were the most natural thing in the world, she straddles me. My heart is beating so fast, I'm sure everyone on the bus can hear it. I feel her weight on my lap, her warmth seeping into my skin, and I can't help but let out a groan.

Damn, it feels good to have her on my lap.

And there's a collective sigh from the audience as she settles into my lap, then a collective gasp as her hands slide onto my shoulders. I feel her fingers dig into my shoulders, and I'm sure she has left her imprints on my skin.

But then, just as I'm about to lean in and kiss her, Penelope leans back, the mischievous glint in her eyes telling me that she has something else planned. I watch, tongue-tied, as she starts to move her hips, grinding against me in a way that sends electrifying jolts through my body.

You might think, given my marine training and all, I would weather this sexy storm whipped up by the world's most tantalizing royal. But let me tell you, the fairy tale-loving little girl inside of me is relishing every moment of this.

My intellectual debate with myself about crushing on Penelope can wait.

Right now, all I want is to give our eager spectators a show. I take hold of Penelope's hips, thumbs tracing her pelvic bones, over that revenge dress. She gasps, and I can't help the slow, predatory grin that stretches across my face.

"Another Oscar-worthy performance, Princess," I murmur, voice laced with mock innocence.

"Yeah, but you need to pick up the slack as well, marine. You don't seem invested enough."

Challenged, I let my hands travel south to the underside of her thighs, fingers brushing the hem of her dress. "Should I ask for permission?" I question, though it's more rhetoric than a genuine query.

"No," she answers, punctuating it with a calculated roll of

her hips.

"Should I ask Alexa's permission?" I tease, my hands exploring the territory under her dress, skimming lightly over her skin.

"No, she isn't my girlfriend yet. And the future queen of England does what she wants."

"So what does she want?"

She captures my lower lip between hers, a seductive tug following a brief suckle. "For you to reenact the scene from the night of the diplomatic ball. It was quite the show."

"The one where I feigned interest in your ass?" I joke, even as my hands make a bold move upwards, hiking her dress up along with it.

A peal of laughter escapes her and I feel her legs tighten around me. Her body language is clear - she's enjoying this as much as I am.

"Just do it before I get off."

I did not want that.

I suck in a sharp breath, and then I find myself moving my hands further up her thighs, the hem of her dress riding up with them.

Inside her dress, away from the eyes of the passengers, I grab more than a feel of Penelope's ass. I see the reaction on Penelope's face, as she sucks in air and stifles a low moan.

People around us are getting bolder with their cat calls, and in the back of my head, I know we need to stop now.

But how can I?

Not when two of my fingers have slid inside the cutouts of her panties, not when Penelope is so close to surrendering to me, to begging...

And then she is off.

"Alright, that's enough. Somewhere in England, the queen, my mother is having a stroke!"

Penelope unwraps herself from around me, and I feel like a little kid who has just been told she can't go to the playground because the sun is setting.

∞ ∞ ∞

Penelope and I are sitting hand-in-hand, like the other couples around us.

Now if you ask me, the feeling of Penelope's hands, small, dainty, royal, in my much larger, worn-out, calloused marine ones? Yeah, that's going to be my new favorite thing in life. It's like having a piece of the most exquisite porcelain in my hand. Fragile and priceless, yet searingly bold.

The rest of the game pretty much goes downhill from our little performance. The other couples throw their hands up, claiming they can't put on a show to match ours, and honestly, who can blame them? We really did set the bar too high, didn't we?

The intriguing part is how Penelope doesn't miss a single question about me from that point. It's as if she's suddenly gotten access to this database about me that even I didn't know existed. And all of it, the right answers, the intermittent pecks, the sly winks – they're all turning me into this gooey mess of a marine that I didn't think I could ever be.

Those kisses?

They turn into something else now. They're no longer a performance for the audience. They're short, sweet, and carry a promise – a promise that there's more to come, perhaps.

It's funny, really.

How something as simple as a game could make you see someone in a whole new light. I mean, sure, I've seen Penelope as the royal, the party girl, the gorgeous woman she is. But I've also seen her as a scared little girl wanting to make her mom proud. But this? This is a side of Penelope I didn't know existed. The Penelope who knows me, who pays attention to me.

And believe it or not, this discovery isn't making me run for the hills. On the contrary, it's making me want to stick around and find out more.

I guess my cynical, lone guardian self has met her match. Who would've thought it would be the princess of England, of all people?

You'd think after putting on an X-rated show like that, we'd have a lot to talk about. But, nope. We're back to that weird silence that had ensued between us after the kiss at the parade. Except this time, it's not just awkward, it's loaded. Loaded with unspoken words, with unsaid confessions, with the fear of the unknown.

And let me tell you, the fear of the unknown? Yeah, that's a bitch. Because that's when your mind starts playing tricks on you. It's like being stuck in the middle of the ocean with no land in sight, and all you can do is float aimlessly, hoping you're going the right way.

So, here I am, a hardened marine, a woman trained to brave storms and fight battles, suddenly feeling like I'm at the mercy of this terrifying unknown. I'm out there in the open sea, no land in sight, and my life preserver is a princess with a penchant for playing games.

And that's the thing, isn't it? Is this just a game to her? Is she just getting her kicks by pushing my buttons, seeing how far she can take this? Or is there something more? I look at her, sitting there next to me, her hand still clasped in mine, and I don't know. I just don't.

And that brings me to the other bit of this mindfuck - Alexa. Penelope is on this road trip because of her. Because she fell for her.

Or did she?

I look at Penelope again, look at her beautiful face, her sparkling eyes, and I don't see a woman in love. But then again, what if that's what she feels for me? What if this is just another frivolous adventure for her?

I mean, why the hell not? She's young, she's rich, she's beautiful. Why wouldn't she want to have a little fun?

Among the barrage of questions invading my brain, I grapple with the most formidable one: what's the bloody point of all this?

Am I equipped for a relationship? Hell no.

Am I primed for a love affair with the future Queen of England? Not even in the weirdest of alternate realities.

So, what's the end game here?

Maybe I should just kick back, soak in the moment, and tuck all this away as a tantalizing memory for later, a sweet nectar to sip on, something to counterbalance the bitter aftertaste of my PTSD-haunted nightmares.

I mean, it's not like I'm booking tea dates with her once we're back in the city, right?

It's a downright alarming sign when I find myself nursing hopes of crossing paths with her again. That's the unmistakable red flag of sanity deserting you, packing its bags and sneaking out the back door while you're busy falling for a princess.

And the horrifying truth? I am losing my marbles. Piece

by bloody piece.

Bullet by bullet.

And the one firing the gun? She's got her delicate royal hand firmly clasped in mine.

Alexa

The vibrations of the bass reverberate through the entire studio. The sweet chorus of my latest track, "Venomous Love," echoes off the glossy walls and buzzes in my ears.

Over in the mixing booth, Tommy, my overpaid but golden-eared producer, tweaks the dials of the soundboard like a maestro conducting an orchestra. To my right, a gaggle of assistants scramble around, securing schedules, and coordinating with stylists for the album cover shoot.

Just when I'm about to hit the high note, my phone buzzes on the glossy table.

It's Penelope, Her Royal Highness, finally gracing me with a text. It's about time!

I glance at her message, and a smirk adorns my face. So, the princess is crawling to me via a pride bus? Now, that's what I call grand. I flicker through my thoughts - Penelope arriving late translates to less time for a media frenzy around our 'friendship.' Less buzz, fewer headlines, that's a bit of a dampener, Penny!

I quickly type a response, my perfectly manicured fingers clicking away on the screen. "Playing hide and seek on a bus, are we? I'm getting impatient here, Penny. Can't wait to taste the sweetness of your lips again."

A little scandalous, perhaps, but that's just my style.

As I press send, the ticks turn blue almost immediately. I chuckle to myself. The princess is glued to her phone, eagerly awaiting my messages.

But as the seconds turn to minutes, no response comes.

Well, isn't this a royal snub!

That's new. And slightly annoying. I return to my music, my eyes darting towards the phone, not quite sure what to make of this silent treatment. But hey, divas can wait too, right?

I wrap up the studio session with my usual flair. All day, we've been belting tunes and refining tracks, transforming the raw beats into scintillating melodies. Oh, the excitement of it all! But while the rhythm pulses around me, my thoughts are elsewhere.

Penelope.

Her name sends a shiver down my spine. I remember the nights in Highgrove, tangled sheets and stolen kisses. I had charmed the princess, had her falling at my feet. The image of walking the red carpet with her, hand in hand, the world watching us, it's intoxicating. The perfect ingredient for my album's launch.

My plan? Oh, it's simple. Get her to Los Angeles, have one final whirlwind romance, let the media play with it. And when the album's a hit, I'll leave her, just like that.

A little harsh? Maybe.

But it's a diva-eat-diva world out there, sweetheart.

I saunter out of the studio, sliding into my sleek sports car. It purrs into life, and I merge onto the star-studded roads of Hollywood. It's here that the music meets the madness.

Just then, my phone rings, interrupting my thoughts.

Tyra.

"Hey, Alexa," she greets. Her voice sounds shaky,

something I'm not used to.

"Tyra, babe," I respond, rolling my eyes. "What's up?"

"Just checking if you've left the studio and how was the session?" she stutters.

"Smashing, darling," I assure her, "as always." I can't help but feel slightly irked at her nervousness, but I shake it off. That's Tyra for you, always high-strung.

After a smidgen of small talk, I disconnect the call, my gaze now drawn to the rear-view mirror.

There's a blacked-out Cadillac trailing behind me. Paparazzi, no doubt. I smirk, deciding to give them a good chase. They're the uninvited guests to my publicity party, after all.

But then, trouble strikes in the least expected form. My car splutters, coughs, and grinds to a halt. Dammit, not tonight! The Cadillac pulls up beside me, and out step two men, clad in resort shirts and shorts, looking far too eager to help.

"You need a hand, miss?" one of them calls out.

I hesitate.

It's past midnight, and this street is deserted. But I need to get home, and these guys might be my only chance.

It's better than waiting for a mechanic to arrive on a deserted road.

"Yeah, sure," I agree, stepping out of the car. Their smiles seem harmless enough, until one of them steps closer, pulling a cloth from his pocket.

The world blurs as he clamps the cloth over my nose. The smell is sickening, the sensation terrifying. I try to pull away, but the world is spinning, and then everything goes black.

Chapter Nine

Penelope

The moment we roll into Hot Springs, I'm struck by the raw, untouched beauty of the place. Nestled in the heart of Arkansas, it's a scene straight out of a fairy tale. Majestic mountains frame the horizon, their peaks brushing against the vibrant azure sky. The air is crisp and fresh, tinged with the tantalizing aroma of pine.

Our campsite, Gulpha Gorge, is nestled within a carpet of lush green, broken only by a narrow strip of crystal-clear water meandering through like a playful child. On either side, thick clusters of trees stand tall, their leaves rustling with the whispers of the forest. It's serene, tranquil - a world apart from the chaotic bustle of my everyday life.

As we disembark from the bus, I can't help but stand in awe. I hear Sharon's voice snapping me out of my wonderment, and I turn to find everyone being divvied into groups.

Tent setup. Of course. Leave it to Rita and Sharon to be our campsite managers.

My gaze flicks over to Jessica, and my heart does that annoying flutter. There she is, dressed down in leggings and a sports bra, effortlessly hauling camping gear around. She's got that 'I've-done-this-a-thousand-times' air about her. And judging by her deftness in setting up the tents, she probably has.

Determined to shake off the strange magnetism, I wander to the periphery of the campsite. The gentle murmur of the Gorge is soothing. I find a spot, away from the busyness, and settle down. The dampness of the earth seeps through my jeans, but I don't care.

A soft sigh escapes my lips as I replay the day's events in my mind. Jessica's taste still lingers on my lips. I touch them absentmindedly. No, no, no. I cannot fall for her. I cannot. Yet the very thought of not wanting to... just makes me want to.

I remember my mother's cold words when she discovered my secret - homosexuality had no place in the monarchy. Fun is okay, she had said, but you will marry a man. The words echoed in my ears, a harsh reminder of my reality.

Looking at Jessica now, helping Stella with her bags, the old woman chattering away and Jessica, smiling genuinely at her, I can't help but think - she's more of a man than most men I've known.

Strong, caring, protective. More real, more...everything.

Alexa and Jessica.

The two names seem to swirl in my mind, like opposing sides of a spinning coin. A mental table forms as I start weighing the pros and cons, a decision process as formal as a royal dinner and yet undeniably vital.

Alexa is like an adrenaline rush, always pushing the boundaries, always making me feel like I'm on top of the world. The sex, God, it was scorching. Like a hot flame that burns and teases, leaving a trail of desire in its wake. But then again, that's all I've known. I've never been with Jessica in that way.

Yet even our kisses, just a simple mesh of lips and tongues, have felt... electrifying, like my entire being is engulfed in a storm of sensations, each one more intense than the last.

Age, the merciless factor of time, is another thing to consider.

Alexa and I are of the same age, immersed in the same cultural context. We resonate on the same frequencies of the pop culture - the singers, the bands, the movies... and that's comfortable. It's easy. Yet, with Jessica, despite our ten-year gap, our conversations have delved into the depths of life, echoing within my soul.

A depth Alexa and I never managed to reach. And it's left me aching for more.

Alexa... she's a thrill, an endless party, but she's just... fun. Jessica, on the other hand, is an enigma. She's intriguing, her spirit ablaze with a kind of passion I've never seen before. She's inspiring, her strength a beacon that draws me in, and she's... unique. A word unto herself. But she's also ten years older than me.

A woman.

A relationship with her means defying my lineage, my duty, and my family.

It means abdicating the throne.

Is she worth it? Is any of this worth it? The questions hover in my mind like specters, and I'm left torn between two worlds - a world where I fulfill my duty, and a world where I follow my heart.

But...What about Jessica? My mind asks me.

Does she want anything to do with me beyond this trip? Maybe I'm just a fun distraction for her, a way to break the monotony of her job. Or worse, a youthful fantasy come alive. After all, it's not the first time I've been an experiment for women curious about their sexuality, women who like the idea of being with a princess in secret but would never consider a real, long-term relationship with me.

And why would Jessica be any different? She's a tough, disciplined, and experienced Marine.

What could she possibly see in a spoilt, flighty princess like me? Sure, we have our fun moments and intense exchanges, but at the end of the day, she's a woman who values duty, responsibility, and reality. Aspects that my life, despite its regality, lacks significantly.

Jessica would need someone solid, grounded - a person who could weather storms with her. And what am I? A pampered princess who has spent most of her life in a golden cage, shielded from the real world. Our lives are worlds apart. I've never had to fight in a war or protect a life. I've never even held a job. All I've done is float through life, fulfilling royal duties and expectations.

I let out a sigh, the cool breeze carrying it away. It's just so frustratingly confusing. My heart pulls me in one direction, towards a woman who could potentially give me everything I've been craving - love, authenticity, adventure. Yet, reality pulls me in another, towards a world of duty and decorum, a world where my love has no place.

Night descends on us, with the Arkansas sky putting on a dazzling display of stars. Not that I'm getting all poetic or anything, but there's something about the American night sky that has an uncanny knack of making you feel like a tiny dot in the grand scheme of things. It's both humbling and annoying, like those 'larger-than-life' Hollywood blockbusters.

As couples snuggle closer around the campfire, Jessica

and I are wrapped up in a blanket too.

A 'pretense' as Jessica calls it.

But she's acting more like we're two plague victims forced to share the last remaining bed in a quarantined zone. I mean, come on, we're under a blanket, not in a bloody minefield.

"Got a problem, Jess?" I quip, nudging her gently.

She looks at me, surprise flashing in her eyes. "N-no... why?" she stammers. But it's there, clear as day in her gaze – the unease, the caution.

"You're all tense," I continue, a playful smile on my lips. "Is it because you're scared you might jump me?" Her cheeks flush in the firelight, but she doesn't say anything.

"Come on, Jessica. It's freezing," I pout, making a puppy face. "I won't bite."

I can see her fighting a smile as she gives in, her arms wrapping around me and pulling me closer. The awkwardness begins to melt away as her warmth seeps into me, her heart beating a rhythmic lullaby against my back.

Suddenly, the smell of roasting marshmallows wafts our way. It's a novelty for me. I mean, the closest I've gotten to making food is calling for takeaway. So, Jessica offers to teach me how to roast one.

My first attempt? Let's just say it turned out like my cooking skills, completely disastrous. But the next one? It's so perfect, it could be on a postcard for 'Marshmallow roasting 101.'

Feeling triumphant, I feed the golden-brown puff to Jessica. It's funny how a woman who can shoot targets from a mile away, wrestle burly men twice her size, and strategize security for a royal turns beet red when fed by a 'helpless' princess.

"Are you blushing, Jess? You could grope me twice, without blinking an eye, but a marshmallow gets to you? My, my, who'd have thought?" I laugh, and Jessica rolls her eyes at me for what feels like the one-millionth time on this trip.

"It's the romantic gestures that unsettle you, isn't it?" I question, nestling further into Jessica, while she maintains a cautious boundary around my waist.

"Penelope..." she whispers, the warmth of her breath teasing my ear, "stop trying to figure me out."

"Decoding you has been the most entertaining part of this trip for me so far. That, and grinding against you, of course. That was highly enjoyable," I tease, offering her a playful grin.

"I wish I could share your sentiment," Jessica quips, prompting me to shake my head in disbelief.

"You still won't admit that I arouse you more than anyone else ever has."

"If that was true, Your Highness, we wouldn't be out here roasting marshmallows," she retorts.

"Really? Where would we be then?" I inquire, intrigued.

"Inside the tent, with your summer dress discarded in a corner," she replies matter-of-factly.

"And what makes you so sure I would let that happen?" I challenge.

"Perhaps the wetness of your panties while I had my hands on you?" she suggests, leaving me momentarily breathless.

How did she know?

"Don't flatter yourself, marine. Your hands never ventured that far."

"But your excitement did," Jess counters with a smirk,

placing a tender kiss on my cheek. "For Sharon and Rita, they were watching," she mimics my earlier excuse, causing my heart to race.

Without a warning, I seize her chin, yanking her face back into mine, for another wild kiss. My mouth opens, my tongue darting out to taste her lower lip, the second most delectable thing about her.

Jessica's taken aback, but recovers quickly. She parts her lips just enough, granting me access for my adventurous tongue.

God, her taste!

Our tongues tangle in a fierce dance, echoing our verbal sparring. Our mutual need to dominate shines through the frantic dance of tongues, bites, and jaw movements.

"Bet your royal panties are soaked...again," Jessica murmurs against my mouth, her hand slipping under my top to explore my bare back.

Caught in the fog of desire, it takes me a moment to process her words. "No, this show is for Rita and Sharon's sake. I am as arid as the Sahara down there..."

"Can I verify?" Jessica teases, nipping at my ear, while her fingers trace a tantalizing path along my waist.

"Not until I get to touch yours," I retort, pressing my hips into hers and breaking off the kiss.

God, I want to devour those swollen lips of hers. But I resist, ignoring the urge to have her carry me back to our tent.

"You can touch mine," she whispers, her breath on my shoulder, sparking sensations I've never known.

"All set to beg, marine?"

Jessica laughs, her touch evaporating from my skin, leaving me craving for more.

Damn you, woman!

Suddenly, she captures my wrist in a firm grip, directing my hand between my legs, pressing my palm against my sodden underwear.

England's weather has nothing on me.

"How's the weather, Princess?" she growls in my ear.

"Why don't you find out yourself?"

Extricating my hand from the blanket, I command, "Open up."

Confusion crosses her face until she notices my fingers coated in my essence.

Understanding dawns, and she parts her lips.

I smear my arousal all over her lips, savoring the surprise morphing into pleasure on her face.

"Taste me," I pant, completely lost in her.

"Enjoying it?" I ask as Jessica devours my finger like it's the finest delicacy.

"So good, I was almost ready to beg... almost!" She grins, a wicked sparkle in her eyes.

I'm drawn out of our enticing banter by the melodious notes of a guitar. Hank, donning a cowboy hat that appears out of nowhere, has found his trusty guitar and started serenading us with the romantic verses of Eric Clapton's 'Wonderful Tonight.'

Hank, the macho bloke, crooning out romantic lyrics is a sight I didn't see coming. His voice is surprisingly soothing, and the way he looks at Gary while he sings — it's pure, unadulterated love.

He fumbles midway, forgetting the words, and the music stops abruptly. A sheepish smile plays on his lips as the campsite dives into silence, save for the crackling of the fire and the nocturnal symphony of the woods.

That's when I hear it.

Another voice, strong yet velvety, picking up where Hank left off, "We go to a party, and everyone turns to see, this beautiful lady, that's walking around with me." I whip around to find Jessica, eyes closed, continuing the lyrics with an ease that leaves me stunned.

She's singing.

My marine, my... bodyguard is singing.

And she's bloody good at it! Hank joins in, their voices harmonising, filling the night air with an enchanting melody. Alexa might have had singing over Jessica, but now, she's lost that too.

I let myself sink further into Jessica's strong arms, letting the mesmerizing rhythm of her song and the soothing strum of Hank's guitar wash over me. With every note she sings, every vibration I feel, I feel my worries about Alexa, the throne, and my twisted royal life fading into insignificance.

The fire dances, casting long, flickering shadows as Jessica's voice winds down. Her body is warm against my back, the heat seeping into me, chasing away the night's chill. My eyes are heavy, my heart is light, and I snuggle further into Jessica, whispering against her neck, "You never cease to amaze me, marine."

"You recognizing the song amazes me as well, Princess," she replies, as Hank takes over from her.

When the song dwindles down to its beautiful end, applause erupts around us. Everyone's clapping, cheering for the impromptu musicians. "Another one, Hank!" shouts someone from the crowd, but Hank, basking in the adulation, just shakes his head.

"That's all for tonight, folks," he calls out, playfully deflecting the groans and good-natured booing that follows.

The crowd, reluctantly appeased, starts breaking up. One by one, the tents begin to swallow up their occupants. I look around and notice that it's just Jessica and I left by the fire, alongside Kriti and Maria, who have been shamelessly making out all evening like teenagers.

Then Maria pipes up. "Umm... guys, I think we'll head off too," she says, her cheeks a lovely shade of pink, causing Kriti to mumble a quick, "Yeah, me too. I'm very...tired."

Jessica lets out a short laugh, rolling her eyes. "Just go and fuck already," she advises them, but adds in a mock-stern tone, "Just keep it down, okay? I'm not in the mood for a R-rated lullaby."

That sets Maria off into a fit of giggles, while Kriti, face as red as a beetroot, buries her head into her girlfriend's shoulder, managing a weak wave in our direction before they scamper off to their tent.

The crackle of the dying fire and the distant sounds of the night are the only sounds that punctuate the silence that falls around us. Our little campsite feels like an oasis, a tiny bubble of warmth and light, enclosed by the cool darkness of the night.

Jessica turns to look at me, her eyes reflecting the glow of the embers. "Don't you want to sleep?" she asks.

I turn to meet her gaze, my heart thudding a rhythm against my chest.

I could sleep.

I *should* sleep.

But the night feels too precious to waste on slumber.

And I have no idea when I would be allowed by my duties,

and my mother, to enjoy another such night in England, let alone America.

"I'd rather watch the stars," I reply.

Realizing we are the only people at the campsite, I gently wiggle myself out of Jessica's arms and sit next to her, now wrapped around my own blanket.

The intimacy had suddenly started feeling very odd without other couples around us, like we were really a couple, and I wasn't ready to feel like that just yet.

"Hey, Jess?" I begin, my words laced with hesitation. "Do you miss... you know...the battlefield?"

She stiffens beside me. I feel her long inhale, her pause as she chooses her words carefully. "It's a loaded question, Penny."

"I know," I confess, tracing my finger absently along her bicep. "Just...humor me."

Jessica sighs and leans back, her gaze wandering to the dying embers of the fire. "There's a part of me that always will, I suppose," she admits, her voice dropping to a whisper. "It's hard to explain."

"Try me," I encourage her, nudging her shoulder gently with my own.

She turns to look at me, a somber glow in her eyes that I rarely get to see. "It's the rush, Penelope. The adrenaline. The purpose. The knowing that every choice you make matters, and the decisions you take could mean life or death, not only for you but for your comrades."

I can hear the passion in her voice, the yearning for that sense of purpose, and the harsh edge that comes with being in a war zone. I can't understand it, not fully, but I see the raw intensity in her gaze, and I respect it.

"But you're here now," I say, squeezing her hand, trying to

offer some semblance of comfort. "Isn't it a relief to be away from all that danger?"

"In a way, yes," Jessica admits, her gaze shifting back to the fire. "But it's also been... tough."

"Tough?" I echo, intrigued. "How so?"

"Out there, on the battlefield, I was...important. My skills were valued. Here... it feels like I've lost a sense of my worth. I was a woman who mattered to her country, and now..." She trails off, shrugging nonchalantly, but I can sense her struggle.

Feeling a tad melancholic, I find myself musing, "You know, monarchy in Britain... it's been gradually turning into a relic. Sometimes, I can't help but wonder, what's our worth? My mum, bless her heart, has done some extraordinary things for England in her time, but now she's reduced to a... well, a marionette, dancing to the tune of the government. And that's all I'm pegged to be. You, on the other hand, you served your country, body and soul, before they summoned you back. I... I'll just be a posh ornament from the very beginning."

Her eyes, smouldering embers in the night, meet mine. "How can you call yourself a mere ornament when a whole crowd of people, the entire queer community, look up to you?" she says, her voice a low rumble that stirs something in me.

"But, they're cheering me on because they expect me to kick up a ruckus, to stand my ground when push comes to shove. I'm not sure if I have it in me to meet their expectations, Jessica. It's a constant tug-of-war inside."

A cloud of confusion paints itself across her features.

"But I thought you had your heart set on refusing the throne if they can't embrace you for who you truly are?"

"I had," I admit, "but take a look at me. I can't even get my mum to agree to me gallivanting around America as I please. How do you think I'd stand against the entire British

Monarchy?"

"I know a way," Jessica murmurs, her gaze shifting to the charred remains of the once lively fire.

"How so?" I ask, curiosity piqued.

"Fall head over heels for someone, someone you simply can't live without. Then, Princess, you'll have no choice but to rebel. Love will drive you to it... It'll lend you the strength," she offers, her voice barely above a whisper.

Caught off guard, I chuckle. "And how would you know so much about love, soldier?"

"I just do," she whispers back, leaving me with more questions than answers.

"Maybe you're onto something. Maybe the right person will be the catalyst," I muse, my gaze lingering on the faint scar gracing Jessica's lips. "How many of these scars adorn your body?" I ask, steering the conversation away from the daunting realm of emotions.

"Too many to keep count," she replies, her voice stoic.

Intrigued, I lean in, grazing my thumb over a crescent-shaped scar below her right nostril. "Tell me about this one," I request, yearning for a glimpse into her past.

Jessica chuckles lightly, an ironic twist to her lips as she looks into the fire. "This one," she says, tracing my fingers on her scar with her own. "This is an old battle wound."

Curiosity piqued, I lean in closer, the warmth of her body mingling with mine under the blanket. "Tell me more," I prompt, my voice barely above a whisper.

"Well, it was during one of our deployments in Afghanistan. We were stationed at a remote outpost, tucked away in the middle of nowhere. One day, a local stray dog wandered into our camp. This skinny, mangy little thing with the spirit of a lion. We named her 'Sasha.'"

I can hear the fondness in her voice, and I can't help but smile. "And Sasha gave you that scar?"

"Indirectly," Jessica admits, the corners of her eyes crinkling in amusement. "I got a bit too attached to her, started feeding her scraps from our rations. The others weren't too thrilled about it, but I didn't care. Sasha was a survivor, and I admired that."

The fire crackles and pops, throwing shadows on Jessica's face. I hold my breath, waiting for her to continue.

"One day, during a surprise insurgent attack, Sasha got scared and ran off into the chaos. I, being the idiot that I am, decided to chase after her. I ran straight into a line of fire, bullets whizzing past me. And as I was diving to grab Sasha, a piece of shrapnel sliced through my cheek. It hurt like a bitch," she concludes, her gaze distant, lost somewhere in the past.

I squeeze her hand, offering silent comfort. "And Sasha?" I ask, fearing the worst.

"She made it. We both did. I still have a picture of her somewhere," Jessica replies, a soft smile curving her lips. "That scar is a reminder of the lengths we go for the ones we care about, even if it's a scruffy stray from a war-torn country."

A gentle silence falls between us, punctuated only by the distant hoot of an owl and the crackle of the dying fire.

"What about the other marks on you?" I ask, a curious tilt to my voice.

Each scar on her is like a cryptic map leading to a part of her history, a testament of her trials and tribulations.

The question seems to amuse her, as she gives me this look, her smile quirking up at the edges. "Princess, are you asking for a tour of all my scars?" She's half-teasing, her words dripping with a sass that's undeniably Jessica.

"No, not all," I answer, rolling my eyes for effect. "Just the...key ones. The ones that hold stories that matter."

"Every scar is a story," she replies, her tone firm but gentle. "Each one is a piece of my past."

"I get it, but surely... some mean more to you than others?" I press, and there's a pause. Her eyes bore into mine as if she's trying to gauge if I'm ready for what she might reveal.

With a sigh, she concedes.

Swiftly, she pulls down the edge of her sports bra, revealing a small arrowhead scar barely missing her nipple. My breath catches at the sight, as the dance of revelation continues under the starry night sky.

As I take in the sight of the peculiar scar, Jessica seems to fall into a distant memory, her eyes glazed over with remembrance.

"This...this was in Afghanistan as well," she begins, her voice barely a whisper as she gently traces the arrowhead shape on her chest.

Seeing my unasked question, she dives into the story. "We were stationed in a small town on the outskirts of Kabul, Afghanistan. There was a local girl there, Afreen, who had taken a liking to our crew. She would run up to us every morning, her little hands offering us hand-picked flowers from the meadows. A tiny ray of sunshine amidst all the chaos."

Her gaze grows distant, reliving those moments. "One day, Afreen comes sprinting towards me, excitement bubbling over in her bright eyes. Clutched in her hands was a toy, a wooden horse, about the size of a basketball. It was intricately carved and clearly a work of skilled craftsmanship. That was what set the alarms off in my head. I knew for a fact there were no toymakers in that small town."

Jessica's hand unconsciously traces the outline of her scar, her voice a mere whisper. "Then, I heard it. A soft, rhythmic ticking sound coming from inside the wooden horse. Time seemed to slow down. I pulled Afreen close to me, shielded her with my body, and hurled the horse as far away as I could. And then, it exploded."

A shudder runs through me. "And Afreen?" I whisper, my throat tight with tension.

Jessica smiles, a little more forcefully this time. "She was scared, but unhurt. Me, I got this." She taps the scar. "I was lucky; the explosion was in mid-air, far enough to just cause some superficial damage. This scar is a part of that day. Courtesy a little splinter of wood from the horse that flew at me. It's a remnant of the chaos, but also the doctor's skill in fixing me up.

"I wouldn't trade this scar for anything. It's my reminder of Afreen, her innocence, and the life she now gets to live because I was there," she murmurs, her gaze finding mine.

In her eyes, I see a depth of experience and a strength that I can only marvel at. The woman who seemed so tough on the surface has such a tender heart. I realize then, that these stories, these pieces of her, are gifts, given to me to understand her better.

"Do you want to know more?" Jessica asks, and I shake my head.

"No. I don't want you reliving all that...trauma."

A dry smile appears on Jessica's face. "I will relive these traumas one way or the other. There is no running away from them."

"Maybe there is," I say, running my fingers over the scar on her breast, "Maybe you need love as well. Someone who loves you so much, that they heal you with all the love that they give you. Maybe both of us need love."

"I don't know about me, Penelope. Maybe I am fine like this."

"No, you are not," I say, my fingers tantalizingly close to sliding inside her sports bra and grazing her nipple that my eyes are thirsty to gaze upon.

I imagine the shape of her areolas, the feel of her hardened nipples on my tongue.

A shudder runs through me, and I pull my hand bank, worried I might do something I'd regret later.

"Should we sleep now?" Jessica eyes me, the pain of the past giving way to a shadow of care and concern for me, "You must be tired."

"Then take me to the tent."

"What?"

"Yes, I am tired, marine, so I want you to carry me back to the tent."

Jessica nods solemnly, "As you say, Princess."

An orchestra of night sounds serenades the encampment, their melody a quiet lullaby that should have been a comforting blanket of tranquility.

But sleep, that elusive minx, skitters out of my grasp. My mind is a whirlpool, whirling with stories etched into Jessica's skin, her tales of the battlefield, of Afreen and the wooden horse. The vivid images make my heart clench in sympathy and my eyelids too heavy to dream.

Our tent is just wide enough for the two of us.

Close enough that I can feel the heat radiating off Jessica's tall, athletic figure. I can't help but steal glances at her as she lays by my side, lost in slumber. Her uniform of the day is tight black athleisure shorts and a low-cut white tee, both hugging her sculpted body and highlighting the contours that define her.

The glow from the moon filters in through the mesh of our tent, adorning her in a silver halo that makes her blonde hair seem even more chaotic, the tangled curls splayed on her pillow, a crown fit for this warrior princess.

Yet, it's not just her physical attributes that draw me in.

It's the strength, the determination, and the utter tenderness that I've come to associate with her. The unvarnished honesty with which she wears her scars and the stories they tell, it's all incredibly mesmerizing.

To distract myself from the haunting images of war, my gaze trails along her lithe figure, mapping the journey of her scars. She is turned toward me, her face relaxed in sleep. There's a softness about her now, a vulnerability that she rarely shows when awake. Her chest rises and falls rhythmically, her every exhale a silent melody in the quiet of the night.

I find myself ogling, not in the basest sense of the word, but in sheer admiration.

Okay, I am ogling a little perversely as well, but can you blame me?

I find myself imagining scenarios that could have played out in this small tent between this sexy marine and me.

Or, scenarios that can still play out, if I wasn't such a confused, egoistic little rascal.

I could just brush her fiery blonde hair off her chiseled cheekbones, lean over, and kiss her lips.

Or I could just let my hands wander over her toned body, feeling every curve and dip.

But as much as I want her, I know that she deserves more than just a physical connection.

She deserves someone who will love and cherish her, someone who will be there for her when the memories of war become too much to bear.

And I do not trust myself to be that person.

I am too young, too inexperienced to be the cushion of support that Jessica needs, after years of being alone and isolated in places that can only be termed as hell on earth.

In fact, I need *her*.

Or someone like her.

To hold my hand through the storm that is waiting for me back home, a few years down the line.

The serenity of the moment shatters like fragile crystal as Jessica suddenly groans, her body beginning to thrash subtly on our shared bedding.

An expression of agony twists her peaceful features, sending a rush of ice-cold worry through my veins. Her usually strong and stoic countenance morphs into a mask of terror, her demons brought to life by the shadowy talons of nightmares.

Her breath comes in ragged gasps, punctuated by soft whimpers that strum against my heartstrings. My mind races to understand the situation, but the answer comes to me unbidden – she's caught in the throes of a PTSD-induced nightmare. My heart breaks a little at the realization, the quiet strength of Jessica laid bare by the horrors of her past.

My instincts scream at me to wake her, to drag her away from whatever terror grips her in the realm of sleep.

But my efforts to stir her go unnoticed, her nightmare firmly clutching her in its icy grip. My heart pounds in my chest as her agony amplifies with every passing second. The feeling of helplessness gnaws at my insides. I need to do something.

So, I do the only thing that comes to mind - I pull Jessica into my arms, enveloping her in a hug that tries to combat her unseen tormentors.

I whisper reassurances in her ear, my voice a low soothing mantra in the silent tent, "You're not alone, Jessica. You're not in Afghanistan... not in Iraq... you are safe, you are loved."

Slowly, as if my words are a balm to her haunted mind, her body begins to relax, the creases of pain on her face softening. She falls into a more peaceful sleep, her breath evening out. I continue to hold her, my arms a shield against her inner demons.

Seconds stretch into minutes, and Jessica comes back to the realm of peace.

My own heart relaxes, and I breathe a sigh of relief.

In the dark, close-quarters of our tent, it's a whole different world. A world where everything is stripped down to its core, no frills, no disguises.

Jessica, unconscious in her sleep, curls into me. Her arms find their way around my neck, secure and snug. Her face presses against my chest, her lips brushing my chin, lighting up my skin with little sparks. I hang onto her, grappling with a tornado of emotions inside me. Amid the quiet night, my heart bangs out a mad rhythm, echoing the new realizations flashing like neon signs in my mind.

All of a sudden, the rules I've lived by seem pointless.

Who said we need to be rock-solid to hold our lovers up? Why can't we just be, well... us, complete with all our rough edges and raw nerves? Why can't two people come together in their hurt, share it, and maybe, just maybe, find some strength in that very sharing?

These thoughts are pretty new to me. It's like being slapped awake from a long sleep.

I've lived a sheltered life in England, safe in my own little bubble. But Jessica's the game-changer. She's the one who pushes me, prods me to step out of my safe zone, forcing me to see things I've ignored all along.

Jessica nestles closer to me, and I can't help but grin. I'm picturing her waking up to the news of her turning into my teddy bear in her sleep. But then, do I really want to share this? Or should I keep this sweet memory for myself? After all, the cold truth is, I was just there for her in a tough moment. Would she have reacted differently if it was Maria there instead of me? Or anyone else?

Man, my brain just won't shut up!

It's like a hamster on a wheel that won't quit. I pull Jessica closer, my leg thrown over hers, creating our own warm, safe bubble. The rhythm of her steady breathing becomes my lullaby, calming the chaos in my head.

Gradually, the tent fills up with the sound of her peaceful breaths and my silent musings. The thump-thump of our hearts combine into a sweet melody that coaxes my eyes to close, surrendering to the pull of sleep. It's a different kind of sleep, something I haven't experienced before. It's warm, a little scary, but most of all, it's filled with hope.

Chapter Ten

Jessica

Coming back to consciousness, the first thing I notice is the strange warmth on my side.

I crack open my eyes to find a head of dark hair nestled against my shoulder. It's Penelope, fast asleep, holding onto me like a lifeline. I rack my brains for any memory of what happened last night, but all I remember are nightmares. Nightmares that have been my faithful bed partners ever since my return from the hellholes called Afghanistan and Iraq.

Did Penelope witness my nocturnal torment?

Did she hold me through it?

A wave of embarrassment and a strange sense of weakness wash over me. I'm supposed to be her protector, the guardian angel in black combat boots, not some damsel in distress.

I slowly disentangle myself from her grip, ensuring I don't wake her up, and exit the tent.

Outside, the rest of the gang are already up and about, brewing coffee, packing up.

I find Maria, her hair sticking up in all directions, a goofy smile plastered on her face. There's something about that smile that makes me want to wipe it off her face.

"So, how was your night?" I drawl, leaning against the Jeep, "Did you and Kriti manage to… score?"

"Yeah, right up to second base, and then she fell asleep," Maria retorts, rolling her eyes, "What about you? How far did you and the princess go?"

I snort, raising an eyebrow. "Oh, we had a lovely chat about my war wounds, then I carried her sleeping form back to the tent where I promptly passed out. Woke up with her cuddled up to me like a koala, though. Possibly got some PTSD-triggered action there."

Maria chokes on her coffee, laughing, while I stroll away, feeling lighter despite the heavy thoughts.

On the Pride bus, heading to Dallas now, the atmosphere is relaxed, subdued. Everybody's drained after last night's camping adventure. Princess Penelope and I have our usual seats, and the silence between us is comfortable, loaded with unspoken words.

Penelope's gaze keeps flickering towards me, her lips curved into a teasing smile. Curiosity piqued, I ask, "What's with that look, Princess?"

She merely shakes her head, her grin broadening, dropping not-so-subtle hints about last night. I choose to play it cool, not giving her the satisfaction of a reaction.

As the journey continues, Penelope's eyelids grow heavy and she drifts off to sleep. I'm left with my thoughts, my eyes glued to the passing scenery, until Stella, the old lady who runs the bookshop in town, shuffles over.

"Is she asleep?" Stella whispers, pointing towards Penelope. I nod, curious about her secretive demeanor. Stella pulls out her phone, showing me her GoFundMe page.

I blink at the huge amount donated by an anonymous

supporter, a whopping $50,000 for her dream Italian café.

"I have a sneaking suspicion that our anonymous benefactor might be her." She points a wrinkled finger towards the sleeping Penelope, a look of deep gratitude on her face.

I glance at Penelope, snuggled against the window, looking innocent in her sleep.

Stella's eyes well up with tears, her fingers trembling slightly as she navigates her phone to show me the anonymous donation that just saved her dream. Her voice wavers as she starts, "I mentioned the café to Penelope yesterday, while we were sitting together."

Her eyes are distant, reminiscing the conversation. "I told her about the financial struggles me and Grace were going through to get the café started. I even showed her my GoFundMe page. I never..."

She wipes away a tear, her lips trembling with the effort of holding back a flood of emotions. "...I never thought she'd actually do it. This...this is so much."

Stella sniffles, clearing her throat before her gaze meets mine. There's a raw honesty in her voice, a motherly wisdom that seems out of place in the boisterous bus around us. "She's special, Jessica, your girl. Despite her silver-spoon upbringing, despite being a princess, she's got a heart of gold. More genuine than most girls her age. Heck, than most people."

Stella's eyes bore into mine, her voice growing more earnest. "Promise me you'll take care of her, Jessica. Don't let her get lost in this big, bad world."

I nod, my voice finding strength despite the lump in my throat. "I will, Stella. I promise."

Stella seems to breathe easier, her smile returning. "I'll thank her myself."

I shake my head, offering a different perspective. "Stella,

if she wanted you to know, she wouldn't have done it anonymously. She didn't do this for thanks, or to play savior. She did it because she cares. Because that's who she is."

Stella looks at me, her eyes full of understanding, and she gives a nod of agreement. "Alright. But you both will have to visit our café when it's up and running. And I won't take no for an answer."

I can't help but chuckle, "Sure, Stella. Maybe for our next anniversary, Penelope and I will drop by and celebrate with you."

The words hang in the air as she shuffles back to her seat, leaving me alone with Penelope who is still lost in her dreams. Anniversary. My words linger in my mind, stirring a strange sensation in my heart.

What would it be like being in a relationship with this ball of energy? I think to myself, gazing at Penelope, who is currently the farthest thing from being energetic.

Charity Balls, crowns, cups of teas, Rolls Royces, tradition and bed-breaking sex...

I sum up the relationship in my head, and add one last thing...*Controversy.*

As the bus speeds towards Dallas, I park my butt at the very back, engrossed in a level of Candy Crush. The game is simple enough, but it's keeping me from overthinking the last night's events. My mindless bubble-popping is interrupted when Kriti flops down next to me.

"What's up, Jessica?" Kriti's accent, a charming blend of British and Indian, fills the quiet space.

"Just trying to score big on Candy Crush," I say, gesturing at my screen.

She laughs, a sound that's warm and familiar. "I could use a distraction too. Maria is mad at me."

"Mad at you?" I can't help but raise an eyebrow.

She grins. "Yeah, she's upset because we didn't get beyond second base last night. The woman has a stronger libido than I thought."

I chuckle, shaking my head. "When she wants something, she doesn't rest until she gets it."

"I am not that easy to get." Kriti winks at me.

"Please don't make her wait too long. I don't want a grumpy...and horny Maria in my car. We still have a long way to go."

Kriti giggles. "No, I plan to drip-feed her along the way. I still need time to prepare myself for the dive-in. You know, I have never been with a woman before."

"It's not that complicated. Think sex with a man, but longer, better, more fulfilling," I say, catching a glimpse of Penelope's hair through the gap between the back of her seat and the window.

She is still asleep, and I find myself waiting impatiently for her to wake up.

Wow, I am actually looking forward to conversations with someone who isn't wanted in a bunch of countries.

That's self-growth, I think?

"Where the hell is our car?" Kriti asks, "How are we going to drive from Dallas to LA?"

"Wow, as Penelope's PA, don't you think you should've been asking me this a lot earlier? I guess Maria proved to be a bigger distraction than you thought, eh?" I chuckle.

"No, I...Oh, just tell me!"

"Our car will be waiting for us at the hotel in Dallas. I had asked one of my contacts in Nashville to drive it there," I say, and then weigh whether I should say the next thing that pops in my mind. "Don't worry Kriti, Penelope now has two people to look after her," I decide to say it.

"I know," Kriti says and looks at me with a weird smile. I've seen that smile before on the face of terrorists with hidden secrets, relishing the feel of toying with me.

"And Penelope knows as well," Kriti continues, "and she is grateful for it."

I give Kriti half a smile, because I don't want her knowing how happy her sentence has just made me.

I decide to ask her something else. "Kriti, is it true that Penelope funded Stella's GoFundMe?"

She looks at me for a moment before nodding. "Yes, she did. That's Penny for you."

I lean back in my seat, looking at her. "Tell me more."

Kriti takes a deep breath before she starts talking. "I'm the daughter of Penny's former math tutor. I used to go to the palace with him and that's how we became friends. When she found out that I couldn't afford her school, she pleaded with her mom to get me a scholarship."

"Penelope did that?" I ask, surprised by this revelation.

"Yes, and she didn't stop there. When my father died, Penny stepped in. She made sure I was taken care of, that my mother was taken care of. I wouldn't have made it to Oxford without her."

"Sounds like Penelope has a habit of playing the savior," I can't help but comment.

Kriti shakes her head. "No, Jessica. She doesn't play anything. She's genuinely kind. She cares, and she does what she can to help."

Her words make me pause. I look at her, really look at her.

"You love her."

Kriti smiles. "Yeah, I do. She's more than a friend to me, Jess. She's family."

Then Kriti fires a bazooka at me, and catches me off-guard, "Do *you* love her?"

"What?" I say louder than I intend to.

"Don't look so scared, Jess, I just wanted to know whether she has grown on you since you first met her. You guys didn't get along in the beginning, so I was just wondering..."

"Yeah, of course, she has grown on me. She is a nice girl."

Kriti bursts into a loud giggle, almost mocking me. "Nice girl? That's how you wanna describe the girl who has you questioning your life's entire philosophy?"

"What?"

"Jessica, use words other than 'what'," Kriti keeps poking me.

I can see she is enjoying this.

Who doesn't like making an ex-marine nervous?

But...why the hell am I nervous?

"Look, I don't know what you are talking about. We have our little games that I enjoy, but...you are going down the wrong road here."

My fingers start swiping over the screen, continuing the game, while Kriti keeps staring at me with a grin. "I am rooting for the marine, and not the singer in L.A., just letting you know," she whispers and leaves me staring at my phone, while my mind grasps the meaning of her words.

The Pride Bus rolls into Dallas around noon, the Texas heat already rising in waves off the asphalt. We're all a little disheveled and road weary, but the air is thick with camaraderie and reluctant goodbyes. Penelope, who managed to sleep the entire way, is rubbing at her eyes, her other hand fumbling for her baseball cap and shades.

It's a long, drawn-out farewell, filled with lingering hugs and heartfelt promises. Penelope, suddenly all wide-eyed and soft-hearted, moves through the bus like a sunbeam, touching every person with her warmth. She tells each one of them, "I'll be here every Pride month, I promise you that." The words, so filled with determination, make more than a few eyes water.

When she reaches Stella, there's a pause.

The older woman takes Penelope's face in her hands, eyes misty behind her glasses. "You are the daughter I never had, darling. I want nothing more than for you and Jessica to become a beacon of love for the world."

The moment stretches on as Penelope hugs Stella, their quiet sobs filling the silence. As they break away, their eyes are red, but their smiles are brighter. Stella steps back and ushers me forward. I wrap an arm around Penelope, pulling her into me. Stella hugs both of us, whispering a quiet, "Take care of each other."

As the bus halts in front of a gleaming Marriott, Penelope looks at the grandeur of the place, confusion clear on her face. "Why are we staying in a five-star?" she asks, dropping her voice to a whisper.

"Made a few calls," I say, tipping my hat at the doorman. "They won't be needing all our IDs. Just mine will do."

She squints up at me, her lips pursing in a mock pout. "And why couldn't you have done that back in Nashville?"

I smirk down at her, my arm slipping from her shoulder to

her waist. "I didn't like you then."

Her gasp of outrage is swallowed by her laughter, her fingers digging into my sides as she tries to tickle me.

Our suite is all about plush upholstery and panoramic views of Dallas. Penelope sinks into one of the couches, a look of awe on her face. "Being with you has its perks, huh?"

"Perks?" I huff, dropping onto the couch next to her. "Princess, you ain't seen nothin' yet."

We spend the rest of the afternoon lounging in our suite, our chatter filling the silence.

"Alright, now what?" Maria asks, sulking in a corner, apparently still upset with Kriti.

"We leave in the evening. I need to risk traveling at night because we are behind schedule," I inform our little group, which has quickly become a tension-filled bubble ready to burst.

I analyze the situation.

We have two ex-marines, both with a penchant for casual, no strings attached relationships, possibly falling for two women they'd never imagined falling for. One of them is as royal as you can get, with a 10-year age gap between her and one of the marines, and a rebellious streak that overlaps with a soft heart. Her ego is stopping her from making a 'real' move on the marine.

Great.

The other woman is her PA, and a loyal friend, who has decided to slowly play her own marine, letting her desires for her simmer while she wrestles with impatience and frustration.

Great.

All of us are playing games of seduction, but in the mix,

real feelings are getting involved. I'm unsure whose feelings are more genuine. The princess's or the PA's? Mine or my friend's?

I lean back into the plush couch, smiling to myself. I can't deny that I'm enjoying the thrill, but I'm also worried about my heart because I know it's not just a game for me anymore.

"So, how was it playing a fake couple?" Maria asks, stretching her leg on the coffee table and sipping on a mojito.

"I had fun," Penelope answers before I can.

"And you, Thompson?" Maria gives me a mischievous look.

"Yeah, it was...interesting," I admit.

"What was your favorite part of the whole thing?" Kriti asks as Penelope rests her head in her lap and Kriti starts stroking her friend's hair.

Unsurprisingly, I'm jealous.

"I want Jess to answer first," Penelope says, turning on her side to face me.

I contemplate.

Kissing you repeatedly on the pride bus?

Tasting you on my lips, on your fingers?

Sharing my scar story, opening up to someone for the first time in a while?

I decide on the last one.

"Sitting by the campfire and telling Penelope about my scars. It wasn't really a 'couple's moment', but it was one of the highlights of the road trip for me. It was the moment that helped me see Penelope as a friend, not as a princess."

"Aww! That's so sweet," Kriti says, brushing Penelope's dark hair off her face. Meanwhile, I sit imagining myself in

Kriti's place.

"I was expecting something else," Penelope says with a grin.

"What?"

"Oh...you know!"

"No, we don't know! I...don't know!" Maria squeals, sitting upright, "Tell us, Thompson. What is the princess talking about?"

"Nothing that concerns you, Sanchez," I retort, throwing Maria a stern look.

"You can tell her, Jess. You don't have to be embarrassed about it," Penelope suggests, tucking her legs in.

Her skirt rides up her thighs, and my imagination runs wild...

"I'd like to abstain, please," I say, taking a sip of the mojito, which is seriously lacking in alcohol content.

"Did you guys...fuck?" Maria asks, her eyes darting from me to Penelope, who giggles like a schoolgirl.

"Perhaps, perhaps not," Penelope purrs, locking onto my gaze.

"Alright, I haven't hit the gym in three days, and I already feel my abs morphing into a potbelly," I announce, standing up abruptly, my mojito drained in one long gulp.

"I thought setting up those tents was enough of a workout?" Penelope challenges, an eyebrow arched mockingly.

Maria chuckles in her corner. "For Jessica? I doubt it. Her heartbeat probably didn't break 80 the entire time we were wrestling those tents into place."

I smirk.

I understand what Maria is doing – playing up my cool

factor in front of Penelope. An amateur move, sure, but oddly it sparks a warmth in my chest.

"I'll tag along. I need to shake off those extra calories before I face Alexa."

The words slice through the air like arrows, straight from Persian archers to Spartan shields. They cut deep, they wound, and they make me feel what it's like to have your heart sting like a son of a gun.

"I mean, not for Alexa...but for LA, in general..." Penelope fumbles, hastily backpedaling, her eyes flashing an apologetic look.

Why is she even bothering with this charade? She might as well own up to it.

"Can I join you?" Her voice is tiny, innocent, irresistible. And just like that, I find myself incapable of saying no to her.

∞∞∞∞

The drone of modern machinery and the sporadic grunts of other gym-goers form the background score to my workout. I'm pushing myself hard, trying to turn the sharp sting in my heart into a manageable burn in my muscles. Steel clashes against flesh as I lift the loaded barbell from the rack, my fingers gripping the cold metal tightly.

My mind is a battlefield, a swirling storm of Penelope, Alexa, and LA - a mantra, a curse, a list of questions with no straightforward answers. How did I let myself get so entangled in this emotional mess? The princess, her world, it's all so alien to me. And yet, here I am, grappling with feelings that have no business occupying my mind.

Every time I hoist the barbell, I attempt to silence the echo of Penelope's words.

Alexa.

Her crush.

My competitor.

The irony is almost suffocating. Is she trying to slim down for her? Is this all just some game for her? My teeth grit against each other, my muscles strain harder. Sweat pours, my heart pounds, but it's not enough to extinguish the fiery questions in my mind.

Despite my best efforts to focus on the barbell and the unyielding resistance of the iron, my gaze betrays me. In the mirror ahead, I see her - the rogue royal running on a treadmill.

Dressed in a skintight, pink Victoria's Secret sports bra and black leggings, Penelope is the embodiment of youthful energy and unabashed vitality. The blonde wig I gave her before leaving our suite gives her an alluring, beach-girl look, which is amusingly counteracted by the nerdy owl glasses perched on her nose.

With every stride, her silhouette becomes more pronounced, a siren call drawing the attention of every man, woman, and mirror in the room.

I curse under my breath, my determination wavering.

My grip on the barbell slips momentarily, and the weight comes crashing down. I catch it just in time, my knuckles turning white.

Get a grip, Thompson.

Focus.

Breaking my stare, I add more weight to the barbell. The heaviness is strangely comforting, the strain in my muscles a welcome diversion from the turmoil in my head. I grunt, pushing harder, letting my frustration fuel each lift, each rep.

Suddenly, Penelope is beside me. Her forehead is slick with sweat, her breath coming out in rapid pants. She looks up at me, her eyes questioning. "Why are you pushing yourself so hard, Jess? You're practically punishing yourself."

I meet her gaze, my eyes hard, determined. This is my space, my sanctuary. Here, I don't need to smile politely or engage in idle chatter. Here, I can be myself - a former marine with a weakness for iron bars and early morning workouts.

"Are you upset?" she asks, her voice lined with worry.

Upset? I almost laugh. "Upset?" I parrot back, raising an eyebrow in feigned amusement. "Why would I be upset?" I ask, my voice oozing sarcasm. I force a dry smile onto my face and hoist the barbell again. The burn in my muscles is satisfying, real.

Penelope doesn't seem convinced. She shifts on her feet, her eyes narrowing slightly. "The moment I mentioned Alexa," she starts, her voice steady despite her heavy breathing, "you changed."

I scoff, the sound escaping before I can stop it. The weight I'm lifting suddenly feels twice as heavy, the air around me twice as thick. "I think you're overthinking things, Princess," I tell her, my voice flat. My hands tremble slightly, but I keep lifting.

Push and pull, rise and fall.

It's that simple.

"Am I?" she retorts, her voice now carrying a frustratingly accurate certainty. "Or is it just a coincidence that you decided to torture your body right after I mentioned her?"

Frustration bubbles up inside me, replacing my carefully cultivated indifference. Being questioned, being seen in such a vulnerable, weak state - it's unsettling. "Princess," I start, laughing dismissively, "I couldn't care less about Alexa. Or you.

Or both of you together. You're reading too much into our... whatever it was."

"I don't think I am," she shoots back, her gaze steady. There's a stubbornness in her eyes that I haven't seen before. It irritates me. It intrigues me.

"Enough, Penelope," I snap, standing up abruptly. The barbell hits the ground with a thud, the sound echoing in the silent gym. "I'm not in the business of being anything more than a bodyguard to a princess who can't keep her legs shut for five minutes."

I see her flinch at my words, but she quickly hides it, her eyes flashing defiance.

"And if we're being honest," I continue, my voice as cold as ice, "the idea of fucking a royal princess is hot, yes, but since you've been playing the 'I won't make the first move' card, I'm frankly bored. I just want to finish this job, get you to your singer girlfriend, and be done with it."

Her face is unreadable, a mask of calm in the midst of the storm we've conjured. "You could've said that more politely," she says, her voice quiet but firm, "I thought we were friends."

"Oh, and now we're friends?" I retort, not bothering to hide my bitterness. "Friends who politely tell each other they want to fuck each other?"

Her gaze softens, a hint of hurt creeping into her eyes. "I thought we were friends, yes." Her voice is barely a whisper. "I thought you cared."

"I don't," I say, the words cutting through the silence of the gym. "I don't care, Penelope. That's how I am. And I won't change. Not for you, not for anyone."

She holds my gaze for a moment longer, her eyes searching, probing. Then, she just nods, the movement barely perceptible, and turns on her heel to walk away. As I watch her leave, something clenches in my chest, an unexpected feeling. Guilt? Regret?

I glance at the weights in front of me. Push and pull, rise and fall. I add more weight to the barbell. The physical pain is nothing compared to the ache in my heart. It's easier to deal with, easier to understand. I'm not built to handle emotions. I'm built to lift.

So, I do.

Penelope

With a huff, I storm into the suite, my footsteps echoing my frustration. I fall onto the plush couch, the cushiony surface doing little to ease the turmoil within me. Kriti looks up from her laptop, her brows furrowing in concern.

"What happened?" she asks, her voice laced with genuine worry.

"In no mood to share," I mutter, the residual anger from my gym encounter with Jessica tinging my voice. I glance at her and ask, "Did my mother contact me?"

Kriti hesitates, her lips pressing into a thin line before she answers, "She has been taking updates from Uncle Robert... about your 'illness'."

"But did she ask to speak to me?" I question, my heart sinking in my chest at the evident avoidance.

Kriti glances down, her silence giving me the answer. "No, she didn't," she finally says.

The affirmation of my mother's lack of concern is a punch to my gut. The hurt is overwhelming, and I quickly excuse myself, retreating to the sanctuary of my bedroom before the tears threaten to spill over.

I flop onto the bed, my heart heavy and the room a little too quiet. A knock on the door and a voice announcing 'housekeeping' pull me back from the precipice of a breakdown. I hastily wipe at my eyes and swing open the door, revealing a boy of about twenty.

Ignoring him at first, I let him in and retreat back to the comfort of the couch. My eyes wander to the name tag on his uniform - James Thompson. A chill runs down my spine as I read the surname, memories of Jessica's curt words echoing in my ears.

"You share your last name with a person I would love to kill right now," I joke, though my tone is far from light-hearted.

The boy, James, flashes a surprised smile before chuckling. "And I have a cousin I'd like to do the same to."

The mention of a cousin intrigues me. "What's her name?" I ask, my heart pounding in my chest.

"Jessica Thompson."

The world around me blurs as I absorb the revelation. It feels as though the ground is shifting beneath me. I look at James, seeing him in a new light. "Jessica's your cousin?" I ask, though it's more of an affirmation.

"Are we on about the same Jessica Thompson?" James queries, his eyes wide with disbelief, a glimmer of familiarity reflected in them. They hold the same shade of blue as Jessica's.

"I mean the Jessica Thompson who used to be a marine and looks more like a supermodel than a bodyguard," I clarify, rising from the couch and fixing him with a questioning gaze.

He blinks in surprise. "I do have a cousin named Jessica Thompson, also an ex-marine. And yeah, she does look strikingly similar to that Dutch model...Romee Strijd."

"Ridiculous, isn't it? Jessica has a cousin!" I exclaim, the discovery prompting a mirthless chuckle from me.

His gaze shifts, landing on my disguised face. "And who

might you be?"

Could I trust him? But then again, he is Jessica's family. Swiftly, I reach for my wig and glasses. "Can you keep a secret, James?" I ask, pulling off the wig and letting my familiar curls fall freely. As I remove my oversized glasses, his eyes widen comically.

"Penelope Windsor?" he gasps, making a clumsy attempt to bow. It's clear he's never performed a curtsey before.

I can't help but laugh. "Guilty as charged. I'm currently on a covert road trip across America. And your cousin...well, she's my bodyguard."

He splutters, clearly taken aback. "No way!"

"Way," I affirm, my grin widening at his astonished expression. "Pretty mental, innit?"

"Pretty damn mental!" he echoes, his eyes still bulging.

"Where is she? I'd love to see her," James asks, his excitement evident.

"She's in the gym, indulging in a love-hate relationship with the weights," I answer, pausing before adding, "Until she's back and finds what I'm hoping will be a pleasant surprise, could you share more about Jessica? And why do you think she would hide her cousin brother from me?"

I am truly puzzled, my heart aches a little too. Here is a family tie Jessica never mentioned, and it makes me wonder what else is there in her life that I don't know about.

James shrugs, his expression somber. "Jess has always been very private. She doesn't like to talk about her past."

He starts to explain how Jessica decided to join the marine school when she was 18, causing a huge rift between her and her uncle, who had promised Jessica's father he would always take care of her. But being a marine meant she would always be in danger. The fight led to Jessica leaving their house, leaving behind a heartbroken family.

"But she never stops caring," James says, his voice breaking, "Even when she told me she wasn't coming back, she would always ask how my parents were."

"And has she visited your parents... her uncle and aunt... since?" I question, my curiosity piqued.

"No," James' voice filters through the room, the heavy note of melancholy making my heart ache, "Dad's a proper southern guy, you know. And when he found out about Jessica's...choices... he became even more dissatisfied with her. Since then, he misses her every day, talks about her, but hasn't picked up the phone once to give her a call. I speak to her, but once a year or something like that, because most of the times, I have no idea where she is posted, and it's not like she has an Instagram or something..."

I nod, my mind racing.

Jessica's life seems to be a complex tapestry of secrets, each more baffling than the last.

"And has Jessica tried to contact your father?" I ask, hoping to untangle the mystery further.

James shakes his head and I can't help but sigh. "Your cousin is a remarkable person, James. In the short time that I've spent with her, I've started admiring her a lot. She's really awesome."

"I know." James grins, his voice taking on a brighter note. "She paid for my hotel management course, which landed me this gig. But I couldn't tell her because I have no idea where she is."

"Well, now you do," I say, a smile playing on my lips. "And when she comes back from the gym, you tell her all about your job. And after that, we are going to go to your house and meeting Jessica's aunt and uncle."

"Jessica won't come," James warns, but I simply shrug.

"She'll have to. It's her duty to follow me around," I reply, a lazy smile playing on my lips. "After all, I am a royal, and she is my bodyguard. She follows where I go."

Jessica

Walking back to the suite, I grapple with the churning emotions within me. I don't do apologies well. I don't do apologies at all. But I am about to. For Penelope.

As I stride in, Kriti, Maria, and Penelope are huddled together in the living room, their faces solemn.

That's odd.

"Pen, can I talk to you?" I ask, using a shorter version of her nickname which startles her. She nods, and follows me to the balcony that overlooks Dallas.

I take a deep breath, the city lights twinkling beneath us providing a small semblance of comfort. Apologies and Jessica Thompson usually don't mix. But here I am, about to make a sorry attempt. Pun intended.

"Penelope, I...I am sorry for what I said in the gym," I stammer, "I was harsh. I...I shouldn't have said those things."

There it is, my admission of guilt. And you know what's worse? I actually mean it. How's that for irony?

"From now on, I will be more professional and promise to keep my personal feelings out of this. You're...You're important to me...as...as my duty, and... and I will ensure your safety," I vow, swallowing the odd lump that's formed in my throat.

She looks at me, a mix of surprise and curiosity in her eyes.

I don't blame her. Hell, I surprised myself. Who knew Jessica Thompson could apologize? And that too to a girl she met barely a few days ago?

"I was hurt, Jess," she confesses, her voice barely above a whisper. "More than anything, I was hurt that you don't consider me a friend." She swallows hard, looking down at her feet.

"And I'm sorry too," she continues, raising her head to meet my eyes, "I was playing these games, trying to see if I could make you beg for me... which was all childish. I know we have sexual chemistry, but I'd like to be more a friend to you than just a partner for exciting games that could ruin any chance of friendship."

"I want to be your friend as well," I mutter, not meeting Penelope's gaze, "Although, it hurts to know I won't get to feel your ass again." I smile as I return my gaze to Penelope.

"You can do that anytime you want. Hell, Kriti does it sometimes."

"Really?" I ask, amused, "Do all your friends touch your butt?"

"No, only the ones that have made a special place in my heart."

I have a special place in her heart.

Wow, and here I thought the only place I would ever call home would be the barracks.

Her words ring in my ears, the truth of them piercing my defenses.

"But," she continues, her voice barely a whisper, "I'll only forgive you on one condition."

"What is it?" I ask, my heart pounding in my chest.

"To know that, you'll have to go into the bedroom." She grins, her tone mischievous. "There's a surprise waiting for you. And the surprise will tell you what you have to do to earn my forgiveness, because you did call me a slut."

"I did not call you that," I defend myself, my face heating up. "I just said you can't keep your legs shut, which is... bad also, but not the same thing."

"Yeah, I don't care." She shrugs nonchalantly. "What's wrong with being a slut? But now, go into the room."

With that, she waltzes off, leaving me standing there, taken aback.

So, here I am, a trained marine, a professional bodyguard, about to face a surprise in a hotel room. Am I nervous? Hell yeah. Why? Because Penelope Windsor is unlike any other human I've faced. She has a knack for shaking up my world, and from the look on her face, I have a feeling this 'surprise' is about to do just that.

So, I take a deep breath, square my shoulders, and with a final glance at the twinkling city below, I stride back into the suite. I can feel the anticipation in the air, can see the secretive glances exchanged between the trio.

I open the door to the room, and there he is.

James.

My cousin.

My little cousin. The spitting image of the photos he'd been mailing me all these years. I can't breathe, can't move, can't think.

As if sensing my shock, he strides across the room and pulls me into an embrace. It's been years, but his scent - something earthy with a tinge of the cologne he used to steal from Uncle - is too familiar, too comforting. I find myself melting, my walls crumbling like sandcastles against the relentless waves of emotion. I hug him back lightly, feeling the raw vulnerability of the moment seeping into me.

"Jessie," James chokes out, pulling away. His eyes are brimming with tears, his smile wavering. "I've missed you so damn much."

I blink, fighting back my own tears and manage a small, shaky smile. "I've missed you too, squirt."

We move to sit on the couch, his knee bouncing nervously, his eyes never leaving my face. "So...tell me everything," I urge, wanting to hear about his life.

His face lights up and he launches into stories. About how he aced his hotel management degree, how he landed this job, how he spent his first paycheck treating Aunt and Uncle to a fancy dinner.

I listen, my heart clenching with a pang of homesickness I never thought I'd feel.

"Hell, you should've seen Uncle's face when I pulled out my card to pay," he chuckles, his eyes distant and happy. "He raised his glass and toasted to you. Said he wished you were there."

I grin, a painful tug in my chest. "And Aunt? Did she manage to perfect Grandma's cookie recipe yet?"

James' laugh echoes around the room, the sound so familiar it's uncanny. "No one can beat Grandma's recipe. But she's close. You should try them sometime."

I fall silent, thinking about Aunt and Uncle, about the home that was once mine. I can almost taste the familiar aroma of those cookies and hear Uncle's boisterous laugh.

But the comfort is fleeting, quickly replaced by a sense of dread. How do you reconnect with a past that you've ruthlessly cut off?

As if sensing my turmoil, James turns to me, his eyes softening. "Jess," he says quietly, "Why didn't you tell me you were back? That you've... retired?"

I open my mouth, scrambling for an excuse, but he raises a hand, stopping me mid-sentence. "I get it," he says. "But, Jess, they miss you. Uncle, Aunt... me. We just... we miss you."

The weight of his words pulls me down. But then, he adds, "Her Highness told me about your... PTSD. How you need... family."

I stiffen.

How dare Penelope... But before the anger takes hold, he continues, "Don't be mad at her. She cares about you. And she's right."

He looks at me, his eyes intense. "I want my cousin back. I want the sister who taught me how to ride a bike, showed me Jackie Chan movies, and fought off bullies. We want you back, Jess."

His words crash over me, leaving me gasping. I swallow hard, blinking away the hot tears that spring to my eyes.

"Uncle and Aunt, they're...they're getting old."

My heart lurches at his words. "What do you mean?"

"Dad... he's starting to forget things. Not you though, never you. He can't remember his best friend's name or where he placed his keys, but he remembers you. Your cowboy outfit, your victories in the 100 meter races... and Mom... she's got arthritis now. But she still tries to bake cookies, hoping you'd come by and taste them someday."

His voice cracks on the last word, his eyes filling with tears. The impact of his words leave me breathless, my own eyes welling up with a mix of pain and regret.

"But they still talk about you, Jess," James continues, his voice shaky. "They miss you... I miss you. I...I don't know how much time they have left and..." He swallows hard, his eyes pleading. "I want you to see them, Jess. Can you do that? Can you visit them... for me?"

His words crash over me, leaving me gasping. I swallow hard, blinking away the hot tears that spring to my eyes. I reach out, pulling him into a hug. "Okay," I whisper, my voice barely audible, "I'll come."

As his arms tighten around me, I can't help but let the tears flow. James is right. I need this. I need my family. And for the first time in a long time, I'm allowing myself to want it, too, even if with a pinch of fear that comes with being vulnerable. I owe my Aunt and Uncle and my cousin this much.

Penelope

As I recline in my chair, watching the emotional tableau unfold, it hits me - this is a Jessica I've never met before. She's not the stern, unyielding marine, but a laughing, jovial woman. She's home, surrounded by her family, and there's a touch of sweetness about her that I've never seen.

Uncle Steve, a tall, lanky man with the same piercing blue eyes as Jessica, can't seem to let go of her hand. The sparkle in his eyes, though red and swollen from crying at seeing his beloved niece entering his house, speaks volumes about his joy.

Then there's Aunt Lily, a robust, jovial woman who embodies the spirit of Southern hospitality. Her shock of curly hair, just like James', bounces with every move she makes in the kitchen. She's practically inundating us with an avalanche of comfort food. It's like she's on a mission to fill us up until we can't move. And by the looks of it, she seems to be succeeding.

And James, oh dear James. His happiness is infectious.

He's practically vibrating with glee, his words a flurry of excitement as he chatters away. His eyes, practically mirrors of Jessica's, hardly ever leave his cousin, capturing every smile, every laugh. It's as if he's making up for all those lost years in just this one afternoon.

It's endearing, to say the least.

Amidst all this, I feel somewhat like an unexpected guest at a family reunion. But, for Jessica's sake, I wouldn't want to be anywhere else. It's refreshing to see her like this. She's not my guardian, she's not my protector. Today, she's just Jessica, the long-lost niece, the loving cousin, and the doting daughter.

It's only when Aunt Lily brings out her secret weapon, a batch of freshly baked cookies, does Uncle Steve finally address me, after being inundated by Jessica and her tales. "Your Highness," he begins, his southern accent thicker than Aunt Lily's gravy, "We didn't know we would be hosting the future Queen of England today, or we'd have put on a bigger show. We apologize if the hospitality has been less than what you're used to."

Grinning, I shake my head. "Uncle Steve, the warmth of your hospitality beats any royal treatment. And frankly, I'm just happy to see Jessica smiling. She's got the temperament of a cactus, but today, it seems she's more of a daisy."

That elicits laughter around the table and an amused smile from Jessica.

After lunch, I ask Uncle Steve about Jessica's childhood room, and they tell me it's still the same, and that they haven't moved a thing since she left for marine school at 18.

So, the universe grants me an exclusive tour of Jessica's past – her childhood room, frozen in time, how an 18-year-old Jessica left it. I can feel my heart flutter with anticipation.

Jessica, being Jessica, is displaying a strange blend of nostalgia and nonchalance, her version of excitement, which is entirely unlike the rest of the human race. As she opens the door to her old kingdom, we find ourselves stepping into a time capsule.

"No way!" Jessica gasps, the moment she enters, "They haven't even taken down the posters!"

Her reaction surprises me a bit, making me chuckle.

There are many posters adorning the off-white walls, and they are the first things I notice as well.

The room is a mishmash of memorabilia and teenage rebellion. Off-white walls sport a vast array of posters ranging from the psychedelic realm of Led Zeppelin to the pugilistic wisdom of Rocky Balboa. The aqua-blue dresser, a sassy rebel in its own right, is a discordant note in the room's symphony.

Above the single bed, hangs a poster with the quote 'It's not how hard you hit, but how hard you can get hit and keep moving forward' from the film Rocky, and all around it, smaller A4-sized posters depicting other monumental scenes from the movie, are arranged in an abstract pattern.

Books, her father's legacy, occupy a cozy nook, a testament to Jessica's inherited love for literature. A whiteboard stands at attention, the ghost of algebraic conundrums still evident in the bottom corner. I try to picture a younger Jessica, wrestling with math problems, and it sends me into a fit of giggles.

The room breathes history, a frozen tableau of Jessica's formative years. School trophies, high school photographs, and childhood knick-knacks offer a silent narrative of a girl on the precipice of becoming a woman, a transformation that would eventually take her to marine school and the life she leads now.

The charm of this room is akin to a vintage photo album - it's heartwarming and melancholic, all at once. It is as if her childhood is locked in these four walls, waiting for a chance to be let out and relived.

My attention gravitates towards a sticky note, hidden like a secret message beneath the study table. "One day, you will stop running and find peace. One day." The words, in Jessica's crisp handwriting, hint at her inner struggle. A strange sadness seizes me, and, without thinking, and acting out of reflex, I pocket the note, and wonder right after why I did that.

I turn around and find Jessica flipping through her yearbook, and I can almost see her lips curved into a smile.

Watching Jessica soak in nostalgia, I can't help but marvel at how the layers of her personality have slowly unfolded before me. From a stone-cold marine to someone softer, someone human - I've seen her metamorphose, and it's filling me up with hope and a sense of camaraderie.

A thought flits across my mind then - if Jessica, the untouchable, iron-clad bodyguard can reveal her softer side, then maybe there's hope for the rest of us too. I think about Mum, all royal and propriety. My heart tugs at the thought of her letting go of her queenly mask and embracing her humanity, embracing me.

Maybe one day she'll see that her little girl is human too, with dreams of her own, with a life of her own to lead. I find myself warming up to the thought, a glimmer of a future where we're not just the queen and her successor, but a mum and her kid. With Jessica's transformation happening right in front of my eyes, that future doesn't seem so unrealistic anymore.

I walk over to Jessica, my mind abuzz with thoughts of future, past, and the present.

Snagging the chair next to Jessica, I plop down just as she's staring at a photo. A striking girl with sun-kissed skin, vibrant, green eyes, and a mess of chestnut curls graces the picture. Her features seem to dance with mirth, matching the playful twinkle in Jessica's young eyes. The two of them look cozy together, arms slung over each other, smiles brighter than the Texas sun they're under.

"Who's this?" I jest, nudging her with my elbow, "A teenage romance, perhaps?"

Jessica's eyes flicker to me briefly before she shuts the yearbook with an unexpected sense of finality. Her gaze, when it returns to mine, holds a tinge of pain.

"Just a friend," she mutters, her fingers gently caressing the now-closed yearbook. Her words hang in the air between us, an invitation to not probe further. But she adds anyway, "Perhaps the only one I've ever had. She died in a car crash right after I left for marine school."

Silence blankets the room, the once vibrant nostalgia replaced with a sudden heaviness.

For a while, we sit there in silence, the only sound being the occasional creak of the old wooden floor under our weight. Then, Jessica clears her throat, breaking the silence. "You know, Penelope," she starts, a hint of gratitude lacing her words, "I've got to say thanks. For today, I mean."

"Thanks?" I raise an eyebrow, "What on earth for?"

"I felt something today," she continues, ignoring my interjection, "Something I haven't felt in a long time. Peace." The word hangs heavy in the room, reverberating with a sense of importance. She takes a deep breath before adding, "And for the first time, I feel there's still hope for me."

Without a second thought, I reach out and take her hand in mine. She looks surprised, her blue eyes widening ever so slightly. But I just shrug, as nonchalant as I can manage.

"You know, seeing you being vulnerable, something you feared, hated, and accepting emotions, gives me hope too," I tell her, my voice soft but firm. "Hope for others like you in my life."

Jessica looks at me, her gaze piercing. "You're talking about your mother, aren't you?"

I remain silent, but my lack of denial is answer enough. Jessica, to her credit, doesn't push. She simply gives my hand a light squeeze.

"Do you miss her?" she asks, her voice barely above a whisper.

My breath hitches at the question, the reality of it settling heavily on my heart. "A lot," I manage to choke out, the words strangled by the lump in my throat.

Jessica's gaze softens, the icy blue of her eyes seeming to melt with empathy. "Has she tried to contact you?" she ventures to ask, her grip on my hand growing a little tighter.

I shake my head, a bitter laugh escaping my lips. "No," I confess, my voice coming out more vulnerable than I would have liked. "But Kriti told me she keeps taking updates from Uncle about my health."

Jessica waits, watching me with a patient gaze. "And?" she prompts gently.

"And..." My voice trails off, a swell of tears threatening to spill over. "And she hasn't once asked to speak with me."

It's almost as if the room shrinks around me, the walls closing in as my heart feels a familiar, painful squeeze. My vision blurs, the corners of my eyes pricking with unshed tears. Why can't she understand? Why does she act so tough, so stone-hearted, hiding behind a royal facade? Why can't she just be my mother?

"Why... why does she act like this?" I mutter, more to myself than Jessica, frustration pouring out of every syllable. "Why can't she show her real emotions?"

Jessica remains silent for a moment, deep in thought.

Finally, she lets out a sigh, her thumb tracing circles on the back of my hand. "Maybe," she begins, her voice so soft I have to strain to hear her, "maybe she thinks you don't want to talk to her."

That might be true, but aren't mothers supposed to see beyond all that? Aren't parents supposed to see through their kids?

Or maybe, they are just humans, like their kids, a fact that kids sometimes overlook, because, for them, their parents are superheroes.

"How about you give her a call, Penelope?" Jessica whispers.

I blink back at Jessica, stunned by her suggestion. "Call my mother?" I echo, my voice laced with surprise and a hint of indignation. "She hasn't asked about me in days! Why should I be the one to make the first move?"

Jessica just shrugs in response, her steely gaze unwavering. "Because you're not doing this for her, Penelope," she says. "You're doing it for yourself."

Her words hang in the air, cutting through the tension like a knife. I can feel the heat rising to my cheeks, my ego feeling bruised. But she isn't finished.

"I've seen you," she continues, her voice softer now. "Hidden behind your charm, your beauty, that distracting mole above your lip, your royal stature, and that rogue persona, is a woman who craves to be seen, to be acknowledged. By her mother. But you're afraid, aren't you? You're afraid of showing your true self."

I swallow hard, feeling my defences crumbling under her discerning gaze. She's right. I'm just as much at fault for this distance between Mother and me. I've been so busy acting the part of the defiant princess, refusing to bow to the demands of royal life, that I've forgotten what it means to be a daughter.

To be human.

"I... I miss her," I confess, my voice barely above a whisper. "But I don't know how to tell her that."

"Then don't overthink it," Jessica suggests, a glimmer of sympathy in her eyes. "Just text her. Tell her exactly that. You miss her."

Taking a deep breath, I pick up my phone from the bedside table. It feels heavy in my hands, weighed down by the responsibility of this one message. But as I start typing, each word feels like a tiny step towards bridging a chasm that's been growing for far too long.

"Hi, Mum," I type, pausing for a moment before adding, "I miss you."

With a final sigh, I hit send. It's done. The message is out there, floating in the ether, waiting for my mother to receive it. Now all I can do is wait for her response. But no matter what it is, at least I've taken this first step. And for that, I have Jessica to thank.

"Thanks for making me act like a pussy," I chuckle, throwing away my phone, too afraid to check for a reply.

"Yeah, same here," she says, and for the first time, she locks her eyes on mine like she never has before.

She looks at me, without fear, without hesitation, but with longing. Her eyes don't flinch; her face does not look away.

She just stares at me, and I stare back at her.

On her childhood bed, in her teenage room, Jessica Thompson, the marine, the warrior princess, pulls me in for a kiss.

We are not faking anything anymore...for anyone.

This is real.

Jessica's lips press into mine, and I reply with a deep, satisfactory sigh.

My world flips on it's head, and pure passion grips me like a frenzied fever.

In a split second, I am climbing onto Jessica's lap, like a cat demanding attention, like a girl finally letting go, like a woman desperate for her lover's touch.

"Took you long enough," I break the kiss and purr into Jessica's ears.

Jessica slides her hand over my lower back, and pulls me into her hardened, marine body. "I know I said I'd act professional and all," Jessica is breathing hard, while I run my tongue over her earlobes, "but if today is embracing the reality, then the reality is, I have been aching for you, my princess..."

I grunt as Jessica rips open my sports bra, the sound of the hooks snapping more erotic than any noise I have heard in my life up to that point.

And then, her hands take over.

I can feel how strong they are, how they can maul me if they wanted to, but for the moment, they are sliding, grazing, caressing and feeling my now exposed back.

Still straddling Jessica, I push into her, and Jessica falls back onto the bed.

My breasts hover over her, and she eyes them like a hungry wolf.

Jessica

I eye her breasts like a hungry wolf, and don't waste a second in reaching out for them.

Hours of staring at them, lusting after them finally lead to me feeling them all over my palms.

"Oh...fuck..." the princess sighs and closes her eyes.

She is a picture of unrealistic beauty and intolerable seduction.

She is the hottest girl in the world, and she is sitting on top of me, urging me to unleash the beast within me.

But I am scared.

What if she does not like what I show her? What if my lust is too much for her? But the thought is only fleeting, because I am *way* in the deep end now, and I know I can't hold back, even if I wanted to.

"You are so hot..." I tell her, and begin flicking her hard nipples with my fingers, pinching and twisting them in her desire.

"Oh fuck...Jess..." she moans, and arches back.

The sound of my name from her mouth is pure magic. I do not realize how much I needed to hear her moan my name...until she finally does.

With my hands down holding onto her waist, I pull her in, as she thrusts her chest forward, pushing her magnificent breasts towards me.

I take one of her breasts in my mouth and begin sucking on it hard.

Oh...the taste of her.

Her skin is so soft, so warm, so silky...I can't help but bite her.

Like a hungry beast, I sink my teeth into her, and begin to suck on her hard.

The princess moans and yelps. She pushes her chest further into my mouth; she pulls me in.

The seduction is too much.

"Don't go easy on me...Don't fucking go easy on me..." she says through lust-dipped moans.

"I wouldn't be able to even if I tried..."

I smile back and continue sucking hard.

The princess moans louder and pushes harder, "Go harder...harder...harder..."

I slide my other hand up her legs and reach for her shorts. I begin to pull on them, and the princess raises her ass into the air, helping me out.

"Oh fuck, Jess..." she moans, as I hook my fingers into her shorts and pull them off.

Penelope

Jessica pulls down my shorts with an impatient tug, and I help her get rid of them.

In the next moment, I am ripping open her shirt, and flinging it aside, while Jessica takes off her gym leggings that she still had on after her workout.

Naked, nervous and nearing a trance like state, I fall down on Jessica's toned body and grip her shoulders. I look into her icy blue eyes and kiss all over her gorgeous face.

I kiss the scar above her lips.

I kiss the corners of her mouth.

I kiss every inch of her, until I find myself craving her swollen lips.

"You've made me so wet, marine..." I husk, while Jessica grabs my ass, and gives it a light squeeze.

"This time, I will be checking for myself," Jessica says, now grabbing both my butt cheeks with her hands and pulling me in as if any space between our bodies is a direct insult to her desire for me.

I kiss her hard and place my thigh against her clit.

She is wet.

Oh my god, she is so fucking wet for me.

I can't believe it.

"Ohhh...ohhh..." Jessica moans, as I slide my thigh up and down her crotch, rubbing myself against her. "Ohhh..."

"You like that?" I ask, taking my mouth away from hers and beginning to kiss her neck.

Jessica replies by grinding her crotch against my inner thigh like a maniac.

The bed creaks, and I find myself matching Jessica's thrusts by moving my legs in a rhythm with her.

"Yes...Yes...yes...ohhh fuck."

Jessica arches her back, and I bring down my mouth on her hard nipples.

"No, no...not yet," Jessica grunts, and suddenly, I find myself being thrown around on the bed like a rag doll.

Switching our positions, and now pinning me under her, Jessica gives my chin and jawline a lick, before saying, "It's not the princess's job to do all the work. Her job is to...get fucked...hard."

Jessica's words work as an aphrodisiac, and I find myself becoming delirious with pleasure.

But I want more.

I want more of Jessica.

I want to be taken, subjugated, and owned by this sexy, strong woman.

I want to submit to this wanton Valkyrie.

Jessica

It seems like all my life has been leading up to this.

The visual of Princess Penelope Victoria Windsor, the future Queen of England, parting her milky white legs for me, begging me with her dark brown eyes to fuck her crazy.

I lick my lips at the thought of what I am about to do to her, and my heart feels more alive than I could ever remember it.

I push her legs apart and look down at her wet crotch.

"Oh fuck...wet...aaahh..." I moan as I see streams of her juices flow down her inner thighs.

I can't wait any longer.

I bend down and begin licking the inside of her thighs.

"Ohhhhh...ohhh fuck..." she moans, and I work my way up to her crotch.

As I kiss her inner thigh, I begin rubbing her clit with my thumb.

"No...no...no...oh...oh god..." she moans, and squirms under me.

I chuckle and push her legs up and apart, until her knees are against her breasts.

"Oh fuck...Oh fuck..." she moans as I bring my mouth down over her pussy.

I push my tongue into her and slide it in and out of her while rubbing her clit hard with my thumb.

In and out, in and out, in and out, I fuck her with my tongue and rub her clit with my thumb.

"Don't stop Jess...iccaah! aaah...yes, baby!"

I don't stop until I feel her juices coat my tongue, and I don't stop until I feel her legs begin to spasm uncontrollably.

"Ohhhhh...ohhhhh...ohhhhh..."

I take my mouth off her crotch and let her moan out her orgasm.

"Oh fuck...Jessica...Jessica..." she moans and arches her back.

I bring my head under her and kiss her on the mouth.

"Oh fuck...oh fuck..." she moans again, as I ask her, "Ready to go again?"

"What? No! Someone can walk in at any moment!"

"I can lock the door."

"Babe," Penelope says, catching her breath, "you need to be pampered too. You are a national hero."

"An American national hero. You don't need to award me anything for my services, Princess of England."

"Well, I need to atleast award you for the awesome work you just did on my body," Penelope says with a sly grin.

"That was hardly my best work. I was just getting started."

"Lock the door," Penelope orders me, and I oblige.

When I turn around after locking the door, I find Penelope on her knees, perched cutely in front of the bed.

"Come over," she says, beckoning me with her finger.

I could cum just looking at her sitting like that!

Oh lord, have mercy!

I tiptoe seductively to my princess, who has her eyes locked onto mine.

"Hurry up, marine, don't make me wait."

Penelope lunges at me, grabs my waist, and pulls me to her.

I stagger and let out a long, drawn out moan as Penelope clasps her mouth on my pussy.

"Ohhh fuck..." I moan, as Penelope laps at my snatch with her tongue.

My knees turn weak, but I stand, as Penelope brings her mouth away from my pussy and starts to kiss my legs.

I press my hands on her head, and try to guide her mouth to my pussy, but she resists and continues kissing my legs.

"Fuck..." I moan, and she replies by licking my inner thighs.

I bring my hands down and find her head. I push my fingers into her hair, and she pulls away.

I pull her hair back, and she looks up at me with her sexy eyes.

"You are so fucking sexy, baby," I say to her.

"Not as sexy as you," she replies and goes back to eating me out on her knees.

Penelope

I have never gotten down on my knees for anyone. Other people have, for me, but not me.

I always thought 'a princess never bends the knee'.

But I do now.

I do it for her, because I can't imagine doing anything else.

I want nothing more than to kneel before this woman and to please her.

I grab her by the back of her thighs and inhale her scent.

I look up at her one last time and imprint her beauty on my brain, before closing my eyes and diving back into the depths of her arousal.

I start lashing her with my tongue, and she starts thrusting into me with abandon.

She begins thrusting into my mouth with such force that I have to put my hands on her thighs to steady myself

"Fuck...Oh...oh...oh fuck..." she moans, and I feel her hands grip my hair, and she pulls me into her.

I feel like my tongue will go numb any moment, but I don't stop.

I can't stop.

She tastes too good.

She tastes like a woman.

I could spend my entire life between her legs and never tire of her.

"Oh fuck...oh fuck...oh fuck..." she moans, and I feel her legs begin to tremble.

Suddenly, I feel her walls tighten around my tongue, and she starts bucking into me.

"Oh, fuck, Penny!"

She collapses into my arms, and I hold her up, offering her a naughty smile.

"Steady there, marine, a national hero like you can't be crumbling because of an orgasm."

Jessica laughs, like really laughs, and in that moment, I find her prettier than ever.

"Don't tell my superiors about that," she whispers, her face buried in my neck.

"So, shall we go out and risk embarrassing ourselves?" I say, steadying Jessica, as she is still wobbly after receiving my world-class oral.

"I am pretty sure my uncle and aunt heard that. Man, I come back home after years and traumatize them on the same day. No wonder I was better off alone!"

Chapter Eleven

Penelope

As James chauffeurs Jessica and me back to the hotel, there's a distinct, sly grin plastered on his face, as if he's got our secret by the tail. "Umm...don't mind me asking, but, if we are going to be rich soon, then I would like to know. I'd go easy at work then," he asks.

"What do you mean?" Jessica asks, and I lean forward from the backseat to hear the conversation better.

"I mean, from what I heard...I think Jessica is close to pulling off a royal heist, if you know what I mean." James looks at me in the rearview mirror, a silly grin plastered on his face.

Yup, he heard.

I wonder how much it would hurt to jump out of this car and escape the embarrassment.

Jessica is stunned as well. "Just get us back to our hotel, James, and don't have an overactive imagination."

"Says the girl whose overactive libido just traumatized Dad and Mom!"

Jessica leans back into her seat nonchalantly and eyes me in the rearview mirror as she says, "Good. they should know that their niece is doing well in life."

"I know, and I am happy for you," he says, giving his cousin a look brimming with warmth and affection, "but give me a heads up the next time you two visit. I'll soundproof your room, sis!"

∞ ∞ ∞

James hits the brakes, and the car screeches to a halt outside Marriott.

As we spill out of the car, Jessica engulfs James in a hug, her eyes glossy with emotion. "Take care of yourself, little cousin," she murmurs, her voice choking a little. James grins affectionately, promising to be on his best behavior until her next visit.

"You are really cool, Penelope. I will be tuning into your coronation ceremony along with all my friends," James says, curtsying horribly once again.

I hug James, and as I let go, I whisper in his ear, "Don't worry. I'll get you front row seats."

This makes James turn red and curtsy again. "You need to stop doing that, James," I laugh and hug him again.

Inside our suite, Maria and Kriti are entangled on the couch, their lips locked together.

Jessica clears her throat, the two of them springing apart like guilty teenagers. Maria's scowl is fierce, but there's a glint of amusement in Kriti's eyes.

"Well, well, well. The bickering lovebirds have finally patched things up." Jessica smirks, crossing her arms.

"Seems like it," I add, trying to suppress a grin. "Though you two were hardly discreet about it."

Kriti blushes, her words coming out in a squeaky stammer. "We... we just... I mean..."

Maria cuts in, her fiery spirit blazing. "Yes, we did. Problem?"

My eyebrows shoot up in amusement. "Not at all. Just curious about the details. Mind sharing?"

Kriti blushes harder, but Maria grins wickedly. "Not unless you share yours first, Princess."

My eyes dart towards Jessica, who looks away quickly. I take Kriti by the arm and guide her away from the prying eyes of Jessica and Maria.

"You won't believe what's happened, Kriti," I say, spilling the beans about the mayhem Jessica and I caused in her old, teenage room.

As I recount our conversation, the fears we helped each other overcome, and the barrier that shattered between us, Kriti's eyes grow wider. But she remains silent, absorbing my story like a sponge.

"So, you two haven't... talked after that?" she finally asks, her teasing tone replaced by sincere concern.

"We haven't. I just need to know if she feels the same or if this was just... a moment of weakness."

"What do you mean by 'if she feels the same?' What are you feeling?"

"I don't know, Kriti. But something very strong. I just feel like I am not ready to say goodbye to her. I feel like spending every waking moment with her.

Kriti offers me a supportive smile. "You need to talk to her, Penny. As someone who's seen you with your rockstar and now with Jessica, trust me, Jessica suits you better."

I feel a warmth spreading through me. "Thank you, Kriti. But...what does that even mean? I wasn't really looking for a relationship with Alexa. But now, I feel like taking a chance on Jessica." I feel myself sinking into a quicksand of my own thoughts.

Get a grip on yourself, Penny!

"Listen, I need a favor from you."

Kriti cocks her head in curiosity. "Yes?"

"I need you to take another car with Maria. I want to ride alone with Jessica."

"But why..."

I cut her off. "I don't want Jessica to know that we've had this conversation. I need to approach this on my terms, and you asking Maria for a separate car provides the perfect opportunity for that."

Kriti's eyes glimmer with understanding. "I see. Your secret's safe with me, Penny. Now go on, talk to her. We'll handle our own transport."

And as Kriti saunters off to Maria, I turn towards Jessica. Her marine-blue eyes meet mine, a silent question echoing between us. It's a conversation we're yet to have, but for now, I bask in the warmth of her gaze, silently promising her that the discussion, as overdue as it may be, will soon unfurl under the gentle cloak of our shared solitude.

As we bid Dallas goodbye, our car hits the freeway in a shared silence.

Jessica's hands grip the wheel, her gaze steadfastly fixed

on the road ahead. Kriti and Maria trail us in a rental, their chatter probably filling the car as they catch up, their initial friction dissolved.

Jessica's deep in her thoughts, her face a fortress of stoicism. I find myself stealing glances at her, our shared secret creating an invisible thread, tugging at my heart. I know she's processing, the magnitude of our actions not lost on either of us. So, I wait. Patience has never been my virtue, but for Jessica, I'd move mountains.

As the Dallas sun paints the sky in hues of oranges and purples, my mind wanders back to the text I had sent my mom, the Queen. A bundle of nerves knits in my stomach at the thought.

What if she has ignored my message?

Worse, what if she has read it, and decided to go all 'Queen of England' on me, and not 'motherly' as my heart is desperately hoping.

I rummage in my bag for my phone, the cool device bringing a semblance of comfort. As I unlock it, I see the notification that makes my heart leap into my throat - a reply from Mother.

"Jess," I croak, my voice barely audible over the hum of the engine. "She replied."

I see Jessica's knuckles whiten on the wheel, but her gaze never leaves the road. "Well," she replies, her voice steady as a rock. "I suppose we best see what the Queen has to say."

With a shaking hand, I lift my phone, my mother's unopened message glowing on the screen. But at the last second, I lower it again, a sigh escaping my lips.

Jessica throws a quick, surprised glance my way. "Not going to read it?"

I shake my head, my heart thudding in my chest. "No.

There's... there's a lot on my mind right now. I don't want to add to it."

"Really?" Jessica's voice carries a note of surprise, her eyebrows lifted as she teases, "And here I thought your mind was a picture of zen and tranquility."

I roll my eyes at her sarcasm, biting back a smile. "Don't act so innocent, Thompson. You know perfectly well what's on my mind."

She keeps her eyes on the road, a smug smile playing on her lips. "Do I now? I have no idea, Penelope."

My gaze narrows at her playful tone, my mind a whirlwind of emotions. "Jessica!"

Her laughter fills the car, the sound bouncing off the windows. "Alright, alright. I was just messing with you, Penny. No need to get all high and mighty on me."

"Then what do you think is on my mind?" I ask.

Jessica takes a moment and replies in a softer tone, "Us?"

"Bingo! Who said lifting weights makes you dumb?" I quip, trying to lighten the heaviness that has suddenly filled the car.

"Umm...no one?" Jessica replies with scrunched eyebrows.

"Yeah, I am thinking about us. I am thinking about the...time we shared in your old room, and how that made me feel."

"And how did that make you feel?" Jessica asks, and I can feel the anticipation in her voice.

Do I lay open all my cards, or do I play it safe and coy?

"How did it make *you* feel?" I counter-question, deciding to test the waters.

"It made me feel very good, Penelope. It was the best sex

I've had, by far."

"So, it was all about sex for you?"

I see Jessica's face contorting into a grimace. "I haven't given it much thought. I am incredibly attracted to you, somehow, against all odds..."

"Thanks for the kind words," I cut in, with a sarcastic smile.

"...and I have never felt more comfortable sharing my feelings with anyone else, like I did with you, which is a big thing for me, as you might have guessed from my overall...demeanor."

"I know," I say.

"But, we aren't normal people, with normal lives, are we? And that raises a lot of complications." Jessica's voice drops, and her words end with a sigh.

"What would you have done if we were normal people?" I probe, sitting cross-legged on the seat, facing Jessica.

"I haven't felt normal since 9/11, Penny. I don't know how to answer that question."

"Sorry, but...you know what I mean. What if I was a normal college girl, and you were a marketing manager in a big company?"

"We would still have the issue of age," Jessica says, stepping on the accelerator and overtaking a bus.

"That's a non-issue in today's world. Age is just a number."

"Homosexuality is also a non-issue in today's world, but the world of royalty is different, isn't it?" Jessica looks at me, and just like always, her eyes cause a sudden uptick in my heartbeat.

"Forget about all that for a minute, Jessica. Imagine a

world where I am not a royal, and you are not a marine. What would you have done then?"

Silence, and then a soft whisper from Jessica: "I would have asked you to stay in America for a little longer."

"That must have been hard for you to admit," I say.

"No, it's not. I am very aware of my emotions. I am hardly ever confused about what I am feeling. It's accepting those feelings that's always been hard for me. I have been fighting these feelings a lot lately. Feelings that...I have been having for you. They are special."

I can't stop the grin that spreads on my face.

"I have special feelings for you too, Marine. It's taken only a week for me to realize how superficial and flimsy my feelings are for Alexa. What I feel, talking with you, is deeper and far more meaningful than any conversation I've had with anyone."

"So...should I take a U-turn?" Jessica says, with a smile.

"No, I'd still like to meet Alexa and tell her personally that we won't be proceeding further...romantically. I don't want to waste my time with flings and random hook-ups anymore, Jess. I want someone who can become the reason I go against my family and the monarchy, and Alexa is not that person."

Jessica does not reply.

My heart thunders in my chest as I add, "But I think it could be you, Jessica."

Jessica does not look at me, but I desperately want her to.

I want her to tell me she feels the same.

"It won't work, Penelope. I am a fractured soul. I like being alone. I like taking risks, and putting my life on the line. That's the only time I feel alive."

"But...you've retired, right? You don't do that anymore," I

say, my heart breaking a little.

"I...have an offer from the CIA, to work with them as an undercover spy in Taiwan, and I am thinking of accepting."

Her words hit me like a punch to the gut, derailing my train of thought.

"But...why? You've just reconnected with your family, you're pursuing a degree in psychology, the future looks promising for you. I don't get it! Why do you want to go back to the trauma that keeps messing with you all the time?"

"Because when I'm in the middle of a mission, the nightmares go away. It's only when I'm safe, leading a normal life, that they haunt me."

"That doesn't mean you should keep throwing yourself into danger, Jessica! This is toxic and unhealthy!" I am irritated and feel helpless.

Why can't she just act like a normal person for once?

Jessica remains silent, her eyes fixed on the road ahead.

The car falls into a tense silence, and I can feel the weight of her decision hanging in the air between us.

"I can't change who I am, Penelope," she finally speaks, her voice low and strained. "I've tried, believe me, but it's like a part of me is missing when I'm not in the field. I need the adrenaline, the rush, the sense of purpose that comes with the job."

"People change their purpose over time. Maybe you'd find fulfillment in something else?"

"I tried. I thought getting a degree in psychology and helping other soldiers with their PTSD would be fulfilling, but to be honest with you, it's messing with my head even more. It's a failed attempt at finding that purpose you're talking about. My life, Penelope, my destiny...is already written. I'm going to die on the battlefield. I know that. And I'll happily embrace death because I would have died doing something I love."

"Bullshit," I snap, and Jessica looks at me, surprise shimmering in her eyes. "You don't love it. You do it because it offers you an escape. You love peace. You want peace, and the only way you know how to get it is by putting your life in danger. That's what you have ever wanted. Peace of mind. And you know what, falling in love can get you there, but you're too scared to choose that option."

Jessica glares at me, her jaw clenched. "You don't know anything about me, Penelope. You don't know what I've been through, or what I've seen. Love won't fix me. It won't fix any of the shit that's wrong with me."

"I know you better than you think, Jessica. I know you're strong, and brave, and capable of so much more than you give yourself credit for. You don't have to keep putting yourself in harm's way to prove your worth. You don't have to be alone."

Jessica's hands grip the steering wheel tightly, her knuckles turning white. "You don't understand," she says, her voice barely above a whisper.

"Then make me understand," I plead. "Let me in. Let me help you. Please, Jessica."

"Penelope, finding purpose, or peace of mind, or the strength to take on your family, or monarchy shouldn't be the reason to look for love. You should just...love because you want to be with the person you love. And we hardly know each other. Hell, until a few days back, I thought you were a snobbish little brat."

"But am I?" I ask, glaring at Jessica, "Do you still think that's how hollow I am?"

"No, I know you're so much more, and that's why..."

"That's why what, Jessica?" I'm almost screaming.

"Let it go," Jessica whispers.

"No, I won't let it go. I need to know. That's why what?"

"That's why it's so hard for me," Jessica says, her voice barely audible over the sound of the car's engine. "That's why I can't let myself give in to these feelings. Because I know that if I do, I won't be able to let you go. And I can't have that kind of attachment, not when I'm constantly putting myself in danger."

"But...who the heck knows if you'd even feel that strongly in the future for me?"

"I know. I told you, I'm very aware of my feelings, and I know once I decide to go all in, I will fall in love with you," Jessica says, taking a deep breath and fixing her gaze on the horizon.

"And so, you'd rather say goodbye, than see how being in love feels?" I ask, my voice dropping.

"Yes."

I'm stunned into silence by Jessica's words. It's as if something inside of me has been ripped apart, leaving me feeling exposed and vulnerable. I don't know what to say or do. I thought that maybe, just maybe, Jessica could be the one for me. But now, it seems like that possibility is slipping away from me.

I stare at Jessica, my heart aching with the realization that she is willing to let go of something that could potentially be beautiful and life-changing.

I want to scream, to shout, to make her understand that she deserves to be loved, to be happy, to be at peace. But I know, deep down, that her decision is hers to make.

Silence descends upon us once again, the only sound

being the whirring of the car's engine and the faint hum of the radio. I glance out the window, watching the scenery blur past us, lost in thought.

"Can I ride with Kriti? I'd like to be away from you for a while," I say finally, breaking the silence.

"Sure," Jessica says, her voice tight.

Jessica pulls out her phone, her fingers swiftly tapping on the screen. I hear her muffled conversation with Maria, asking her to pull over their rental. She explains that I'd like to switch cars for a while and ride with Kriti, a statement that triggers an odd pang in my chest.

My mind is a whirlwind of thoughts and emotions. Disappointment, anger, sorrow, they all blend together into a bitter cocktail that leaves a sour taste in my mouth. The warmth of Jessica's presence, which used to comfort me, now only amplifies the pain.

The car gradually slows down as Jessica maneuvers it to the side of the road. I glance outside the window, catching sight of the rental car that Maria and Kriti are in, parked just ahead of us.

Without uttering a word, Jessica switches off the engine. The sudden silence feels heavy, filled with unspoken words and a tension that is almost palpable. I unbuckle my seatbelt, gripping the door handle with more force than necessary.

"Penelope." Jessica's voice is low, filled with a kind of regret that's contagious. She reaches out tentatively, her hand hovering above mine that's resting on the car door handle. I feel a strong urge to grasp her hand, to seek comfort in her touch, but I force myself to resist.

"I'm sorry," she says, her words barely audible. They hang in the air, adding another layer to the melancholic silence.

I don't respond.

I simply exit the car, letting the cool wind whip around me as I walk towards the rental. Behind me, I hear Jessica get out of the car too, but I don't look back.

I can feel tears pricking at the corners of my eyes as I approach the rental. But I refuse to let them fall, not here, not now. As I climb into the car, Kriti gives me a look of concern.

"Don't ask," I say, cutting off any potential questions. I simply lean back into the seat, shutting my eyes as I try to gather my thoughts. I don't know where this leaves me, or us, or what the future holds, but one thing's for sure: my heart hurts, and I need some time to heal.

Maria looks between me and the car I just exited, her eyebrows knitted together in a concerned frown. "Should I ride with Jessica, or does she need to be alone?"

"She'd appreciate the company," I reply, my voice sounding hollow in my own ears. "Kriti can drive for a while. She has an international license."

Maria's eyebrows shoot up in surprise, but she nods, understanding the gravity of the situation. Her gaze lingers on me for a few seconds longer before she walks towards Jessica's car.

With Maria gone, Kriti shifts from the passenger seat to the driver's seat, her movements slow and deliberate. She adjusts the mirrors and buckles her seatbelt, all while sneaking concerned glances my way.

"Are you okay, Penelope?" she asks.

"I will be," I respond, closing my eyes and leaning back into the seat. "Just... give me a while. I need to be alone with my thoughts."

Kriti nods, understanding the unspoken plea for silence. The car comes to life under her touch, and the quiet hum of the engine is the only sound that fills the silence. I can sense her curiosity, her worry, but she respects my wishes, allowing me the solitude I crave.

As we merge back into the traffic, I can't help but steal a glance at the rear-view mirror. Jessica's car is right behind us, and I can just about make out her figure in the passenger seat.

My heart aches at the sight, but I force myself to look away.

An unfamiliar pang of disappointment settles in the pit of my stomach as the conversation with Jessica replays in my mind. I take a deep breath, the cool air doing little to soothe my frayed nerves. Kriti's questioning gaze pulls me from my thoughts, and I decide to let her in on the complicated narrative I've been juggling.

"Jessica... she rejected the idea of us," I admit, my voice barely above a whisper. Kriti remains quiet, her fingers gently drumming on the steering wheel. The silence that follows is heavy, loaded with a million questions, but Kriti doesn't ask any of them. She gives me the space to elaborate, to explain, to vent, and I appreciate it.

"She did admit to having feelings for me. Feelings which mirrored my own."

I see Kriti's eyes widen, the surprise evident in her gaze. "Then, why...?" she begins but I cut her off, finally allowing the words to flow freely from my mouth.

"She has been offered a chance to be an undercover agent for the CIA in Taiwan. She's drawn to the danger, Kriti. She told me it gives her a thrill, makes her feel alive, feel free from her past."

Kriti absorbs this information, her expression unreadable. I continue, my eyes staring at the gentle slope of the road ahead, "She said it's her destiny, her way of life. And she fears if she grows too attached to someone, it will make it harder for her to accept that danger. And that someone... it's me, Kriti."

"Have you thought about what you want?"

I ponder her question for a moment. "I...I don't know. Part of me wants to try to make it work, to fight for her. But the other part of me knows that it's not fair to either of us if she's not fully committed."

Kriti nods in agreement. "It's important to prioritize yourself, Penelope. You deserve someone who can give you their all."

I let out a small laugh, the sound bitter. "And what if that someone was Jessica all along? What if she's the one I've been waiting for?"

Kriti's expression softens. "Then you fight for her. But remember, you can't force someone to change their mind. All you can do is be honest with yourself and with her."

I nod, taking in Kriti's words. "I know. And I don't want to force her into anything she doesn't want. But it's hard, Kriti. It's hard to let go when you feel like you've found something special."

"I know," Kriti says softly, placing a comforting hand on my shoulder. "But sometimes, letting go is the best thing for both parties involved. It may hurt now, but in the long run, it could be the best decision you ever make."

I sigh, knowing Kriti is right.

But my heart still aches, and the thought of letting go of Jessica feels like a sharp blow to my chest.

"So, the sex was really good, huh?" Kriti asks, making me smile after what seems like an eternity.

"It was phenomenal, even though it lasted for a few minutes."

"It had to be, for you to start imagining a life with a woman you met a week ago," Kriti says.

"Seven days is a long time, Kriti. How long has it taken you to be fangirling over Maria? You were sure you are straight before you met her, right?"

"Well, actually, it was Jessica who planted the doubt in my mind, when you sent me on that mission to seduce her. Maria just confirmed it."

I smile. "What is it about women in uniforms?"

"We haven't even seen them in their uniforms, Your Highness," Kriti reminds me.

"I hope I don't. Not after I have been aired by Jessica," I joke, using humor as a coping mechanism like a psychopath.

"You've just had the best sex of your life with her. If that's her airing you, then by god, I would love to be aired by Maria every day."

The best sex of my life, followed by the worst heartbreak of my life. *What a day.*

"So, what are you going to do now?" Kriti asks me the question I have been dreading asking myself.

"I am going to go to L.A. and meet Alexa."

"Penny, don't go making bad decisions just to get back at Jessica," Kriti warns me, and I scowl.

"Who do you take me for? I am not a kid! I want to meet Alexa and tell her we are over. At least Jessica made me realize what I should be looking for in my soulmate, before breaking my heart, and it is not Alexa. I just want to tell her personally."

"Okay, and then?"

"And then, we fly back from L.A. and I say goodbye to Jessica...forever."

"And you are sure you don't want to try and ...change her mind?" Kriti asks tentatively.

"No, I don't want to convince anyone to give me a shot. That's not what I deserve."

Kriti nods, while I close my eyes and try to sleep.

But I don't.

Instead, I am tortured by images, flashes, memories of Jessica and I making love.

The flashes are blinding, each one more painful than the last, reminding me I am soon going to lose her forever.

"Kriti," I whisper, eyes closed.

"Yes?"

"Can you do me a favor?"

"Yeah?"

"I want you to read a text from Mother that I haven't read yet. Don't read it out loud, but just tell me, on a scale of ten, whether I should read it or not."

"What? Why?"

I tell Kriti about the text that Jessica made me send to Mother, and she sighs. "What if the number is 3...or 4?" she asks me.

"Then I want you to delete the text and never tell me what it said, no matter how much I ask you to, okay?"

"Okay."

My eyes are still closed as I hand Kriti my phone.

"There's a text from Jessica as well," Kriti says, and I open my eyes and look at her.

"Do I dare having my heart broken by two people at the

same time?" I ask Kriti, who has one eye on the road, and the other on the phone.

"I have already read the text from Jessica, sorry," Kriti says.

"Give me a number...one to ten," I say, and close my eyes again.

"Why do you keep making me do weird things, Penny. Just read the texts on your own. I am not rating your texts."

"You are my PA. You will do what I ask you to, or else I will tell your orthodox Indian mom you like making love to strong, Latina women now."

I hear Kriti groan. "Jessica's text reads, 'we will be stopping for the night at a ranch owned by one of her colleagues. She has decided not to risk driving in the night after all'."

"Tell her I want to reach L.A. as soon as possible, and I do not wish to spend another night with her in the same room."

"Penelope..." Kriti tries to argue.

"Do as I say, Kriti."

I hear Kriti pulling the car to the side. The sound of the engine dies, and I hear Kriti typing away on her phone.

"Why would I now want to spend even a single second with her in my sight?" I scoff.

Kriti's fingers dance across the screen for a few moments before she lifts the phone to her ear, presumably dialing Jessica's number. I keep my eyes closed, the dread of what's to come making my heart pound.

"Jess, it's Kriti," she starts, her tone placating. She listens for a few moments, her eyebrows furrowing. "Look, Penelope insists we drive through the night. She doesn't want to stay at the ranch..."

The silence that follows is filled with tension, and I can

almost hear the icy tone in Jessica's voice as she responds. Kriti swallows, shooting me a glance. "It's not negotiable?" she repeats, her tone incredulous. My eyes fly open and I sit up, my blood boiling at the audacity.

"Give me the phone, Kriti," I demand, my hand outstretched. She seems hesitant but hands it over, her gaze wary.

"I've had enough of her calling the shots," I snap, pressing the phone to my ear. "Jessica, listen to me, I'm done playing by your rules. I'm not staying at the ranch, I'm not spending another night in your company. You don't get to decide for me anymore."

"Penelope..." Jessica begins, her voice calm and infuriatingly collected. I cut her off, my anger rising to the surface.

"No, Jessica, it's my turn to talk. It's been one-sided for too long. I've danced to your tune for the last time. I've tried understanding your side, accommodating your wishes, and respecting your boundaries. But what about me, Jessica? What about my feelings? What about what I want?"

"Penelope, I..." she tries to interject, but I'm not having any of it.

"No, Jessica! I'm driving through the night. I'm going to L.A., and I'm doing this my way. You can join if you want, or you can stay behind. I don't care anymore."

And with that, I end the call, the silence in the car echoing my pounding heart

"What the hell was that, Penny?" Kriti asks, her voice thick with worry.

I remain silent, my fingers gripping the edges of my seat. Before I can respond, the distant hum of a car engine grows louder, and we see headlights approaching from behind in the rearview mirror. Kriti tightens her grip on the steering wheel, her knuckles turning white. "Oh, shit."

The headlights belong to Jessica's car, which comes to a halt a few feet behind ours. The car door opens and Jessica steps out, her silhouette illuminated by the car's interior light before it closes with a soft thud.

"Please, Penny, don't fight. Stay calm," Kriti pleads as I unfasten my seatbelt. Her eyes flicker nervously between me and the rearview mirror where Jessica's reflection looms.

"Don't worry, Kriti," I say, my voice flat. "I'm going to be very calm." Despite my words, Kriti doesn't look convinced. I can't blame her. My blood feels like it's buzzing with electricity, my heart pounding with a mix of anger and anticipation.

The cool night air wraps around me as I step out of the car, the scent of the surrounding pine trees filling my nostrils. The sky above us is a deep, velvety black, speckled with countless stars that cast a soft, dim light over the deserted road. There's an eerie stillness in the air, the kind that only exists in the deep hours of the night, broken only by the distant hooting of an owl.

Jessica is standing by her car, her figure bathed in the glow of the streetlight. Even from here, I can see the rigid set of her shoulders, the determination in her stance. As I begin to approach her, I hear Kriti and Maria exiting the cars as well, trailing behind like wraiths in the night.

The moment we step out of our cars, the tension is palpable. The quiet night hums around us, pierced only by the distant croak of a night bird. Maria and Kriti look like they'd rather be anywhere but here, caught in the brewing storm between Jessica and me.

"Why are you being so obstinate, Jessica?" I start, frustration knotting my brows. The chilly wind flutters my hair around my face but my gaze stays locked on hers. "We can't just waste time lounging in some ranch. We need to reach LA as soon as possible."

"I am not being obstinate, Penelope," Jessica retorts, her arms folded across her chest. Her face is a canvas of stern pragmatism, a mask that hides whatever she might be feeling. "I'm being sensible. It's late, we've been driving for hours. It's not safe to travel through the night."

"Sensible?" I scoff, stepping closer, our shadowy figures illuminated by the car's headlights. "Or is it that you just don't care about reaching our destination in time? That you're not invested in this, not like I am?"

Jessica's expression changes, hints of confusion and hurt flickering in her eyes. "Penelope, what...?"

"No, Jessica," I cut her off, my heart pounding as a surge of bitterness washes over me. "It's not just about the drive. It's about us. It's about you accepting...me."

There, I've said it. The words hang heavy between us. I see Jessica take a step back, surprise etched across her face.

"Penny, this...this isn't the time to..."

"Well, when would be the right time, Jessica?" I press on, my voice trembling with pent-up emotions. "When would it be the right time for you to stop running? To stop hiding behind your job, your sense of duty?"

"Penelope, you're being unfair," Jessica protests, her voice wavering. "This is about our safety, not about...us."

"But it is, Jessica! It always has been!" I shoot back, anger mingling with desperation. "Every delay, every avoidance - it's not just about the drive, it's about you avoiding the fact that you can't accept me, can't face your feelings for me."

My chest heaves as I finish, my heart heavy.

Jessica stands still, her face a maelstrom of emotions she's not willing to display. The night holds its breath as the echo of my words fade, leaving a silence that somehow feels even louder.

"It's always about more than the road ahead, Jessica," I murmur, almost to myself. "It's about the journey, our journey... and whether you're brave enough to undertake it with me."

Jessica, having watched me retreat to the car, calls after me, her voice steady despite the sudden downpour of my heartache. "Penelope! Penny, wait... We can talk about this. Just... not now. Right now, we need to figure out how to get to L.A."

I halt in my steps, my back still turned to her. My mother's words echo in my mind, "A princess never shows weakness." I pull myself together, swallowing the lump in my throat. "You're right," I call back, my voice hoarse yet firm. "We have a journey to finish.

"I need to get to L.A. as soon as possible, Jessica," I continue, my words laced with a tired surrender. The gentle moonlight shines down on us, casting an almost ethereal glow around the scene. "I just want to end this journey as soon as possible. It's... It's not about us, not right now."

A heavy silence descends once again, my admission lingering in the air. I don't have to turn around to know that Jessica's stunned, her sharp intake of breath piercing the quiet night.

"All right, Penny," she finally says, her voice subdued. "We'll drive through the night."

The night turns colder, but I feel strangely warm inside. It's not the victory of getting my way. Rather, it's the relief of having voiced my feelings, of letting Jessica know how deeply this journey - our journey - affects me.

I walk back to the car, my posture regal, my face a mask of calmness.

A princess never shows weakness, I remind myself.

As I slide back into the passenger seat, I take a final glance at Jessica. She stands there, looking lost and alone under the moonlight.

My heart aches for her, for us. But there's a road ahead, a journey to finish. There will be time to heal, to make amends, to confront and perhaps even reconcile. But not tonight.

Tonight, we drive. We drive through the darkness, towards the dawn that awaits in L.A.

Chapter Twelve

Jessica

Settling back in the driver's seat, I feel the hum of the engine vibrating through the soles of my feet, the rhythm an odd source of comfort after hours of relentless driving. Dawn's first light is now stretching out across the sky, a welcome change after a long night.

Kriti stirs beside me, having switched with Maria, who is driving Penelope in the Range Rover behind us.

Rubbing her eyes, she lets out a yawn. "You must be tired, Jessica. How far are we from L.A.?" she asks, a hint of concern edging her words.

"I'd say another three hours, give or take," I reply, the hours of solitude behind the wheel giving my voice a rougher edge than I'd like.

Her eyes dart to the digital clock on the dashboard before looking back at me. "And we're heading to a hotel in Beverly Hills?"

"Yes," I nod, blinking away the fatigue that threatens to pull my eyelids closed. "We have a place booked. A chance for everyone to freshen up and rest."

For a moment, Kriti just watches me, her gaze

questioning. I'm too tired for this, and part of me is glad when she breaks the silence.

"How are you feeling, Jess?" she asks, her voice soft.

Her question hangs in the air, leaving an echo that stirs my weary heart.

For a while, I don't answer. I keep my gaze locked onto the open road ahead, taking in the spreading blush of dawn and the desolation of the scenery rushing by. With each passing mile, the weight of everything that's happened – my confession, the strain between Penelope and me, the CIA offer – seems to grow heavier.

How am I feeling? That's a million-dollar question. But I'm too tired, too worn out to begin untangling the knot of emotions lodged in my chest. So instead, I just shake my head and push the accelerator a little harder.

"Don't mind Penelope. She's just not used to being denied what she wants," Kriti says, breaking the silence that had built up in the car.

"Not upset with her," I murmur, eyes on the road. "I'm upset with myself."

Her voice betrays her curiosity when she asks, "Why?"

I suck in a breath, not sure how to explain the churning feeling in my gut. "Because I couldn't adapt after I retired. I couldn't...normalize myself. And that inability is now affecting those around me."

There's a pause.

Kriti mulls over my words, her expression unreadable. "You're so used to doing things your way, Jessica," she starts slowly. "You're not allowing yourself to admit that you might be...lost. That you don't have all the answers."

There's a prickling defensiveness at the back of my mind,

but I tamp it down. "My ways have worked for me. Kept me alive. Why would they fail now?"

But Kriti doesn't back down. She turns to me, her eyes probing. "Have you ever been in love?"

The question throws me off-guard. "No."

"Then you're in unfamiliar territory, Jess," she says gently. "You might be an exceptional soldier, but you're not infallible. You don't know what love can offer you. You think you know how a relationship - or hell, even the possibility of one with Penelope - would turn out. But you don't have any evidence to back that up. You're a Marine, right? You're trained not to make decisions based on emotions. You're supposed to use past data, probability, and other variables to construct a likely outcome. But you're not doing that with Penelope. You're just going off on what you think might happen, without having a real conversation with her...or with yourself."

Her words hang heavy in the car, a brutal honesty that's hard to swallow. This isn't a battlefield or a mission. This is love, or the possibility of it. And in that, she's right.

I am lost.

But admitting it is a battle of its own. I sigh, my grip tightening on the steering wheel. But I can't deny the truth in her words. This is one fight I can't win with my usual tactics. And that terrifies me more than I care to admit.

I steer the conversation away, unable to handle the rawness of my own vulnerability. "What's going on with Penelope?" I ask, hoping to shift focus.

Kriti's not fooled, though. "See, you're still running away."

"Kriti," I huff, an edge of desperation in my voice. "If you want me to look at the situation practically, let's do it. I'm thirty-one, she's twenty-one. A decade apart, for god's sake. We don't really know each other, not in a way that counts. Not in the way you need to when you're...involved with someone."

I take a breath, glance briefly at Kriti, then back to the road. "We're two people who find each other physically attractive, who enjoy verbal sparring, and who've somehow found a measure of comfort in each other's company. That's it."

The words hang in the car for a moment. I swallow, realizing the weight of the next ones.

"She's the damn Princess of England," I blurt out. "An internationally known public figure. And me, I'm an American marine. Dating her means losing any shot at future missions. That would leave me jobless, afloat without a purpose in life."

I let out a sharp breath, feeling the bitter taste of reality. "And then, to top it all off, I'd find myself in a relationship scrutinized by the entire world. Look at me, Kriti. Do I strike you as someone who enjoys attention?"

Kriti says nothing, watching me quietly.

"So, am I supposed to take this massive risk for the slim chance of finding love? With all my Marine training, all my practical thinking, it's a negative, Kriti. It's just...it's not practical."

My words fill the car, hanging heavy and undeniable between us. Even as I say them, a part of me aches at the harsh truth they carry. But they're real, and they're mine, and as much as I wish things were different, this is the reality I have to live in.

"Wow," Kriti finally breaks the silence. Her voice is an odd mix of awe and amusement. "I never thought the tough Marine would be the one scared out of her mind."

A flash of anger burns my cheeks, but it quickly cools.

I recognize her teasing for what it is - a friend trying to do right by Penelope. Even if it means ripping into me. I've never been good at being the target of jokes, but I swallow down the bitter taste and let her have her fun. After all, I'm just as frustrated with myself.

Why do you always have to be so damn complicated, Jessica?

I know where my answer lies. It's hidden deep, tucked beneath years of heartache and tragedy.

It's in the dust of the fallen twin towers, in my military bearing, in the hard glint in the eyes of Afghan girls just trying to make it through one more day.

I yearn to break free from my past, from my demons, but they've got a stranglehold on me. And the worst part is, I don't want to drag Penelope into my hell. She doesn't deserve my nightmares, my baggage. That's my cross to bear, and likely, to be buried under.

The skyline of Los Angeles begins to peek over the horizon, and it hits me that the end of this journey is near. This trip that's been filled with more laughs, tears, and heart-to-hearts than I've had in a decade will soon be just a memory.

I can't help but wonder what kind of memory it'll be. A fond one? A regret? Only time will tell. But one thing's for sure - I'll remember this road trip for the rest of my life.

Penelope

I'm perched on the edge of my hotel bed, alone with the echoing silence of the empty room. The buzzing city of Los Angeles sprawls beyond my window, but it feels a world away. I am still staring at the unopened message from mother. My fingers hover over the screen, poised with indecision.

The sudden ring of a call diverts my attention, the bright screen flashing with Alexa's name. Alexa, lead singer of Pink Poison, the unabashed rebel. My heart sinks a fraction, a reminder of another unresolved thread in my life.

"Penelope! Tell me you've arrived in L.A." Alexa's voice is a jolt of energy, vibrant and loud, demanding my attention.

"Yes, Alexa, I'm here," I reply, attempting to match her enthusiasm. But exhaustion colors my words, hinting at the truth I'm about to reveal.

"Great! So, you're coming to the listening party tonight?" she asks, excitement woven into her question.

A heavy sigh escapes me before I can stop it. "Alexa, I'm sorry," I begin, steeling myself for the fallout, "I don't think I can make it tonight. The drive was... draining."

I brace for her reaction. There's a pause, and then, "But Penelope, you have to come!" she exclaims, desperation threading through her words, "This is the perfect way to stick it to your monarchy, to show your mother you won't be controlled."

The sentiment should resonate with me. But instead, it feels hollow, a tinny echo of my previous rebellious spirit.

"Alexa," I say quietly, "I'm just...really tired."

Her response is immediate and sharp. "I had already informed my team that you'd be arriving. We had already decided on poses for the red carpet, and a great joint media statement from both of us. You being at the party was supposed to help me bag the world's attention, Penelope," she says, her voice hardened.

The candid admission stings, but it doesn't surprise me. In this world of fame and fortune, everyone has an agenda. My being royalty is both a boon and a curse.

Instead of getting angry, guilt settles in the pit of my stomach. I'm about to break things off with Alexa, after all. I owe her something.

"Okay, Alexa," I concede, a plan forming in my mind. "I

can't come to the party. But I'll help you. I'll post about the album, make a video listening to it. We can even be seen around L.A. together. It'll be my first public appearance since I arrived."

Alexa is silent for a moment. "You'd do that?" she asks, her voice softer, doubtful.

"Yes," I answer, trying to reassure her, "And I'll visit you later tonight. We can talk."

Her response is far from enthusiastic, but she agrees.

I lean back against the plush hotel bed, my gaze lost in the high-ceilinged opulence of the room.

People truly are curious creatures, I muse. They wear masks, dance to the tune of pretenses until something doesn't go their way. And when that happens, they peel off their disguise, revealing the bare, often ugly truth beneath.

A wry smile tugs at the corner of my lips. I consider myself lucky. Lucky to have seen Alexa's true colors before I ended up dancing to her tune, caught in a glittering, but false symphony of false pretenses.

Pushing myself off the bed, I walk over to the floor-to-ceiling window, my eyes tracing the sprawling expanse of Beverly Hills. Nestled amidst lush greenery, luxurious villas dot the rolling hills, each grander than the last. A picture-perfect snapshot of wealth and glamor, and hiding beneath it, a world teeming with facades and shallow relations.

A wave of melancholy washes over me as I realize the relationships here aren't much different from the ones back home in the UK.

It's the same story, different setting. I've always been a ticket to privilege, a stepping stone to greater heights. From my childhood, I've found myself surrounded by those who saw me more as a golden ticket than a friend, their affections conditional, their loyalty questionable. All except one.

Kriti.

She was, is, the only one who saw past the royal, to the girl underneath. Her friendship is one of the few things I treasure in this whirlpool of royal obligations and public expectations.

And Jessica…

No. I push that thought away. I've closed that chapter, haven't I? That was just a fleeting moment, a break in the clouds. I'm back in the storm now.

Deciding to escape into slumber, I collapse onto the bed, burying my face into the soft pillow. Sleep, my old friend, offers me the perfect escape from the haunting silence of the room and the turmoil of my thoughts.

But even in the realm of dreams, I can't escape her. Jessica's face comes unbidden to my mind. Her guarded smile, her intense gaze, they follow me, haunt me. Like an echo, she lingers, in the corners of my dreams, a shadow I can't shake off. I'm ensnared in a labyrinth of dreams and desires, where every path leads back to her and every road away feels colder and lonelier.

Alexa

The regal confines of my Calabasas mansion are closing in on me, the luxuriously appointed rooms feeling stiflingly narrow. I'm pacing the floor, a restless tiger trapped in a gilded cage. My fists clench and unclench at my sides, the usually sparkly diamond-studded knuckle rings digging into my palms. This mansion, once the scene of raucous parties and wild nights, is now my prison.

The world I once swayed with my voice, the world I once dominated with my sassy lyrics and pulsating beats, is now turning on its axis.

It's not just about the songs or the concerts anymore. It's a goddamn whirlpool of international politics, and I've been tossed in without a life vest. The fickleness of the Americans is suffocating, their loyalty as volatile as their ever-changing music charts. I am a traitor, they say.

Why? Because I, a Russian, dared to keep my mouth shut on my homeland's actions. Hypocrisy stings more than a venomous snake bite.

My parents, the only constant in my mercurial life, have been deported already. Our home, our sanctuary, ransacked and violated by government agents. All the intimate remnants of our life treated as mere evidence, handled by strangers with rubber gloves. A shudder courses through me. I feel exposed, naked.

Even my own band, 'Pink Poison,' my co-conspirators in all the musical madness, is looking to replace me. The stage that once felt like a second home now feels as distant as a fading dream. It feels like I'm standing on a crumbling precipice, with my life falling apart brick by brick, carried away by the relentless tide of public opinion.

A memory flickers in my mind, like a faintly glowing ember in the darkness.

The whispered offer made by the stern-faced KGB handlers, their icy eyes full of promise. A safe haven. A reward that would keep me drowning in luxury.

My initial denial seems laughable now. In the face of the storm raging through my life, their offer appears as a lifeboat.

I had banked on Penelope. The blue-blooded princess. The one whose slightest whim could change the public's perception. She was my lifeline, my ticket to claw back into the limelight, to salvage my career.

But she turned me down, her refusal echoing in my ears like mocking laughter. Her rejection was a push, propelling me towards the edge.

A dark thought blooms in the back of my mind.

If Penelope, the darling of the tabloids, the charming princess, chose to leave me in my hour of need, why should I stand by her?

The thought solidifies into a decision. Resolute and determined, I dial the secure line. The secure line that was my insurance, my emergency exit. "I'm in," I state, my voice resonating with a sense of finality. I relay the details of Penelope's planned late-night visit, laying the trap, baiting the hook. I listen to the handler's curt instructions, each word etching into my mind.

"Make it look real, and leave no traces of all this leading up to me," I demand, my voice barely above a whisper.

As I disconnect, I'm swept with a rush of adrenaline, a potent cocktail of fear, desperation, and vengeance. It's intoxicating, more potent than any drug I've ever indulged in. My reflection in the full-length mirror stares back at me, fiery and unbroken. I'm not just Alexa, the singer. I'm Alexa, the player in a high stakes game of survival. And I'm ready to play, ready to win, ready to reclaim my life.

Penelope

In the dead silence of midnight, the suite feels more like a museum exhibit than a lived-in space. I stand in front of the mirror, observing my reflection. It's been a long time since I've dressed to kill, but today, I'm in the mood for a bit of drama. A smirk plays on my lips.

Oh, the things we do for a bit of juvenile fun.

I've chosen a dress that does wonders for my curves, the royal blue silk hugging my body like a second skin. The neckline plunges daringly, and the high slit allows a generous view of my legs. My chestnut hair cascades in loose waves down my shoulders, a splash of vibrant contrast against the blue. I add a pair of sky-high heels for good measure. One look at me and no one would guess I'm a princess.

Tonight, I'm a femme fatale, a woman on a mission.

I step out of my room and into the living area, the lights of the LA skyline twinkling through the expansive windows. Kriti is sprawled out on one of the plush couches, engrossed in some show on Netflix. Jessica, on the other hand, is curled up on an armchair, a look of surprise blooming on her face as I make my grand entrance.

"I'm off to meet Alexa," I announce, delighting in the sudden tension that fills the room. I catch Jessica's weird look, a delightful mix of shock and confusion.

Ah, victory. Just as I had planned.

A small part of me feels guilty for the mischief, but then again, all's fair in love and war, isn't it?

"How are you getting there?" Kriti questions, her gaze flitting between me and Jessica.

"She's sending a car for me," I reply nonchalantly, enjoying the undercurrents of jealousy that are starting to become more pronounced. Jessica offers to drop me off, but I shrug it off, the thrill of control too irresistible to resist.

"You shouldn't be going alone at this time," Kriti voices her concern, her gaze filled with worry. Jessica chimes in, cautiously agreeing with Kriti, careful not to overstep her boundaries.

My smile fades, replaced with an expression of determined resolution. "I'm not a damsel in distress, ladies," I retort, the shadows in the room casting an ominous tone to my words. As a princess, I've lived a life wrapped in cotton wool, but as Penelope, I'm made of sterner stuff. "I can handle myself. It's just a friendly visit." I stress the last part, my gaze never wavering from theirs.

There's a knock on the suite door, punctuating my statement. My ride's here. As I stride towards the door, the feeling of foreboding threatens to consume me. I push it aside, channeling the courage that's been my armor all these years.

The drive to Alexa's house feels like an impromptu tour of a Los Angeles shrouded in night.

Lights twinkle like fallen stars on the empty streets, a quiet symphony of silence reigning over the city. The man driving me speaks little, his stony expression unchanging as we navigate through the maze of roads. His silence offers me an opportunity to be alone with my thoughts.

A wave of nostalgia washes over me as I think of Jessica. She had been my constant companion during the past seven days. Despite the turbulence of our relationship, she had been there for me. My heart aches a bit, a longing for her familiar presence. Part of me had wanted her to drop me off at Alexa's, but my ego, that obstinate little part of me, had won.

As the car pulls into the driveway of Alexa's mansion, my heart flutters with nervous anticipation. This is the first time I'm truly alone - no Jessica, no Kriti, no bodyguards. It's just me, the rogue royal, and I love the thrill of it. Alexa and I could have fun tonight, one last hurrah before we part ways.

Perhaps it's not the wisest idea, but then again, since when have I been known for wise decisions?

As we drive up the winding road, I absentmindedly scroll through the news on my phone. A breaking news headline makes my heart lurch - British troops have landed in Ukraine to assist in the fight against Russia. I feel a pang of anxiety

- the world outside my little bubble is a mess, and I'm here, indulging in my personal dramas.

A smaller news piece catches my eye – Alexa Ivanova's career teetering on the brink as her silence, and her subtle support to Russia, has incited public outrage. Industry bigwigs had boycotted her album listening party. I feel a stab of regret. I should have been there.

She's my friend, after all.

My mind spirals into an abyss of 'what-ifs.' If there were no wars, would Jessica have chosen a different path? Would she have been with me? The thought makes my heart flutter with a painful longing. I chastise myself for entertaining such fantasies. Jessica's chapter is closed.

The car lurches to a stop, bringing me back to reality. The grand entrance of Alexa's mansion looms ahead, the towering structure a stark contrast against the inky night. The quietude of the scene sends a chill down my spine, the feeling of foreboding returning tenfold. I take a deep breath, steeling myself for what's to come.

Jessica

The first inkling of unease creeps into me the moment Penelope sashays out of her room, all dolled up for her midnight escapade. She is beaming, radiant even, but there's something about her nonchalant disregard for safety that sets my senses on high alert.

It's not jealousy – I won't allow myself that indulgence, not when there's so much more at stake. No, it's that hard-earned instinct, drilled into my very marrow during my marine days, whispering warnings.

Kriti is sitting next to me on the plush couch, eyes glued to the Netflix dramedy flickering on the big screen. But my gaze is on the glass door, where Penelope's shadow just disappeared. The LA skyline beyond glimmers with a million stars, hiding the beasts of danger beneath its glamorous façade.

Something is not right.

The sensation grips me, cold and relentless. I can almost taste the metallic tang of unease.

I've spent too long on the battlefield to ignore this sensation, too long surviving in the wild to dismiss it. An inner voice whispers, urging me to act. Because if I don't, Penelope, the woman who is more than just a protectee to me now, could be in danger.

"Kriti." I turn towards her, my words slicing through the comedic dialogue blaring from the TV. Her attention shifts towards me, an eyebrow raised in curiosity. "There's something I've been thinking about."

She hits the pause button, eyes curious. "What is it?"

"It's Alexa," I start, my words filling the room, painting a picture of the uncertainty brewing inside me. "She seemed too miffed about Penelope skipping the album launch party. More so than her realization that Penelope isn't as interested in her as she was."

Kriti ponders over my words, tilting her head slightly, considering. "She's Russian, isn't she? Her career's spiraling downward, and yet, instead of prioritizing her image, she is more concerned about Penelope. And why did she insist on meeting her so late at night?"

Kriti narrows her eyes, digesting the implications. After a pause, she ventures, "You think this could be...dangerous?"

"I can't shake off the feeling, Kriti," I admit. "And I am not taking any chances."

Before Kriti can interject, I am already pulling out my phone, dialing a number memorized by heart.

It rings once, twice before there's an answer. "Hey, it's me, Jessica," I greet, my voice a practiced calm. "I need a favor. I need call details of a certain someone. Can you help me out?" The tension hangs in the air as I wait for a response.

∞ ∞ ∞

The silence of the room is punctured by the steady click of keys on my laptop as I begin to dissect the call logs. I'm a woman on a mission, driven by an instinct that is as much a part of me as my own skin.

Kriti's voice breaks through the intensity of my focus, an unexpected lightness in her tone. "Please tell me you're not doing all this out of jealousy, Jessica. Penelope won't appreciate this."

I huff a laugh at the absurdity of her suggestion, glancing at her from the corner of my eye. "If I were acting out of jealousy, Alexa would be six feet under right now."

The humor doesn't quite erase the tension that has insinuated itself into the suite. I return my attention to the task at hand, sifting through the details that my CIA contact had sent over.

Most of the calls are to numbers that I can immediately associate with various PR companies and talent agencies. There's one to a sushi restaurant, another to a vocal coach, all mundane calls.

But then, I notice something odd, something that has my gut clenching with unease.

"Kriti," I speak, my tone sharper than intended. I lean back in my chair, and she shifts closer, curiosity piqued. "There are a few calls made to a hidden number." I spin my laptop around to show her.

Her eyes scan the screen, confusion crinkling her brow. "But why would she call a hidden number? That's…weird."

The cogs in my mind start to turn, the unease transmuting into suspicion. I don't know what Alexa is playing at, but I have a bad feeling that Penelope is caught up in it.

Inwardly, I wince at the thought of what I must do next. I need to call in a favor, but it's not going to be easy.

"Alright," I sigh, closing the laptop and pulling out my phone once again. The contact flashes on my screen - Jacob, a CIA officer and the man who'd made me an offer that could change the course of my life.

I hear the click as he answers. "Jessica," his voice comes across, professional as always. "To what do I owe this pleasure?"

"Jacob," I say, my voice gruff. "I need your help." I give him the number that Alexa's been calling. I don't tell him why, but I don't have to.

He's silent for a moment, then says, "I'll see what I can do."

With that, I end the call. The silence in the suite is deafening. The tension, palpable. Kriti and I sit in silence, our shared anxiety hanging in the air. All we can do now is wait.

Penelope

The sound of my high heels echo through the mansion, bouncing off the high ceilings and ornate walls. Despite the grandeur of the place, it's eerily quiet, like an abandoned cathedral. No staff milling about, no guards standing watch. The only other presence is the silent driver who escorted me to this fortress of solitude.

I can hear my own breaths, too loud in the stillness, and it sets my heart to racing. Why the devil am I so jittery? I mentally shrug it off. I suppose it's the lack of familiar faces, the lack of my usual entourage. It's not often that this princess finds herself unescorted.

As I'm led into the living hall, I see her - Alexa.

Despite the night's hour, she looks as though she's ready for a high-fashion photoshoot. A plaid skirt cinched at her waist, a corset teasing the imagination under a figure-hugging blazer left open. She's a sight for sore eyes, but underneath that allure, I spot telltale signs of strain - swollen eyes, shadows cast deep under them. Evidence of a broken heart? Or something far worse?

Our greeting is warm, a hug that lingers, carrying an undercurrent of tension. We pull away, her dark eyes looking into mine. "I'm glad you came, Penelope," she says, her voice velvety.

"I couldn't miss the chance to see you, Alexa," I reply, forcing a lightness into my voice that I don't feel. I deflect the tension by asking about her album launch. Her response is heavy with sarcasm.

"Oh, it was marvelous," she drawls, a bitter smile on her face. "The press barely showed up, and most of the industry decided to give it a miss. It was just wonderful."

My heart clenches at her words. "I'm so sorry, Alexa," I manage, holding her gaze. "Is there anything I can do to help?"

Her eyes soften for a moment. "I appreciate the sentiment, Penelope." Her gaze drifts to the side, as she changes the subject. "What will you have to drink?"

"Whatever you're having is fine," I respond. But then, a new thought strikes me. "Where is everyone? Your staff, security? It's unusually quiet here."

She gives a short, harsh laugh. "I sent everyone home after the farce of the launch. I just wanted to be alone."

"So, there's no one here at all?" I can't help but press. "No security?"

"Mathew's around," she replies, referring to the driver who brought me here. A single security guard for a mansion of this size? The thought sends an uneasy chill down my spine.

My heartbeat echoes in my ears, each thump a pounding reminder of the silence in the mansion. I tread across the large, shadowed living hall, gravitating towards Alexa and the promise of warmth radiating from her. Her fingers wrap around two glasses, a bottle of whiskey poised to fill them.

"You look stunning, Alexa. Better than I remember," I say, trying to smooth over the tension of our meeting.

She snorts lightly, her gaze never leaving the glasses she's filling, "Bags under my eyes? They're all the rage here in LA, didn't you know?"

Her words hang in the air, a reminder of the weight she's carrying. I watch her, my eyes softening. "I can only imagine how hard this is for you," I begin, "Everyone turning against you. The hatred from an entire country just because you're from a place we're at odds with…"

Her movements freeze momentarily, then resume, her grip on the bottle tighter. She slams the bottle on the counter. "No one understands. They're taking away my livelihood, going after my family… all because I chose to remain silent. Can't I just make my music without having to weigh in on politics?"

I sigh, feeling the echoes of my own frustrations in her words. "I know. When you're in the limelight, when you hold influence, people expect you to use it. People expect me to make statements about everything too. I haven't even said anything about the war yet, but they're all over me."

"Your mother though," she shoots back, "I heard she's been supportive of sending troops to Russia. That could lead us straight into World War III. How do you feel about that?"

Caught off guard, I remain silent for a moment. "I'm not in authority there, Alexa. I'm not my mother. But I will tell you this: I don't see you as the enemy. You're my friend."

Her laughter fills the room, a bitter and hollow sound. "We used to be more than friends when we stayed at Highgrove. Things changed during the road trip, didn't they?"

"Something did change," I admit, "But it's complicated. I'm trying to figure out what I want in life."

Her eyes narrow, scrutinizing me. "And it's not me?"

The vulnerability in her voice tugs at me, so I step forward and hug her. "I just need some time, Alexa. It could be you, I just... I'm not sure."

Our heart-to-heart is abruptly interrupted by a loud crash reverberating through the mansion. I pull back, fear making my heart pound. "What was that?" I ask, turning to Alexa.

Wide-eyed and as scared as I am, Alexa yells out for Mathew to check the noise. We wait in the living hall, silence enveloping us like a shroud.

Sitting there, my heart hammering in my chest, I regret leaving Jessica behind. This was supposed to be a personal meeting, an attempt to patch things up. But right now, I can't shake off the feeling of something sinister lurking in the shadows.

Chapter Thirteen

Jessica

Swathed in the raw undercurrents of dread, I catapult myself into the Range Rover, the slam of the door echoing my frantic pulse. Tires screech as I pull off with lightning speed, ripping away from the safety of our suite into the black maw of the L.A. night.

As the cityscape blurs by, I dial Maria.

My voice, usually measured and calm, betrays a hint of the fear gnawing at my insides. "Alexa's been in touch with a known KGB agent. There's a plot at work here; Penelope's in danger."

Maria doesn't miss a beat, her voice steady as she confirms, "I'm en route to Alexa's mansion. Got a few toys with me that might come in handy.

"Informed the Brits?" she questions, but I cut her off, my words sharp with urgency.

"No, we can't risk it. We don't know who might be compromised. Plus, they could panic, pull some idiotic move. We don't have time for that. We need to handle this ourselves."

The call ends but my fear doesn't.

It gnaws, it claws, it pulls at the frayed edges of my

composure. For the first time, I am afraid, genuinely terrified. I can feel my heart battering against my rib cage, a relentless drum pounding out an ominous rhythm. A quick glance at my smartwatch confirms my fear - a heart rate of 180.

A cold sweat breaks out on my skin, making my grip on the steering wheel slick. Why am I scared? I've been in more perilous situations, with hundreds of lives hanging in the balance and my pulse has never wavered above a calm 100. I've been a human shield in the middle of a firefight, I've dove headfirst into insurgent territory and came out unscathed. But now, the possibility of losing Penelope... the mere thought threatens to shatter me.

I draw in shaky breaths, forcing myself to focus on the road ahead. Nothing can happen to Penelope. I won't allow it. I repeat it like a mantra, each word embedding itself into my consciousness, trying to exorcise the specter of fear that's taken hold of me. As I tear through the Los Angeles night, one thought reigns supreme, acting as a beacon in the turmoil of my terror - I won't let anything happen to Penelope.

Penelope

The terror begins with sound—a cacophony of screams and crashes that reverberate through the otherwise serene mansion. The noise descends from the floor above, each thunderous boom causing the crystal chandelier above us to shiver, sending shards of light skittering around the opulent hall. The fear is visceral, paralyzing me to the spot next to Alexa.

Then, a terrifying sight tears through my stupor—Matthew's body appears at the top of the spiral staircase, collapsing over each step, before landing at the base with a sickening thud. The vacant look in his eyes, the spreading pool of crimson around his chest—it's horrifyingly clear that he's been shot.

My screams pierce the silence, reverberating off the polished marble walls. But my cries are drowned out by the ominous crunch of boots on the staircase. Three men, faces hidden behind black masks, burst into view. Dressed in a uniform of darkness, assault rifles swing from their shoulders. The laser sights—cold, red beams—are aimed straight at Alexa and me, holding us hostage in a terrifying limbo.

A primal fear clutches at my chest, but I move.

Survival instinct takes over, prompting me to snatch my phone from my bag. My fingers, slick with sweat, punch in Jessica's number. My shaking hands shove the phone between the cushions of the nearby couch, just as the men advance on us.

Their steps echo ominously in the silent room. From their hands, they wield cans, releasing a disorienting spray into the air. It takes only seconds for the room to swim before my eyes, the edges blurring as a weighty fog descends over my consciousness.

My limbs are leaden, my eyelids drooping.

My world blurs, the imposing figures of the masked men the last sight I can discern before darkness starts to creep in. And right before it claims me, a pang of regret stabs through the fear. I wish I'd read the message from Mum, the one I've been deliberately avoiding since yesterday. A wish that lingers even as the darkness engulfs me completely.

Chapter Fourteen

Jessica

T he mansion looms ominously in the distance as I park the Range Rover a few hundred feet away. Nestled atop a hill, it looks more like a fortress than a home. A low, stone wall marks the boundary, separating this property from the rest of the world.

As I step out of the vehicle, my phone buzzes in my pocket. It's a text from Jacob. The message opens to reveal a satellite image of the mansion with potential entry points circled in red. In my hand, I clutch an M18 gun, its weight a familiar comfort. Behind me, Maria mirrors my actions. A bag filled with high-tech surveillance and military gear is slung over my shoulder.

We crouch together near the mansion, discussing our approach. Maria, ever the strategist, points to the golf course that stretches below the mansion's hill. The open area provides a clear, albeit risky, path to the mansion's backyard.

If we descend to the golf course, we can circle back up the slope and infiltrate the mansion from the rear. The idea is risky, but it's the best we've got. Jacob's influence can get us past the security of the golf course.

Minutes later, Maria and I find ourselves navigating up the

hill, the mansion's stone boundary wall looming above us. We crouch, hidden in the foliage, and I pull out my night vision goggles.

I scan the mansion, my heart pounding a relentless tattoo in my chest. Broken glass glitters ominously from a first-floor window, a silent testament to a violent struggle.

My gaze travels down, catching sight of a scene that causes my blood to run cold. Through the partially drawn curtains of the pool-facing glass doors, I see three men in the living room. They are restraining Alexa and Penelope, their movements brutal as they tie and gag them. The sight fuels my adrenaline, sharpening my senses.

As I'm watching this horrifying scene unfold, my phone buzzes again. A glance at the screen reveals Penelope's name. A rush of relief and admiration sweeps through me. Somehow, she has managed to call me, to alert me of her location. I answer the call, muting myself. Maria and I listen intently as the conversation of the men inside the mansion filters through.

"Heard the truck's due in fifteen minutes," one of the men grunts in a thick Russian accent. The casual banter that follows is chilling in its callousness.

"We've got plenty of time," another man replies, his voice laced with crude humor. "Maybe we can have some fun with these pretty ladies before they get shipped off."

The crude laughter that follows turns my stomach. I can feel Maria's silent fury beside me.

I disconnect the call and start planning the rescue mission.

"Storm the backyard?" Maria ventures, scanning the dense line of trees separating us from the mansion.

"Too open. They'd see us coming."

Maria nods, chewing her lower lip. "A frontal assault? Taking them out from here?" She gestures at our concealed position behind the wall.

I shake my head, frustrated. "We can't guarantee clean shots. Plus, Penelope and Alexa are in there." My voice drops to a whisper at the thought of a bullet hitting either of them. "We can't risk it."

We fall into a tense silence, the weight of our predicament pressing in from all sides. I can feel the seconds ticking by, each one a beat too fast, too loud.

"We could use smoke bombs," Maria suggests, her eyes brightening at the idea. "Create a diversion, use the confusion to get in."

My mind races through the possible outcomes, but each one ends in a probability I don't want to contemplate. "It's too unpredictable. They could use Penelope and Alexa as shields...or worse."

My voice trails off as another idea forms in my mind. "We need more information," I declare, my tone resolute. "We need to know how many men are inside, their positions..."

Maria's eyes narrow in thought, then widen with realization. "Jacob," she breathes out. "He could get us live satellite imagery. We could use the heat signatures to track their movements."

I nod, impressed by her quick thinking. "That's it." I pull out my phone, dialing Jacob's number.

As I relay our plan, Maria keeps her gaze trained on the mansion, her hands restlessly fidgeting with the strap of her bag.

"Once we have their locations, one of us enters through the broken window on the first floor," I lay out the plan, eyes fixed on the layout displayed on my phone, "while the other creates a diversion in the backyard."

"So, split up?" Maria queries, uncertainty edging her tone.

I nod, eyes meeting hers. "Two vantage points. Better coverage."

Maria purses her lips, considering. After a moment, she nods, determination hardening her features. "Let's do it."

With that, we fall into action, our preparations made with efficiency born from years of training. As I wait for Jacob's response, a sense of anticipation fills the air, crackling with tension.

My heart thuds in my chest as Jacob's voice cuts through the tense silence. "Negative, Jess. I can't get you that feed. It will draw the wrong kind of attention."

"But Jacob-" I begin, desperation leaking into my voice.

"I need more information, Jess," he interrupts, his voice carrying a note of finality that brooks no argument. "Tell me what's going on. Who are we trying to save?"

I let out a sigh, my hand clenching tightly around my phone. "I can't, Jacob," I whisper, and with that, I disconnect the call.

Maria looks over, questioning. I shake my head, disappointment sinking heavy in my chest. "No satellite feed. We're flying blind."

Maria blinks, apprehension flickering in her eyes. "Jessica-"

I cut her off before she can voice her concerns. "We don't have time, Maria." My voice is steady, resolute, despite the fear gnawing at the pit of my stomach. "If I fail, you storm in and take them out. Even if..." My voice falters at the thought, the unspoken ending hanging heavy in the air.

Swallowing hard, I climb over the low wall, my shoes

sinking into the soft grass. Silently, I creep along the hedges, my heart pounding in my chest. I reach the first floor window, the remnants of the ropes they used to climb in still hanging loose.

I stop, crouched beneath the window, listening.

All I can hear is the distant rustle of leaves and the eerie quiet of the mansion. Taking a deep breath, I hoist myself up, using the ropes to ease my way in. I drop to the floor with a soft thud, quickly hiding behind a heavy four-poster bed.

I barely have time to steady my breathing when the bedroom door creaks open. My heart leaps into my throat as a man enters the room. He walks over to the window, peering out into the night.

Seizing the moment, I spring into action.

Like a shadow, I cross the distance between us, my hand clamping over his mouth, my forearm locking around his throat. He struggles, his nails digging into my arm, but I tighten my hold, my body pressing him against the wall.

After a gut-wrenching minute, his body goes slack.

His rifle slips from his grasp and I snatch it up, casting aside my M18. Muffled voices reach me from beyond the bedroom, and I move closer to the door. The hallway is empty.

Across the way, a large potted plant stands in an alcove. Perfect for cover.

I hurry over, crouching behind the plant. From this vantage point, I can see the staircase leading to the living room. Three men circle around Penelope and Alexa, their unconscious forms sprawled on the floor. I curse under my breath. If only Maria was here.

The thought of calling her flits through my mind, but the risk of one of the men coming upstairs in the meantime chills my blood.

Glancing around, my gaze falls on the potted plant. With a sudden clarity, I know what I have to do.

Bracing myself, I give the plant a gentle nudge. It teeters for a moment on the edge of the alcove, then crashes to the ground, splintering into pieces and sending dirt flying in all directions. The loud crash reverberates through the quiet mansion, the perfect distraction I need.

I squint, watching the men look up at the source of the noise. I know they can't see me, but I can see them.

"Come on, bastards, take the bait."

One of them points towards the backyard, towards the swimming pool and the outer wall behind which Maria waits with her M18. The men are engaged in a heated debate. Muffled Russian filters up to the first floor, and I can only understand fragments of their conversation.

"Ambush"... "Idiot"... "Needs to be here".

They're discussing how to inspect the source of the noise.

Suddenly, one of them screams at the top of his lungs, looking straight up at the staircase and the hallway.

"Dimitri! Dimitri, you fucking idiot, is that you?"

Dimitri does not respond because he's just been strangled to death by the forearm of an ex-US marine.

Come up and look for your boy, idiot!

After another round of animated conversation, the men decide on a plan. One of them cautiously makes his way up the staircase, his gun pointed in front of him, while another exits through the glass door into the backyard.

"One for me, one for Maria. But what about the third one?"

We'll have to neutralize our preys without making any noise or we risk scaring the third guy and provoking him into doing something crazy. I just hope Maria is thinking the same.

I press my back against the little wall that forms the alcove, hiding my entire body from the view of anyone coming up the staircase.

I will have to act based on noise.

The man is a skilled operative and doesn't make any sound. I have no eyes on him and no way to find out how close he is.

I take a deep breath.

This might end up in a Mexican stand-off.

It will all depend on who can fire first.

Then, I hear it: a short-lived scream, more like a screech, emanating from the backyard. It reverberates off the walls of the mansion, piercing the eerie silence.

"Fuck!"

Hoping the sound will have distracted him for a bit, I jump out of my hiding place and find the man aiming his assault rifle straight at me.

I roll to the side, take aim, and pull the trigger. He fires too, but he's not as experienced as I thought he was.

He doesn't roll.

My bullets pierce his chest, and he collapses onto the ground. His bullets find my shin bone as I'm rolling to the side. The pain is nothing compared to the urgency I'm feeling. The third man must have been alerted. He could be in a state of panic, likely to do something stupid.

I run to the staircase and find the man with his arm around Penelope's neck. His eyes are bloodshot and wide with fear behind his mask.

Penelope is awake, and tears stream down her cheeks as I

stare in horror at the scene in front of me.

"My orders were to kidnap this bitch, and if I'm caught," he screams in thick Russian, "to kill the bitch. This is for Russia..." I see his fingers slide across the body of the gun, coming to rest on the trigger.

Years of marine training and battlefield experience melt away as I watch the woman I love about to die in front of me.

A muffled gunshot from a silencer makes a faint, whizzing noise, and the man crumbles to the ground before he can do anything for Russia.

I break down as I see Maria appear out of the shadows, through the glass door, and stand over the man to check for his pulse. She's in a commando position.

She has just saved the love of my life.

Chapter Fifteen

Penelope

I wake up in a strange, dim room that feels about as welcoming as a crypt. There's barely any furniture; just a tiny lamp that seems to be on its last legs, a table that looks like it has seen better days, and a rickety chair tucked under it. And then there's this shabby couch, hugging a grimy wall. It's the kind of room that screams 'bad decisions were made here.'

But the one bright spot is that I'm alive. Against all odds, I've got my name in the 'still living' column.

I try to get up, but my head is spinning like a roulette wheel. Okay, standing is off the menu. Scratch that. Let's start with something simpler. My phone. Now where the hell did I leave that thing?

Before I can dive deep into the hide-and-seek game with my phone, a figure shuffles out of the shadows.

She's carrying a Cheshire Cat grin that's bright enough to light up this dank room.

It's Jessica.

Her hair is hastily bundled into a messy bun that's hanging on by a prayer. There are dark circles under her eyes that tell tales of sleepless nights. And then there's the bandage wrapped around her knee, that instills a sudden feeling of dread in me. It's quite a sight, this woman.

But in the mess that we find ourselves in, Jessica is a sight for sore eyes. She hobbles over and I watch her, rooted to the spot.

It's like one of those surreal moments in life where everything slows down, and it's just you and this other person in your bubble. She sits next to me on the bed, her knee protesting with a pop. Then, before I know it, I'm being enveloped in a bear hug.

I can feel her warmth seep into me, grounding me. And just like that, the spinning stops. It's just us, hugging each other in the middle of this shithole.

And you know what, in that moment, it feels like the safest place in the world.

"You know, you finally pulled off that thing you were supposed to be doing all along...keeping me in the land of the living," I manage to sputter, a giggle escaping my lips.

The sound of Jessica's laughter echoes mine. And in the hazy light of the lamplight, I notice something unusual – teardrops making their shimmering descent from Jessica's eyes. Or rather, miracles veiled as teardrops.

"Yeah, I guess I finally managed to do my actual job instead of... other activities not specified in my contract," she retorts.

My eyebrows shoot up in surprise. "Oh? And what might those be?"

Her voice is steady but weighted with unspoken emotions. "Falling in love with you, for one."

Silence cloaks us, heavy and palpable. I struggle to process the unexpected revelation.

Could my drowsy mind have played tricks on me?

"Could you... could you say that again?" I ask, leaning in closer to her, my ear almost touching her lips.

With a smirk, she repeats, "I've fallen in love with you, Princess."

Pretending to be still lost, I keep the charade going. "There's a lot of noise in this room, Jess, I might need that one more time."

Before she can respond, she's pulling me into her arms, our lips meeting in a kiss that speaks louder than words. I return the gesture, because, who am I kidding? I'm head over heels for her too.

The world fades away as we remain entangled in our intimate embrace. When we finally break apart, our hands remain interlocked.

"What made you change your mind?" I ask, genuinely curious.

"A handful of Russians and a batshit crazy singer," she answers, leaning her forehead against mine.

"Who knew? All it takes is a potential threat to my life for you to develop a sense of humor."

"And all it takes is me charging to your rescue for you to still be alive," she retorts, the banter between us familiar and comforting.

"Last I checked, it was Maria who made it to me first."

"Guess who put the pieces together and led her there?"

I can't help but tease her. "Still dodging my question, marine. What made you change your mind? Are you over your thrill-seeking ways of courting danger?"

Jessica takes a deep breath, shuffling closer. "I realized

that risking my life to save you was far more rewarding than putting my life on the line for the country."

"Traitor!" I shoot back playfully, a grin plastered on my face.

"I've done my bit for the country. Now, I want to focus on keeping you safe – from threats, from all your issues, from the world."

Before I can process her words, our lips meet again, the kiss so intense it leaves me breathless. I gasp, "How can a simple kiss leave me breathless?"

"When it's with the right person, it can be...breathtaking."

"Where are we? And what happened to your leg?" I ask, my face snuggled against her chest.

"We are in a CIA safe house, and this little thing on my leg will be another scar on my body, one that tells the story of me saving a very special person in my life, along with Afreen and Sasha."

I smile, and then suddenly realize that Alexa is nowhere to be seen.

"What happened to Alexa? Where is she?"

"Under CIA custody. She has quite a bit of explaining to do."

"Wait, what? Why?"

"Turns out, she was the reason the Russians found you. She was working with the KGB."

The revelation hits me like a truck. Alexa, who had looked terrified when those intruders had barged in, was actually working against us?

"But why? Why would she..."

"It's a long story, baby," Jessica interrupts, saying

something more that is lost on me as my mind spins over the fact that she just called me 'baby'.

I shut her mouth by kissing her again, and after a few more minutes of breathless kissing, I let her go and ask about Mum. "Does she know?"

"Yes," Jessica replies.

"And?"

"I think you should read that message that you have been avoiding," Jessica says, handing me my phone.

Curiosity takes hold of me, as I waste no time in finding the text, and opening it.

Finally, I read its contents.

Dear Penny,

I miss you loads. Your absence from my side, after so many years, has made me realize how important you are to me. It made me realize, you are so much more my daughter than you are the future queen of England.

I know about your road trip, and I know you are having loads of fun. I will not be a dampener on your enjoyment, in fact, I would venture as far as to say, 'break a few rules, live a little...perhaps, love a little?'

You are always in my thoughts,

Your Mumma.

My eyes tear up, and the words blur in front of me.

If only I had read the message earlier.

But my own fears had kept me from opening it.

"See, what being vulnerable can get you?" Jessica says, rubbing my arm.

"She knew all along? She knew all along!" I whisper to

myself in disbelief.

"She is the Queen of England, Penny. Do you think she wouldn't know what her rebellious daughter is up to in America?"

"But...how did she change? How are people around me changing so abruptly? What's going on?" I say, half amused and half in shock.

"Well, in the queen's case, I think it was a case of 'absence makes the heart grow fonder' and the way you opened up and sent that text, being vulnerable. And as for me, I think I can finally admit, it was caressing your amazing ass all along that led me to you!"

"Ehm..." a voice that sounds eerily familiar makes me turn my head.

"I was not expecting to be greeted by those words, but as I have decided to loosen up a little, I'll let that slide," the Queen of England, Her Majesty Beatrice Victoria Windsor, and my mother says with the faintest sign of a grin on her graceful face.

"Mum!"

"Your Majesty!" Jessica curtsies, and even in a situation like this, I can't help but find her irresistibly cute.

With the weight of Her Majesty's gaze upon us, Jessica and I become acutely aware of the stale air in the room, our chests heavy with anticipation. We can hear the muted hum of urgent voices outside the door – a stark reminder of the high-stakes world we exist in.

"I... should I leave you two alone?" Jessica asks, her hand

instinctively moving towards the door. I find myself wanting to protest, but it's not my voice that fills the silence.

"Stay, Jessica," my mum says. Her tone isn't commanding, as it usually is, but holds a softness that seems foreign. Her words are an anchor, rooting Jessica to the spot. We exchange a look, both of us a mixture of curiosity and nerves.

And then, without another word, Mum steps closer and pulls me into a hug. It's a rigid and uncertain hug, as if she's handling a piece of fine china that could break at any moment. Not very surprising considering her track record of avoiding physical displays of affection. But, hell, I'll take it.

So, I return the hug with all the strength I can muster, trying to give her a decade's worth of affection we've both been starving for, and at the same time, replaying Stella's words about giving my mother a hug when I see her in my head.

Pulling away, she holds my face and murmurs, "Thank God you are alive and well, Penny." Her eyes well up, but she blinks the tears away, managing a smile. The mention of my nickname – the one she used to coo when I was just a tiny tot – feels like a balm on my soul.

She then turns her gaze to Jessica, who stands a respectful distance away, her usual bravado replaced with quiet humility. "And, Jessica," Mum says, "I owe a debt of gratitude to you, as well."

The moment feels surreal, like we're a part of some alternate universe where the Queen of England thanks a rogue American bodyguard for saving her rebellious daughter.

Jessica stands ramrod straight, her gaze unwavering under the regal scrutiny. "I was merely performing my duty, Your Majesty," she says, her voice as steady as her gaze.

Mum seats herself on the weather-beaten bed, our fingers intertwining in a silent conversation of their own. Her gaze doesn't leave Jessica. There's a playful glint in her eyes - a rare phenomenon reserved for when she's winning at Monopoly, or perhaps playing detective.

"Was that duty borne out of necessity or affection?" Mum asks, and I nearly choke on my own breath.

But Jessica, she's an old hand at this kind of interrogation. "Out of the love for duty, Your Majesty," she retorts smoothly.

Mum's not buying it, though. "From what I've heard, you've developed an affection for my Penny that transcends professional boundaries. Is that true?"

I hold my breath. This is it. This is the moment that will define just how serious Jessica is about me.

"Yes, Your Majesty." Jessica's affirmation comes across as solid and resolute as she is, and it makes my heart flip.

Mum turns to me, her question hanging in the air like a gauntlet. "And you, Penny, are fond of Jessica?"

"Yes, Mum. More than just fond," I confirm, my voice echoing the surety of Jessica's.

"Hmm..." The Queen of England sighs, a contemplative look in her eyes as they scan both of us. "You have my blessing to explore this... fondness. But bear in mind, a week or so is hardly enough to make a lifelong decision. If a year from now, you both feel the same, then I'll do my utmost to ensure you won't have to hide. Until then, discretion is key. Understand?"

Jessica nods before I get a chance to respond. "Yes, Your Majesty. And... Penny will always be safe with me."

Mum offers us a smile, albeit a small one. "That is the one advantage of falling for a soldier, isn't it?"

"Absolutely," I chime in, a shy smile spreading across my face.

With a wave of her hand, Mum calls an end to our

clandestine meeting. "We should return home, Penny. The media is bound to be in a frenzy soon, and no one knows about the failed kidnapping by the Russians. The President assured me he'll keep it that way until we're back in England. Jessica, you'll debrief your seniors and then you're welcome to visit Buckingham anytime."

"But can't she come with us?" I blurt out, casting a longing glance at Jessica.

"I'll join you as soon as I can," Jessica promises, her steady gaze making my heart flutter.

And with that, the Queen rises to her feet, gives me a kiss on my forehead, and says, "I am glad to have you back, Penny."

"I am glad to have you back as well, Mum," I reply.

Epilogue

One Year Later

Maria

Kriti is bent over her desk in her cozy room in the Balmoral Castle, scattered papers and a laptop before her. She's discussing Penelope's agenda for the day with me, now the head of Penelope's security team.

I am lounging against the door frame, arms folded and lips set in a determined line.

"Penelope is insisting on horseback riding to the coast today. Along with Jessica, she wants to visit the lighthouse where she used to hide as a child," Kriti says, shooting a look at me.

I stiffen at the idea, my eyes flitting across the room, then settling back on Kriti. "That's quite a distance from the castle, Kriti. We'll need to send a security detail with them."

Kriti leans back in her chair, her lips curving into a wry smile. "And I suppose that detail would be you?" she teases, challenging me with her gaze.

I shrug, feigning nonchalance. "If need be. I can't risk the princess, can I?"

Kriti stands, her hand resting on the desk for support. "So, what you're saying is, you don't trust Jessica to keep Penelope safe?" She moves towards me, her eyes never leaving mine.

"No, I'm saying we can't take any chances," I retort, my breath hitching as Kriti closes the distance between us.

"Penelope does not like taking no for an answer, and in this case, Jessica will side with her."

"Jessica always sides with her," I say, and wrap my fingers around the back of Kriti's neck.

Dressed in a pencil skirt, her tall frame highlighted by how tight the skirt wraps around her like a second skin, she looks like a doll ready to be played with.

"And you never side with me," she groans, as I tug at her neck, and bring her gorgeous face centimeters away from mine.

"My loyalties lie with the Princess," she husks and gives me a challenging smile.

She is getting brave.

"I though your loyalties lay with whoever could make you scream the loudest in pleasure." I start fiddling with the zipper on her skirt.

"It's been so long since you've made me scream that I have forgotten...how it feels."

I push her skirt down, and it puddles around her knees.

Fuck, she looks gorgeous.

I run my hands over her thighs, my fingers tracing the outline of her lace underwear. "Is that a challenge?" I murmur, my lips grazing her earlobe.

She shudders, her breath hot on my neck. "Maybe," she whispers, her hands trailing up my chest.

I capture her lips in a fierce kiss, our tongues battling for dominance. I push her against the desk, the papers and laptop scattering to the floor. My hands roam over her body, taking in every curve and dip.

"Fuck, I have missed you," I groan, my hands pulling up her shirt, and I run my hands over her smooth, flat stomach.

"Have you?" she asks between deep kisses.

"Oh, I have," I mutter, my hands moving up to cup her breasts.

She arches into my hands, and I can feel her nipples pressing into my palms.

A knock on the door causes us to freeze in our tracks.

"Kriti, are you in there?" Penelope's voice comes through the door.

"Yes, Your Highness. I'll be right there." I pull my hands away from Kriti, and she quickly rights her shirt.

"Are you guys fucking again?" Jessica asks through the door.

"No," Kriti says.

"Yes," I say at the same time.

"Get done with whatever sins you are committing in there, and get our horses ready, Kriti. We have decided to visit the lighthouse earlier than before."

Jessica

Grains of sand rise and fall with the wind as we gallop towards an old, abandoned lighthouse along the rugged coastline of Scotland. The storm-laden sky roils above us, casting a sinister glow on the ocean, the waves crashing violently against the rocky shore. The muscular beasts beneath us, white for Penelope and a jet black one for me, are as different as night and day, and somehow a perfect representation of us.

Penelope, the damned royal, rides her horse with grace and elegance, completely in sync with the animal as if they are one. It's almost as if she's born to this, the wild wind playing with her hair, and the stormy sky setting a majestic backdrop.

Me, on the other hand, I'm struggling.

You'd think a former Marine like me would have no problem handling a horse, but then you'd be sorely mistaken. These creatures and I don't exactly see eye-to-eye.

"Come on, Jessica! You're slower than my grandmother!" Penelope's laughter rings through the air, her words carried back by the wind. I scowl and force my horse to pick up the pace.

Penelope is a sight to behold in her white shirt, soaked through and sticking to her skin, defining every curve of her body. Her khaki pants hug her perfectly, and the riding boots make her look nothing short of a mythical warrior.

My eyes can't help but drink in the sight, my heart pounding against my ribcage.

The lighthouse draws closer, a lone silhouette against the stormy sky. A silent sentinel standing guard over the unforgiving sea, it's an eerie yet magnificent sight.

We reign in our horses and dismount, Penelope with a fluid grace that seems to be her second nature, and me with a grunt and a stumble. Penelope simply laughs, her eyes sparkling with mischief as she takes off, running towards the lighthouse. Her taunt hangs in the air, "Catch me if you can, Sergeant Slowpoke!"

Throwing a reproachful glare at my horse, I take off after

her, up the winding stairs that seem to go on forever. By the time we reach the top, we're both panting and laughing, the thrill of the chase still resonating within us.

The sight that greets us is nothing short of magical. Amidst the raging storm, the top of the lighthouse is transformed into a cozy cocoon. Twinkling fairy lights dance along the railings, a small table set for two in the middle, adorned with a single candle, casting a warm glow around. A picnic blanket lies invitingly next to it, a wicker basket waiting to be explored. Kriti's romantic touch is evident in every detail.

Penelope's gasp of surprise is music to my ears. She turns to look at me, her brown eyes wide with excitement and appreciation. It's then that she unpins her hair, setting free the coppery waves. They tumble down her back, the wind picking up a few strands and playing with them. The sight of her, soaked and radiant, stirs something deep within me. A primal instinct that's been carefully repressed, now rising to the surface. She's undeniably irresistible, and I can't help but be in awe of her.

This is what I've been missing.

I walk up behind her and wrap my arms around her waist, pulling her back against my chest.

Her lips part as I nuzzle her neck, the smell of her tingling my senses. "You look amazing," I murmur, my hands running up and down her chest.

"So do you. You should wear this more often," she murmurs, leaning back into me, her head resting against my shoulder. Her hands rest on my forearms, her fingers caressing the skin.

"I like this though. You in wet things," I whisper into her ears, grazing her earlobe with my teeth. She shivers, and I can feel the goosebumps on her arms.

I turn her around and press her against the railing, my body flush against hers. Her eyes are hooded, and she bites her lip, her breathing shallow. I run my hands up her thighs and up her waist, my fingers tracing the definition of her abdominal muscles.

"You like?" she asks, and I can see the confidence in her eyes.

"I like," I whisper, and trace my hands to her breasts, cupping the soft mounds.

She arches into my hands, her eyes closing as I run my thumbs over her nipples. She lets out a soft moan, and I can see the goosebumps on her arms.

"I think it's time I save my reputation as a bad rider," I whisper into her ear, my hands cupping her breasts, getting ready to take off her top.

"We are talking about riding horses, marine."

Her voice is husky with desire, and she shrugs off her shirt, letting it drop to the floor. She pushes my shirt off my shoulders, and it joins her shirt.

Clinging onto the slope of her cleavage are raindrops that I lick and end up swallowing.

Behind her, the angry ocean matches our passion and whips up massive waves.

She claws at me, ripping off my shirt, and snaking out her tongue to lick the entire expanse of my shoulder blades and then back to the base of my neck.

I grab her ass, the thing that drives me the craziest about her, and give it a hard, impatient squeeze.

She laughs. "A year later, and you still can't keep your hands off my ass."

"Not just my hands, Princess."

I grab her waist and turn her around.

Her torso leans over the railing, and below her, waves crash against mossy rocks, foaming in rage.

I grab her pants and pull them down.

She steps out of them, and I gasp at the sight of her ass in black lace.

I fall down to my knees and press my cheeks against the soft skin of her hips, savoring the moment.

Above me, Penelope moans and wriggles her hips, begging me to grace her posterior with the slickness of my tongue.

My tongue licks up the crease of her buttocks, and she shivers.

"Taste me, Jessica! I need it! I need it now!"

I grab her with both my hands and push my tongue into her, tasting her sweetness.

I push my tongue in and out of her, and her breathing becomes ragged. She pushes her hips back into me, wanting more and more. She's writhing against me, her hips rising and falling, her hands on her breasts, pinching her nipples.

I shove my tongue deeper into her pussy and start lashing her clit with my tongue, thrusting into her with a renewed vigor.

"Oh fuck! I'm going to come! I'm going to come!"

Not so soon, Princess. I still need to show you how well I can ride!

In a split second that catches her off guard, I grab her waist and lift her into my arms.

Carrying her to the picnic blanket, I gently lower her to the floor, and climb onto her.

I pin her hands behind her, and she giggles.

"This doesn't change anything. No matter how well you ride me, you'd still suck at riding horses."

"Shut up, or it will be your face that I will ride."

"And who the hell told you I'd mind that?"

"Let's save something for our wedding night," I say.

I position myself above her, and slowly lower myself onto her, my pussy greeting hers with a gentle kiss.

She gasps, and I can feel her tight pussy clenching against my pussy.

"You feel so good, princess," I whisper into her ear, my hands tracing the contours of her face, and her neck.

I start thrusting into her, my hips rising and falling.

"Harder! Faster! Faster!" Penelope cries out, her hips thrusting upwards to meet mine.

I push her down onto the blanket and start fucking her with an intensity that I've never felt before.

She grabs my breasts and starts massaging them, her fingertips teasing my nipples.

I pick up the pace, the friction between our pussies growing. I grab her breasts, and she grabs my hips, bucking against me.

I am thrusting harder now, and her hips are rising to meet mine, wanting more of me, all of me. I can feel her pussy tightening around me, her gasps becoming more and more ragged. I bite her lip, and she moans.

"Give me everything, Jessica! Fucking give it to me!"

With a final thrust, she comes, moaning into my ear, her wetness mixing with mine.

The waves of pleasure crash down on me, and I bury my head in the crook of her neck and groan into her.

She unlocks her legs from around me, and I roll off her, the both of us lying on the floor of the lighthouse.

Above us, the storm rages on, and the lightning illuminates the sky, and reminds me of the fireworks that we watched last December, during New Year's.

"Check off 'make love in a lighthouse' from the list," I quip, turning my gaze towards Penelope.

"Are you compensating for a lifetime of missing out on the usual stuff?" Penny queries, draping her leg over my torso and resting her head on my chest.

"You bet, and that list of mine is long."

Her curiosity piqued, she props herself on her elbows, a playful glint in her eyes. "And what's next on the agenda?"

I smirk. "Tasting Stella and Grace's pizza at their newly launched café? Making love in the throne room of Buckingham Palace?"

She chuckles. "For that, you'll have to wait until I ascend the throne."

The conversation lulls into a comfortable silence, the stormy backdrop perfectly mirroring the tempestuous journey we've been on.

"It's been more than a year," I say, breaking the silence, my voice barely above a whisper. "I'm tired of hiding, Penny. I want to walk down the street, hand in hand."

Penny's gaze flickers away, her eyes reflecting the turmoil within.

"I'll talk to Mum," she promises, meeting my eyes again. "She's quite fond of you, you know. I doubt she'd oppose us being public."

"Likewise," I admit, "She's got the emotional control of a hardened soldier. The way she handles crisis after crisis with the mindset of a monk...it's amazing."

She stares back at me, anxiety shimmering in her eyes. "Do you think I'll live up to her legacy?"

I cup her face, holding her gaze. "You've got her guidance, and my unwavering love and support. You'll be just fine, Princess."

Her face softens, a small laugh escaping her lips. "We also have Kriti and Maria, don't forget. As long as they can find time amidst their workplace shenanigans, that is."

That draws a hearty laugh from me. "Can you blame them, really? We're not any different."

Right on cue, Penny's phone buzzes, Kriti's name flashing on the screen.

"I bet she wouldn't be disturbing us unless it was important," Penny says, picking up the call and putting it on speaker.

"Penny, sorry to interrupt you and Jess," Kriti begins, her voice strangely solemn, "but this is important. The Queen will be joining us for dinner. She's already en route from London."

A surprised gasp escapes Penny's lips. "Do we know why?"

Kriti hesitates. "Actually, I do. On a scale of ten, Penny, how prepared are you to become the fucking Queen of England?"

Our surprised exclamations echo each other, hanging heavy in the storm-laden air.

A source in Buckingham Palace, reliable enough for Kriti to trust, has informed her that the Queen plans to discuss her abdication in favor of Penny. Just like that, the world turns on its axis.

Penny stares at me, wide-eyed and lost. I break the tension with a nonchalant shrug. "Good. I was growing tired of that personal trainer gig back in London."

Kriti's voice crackles over the phone. "Penny?"

"I'm here," she replies, still in shock. "Thanks for the heads-up, Kriti. And to answer your question, I'm a big, fat zero on that scale."

She ends the call and I rise to my feet, smirking as I drop a curtsy. "Your Majesty," I say, grinning devilishly as I watch her shock melt into a smile.

Penny hugs me, and I hug her back.

I had finally met the goal I had set for myself as a teenager. I hadn't had a PTSD-induced nightmare in over a year.

I was finally at peace.

The End.

Fated To Love You

(Rated 4.5 from more than 300 ratings across platforms. A Certified Bestseller!)

Read the first 2 chapters of A. Goswami's most popular, highest rated Age-Gap Sapphic Romance, from the series 'The Brooklyn Girls'.

"An Astrophysicist falls for her daughter's roomate and best-friend, in this steamy, fun and humorous Les Rom-Com" Read now by clicking here, or read the first two chapters for free from the next page.

Chapter One (Bella)

A bevy of beautiful girls gyrate on the dance floor in front of me, and the usual, often depressing, but mostly routine question pops into my head.

Who should I fuck?

I scan the dance floor.

I spot the blondes that look like me, with cute, innocent faces, but there was nothing innocent about the way their hips were moving.

I had had my fill of blondes. Tonight, I wanted something exotic.

And as the word materialized in my head, so did she, in the corner of my eye.

Yes, she was exotic, but she was also so much more.

A purple beam of light moves through the dance floor and briefly illuminates her gorgeous face.

I only get a brief look at her face, but it is enough.

I know who I am fucking tonight.

She is standing alone, looking bored, looking like she would rather be anywhere else in the world.

Me too, babe. Me too.

My fingers graze the many knobs and sliders on my Pioneer

DJ mixer, finding the one I need.

I twist the knob, and the volume of the trance music that had been blasting through the speakers decreases, and a groan of disapproval flows towards me from the crowd.

I hold the mic close to my lips and lick them once.

I am not usually nervous, but suddenly, I realize I am sweating.

She is unbothered by the sudden decrease in volume.

In fact, the look on her face says she welcomes the unexpected quiet.

"Hello folks, this is your DJ, DJ Aphrodite in the house, can I get a 'hell yeah' if you are enjoying the party, and can you make sure you are loud enough to shake the fucking foundations of Burj Khalifa?"

I point the mic at the crowd.

They scream their approval, and I smile.

I like it when the crowd is responsive and alive, and when it comprises a beautiful, older lady, who I desperately want to see naked.

I flick my blonde hair out of my face.

My ocean-blue eyes are drawn to her once again, and I find her finally looking at me.

She has a glass of whiskey in her hand.

A woman who likes whiskey is a woman who likes danger.

"Those of you who know me, know I like to do this thing during my sets, where I shine the spotlight on someone I either find extremely beautiful, or someone...who looks like they would rather swim with sharks than be at my concert."

I signal with my hand, and suddenly, beams of white

light from above, pierce the darkness of the club and start moving around amidst the crowd, like searchlights searching for escaped criminals.

The crowd howls and starts chasing after the spotlight, like children running after fireflies.

Ms. Exotic is rooted in her spot. She wants no part of this.

Little does she know, I am going to make her a part, whether she likes it or not.

I slowly start twisting the volume knob, gently increasing the volume.

The crowd starts jumping, as the music climbs, and nears crescendo.

"Are you guys ready to be 'spotlighted'?"

Yeah, I know, it's a cringe term, but it's stuck now, and my fans kinda know me for it.

A cocktail waitress climbs onto the little circular stage from where I had been DJing the party.

"Which one?" she whispers into my ear.

"Woman in black, wearing the strapless dress…curly hair, with the glass of whiskey in her hand."

The waitress nods and leaves.

I am now blasting the music at full volume.

People in the crowd have begun dancing.

In a sea of people twisting, grinding, and throwing their bodies around to the beats of music, beats that I produced, Ms. Exotic is standing still, sipping her whiskey as if she is staring at art in an art gallery.

Am I the art?

I signal with my hand once again, and the music stops.

All the spotlights disappear, except one.

One shines down upon Ms. Exotic, illuminating her like a unicorn in a mystical forest.

And now, I can see her clearly.

I can make out her features, and after a few seconds of staring at her blankly, I realize I might have stumbled upon God's greatest creation.

"Hi, I guess the spotlight has chosen you," I say into the mic.

The corners of her mouth curl into a mischievous smile. She looks around, and then back at me.

"The spotlight...or you?"

Even without the mic, her voice carries to me.

"Guilty as charged!" I raise my hands in defense, "Would you like to know why the spotlight chose you?"

"No."

"Because you are both the most beautiful, and the most bored of all the people here tonight, and I have no idea why. Your looks should be enough to cause chaos around you."

"The eye of the storm is always calm."

The crowd cheers for her response and quick wit.

Her smile lengthens to a grin.

"Look at the mouth on this one, and by that I mean, gosh, your lips are pretty!"

The crowd now cheers for me.

"What's your name, honey?" I ask.

"Ava."

"Ava, the rules state that if the spotlight chooses you, then you gotta give a solo dance performance on a track of my choosing."

"What if I don't want to follow the rules?"

A few boos crop up from the crowd.

"Then you would leave this crowd, and me, very disappointed in you. You have a body that's made to dance. And all of us here, would like to see it move, am I right, people?"

The crowd cheers. They are so drunk, they would cheer for Nazis at that moment.

Ava presses her lips together.

I notice the fullness of her mouth, and how thick and juicy both her lower and upper lips are.

I lick my own lips in anticipation.

She is driving me crazy.

"So…Ava…will you dance?"

"I will," Ava takes a step closer to the dance floor, "but not on a song of your choosing, but mine."

"Accepted," I say, making an exception to my rule for the first time since the inception of my 'Spotlight Trick'.

"What kind of music would you like me to play?"

"Something that is out of this world, quite literally."

"What do you mean?"

"I am an astrophysicist, darling. I would like you to play something that brings me closer to the universe."

I laugh, "Can I play the Star Wars theme?"

"I would prefer that over the nonsense I have been hearing ever since I stepped into this club."

"Yo, the scientist coming in with that nuclear heat!" someone shouts from the crowd, eliciting a few chuckles, but I am not laughing.

She might be hot as fuck, but she can't get away with calling my music 'nonsense'.

"Maybe you are too old to understand it, Ava?"

Yes, I went there, although she hardly looks a day older than 35.

"Is it so easy to rile you up? Come on, Aphrodite, show me what you can do."

I suck in my cheeks and stare Ava down.

She glares back.

"Come forward, Ava. I want you on the dance floor."

Ava climbs the three steps, and steps onto the floating dance floor, hanging a few feet above the swimming pool.

No one is allowed here, except the person I want.

Ava affords me the best view of her body ever since I spotted her, and I stifle a gasp.

She is tall, statuesque, and curvaceous.

Elegance drips through her posture.

Her hair is the color of chestnut, and they fall in electrifying curls down to the small of her waist.

Her strapless dress hugs her frame, making me dizzy with desire, and her hands, resting on her waist, make her look like she is modeling for the biggest fashion brands in the world.

Scientists look like this? Well done, Neil Degrasse Tyson, on getting hot women to take up science, man!

"Where are you from, Ava?"

"I am from America. I am an Iranian-American."

A middle eastern beauty. That explains the flawless skin.

"Ava, from America, especially for you...this is my own produced track, 'No Time For Caution' from Interstellar."

I see Ava's mouth part in surprise.

"I want no lights, except the one on Ava. And I want us all to look at the stars outside, from the highest floor, in the tallest building in the world, as the music of 'Interstellar' takes us to a place beyond our imagination. And Ava, maybe after this, you'll think better of my music."

I open the folder titled 'private', on my Mac, and click on 'No Time For Caution'.

My eyes find Ava, who is still confused as to how a Trance DJ had remixed a song from 'Interstellar'.

"Ava..." I call out to the Middle Eastern, "No time for caution, baby."

The synth beats start flowing from the speakers, overlayed with the iconic piano piece from 'No Time For Caution'.

Ava closes her eyes the moment she identifies the track and starts to slowly move her body.

Like a ballerina, she starts to spin, waiting for the beat to drop.

Ava spins, and she spins with full control.

I look in awe, as she keeps spinning, and then she raises one leg in the air, and starts spinning on just one leg.

She *is* a ballerina!

She stretches her arms out, her body now a little blur of black.

And then the beat drops, and picks up again, with electric

guitars ripping through the track, going crazy along with the pianos from Hans Zimmer, and it seems like something has caught hold of Ava.

A ripple runs through her body, and she does the wave with the flexibility of a gymnast.

The crowd stands still, and then erupts when the song comes to a close.

Ava stands panting, clutching her sides.

All the spotlights are turned on, but I wish they weren't.

I was not done gawking at this beauty.

Ava bows, and the crowd goes berserk.

She turns around and walks to my DJ console.

She grabs my hand and raises it in the air, while taking the mic in her hand. "Never have I heard Hans Zimmer's work remixed such flawlessly. Your music *did* take me to a different world, DJ Aphrodite!"

"Bella," I whisper to her.

"What?"

"My name is Bella, and I would like to buy you a drink."

I am alone with Ava at the back of the club, as the party slowly draws to a close.

Another DJ is helming the music, while I lean against the bar counter, as the city of Dubai twinkles below and behind me.

"I think you are really hot." I do not waste time.

"I think you are very pretty yourself," Ava says with a subtle smile.

"Are you single?"

"Yes."

My heart leaps with joy, and my panties become a little wetter.

"I can't help but think of how flexible you are," I say, frantically trying to come up with one-liners that would get me in bed with the goddess in front of me.

"Why would you think of that?"

"Flexibility has its uses, especially in bed."

Take the hint, woman!

"Oh…umm…yeah." Ava takes a sip of her whiskey, and turns her gaze away from me.

She doesn't want me. Good thing I am on the 154th floor from where I can jump to my death!

"Do you like women?"

I guess it's time to be direct to save time.

Better rip the band-aid off as quickly as possible.

"Yes, but Bella, I am not interested in hooking up at the moment."

I nod.

"Am I not your type?"

"Yeah, hot, young blondes with the body of a gymnast are not my type," Ava says sarcastically.

"Then what's the problem?"

"I am here to support my friend, Samantha, and I wouldn't be a good friend if I abandoned her right after the party celebrating her becoming the head at Louis Vuitton."

"Samantha Brooks is your friend?"

"Yeah."

"How does an astrophysicist strike up a friendship with a fashion designer?"

"Long story. It will take time."

"But I won't, in making you…cum."

The missile is away.

Ava blushes and hides her face behind her glass.

The missile has locked onto the target.

"You really want this, don't you?"

"As much as I wanted you to dance."

"Well, blow my mind again, and I might just do…what you want."

Jackpot. Missile has demolished its target.

"Ava, you look like someone who likes being in control."

Ava frowns and looks at me with confusion.

"Why would you say that?"

"I have a hunch," I say, "and I know exactly…what would blow your mind."

I wait for a group of tipsy, staggering girls to pass, and then unzip my clutch.

"Give me your hand," I ask Ava, who extends her right arm, palm facing upwards.

I drop a cylindrical bullet shaped not much bigger than an actual bullet, in Ava's hand.

I look around to see if someone has seen me hand Ava a sex

toy.

"What is this?"

"Power."

Ava looks at the pink bullet-shaped vibrator, her eyes studying the fascinating object like it was material from outer space.

"Ava, you gotta be subtle, babe. I don't want people to find out how desperate I am for you."

Ava smiles. "Who's gonna be using this, you…or me?"

"I am giving you the power," I say and take the vibrator back from Ava, "and I am keeping this."

I glance around, and when I am satisfied no one is watching me, I slip the vibrator inside my skirt, and with a gasp, I insert it inside my vagina.

Ava's eyes widen.

They look prettier than ever.

If only it was my mouth between her legs making her eyes go wide.

"This…is your power."

I search inside my clutch once more, take out a small, rectangular remote, shaped like a Wrigley's Doublemint chewing gum, and thrust it into Ava's hand.

"The controls are easy enough to understand, especially for an intelligent scientist like you. Just make sure you don't start off with max speed. Be…gentle with me." I graze Ava's arm with my fingers.

"I'll be in the washroom." I lean closer to Ava and touch my lips to her cheeks.

She withdraws, but out of the suddenness of my

movements, and not because she did not like it.

Or I hoped so.

I make my way toward the washrooms and feel the vibrator start vibrating the moment I step into a stall.

She did not waste time.

She is eager.

I grab the sides of the stall with both my hands, as the vibrator starts humming intensely inside me.

I close my eyes and imagine Ava, leaning against the bar counter in her black, sparkling dress, her fingers playing with the buttons on the remote, controlling me like a puppet, wondering how soon she wants to burst into the washroom to see the consequences of her actions.

The vibrator speeds up, and I gasp, and then moan.

A knock on the door scares me.

Have I been caught?

"Yes? Just a minute!" I say in my most natural, not close-to-cumming voice.

"I don't think I can wait a minute," comes the voice from the other side of the door.

I unbolt the door and pull Ava in.

She crashes into me, like monstrous waves crashing ashore, like women crashing into a store with end-of-season sale.

She is hungry, and I am ready to serve.

I am pushed against the wall, in the cramped little space, with Ava's body pressed tightly against me.

She searches for my lips with her own, and I offer her my

mouth.

She pulls my lower lip with her teeth and moans when our tongues meet.

Her hands are already on the small of my back, her legs sliding between my thighs.

"What's your age?" she asks, nibbling along the sides of my neck.

"Old enough to show you the time of your life."

She holds me by my throat. "Tell me your age, Bella."

"20." I smirk, while Ava chokes me lightly.

"Fuck, you are too young."

"I am above 18."

"I am 19 years older than you."

"That's hot."

"That's inappropriate." She is slowly backing away from me.

I stop her by grabbing her waist, turning, and pushing her against the wall.

"It's 2023. We are consenting adults, and I don't think I can let you go now before feeling your fingers in me."

I nuzzle the sides of her neck and take a big whiff.

She smells of lust and seduction, mixed with notes of pear, tangerine, and bergamot.

Prada.

I see her battle with her thoughts.

She is deciding whether it would be morally justified to fuck a girl who is 19 years younger than her.

I pull the top of my jumpsuit down, to reveal my left tit, and to help her make a decision.

She lowers her eyes, and I see her lick her lips.

I grab the back of her head and direct her towards my swollen nipples.

She thrusts her tongue out, to taste it, while also coming to a decision.

"We need to go somewhere else." She is hardly able to speak with her mouth stuffed with my breast.

"I know just the place," I say.

∞∞∞

I have VIP access to the observation deck of the Burj Khalifa, which is empty as Ava and I enter it through gold, metallic doors.

The city glitters around us.

We are on top of the world, up in the clouds, and I am with an angel who can't keep her hands off me.

We stumble our way to the very edge of the observation deck, where only a chrome-finished railing separates us from massive glass panes affording 360-degree views of the city.

Ava has me pushed against the railing, which is biting me on the small of my back.

But I couldn't care less.

I am in a daze, numb to everything except pleasure.

Ava is gasping, her breasts rising and falling like musical notes in one of Beethoven's symphonies.

"I had no plans of doing this tonight," Ava mumbles against the skin of my neck, as she kisses upwards, and bites my ear lobe, "but you are so...fucking...hot."

I arch my back and lean backward over the railing. "I had no plans of making out with an astrophysicist, like ever," I say, running my hands through Ava's chestnut-colored hair, "but you are fucking hot as well..."

"I don't have much time. We'll have to be quick," Ava says, taking deep breaths and undoing the knots of my top.

In the few seconds that we stop making out, we look at each other.

Her fingers work frantically on the knots, while her eyes peer deep into my soul.

My knees suddenly falter, and I feel my heart filling up with emotion.

"Your eyes are kind," I say.

"No one has ever said that to me. People mostly think I am a cold-hearted bitch."

"People don't know shit. I know my shit. I can read people."

"What else can you read?"

"That you wish I hadn't tied these knots so tightly." I smile as Ava unties the last knot.

Straps of my dress fall off my shoulders, now revealing both of my breasts.

"My...god," Ava mutters.

She stands and gives my breasts an eyeful, while I smile at her childlike excitement.

"You like them?"

Ava replies by stuffing her face between them.

Her tongue explores my under-boob, and I feel my nipples hardening to their max potential.

I want them inside her mouth.

Behind us, the sound of helicopter blades rotating disturb the silence surrounding us.

Ava stops feasting on my tits for a second and looks past my shoulder.

"We have company," she says, and before I know it, I am pulled down to the floor by my shoulders, behind the opaque part of the balcony running parallel to the glass panes.

"Shit." A searing pain on the back of my neck makes me wince.

"Fuck!" Ava pulls her hand back from my shoulders and reaches for the railing.

"I broke your necklace," she says somberly, holding up my broken 'Aphrodite' chain with the Greek symbol of Aphrodite as the pendant.

"It got stuck in the railing, and broke as I pulled you down. I am so sorry!" Ava hands me the necklace.

"It's okay. Forget it. It's not very expensive."

"Are you hurt?"

"Yes, I am in extreme pain, Ava...pain of not having your mouth and hands all over me! Stop torturing me and continue what you were doing."

"The helicopter is right on top of us," Ava warns.

"Good, let them enjoy a few minutes of excitement in their mostly boring job."

Ava smiles and pushes me flat against the cold, granite floor of the observation desk.

My head rests against the hardness of the floor, but I don't care.

I watch as Ava lowers her face on my tits and starts sucking one again, while palming and kneading the other.

My tits aren't very big, and I feel a little insecure as Ava tries to grab a handful with some difficulty.

But soon, Ava's mouth alternating between my tits makes me forget all about my tiny tits and makes me arch my body in sheer, unadulterated pleasure.

I part my legs and groan, "Fuck me, Ava. Please fuck me!"

Ava sighs and, without leaving the assault on my nipples, pushes the hem of my skirt up my legs, and finds my soaking-wet panties.

She pulls them to the side.

I love it when a woman does that.

It tells me they are impatient.

That they don't have the time to undress me. They would rather make space for themselves, in the shortest time possible.

"Yes!" I moan, as Ava toys with my pussy lips, rubbing the edges of my opening, while swirling her tongue around my nipples.

"Don't…" I gasp.

"Don't what?"

"Don't make me beg for it."

"That's exactly what I want you to do."

"Power…you like power, don't you?"

"I like beautiful girls begging me to thrust my fingers in

them."

"Then do it, baby. Stick them in. As far as they go. Please! Please!"

Ava succumbs to her own impatience and enters me.

I let out a muffled scream as I clasp my arm over my mouth.

I didn't want to be caught indulging in lesbian sex in an Islamic country like Dubai.

Although, I hear prison isn't that bad for lesbians.

It took Ava one finger and a few thrusts to get me cumming all over her hand.

I was embarrassed.

I hadn't cum so soon in months, or maybe years.

"That was quick," Ava laughed, licking my juices off her fingers.

"Thanks for confirming what I was only assuming," I say, feeling my cheeks going red.

"It's okay, I have this effect on girls."

"An assertive woman scientist who is full of herself, do you *want* to make me fall for you hopelessly?"

"No, I want you to help me cum."

"How can I be of help?" I ask.

"By staring at me with your beautiful blue eyes and playing with your tits."

"What? That's it?"

"Yes, I don't need much."

Ava straddles me in a way that my thighs are pressed firm against her crotch.

She lifts her dress, and I feel her pussy on my thigh.

It is wet, leaking, and warm with desire.

Ava starts rubbing herself on my thigh.

"I am ready for round two." I hand Ava the vibrator, who inserts it inside my pussy and presses a button on the remote.

The vibrator comes to life.

So does Ava's need to ravish my thigh.

She starts riding my leg, like a cowgirl on a mechanical bull.

Her expressions change from sophisticated ecstasy to ugly lust.

She is sucking her teeth, groaning wildly, and putting her all into feeling my skin rub against her clit.

"Play with your tits," she commands me.

I grab them hesitantly. I am still insecure about their size.

"They are perfect. They are heavenly. And they are the ones that convinced me to fuck you."

It's like Ava has read my mind, but I don't let my surprise boil to the surface.

Hearing her call my breasts heavenly gives me the boost of confidence I need, and I grab them and press them hard for Ava.

"Is this turning you on? Watching a 20-year-old manhandle her tits for you? Huh? Do you like fucking my leg? You like feeling my young skin?"

"Oh fuck yes!!!" Ava screams and cums.

It's all over.

She collapses on top of me, as the sound of the helicopter

fades into the distance.

Did we really put on a show for them?

Am I really focusing on that right now? What's wrong with you, Bella?

I hug Ava, and suddenly, she backs away.

I am confused.

"That was…amazing. You are really hot, Bella."

Ava stands up, and I am forced to stand as well.

"Are you leaving?"

"I have to meet Samantha at 11 in one of the restaurants in this building. We have planned our own little afterparty."

I look at my watch. It's 10:50 pm.

"But I didn't even get to see you naked?"

"Was it really required?"

I make a face that says 'duh'.

"Maybe next time?"

"Ava, you can't just leave like this."

I try to soften my tone, but I let slip in the frustration anyway.

"I am sorry. I wish I had more time. But I really don't. I… am thankful that your 'spotlight' chose me tonight. Otherwise, this party would have been torture for me. And thank you for the amazing time." Ava extends her hand for a handshake, and I look at it in disbelief.

"You are more Gen Z than me, an actual Gen Z! Are we really going to say bye with a handshake?"

"Why not? Do you want a goodbye kiss? I can give you one if you want."

"What? Not like this! I can't believe this is happening. Anyway, thanks for your time, Ms. Ava, I am glad my legs could be of service to you tonight."

Ava looks at me with pity.

 I hate that.

"I'll see you around, Bella."

"How? We don't have each other's numbers."

"I'll reach out to you."

I scoff.

"No need."

I pick up my broken chain from the floor and stuff it inside my clutch, along with the vibrator and the remote, while Ava watches me curiously.

"What are you looking at?" I ask her.

"How beautiful you are."

"Then why are you leaving me?"

"Because I am 39, and you are 20, and I can read people too. You look like someone looking for love."

Is it that obvious?

"You are wrong," I say resolutely.

"Maybe. But I can't take the chance. Goodbye, Bella, or should I say, Aphrodite?"

Ava turns around and leaves me with the sight of her perfectly shaped hips and the sound of her heels.

"What a night," I murmur and follow behind her.

My phone wakes me up, and I grudgingly look at the screen to see who has dared to disturb me from my slumber.

"Yes," I say in a drowsy, raspy voice.

"I need you!" Sophia whispers urgently from the other end.

"I need sleep, bitch," I say lazily.

"I am at a cafe with my mom, and things are getting awkward at the rate of 36 'umms' per minute."

"Umm...so? How can I help?"

"You can bring your ass down here and help save me from this vortex of awkwardness."

"It's your mom, Sophia. How awkward can it be?"

"Don't you know what's it like between my mom and me?"

"No, because you never speak of it." I lift myself off the bed and sit cross-legged, staring out the window.

"There was a reason. Now, are you coming or not?"

"Do you know I landed at 2 am this morning from a 14-hour flight from Dubai?" I stand up and stretch, admiring the shards of sunlight filtering through the netted window in my room.

"I know, and I also know you had sex with a lovely old lady while you were over there, so I am very sorry if I am not able to empathize with your labors. The Little Sweet Cafe. 77 Hoyt Street, Brooklyn. Be there in the next 15 minutes."

Sophia hangs up on me, leaving me with no option but to visit her and her mother.

I decide to throw on a hoodie and gym leggings, anticipating the cold October weather of New York.

I look at myself in the mirror before stepping out and wonder if the 'old lady' that Sophia had mentioned would still appreciate my beauty if she saw me looking like a homeless teenager, with frizzy bed hair and sunken, sleep-deprived eyes.

Chapter Two (Ava)

T he Little Sweet Cafe looks exactly like it is named. It is sweet, small and cozy, with the aroma of coffee floating all over the place.

I look through the large windows and lazily observe the citizens of New York City go about their business.

I try to spot my daughter in their midst, but she is nowhere to be found.

A young guitarist enters the cafe, her guitar slung over her shoulder.

I watch her take the booth next to mine and start working on her laptop.

I am curious to know what a guitarist does on a laptop, so I try to steal a glance.

She appears to be mixing two tracks on a DJ software, similar to the one Bella had been using at the party in Dubai.

A sudden uptick in my heartbeat reminds me I am still not over what happened a few days back, on the observation deck of the tallest building in the world.

As I remember the heated, passionate encounter I had found myself in, I hope my blush fades away before Sophia returns to the booth.

Bella.

Aphrodite?

Aptly named.

She possessed the beauty and the passion of the Greek goddess for sure, and had somehow managed to infect me with it as well.

I, a 39-year-old scientist, who had increasingly found herself having fewer one-night stands than ever before, had behaved like a cougar on the prowl.

I blush harder than ever before.

I had left Bella in Dubai, but she still prowled the hallways of my brain.

The bell over the entrance to the cafe rings, and Sophia enters with her friend in tow.

Her friend, who she was eager for me to meet.

Her friend, who has light blonde hair, a tiny waist, a small stature, and ocean blue eyes.

"Sorry to keep you waiting Mom, this one wouldn't leave her bed!" Sophia apologizes and slides into the booth, occupying the seat in front of me. "Bella, this is my mom, Mom, this is Bella, my best friend, my roommate, and probably my soulmate."

I meet Bella's eyes, and feel my heart climb up my throat, and lodge itself in the back of my mouth.

I do not blink, and neither does she, I think.

I sit, and I stare.

I hear Sophia calling out my name, but I couldn't give a fuck, because the improbable, the unthinkable was happening right before my eyes.

Bella smiles at me and extends her arm for a handshake.

The damn handshake!

"Hi Ms. Miller, it's nice to finally meet you!" Bella expertly hides any bout of surprise or shock that may have assaulted her.

She acts innocent, which makes her look prettier than ever.

"Hello." I shake Bella's hand and feel sparks of electricity sizzle where our hands make contact.

"Bella has just returned from a week-long trip to Dubai, where she played two parties."

"Played?" I try to act innocent as well, but I have no idea how convincing I look.

Bella smirks, her eyes twinkle, and her thin, rosy red lips glisten as she licks her lips. "I am a DJ, who would like to be known as a producer someday."

"A producer?"

"Of beats...music...tracks, that sort of stuff."

"Oh..."

I try to think of other things to say, sentences, words, anything that would not give away my lust mixed confusion at seeing Bella sitting in front of me.

"That must be an exciting field of work?" I manage to say.

"Yes, I get to travel around the world, meet new people, and make interesting music. I am not complaining."

"That's great."

Cliche and dry replies exit my mouth.

"It is genuinely very nice to meet you, Ms. Miller, because this one keeps mum on anything to do with her family. We had started to think she was an undercover spy running around as a fake model. And I also see where she gets her killer good looks from." Bella turns her head to wink at Sophia, and then rests her youthful blue eyes on me as if challenging me to a duel.

"Thank you. Sophia has been very quiet about you as well. Whenever I would ask her about her friends, she would say, 'Mom, it's better if you just meet them. It's very hard to explain my friends. They can only be experienced and not explained.'"

"Really? I just think she was just too lazy to say anything about me. Well, now that we have met, Ms. Miller, we don't need her to play the middleman, do we? We can now gang up on her, something I had always wanted to do."

Sophia dismisses Bella with a wave. "She is just frustrated Kaylee and I keep pulling her leg, and she can never come up with a good comeback."

"It's hard to go against two bullies," Bella says, rolling her eyes.

My heart vibrates, much like the vibrator inside Bella I had been controlling a few nights ago.

As Bella and Sophia banter, I steal glances at Bella.

She is dressed in a grey oversized hoodie, and navy blue gym leggings, with her hair parted down the middle and her face devoid of any make-up.

I still find her breathtaking.

Especially her cute little butt that I hadn't had the pleasure of exploring in Dubai.

I shake my head.

She is your daughter's friend…best friend! Roommate!

Not an object of desire!

"Mom, are you okay? Why are you shaking your head?"

"Umm…nothing, just trying to get rid of this pain in my

neck. I think I slept weird yesterday."

"It's the pillows of the modern world, Miss Miller. Try sleeping on the floor without a pillow. It's great for your spine. I find myself on the floor most nights."

Bella stares right into my eyes, and they scream silently at me.

"On the floor? Isn't that uncomfortable?"

"Not if you are in Dubai, and on the highest floor in Burj Khalifa."

I almost faint.

My heart thuds and bangs against my rib cage.

"Wha...What?"

"I mean, even the floors there are more expensive than any bed I have ever slept on, so, I was just exaggerating, Ms. Miller... I don't sleep on floors in five-star hotels."

"What the hell are we talking about, guys?" Sophia butts in, "Can we switch the subject to literally anything but floors?"

I smile, and Bella laughs, radiating extra-terrestrial beauty.

I look at her for a few seconds, then tear my eyes from her striking face with difficulty.

"Sophia told me you're an astrophysicist? You must be like, really smart?"

"Yeah, that's one thing I can say about myself confidently."

"Bella is pretty dumb, Mom. Like really stupid. It's really amazing how few brain cells she has!" Sophia laughs.

"Your daughter, Miss Miller, is the biggest whore in the world. I mean, talk about orgies, glory holes, swinger clubs, she has tried everything!" Bella retorts, and Sophia's mouth opens into an 'O'.

"That's you, bitch!"

"But who got me started?" Bella quips, and I can't help but grin at Sophia and Bella's banter.

Fucking my daughter's best friend aside, I feel happy that during the time I was away from Sophia's life, she had the support and care of good friends like Bella and Kaylee, who I was yet to meet.

And then suddenly, I wonder if Bella had told Sophia about her encounter with me in Dubai.

The thought leaves me feeling uncomfortable, and I quickly drag myself away from the thought.

"How is Sophia as a roommate?" I ask.

For the next few minutes, Bella tells me all about living with Sophia, and by the end of it, I am both happy and sad.

Sophia has changed.

She has become clean, organized, and responsible, which was a huge departure from the teenager who used to live with me.

I was happy my daughter had changed, but I was sad I could not see her change in front of my eyes.

A tear forms in the corner of my eye, and Bella goes quiet.

"What's wrong?" she asks, her voice full of concern.

"Nothing, just…regretting a few things. Like being away from her…for so long."

I reach for Sophia's hand and squeeze it.

The ever emotionally awkward Sophia smiles nervously and pulls her hand back.

"It's okay, Mom, you did not miss much."

"Yeah, except for seeing her throw up all over the place after a night out and hearing her bitch and cry over boys, you haven't missed out on much. Her life is pretty boring," Bella tries to lighten the mood, and it works.

I start to feel at ease.

Maybe Bella also realizes the importance of keeping our little sexual soiree under wraps, for the benefit of her friendship with Sophia.

And I didn't have any idea that the hot, little blonde, with perky tits and a bubbly personality was my daughter's roommate.

So, was it really my fault?

I reached a conclusion that acquitted me of any wrongdoing, and I eased into my chair and sliced into my sausage, something we lesbians don't usually do much.

"So, I was thinking," Sophia starts, "how about the two of you come together to my fashion show tonight?"

No, baby girl, what are you doing?

"Yeah, about that, how are you feeling?" Bella asks Sophia.

"I am good. I mean, I am not scared of tripping on the runway or anything, but I *do* feel a little nervous thinking my mom and my bestie are going to be in the crowd. That can fuck with you a little."

"Language, Sophia." My motherly instinct jumps out of me, eliciting a chuckle from Bella, to who I give a side-eye.

"Mom, fuck is like…not even a curse word now. It's so much more than just a word, it's an emotion," Sophia tries to wriggle her way out of her mistake.

"Still…it wouldn't behoove you to speak like a lady sometimes."

"Would I sound like a lady if I used words like 'behoove'?" Sophia says dryly, "Anyway, as I was saying, I have already added both of your names to the guest list. You should have good seats, so come together, okay?"

"Umm…I have work later tonight, so I might show up a bit late," Bella says, and I give her a look of appreciation.

"Okay, but you *will* make it, right?"

"I wouldn't miss it for the world, baby." Bella hugs Sophia, and once again, I feel happy that Sophia has people around her who care for her.

"And you, Mom? Will you come?"

"Of course, why wouldn't I?"

"Because the whole reason I left the house was you not being supportive of my career choices."

Sophia finally addresses the elephant in the room, but I wish she didn't do it in front of Bella.

"I am trying to change my ways, Sophia. I hope you can already see some of the changes."

I almost choke up as I say the words.

Sophia smiles, and this time, it is her who reaches out and grabs my hand. "Yes, I can, but I just don't want anything bad to happen. I am a little cynical like that."

"Nothing will go bad. I won't let it," I say, but I speak too soon as I feel Bella's feet slide up against my ankle below the table.

Shit.

Bella does not care. She wants to continue playing.

I shoot Bella a look of warning, but she is busy talking to Sophia about the fashion show.

And all the while, her toes continue on their path upwards.

Inching towards my knees, and in the process, pushing the hem of my maxi dress along with them.

I plead with Bella with my eyes, but she does not offer me a look.

Her feet are now gently caressing my calf-muscle, and I feel her touch on every square millimeter of my skin.

She looks innocent while talking with Sophia, like a Barbie still in its box, waiting to be played with, but I know she is no Barbie.

She is Annabelle.

A sexy, seductive Annabelle that wants to possess me.

I take a deep breath.

I know I can just shift my position, and I will be rid of Bella and her foot.

But I stay put.

I am hooked.

I am like a fish swimming toward the bait, even though I know it will mean the end of my life.

Bella finally looks at me, and I see a cocktail of mischief and seduction brimming in her eyes.

"Miss Miller, have you gotten something done to your lips?"

What a weird question to ask while playing footsie with your roommate's mother!

"No, why?"

"They are so full, and so…aagghh…just beautifully shaped. Especially your lower lip. Girls I know would kill for thickness like that."

"Yeah, and I never understood why I wasn't passed on these 'lip' genes?" Sophia mutters, as she sips her latte.

"Can I call you Ava, Miss Miller?" Bella slides her feet beyond my knees and tries to slip it between my legs.

My cross-legged posture does not give her access, and her toes keep trying to wriggle their way in.

"No, Bella!" I blurt out.

"Mom, all of your juniors call you Ava, why can't Bella?"

"No, I mean, I said, no, of course, you can call me Ava. Miss Miller makes me sound old."

"But your bangin' body says otherwise, Ava. It says I am the hottest piece of science ass around!"

"Bella, stop flirting with my mom and tell me if I should call Kaylee's new boyfriend to the show?"

Bella and Sophia meander into another discussion, while Bella's toes keep trying to part my legs and slide up my thighs.

"Wait, I gotta take this," Sophia says, as her phone starts ringing.

She leaves the booth, and exits the cafe, leaving my torturer and me alone with each other.

"Open your legs," Bella mouths.

"I need to talk to you," I quickly respond. I know I don't have much time, and I need to make sure Bella understands the gravity of what I am about to say.

"What happened between us in Dubai was a mistake. It was a mistake back when I didn't even know you were my daughter's friend, but now it is more than a mistake. It is a sin."

"It didn't feel like a sin when you were pushing me down to the floor and breaking my necklace to get to my tits. See, I have proof."

Bella pushes her hair to one side and shows me a bruise on the side of her neck, which was almost completely healed.

"You hurt me, Ava. See?"

"I am sorry for that."

"Oh, I am not talking about this. You hurt me when you just abandoned me. I was hoping for so much more."

"As I said, I did not have time."

"We have all the time in the world now."

"We are not doing anything, Bella," I hiss, "I am trying to mend a very strained relationship with my daughter. The last thing I need is her finding out I was boning her best friend."

"Who said anything about boning? I just want my goodbye kiss."

"No."

"Yes."

"Ava...you know you want to."

Bella parts my legs with her foot, and somehow, I don't offer any resistance.

Her feet slide up against my inner thigh and reach my panties.

I am almost half-naked now, my indecency only hidden by a slab of wood.

Bella is disrobing me with her feet, and I am allowing her to.

I am glaring at her, and she is smirking at me. She is enjoying this.

She is a wicked 20-year-old, and I am a desperate 39-year-old, and I can't help but love being lusted after a bombshell like the blonde sitting in front of me.

And then I snap out of it.

"I have to go to the washroom," I mutter and stand up quickly, forgetting my dress has ridden up to my waist.

I sit back down, adjust my dress, and stand up again, while Bella keeps a hand on her lips and watches me with delight.

I almost run to the washroom, which is just a little closet with a single commode.

I close the door behind me, drowning out the chatter outside, and grasp both sides of the sink.

I look at my reflection and wonder how a confident, project-leading scientist on the James Webb telescope, NASA, is being toyed with by a 20-year-old.

Even the interview with the head of NASA for my current position was less nerve-wracking than the last 10 minutes of my life.

I realize I need to get a grip on myself...or maybe on Bella's waist as I push her against a wall and attack her mouth...

No! No! Hell no!

I straighten up, and nod to myself.

I got this.

A knock sounds at the door.

"Occupied," I say.

"I need to talk to you," says Bella from behind the door.

"Okay, give me a minute."

"No, in there. I need to talk to you alone."

"Sophia will be back any minute."

"She won't. She is talking to Kaylee, and they are arguing about her boyfriend. She won't be back anytime soon. Just open up. I swear I won't bite."

I unlock the door, and that's all Bella needs.

She slides in and closes the door, then locks it.

We are cramped inside the little washroom, our breasts almost touching.

"I need that kiss, Mommy," Bella groans seductively.

This time, I am prepared for Bella's nonsense.

I push her back, pinning her against the wall.

"No, Bella. We are done."

Bella takes a few deep breaths, never breaking eye contact with me.

She is the sexist thing in the world.

I can't believe I am rejecting the sexist thing in the world.

"Okay," Bella whispers and starts taking off her hoodie.

"What the hell are you doing? Bella?"

I watch in utter confusion and horror, as Bella pulls her hoodie over her head and clutches it in one hand.

"Kiss me."

She starts massaging her tits, and my mind flashes back to the night in Dubai, when she was doing the same, while I rode her thighs to an earth-shattering orgasm.

"Just a kiss, and we will be done. I promise."

"Why? Why is this kiss so important to you?"

"You broke my necklace, bruised me, and then abandoned me. Don't I deserve this fucking kiss?"

She had a point. Or was I being biased here?

Bella closes the gap between us, and all of her 5 feet 2 inches of sexiness presses against me.

She hugs me.

I glance past her shoulder and notice the curve of her butt in her tightly fitted leggings, and I lose my mind.

I grab her hips with both my hands and start kissing her.

I kiss her hard.

I kiss her with passion.

I kiss her like she was my lover.

She slides her hand inside the neck of my dress and grabs my boob.

I moan into the kiss and caress her hips through her leggings and then start grabbing at them with fervor.

She starts kissing down my neck.

She parts the front of my dress to reveal more of my cleavage and licks up and down the line, and I feel like the most desirable woman in the world.

She drags her lips over my tits, towards my nipple.

She is almost there.

My breath quickens in anticipation.

My grip on her ass hardens.

My mouth opens, and then shuts, and then opens again.

Wordless screams, along with expressions of pure ecstasy, override my face.

I forget every moralistic principle in the world, the age gap between us, the relationship Bella has with my daughter.

All I want is for her to cover the remaining distance of a few centimeters with her mouth and latch onto my nipple.

A knock on the door ensures that never happens.

Like the crumbling blocks of a game of Jenga, everything collapses around me.

Anticipation turns into fear. Lust into anxiety.

"Yes?" I say in a perfectly normal voice, while Bella's face goes white with fear.

"We're waiting to use the loo out here. Can you hurry up?"

It's not Sophia, but it very well could have been.

"We need to get out," I say, and Bella nods.

This is the first time I see her scared.

"And now, we are really done," I say, and Bella nods again.

The expression on her face tells me she isn't faking or lying this time.

I take a deep breath, adjust my clothes, and exit the washroom, followed by Bella.

Sophia is still outside.

Bella and I sit at our booth in silence, waiting for our nerves to settle.

"That was close," Bella finally says.

"I am glad you finally have that notion."

"But, after that kiss, I know it will be fucking hard for me to stop thinking about you."

Me too, I think to myself.

"It will pass," I say.

Bella shakes her head. "Don't think so," she says, while

running a gentle finger on the bruise on her neck.

Click Here To Continue Reading

———————————

Free Lesbian Romance Novel by A Goswami

Hello Dear Readers,

Please don't forget to download your free 300-page Lesbian Romance Novel by me that I would like to give to you as a thank you for reading and enjoying this book.

For paperback readers : https:// mailchi.mp/8f0f411551ce/a-goswami Download it right now by clicking here

Author's Note

Hi Readers,

I hope you enjoyed the romance between Penelope and Jessica, and had fun getting to know their story through this book. If you did, then it would be very helful to me if you could give this book a posive rating or review.

If you did not like something about book, please mail me at **agoswamibooks@gmail.com** , and I will make sure I give heed to your constructive feedback, or you can just mail me to say Hi, i would love to interact with you!

Join my newsletter for new release updates, discounts and free books by clicking here , for papaerback readers, by going to this link : https://mailchi.mp/8f0f411551ce/a-goswami

Happy Reading!

A. Goswami

Books By This Author

The Fire Between Us

Beyond Boundaries

The Queen Of My Heart

Lapdance Love

Printed in Great Britain
by Amazon